MW00679594

RAINY DAY PEOPLE

By

Susan C. Haley
with
Robert J. Delany

ISBN 0-7414-2874-1

Cover Photograph taken by Paul Wamhof © 2002

Editing assistance provided by Michael Garrett

The One © Bernie Taupin / Elton John, All Rights Reserved

Published by:

INFI∞ITY
PUBLISHING.COM

1094 New DeHaven Street, Suite 100
West Conshohocken, PA 19428-2713
Info@buybooksontheweb.com
www.buybooksontheweb.com
Toll-free (877) BUY BOOK
Local Phone (610) 941-9999
Fax (610) 941-9959

Printed in the United States of America
Printed on Recycled Paper
Published November 2005

For Robert J. Delany, who passed on shortly after the completion of this work, and without whom it wouldn't exist. Bob, I dedicate it to you in your own words . . . "I know it's not much for all you did for me that I wasn't even aware of, the love you had for me that I never really got a chance to have for you, just one word . . . Thanks."

* * * *

Always, there are many to thank when an accomplishment is achieved; a goal is met. No man is truly an island.

In Memory of Tag, an orange kitten, who inspired us both.

To Jerry A. Haley, my dear husband, who instilled the Spirit in me. And still does from a higher place . . . Thanks.

To my cousin, Melanie Sue Bowles, who had a confidence in me that I didn't have in myself . . . Thanks.

To Paul Wamhof, dear friend to both Bob and I, and photographer for the cover shot . . . Thanks.

To a staunch group of our friends for the support and encouragement to never give up on this story after Bob's passing. Paul, Linda, Nikki, Jo, Nelson, Connie, Tom, Kathy, Laura, Sharron, Allie, and many more . . . Thanks.

To Michael Garrett who taught me the value of an editor and the tenacity to take a chance . . . Thanks.

And to the readers who now allow me to share our story . . . Thanks.

Susan C. Haley

RAINY DAY PEOPLE

BOOK ONE

Prologue

Dawn. Night clutched its darkness around the fingers of light rising in the eastern sky. Rays of a still hidden sun peeking just above the horizon were quickly shrouded by rumbling gray clouds rolling in off the water. A cool mist hovered around the little house situated on a bluff along the shore. *Sea Fog.*

A dim light flickering inside the house, lantern-like, silhouetted two figures on the long narrow porch that protected the worn dwelling from the east wind. The couple, by habit over time, had their morning coffee on the rickety swing hanging there. They shared reveries, passions, and lately, anguish, before beginning their now kind of uncertain days. Again on this morning, as the scuffle between the elements swirled in the sky, they sat holding their hot mugs and overlooking a slightly angry sea.

"It's building up to something," he said, coaxing the swing into a leisurely to and fro movement with his feet on the old clapboard floor.

Without even a sideways glance, she asked, "You talking about the ocean or . . . ?" She didn't finish her question. She did hear the sigh escape his lips.

And, what's that supposed to mean?" he asked. But he kind of knew. He'd come to know her well.

1

She sipped the coffee, hoping it would dissolve the knot in her stomach and said nothing. She knew him well, too.

They sat quietly for awhile, this odd pair, both lost in private thoughts. Yet, even in their silence, hand found hand and fingers entwined. So different they were, like morning and eve, but the pull between them seemed to cross a lifetime, many lifetimes, yet no time at all.

He eased her around and pointed out over the water, now breaking in little white explosions over the rocks.

"See out there?" he motioned. "You and I are like that ocean. You're the waves ever rolling and ever dreaming of where to crest. And me? I'm the depths grown weary of the movement, yet stirred by it all. But, we are the same sea. One sea." He released her, but not before noticing a tear on her cheek, glistening in the wavering light.

"One sea?" she questioned, annoyed now. "Then why do you have to go off sailing a different one again? You say you're weary of the movement, happy sitting by your damn fire, but you aren't. Not really. You refuse to let go of the past, let it find its place, let its lessons be learned by whoever needs to learn them. You have to go back and try to fix every damn thing you ever did wrong, or think you did wrong." She turned and pushed his shoulder, hard.

"Well, go then. Just go. Take all that damnable responsibility and load it up on those shoulders of yours. The ones you think were made to carry the world around. Relieve everyone else of their own responsibility. Oh, hell yes, martyrdom is such a sweet cape to wrap one's self in. I just hope you're able to wear the damn thing."

Amber stood. "I must go to town while the road is still drivable."

Ben looked up at her, then down at the clapboard floor. He sighed, his face showing lines of weariness. He knew she'd go, had to go, and there was no point in discussing it further.

"Yes. Go now," he answered.

Moments later he watched her trudge up the rocky path, the blustering wind wrapping her windbreaker tight around her tiny body. Noticing her bent posture and unsure if it was just her usual determination or sadness he saw, a thought fleeted through his mind. *She really is like a fragile little bird.*

He rose from the swing and walked through the door to throw a log on the embers of a dying fire. Dying, as maybe they were. He pulled a chair up close and watched the flames come alive. Briefly, he thought of life before her, and since. We'll talk when she comes back, he mused. Oh, how they could talk. Strange almost, for a man and a woman.

"Another rainy day," he said to no one but himself.

Up on the road, the wind was biting and she hugged her jacket tightly to her body. Suddenly angry again, she looked up and implored of the forces above the rumbling clouds, blacker now, "Why? Damn you! Damn him! Why?"

Her only answer was a lightning bolt that struck the earth somewhere ahead. And then its peal of thunder, like laughter mocking her. The rain fell harder as she approached the car. She felt an urge to keep walking, to let the rain wash the tears threatening to spill onto her cheeks yet again. She really had nowhere to go, the trip to town only a pretext to avoid yet another argument. The road hugging the bluffs was slippery in this weather. Perhaps, her excuse to go running back down the path she'd just forced herself to climb? Back to him?

Doing neither, she tumbled into the car shivering from the cold wind. The need to just drive, drive fast on the winding road, took over. To drive away from this place she loved so. And this man, who allowed her the freedom her very being demanded, yet imprisoned her heart and mind. She dug the key from her purse, turned it in the ignition and felt the engine vibrate into life. Something moved inside her; a surge, as she pulled out onto the asphalt, turned the music loud, and pressed the accelerator hard. Now she would ride with the wind and be free for just a while.

3

The loud clap of thunder sat him straight in his chair and he listened for the sound he knew he'd hear. When he heard the car's engine revving a few moments later, he turned slightly in the direction of the sound.

"One of these days she's going to sail that damn fool car off the cliffs," he muttered out loud. His lips parted in a quiet chuckle, but a small fear grabbed at his heart with the thought. "Goddamn crazy woman," he said, slapping the arm of the chair in exasperation.

Amber slowed some, not much but some, as she approached the last set of curves before entering the town that lay in the lower flat land. A town built by the fishermen and whalers who came long ago to find refuge in the quiet bay that pushed back into the cliffs along the rugged coast.

The houses and shops along the narrow streets, tumbling chimneys and missing shingles revealing their age, stood as wooden tombstones in testimony of its history. It was a quiet hamlet except for the spurts of tourism, the seasonal festivals, and the occasional row when a riled sea kept the fishing boats in the harbor and men became impatient with waiting. Now, years later, they'd chosen it for a time. Or, maybe the town had chosen them. Had drawn them there by circumstance or destiny, by the turbulent and unexplained forces so much like the sea and themselves.

She pulled into a parking space in front of the small café and pushed the door of the car open against the wind now invading the harbor and threatening a gale. She hurried toward the open sign hanging on the door. Nearing the entrance, she changed her mind. *No! Get back in the car and just drive.*

Out on the road again, she intended to keep going west, into the rolling farmland where the roads were straight and unbending, but at the edge of town she turned east, back toward the little house on the bluff. Tears burned her eyes again but she drove faster, not to the beat of the music this time, but to the pounding of the pull in her heart.

4

Halfway back and now unable to see because of the rain and the wipers beating furiously on the windshield, she pulled into a small cove, an outcropping, that sheltered the sea birds taking respite from the storm. They became uneasy when she pulled into the cover and turned the engine off, yet didn't fly away.

"It's all right, bird friends," she said. "If you don't mind, I'd like to share your place awhile. Hide a moment from a storm of my own." The birds seemed satisfied, as if understanding what was said just by looking at her. Suddenly tired, she lowered her head to the steering wheel, her long auburn hair falling and covering the sides of her face.

"Damn him," she muttered again, half-heartedly, as her thoughts trailed back to when they first met.

* * * *

It was Saturday. She always spent Saturday morning in her favorite place, the bookstore that had survived the influx of growth ruining seaside towns. It was a quaint little store so unlike the ordered atmosphere found in the better known chains. The wooden floor was polished to belie its age, and the air was faintly scented with the smell of paper and printers ink.

To her this place was a cathedral of thought, a graveyard of energies past, sanctified and almost holy, for it held all she cherished on its dusty shelves. She slipped inside almost in reverence, as she always did. Bach, Emerson, Thoreau, she loved them all, those who wrote from their soul. They had provided her only solace in the lonely months since her husband's death, and she'd heard that Richard's newest book had arrived.

She waved "hello" to the young salesgirl and headed straight to her favorite nook. As she rounded the end case she saw him standing in front of New Arrivals, and was immediately irritated. Damn! A stranger had invaded her solitary corner and he was standing in front of the display of Richard's new book, slowly leafing through its pages.

5

Moving slowly forward, she sized him up. He was about her age, taller, but then everyone was taller than she. He was wearing a plain green European walking hat and casually dressed in jeans, loafers, and white short-sleeved shirt, a cross between aging hippy and something else. Something one might find in a smoky bar, a roadside cafe, or a town meeting. Nothing to look at really, but he had a certain air about him.

She edged closer, curiosity taking over her initial irritation. He was engrossed in his reading and didn't seem to even notice her. She studied him more carefully while pretending to browse. His face was lined and worn inside his slight beard, like an outdoor face, but he didn't look the part. A life lived on the edge, she suspected. He seemed, himself, a story waiting to be told. She wondered of his interest in Bach.

"Excuse me," she said trying to get by, but he didn't seem to hear. Feeling her aggravation returning, she said again, "Excuse me."

"I heard you," the stranger said almost coldly without looking at her. He inched in toward the shelf, giving her room to pass, still reading, still not looking at her.

Rude bastard, she thought, but bit her lip and brushed past him. There was no smell of cologne on him, no aftershave, just a hint of tobacco smoke. She managed another look out of the corner of her eye. He was clean but unkempt at once. No belt on the jeans, no socks for the shoes, but his smaller than normal eyeglasses hinted at fashion, and his ring was as if hand-made from some Arts & Craft. City boy. No wedding ring.

What the hell am I doing studying this man, this rude man, she wondered, as thoughts of her late husband passed through her mind? She unconsciously plucked a book from the shelf and started leafing through its pages.

His deep voice almost made her jump. "My turn," he said. She glanced up and into his face, and there it was . . . all of it, in his eyes. *Oh, God.*

"I'm sorry, w-what?" Her voice was barely audible.

"I said it's my turn to be excused."

She felt foolish and blushed as he looked into her eyes with a calm but piercing directness. "To pass by, I mean."

Now there was no coldness to this stranger, at least in his voice. It was a voice as gentle as deep, but lined with impatience. Or was it arrogance? She wasn't sure. She moved to let him pass and tried to focus on the book, no longer seeing the words on the page. He brushed against her ever so slightly as he moved by, and she felt a tightening rise inside her and lodge in her throat. She closed her eyes and swallowed hard, again focusing on the book in her hands. But her mind stayed riveted on the man and the feeling he'd unexpectedly aroused in her.

"Rude bastard," she mumbled her thoughts, not knowing why, and stole a quick glance toward the counter where the clerk was taking his money. He must have felt her stare, for he suddenly looked straight at her. He was studying her with eyes the color of a vivid sky.

She quickly looked away. She didn't see him leave, but the tinkling of the bell above the door told her he had. The book she was no longer interested in trembled in her hands.

* * * *

The wind was swirling now. Clumps of broken sea oats mimicked tumbleweeds as they rolled down the asphalt. The black thunderheads, yet tossing their bolts of lightning, were heading out over the water.

Raising her head slowly, she brushed the long hair off her face and leaned back against the seat, breathing deeply. She pushed the CD back into the player and turned the key, tossing a little wave to the sea birds still perched on the rocks.

"It's going to be calm in a couple of hours, little ones. Wind's out of the west now," she said pulling out onto the road. The drive back was short.

Gingerly making her way back down the rain-slick path, she knew where she'd find Ben. He was sitting on the swing

7

again, staring toward the water. Her hand found his as she sat beside him, and she felt his tenseness slowly ebb in the joining of their flesh. He turned to face her and she half smiled up at him.

"So what're you doing? Out there chasing rainbows among the lightning bolts in that damnable car of yours? Lunatic, that's what you are." But he was smiling now, too, and draped his arm around her shoulders. He worried for her when she struggled so with his ways.

Leaning into him and resting her head against his arm, once again her fear lost its grip. How well she knew his penchant for evasion, not dealing with issues. Resigned, she told herself to just let it be. In time, she knew, he'd confront her.

"Want some hot soup for supper?" she asked, giving his belly a loving pat. The water was calming, the rain had stopped, and the setting sun was able to peek over the bluff behind them.

"Hot soup? Figures. Next I'll be getting a grape or two for breakfast."

It had taken her awhile to learn the way he kidded her, this man whose moods were often as stormy as the clouds. It was as if the pages in his life had been turned by forces out of his control. Whole chapters were hidden and guarded, and she suspected she'd never be allowed to read them. She could only wonder when she saw the tenseness form in his jaw, or held him close at night and felt the cold sweat of his nightmares against her skin.

But learn she had, and to cherish the times when he'd tease or talk to her of his life. The parts that were an open book. She cherished the deep laugh and sparkling blue eyes, and those times when he'd tell his story by the hours.

"When you get grapes for breakfast, they'll be served on your favorite oatmeal. I promise." She laughed and punched his arm as she rose to go inside to the small kitchen.

"I hate oatmeal," he said in harmony with the creaking screen door. He immediately felt her void as the place beside him on the swing sat empty, as he'd felt it in her absence.

8

And still, he wondered what it was about this woman that had made her come with him, which took them from all they'd known before; that made both know they must.

She was calling him now. Guess I better go slurp the abominable soup, he thought. He got up slowly, not ready to give up his daydreams. As he entered the kitchen, she was bent over the table lighting a candle, and his heart tightened as he sat and picked up his spoon.

Sipping on the hot soup, noticing it was sprinkled with cheese, her little way of giving in just a bit on the diet she insisted would keep him around a while longer, he finally asked, "So, where did you and that fool car go today on your infernal rainbow hunt?"

"Why would you even ask that when you already know?"

"Because you're puzzling, that's why."

"Me? Puzzling?"

"Yes, you. You're always running off in your car and driving like a scalded cat, only to return as if you've merely been for a drive in the country. In the meantime, I have to sit and worry if you've sailed off one of the cliffs because of your reckless abandon. Then you sit, and then you make soup. Shouldn't you be out working on a dragster instead?"

"Oh, pfffttt. I drive fast; you drive like an old lady with trifocals. So what?"

"So what?" His eyes widened at the question.

"Yes, so what? And eat your soup."

He pushed the soup away. "Hate soup."

"Eat it anyway."

"You know, Abby, there's a limit to what we can do, and if that wasn't so, there couldn't be a tree, a critter, or anything else you love so. We'd all walk through walls and walls wouldn't be necessary."

"I don't know any such thing," she retorted. For me, there are no absolute limits. The magic of it all is in discovering our limits and what we only think are our limits. And, wouldn't it be wonderful if walls weren't necessary?"

9

He caught the implication in her last, but ignored it and picked up a small piece of driftwood, a remnant of an earlier walk along the shore. "See this? Look at how, over time, lots of time, it developed this way. Its design shows grace and the intellect of Creation, so to speak." He turned it, revealing its almost grotesqueness from wind and sea water. "Forces made it become as it is since its inception as a tree branch. And this."

She looked at him as he laid the wood down and picked up a pine cone.

"A pine cone's job is to rebuild the forest after a fire's come through to weed out the weak. No fire, the cone lays unfulfilled forever, or until it dies. That isn't chance; something makes it that way. While everything else is burned to death, the lowly pine cone comes into its own. Now why do you suppose there's a need for the weak to perish in all living things? Shouldn't there be a place for all things? Why do you cut your grass instead of letting it take over, which it would? Doesn't it belong, same as you? But it's weaker, in a round about way, so it's controlled. It dies."

"What on earth does any of that have to do with the way I drive?" she asked, becoming irritated.

"This, goddammit. You are weaker than the forces of nature, of steel against rock at 100 miles per hour on a slippery road. Same as the forest is to fire, that wood is to water. Do you want to die? Or, do you think that rainbow of yours will suddenly appear, swoop down, and lift you up above it all?"

She looked down, stirring the soup in her bowl and wondering the exact same thing.

On impulse, he rose, walked around the table, and bent and kissed her cheek lightly. "I'm going to watch the tube." He walked off into the living room and didn't look back. And why should he, since they'd had this discussion many times.

Her cheek tingled where his lips had brushed, and she looked up to watch him cross into the small sitting room and turn on the TV. Picking a grape from the cluster in the bowl, she hurled it in his direction, hitting him square in the chest as he sat back in the chair by the fireplace.

"HEY!"

She burst into laughter at finding her mark, and at his surprise. "Want vanilla in your coffee, or plain milk?" she asked, starting to clear the table.

"Vanilla, and *this*," he said, as the grape flew over her shoulder. The deep-throated chuckle was music to her ears, and caused her to remember the first time she'd heard it.

* * * *

DO YOU BELIEVE IN RAINBOWS?

Sunday dawned warm, covered with a radiant sky, as was common in April. It was the kind of day that demanded coffee and a read by the shore. Grabbing the book purchased the day before, her thoughts drifted back to the unsettling occurrence at the bookstore.

Still not understanding her reaction to the stranger who shared an interest in Bach, she now felt embarrassed at her fumbling in his presence. What he must have thought at such behavior. Dismissing it, she stuffed a Ziploc bag with Cheerios and headed out the door, deciding to walk to the small park by the jetty instead of driving.

Approaching the beach, she saw him. He was sitting on the bench, *her* bench, surrounded by fluttering seagulls. Instead of the previous irritation felt at the bookstore, an unexplained excitement came over her. But quickly, the embarrassment returned.

"Maybe I should just go somewhere else," she wondered out loud. "Aww, hell, it is my bench and there is an empty other half."

She smiled a greeting as she sat on the vacant portion of the bench where he sat throwing crumbs to the hovering, aggressive gulls. Definitely a tourist, she thought, but her heart sensed an animal lover and her embarrassment was replaced with a feeling of camaraderie. "Good thing you're wearing that cap."

"Don't you people ever feed these poor critters?" He sort of chuckled in that deep voice of his, not looking at her. It seemed as if he knew it was her.

"Just happened to bring their dessert," she answered, pulling the Cheerios from her book bag. Their eyes met again, but this time she didn't look down. Both then turned away and continued to feed the ever-ravenous gulls, remaining strangely aware of the other's presence.

"They never fill up, you know," she said, breaking the silence. He nodded, but his gaze remained fixed on the birds. Hesitating, she turned toward him, "Mind if I ask you a question?"

"Yes, but you will anyway." He glanced at her, waiting for a reaction.

"True," she said, smiling to break the ice. He turned back and tossed a bread crumb into the air and one of the gulls caught it on the uptake. "Do you believe in rainbows?"

He was silent for a long moment. "What kind of question is that? Don't you want to know who I am, if I'm married or not, what I do for a living? You know, the usual questions women ask."

"Not really. I just wanted to know if you believe in rainbows."

"Maybe," was his answer, but his tone said otherwise.

"Okay." Rising, she threw all the Cheerios to the birds at once, then turned and walked away without another word.

Almost reluctantly, he watched her go and then turned back to the gulls who were busily eating the crumbs she'd left, and ignoring him. Bothered, he stood and looked to see where she'd gone.

She walked quickly, afraid that if she didn't he might call her back. Or, afraid he wouldn't. She didn't know what she was thinking anymore since this man had so abruptly entered her life, invaded her solitude and loneliness, yet added to it by his unfriendliness. She didn't know, and right now didn't care. She wanted only to get away from him.

She followed the path through the Sea Grapes that would block her view, not wanting to give in to the temptation to look back. Where the trail opened back into the parking lot, she quickened her steps. And there he was, blocking her escape. It startled her. "Oh! Dammit!"

"Sorry," he answered somewhat sheepishly. "I cut across to catch up. Didn't mean to scare you."

Amber backed away, angry now. "Who are you, anyway? You're ruder than hell to me in the bookstore, then aloof to my simple question. Now you scare the wits out of me."

At this, a slight smile formed on his lips. "I'd say you were the rude one, bumping into me in the store like that. You damn near knocked me over."

"What? Why, it was you who . . . ." She stopped. He was grinning now, an obvious joke on his part, and she'd missed it. Unable to stop herself, she began to smile. They both said the same word at the same time.

"Sorry."

She laughed, he chuckled, both slightly self-conscious. There was a long pause as each fumbled, not knowing what to say next.

"I wanted to tell you something," he finally said, his tone sincere now. "I never talk to strangers. Becoming a habit, I suppose. Maybe it comes with aging, getting cantankerous, I mean."

She guessed him to be not much older than herself, but his face said he was older. It was deeply lined, as if permanently tanned at one time, but more like he'd seen too much too soon, lived too hard too fast. Or felt too much, maybe.

This is crazy, she thought. He's nothing like . . . . She stopped, afraid of what she was thinking, then answered, "Neither do I."

"But, you talked to me," he said with a curious tone. "Just now."

She had to admit he was right. She'd been the one to start the conversation.

"But, somehow it's as if you're not a stranger," he continued. "I get this almost eerie feeling I know you, that we've met before."

"Maybe," she said, now playing his game.

"Say, could we just do this over?" he said. I feel responsible for screwing up your plans." He glanced at her book bag. "Here, I mean."

"No, it's not your fault. It was me that interrupted you, and I really must go now." She wanted to go home. She needed time to sort out this strange feeling coming over her.

Stepping aside so she could go on, he said, "I hear coffee and sunsets go well together."

She pretended not to hear him and kept walking.

"I like vanilla in mine," he called after her.

"Vanilla, huh?" she said, but didn't look back. Instead, looking at her watch and continuing on.

He watched her walk away and then turned back toward the flock of gulls, wondering at his feeling of attraction to this woman. Was it because she was so different than most he'd known? Or, had he known her for a long, long time? He made a mental note about the time of sunset.

Walking home, Amber regretted her decision not to drive to the jetty park. The sun was hotter now and she was eager to get home into the cool solitude that had become her haven. Her reaction to this man, this strange encounter, was unsettling. Something rumbled underneath the surface of it all and she couldn't put her finger on it. It wasn't your typical movie plot, lonely woman meets handsome man, stomach ties in knots, and romance bursts forth from bud to flower, kind of a thing for sure. No, it was something much deeper than that, almost as he'd said, eerie.

She opened the door to the rush of cool air in the house and let it soothe her flushed face. The grove of old trees overhead was a canopy of shade, keeping the house comfortable as well as private, and how glad she was now she'd insisted on the trees staying when the house was built.

Kicking off her shoes, she walked over and pushed a CD into the player and threw herself on the couch. She felt safe here; safe in the solitude and the music. Music was to her ears what flowers were to her eyes. Peace.

Pondering the events of the last couple days would come easier now. In the two years since Jeff had passed, she'd pondered much on the workings of the scheme of life, its purpose and meaning. The pain endured then, the pangs since, had forced her to look at things differently in his absence. She no longer held a surface view of life. Now, she was aware of the subtleties, the shadows, not just the apparent. Oh, how she missed him. How often she wondered if they'd ever meet again.

Of one thing she'd become certain, to pay close attention to reactions within herself as they were usually revelations of higher things. The something rumbling deep inside, the intuition, was often more profound than the situation that triggered it. And this man had, indeed, triggered a reaction that she hadn't felt in a long while. It scared and intrigued her at the same time.

She sensed the stranger was as much in the dark about his own reaction to her. She found herself looking forward to the possibility of seeing and talking to him again, exploring this new feeling no matter her previous insecurity. She wouldn't run away again. Sunset, did he say? How did he know sunset was her favorite time of day?

Ben returned to his son's apartment, thinking about the encounter. She's odd but interesting, he had to admit. Not many interested him anymore. He wondered at her age. She certainly made no excuses . . . no makeup, lipstick, or fake eyelashes. She was dressed simply in sandals, shorts and a halter-like top. Her skin was as bronze as her auburn hair. What you saw was what you got, and he liked honesty. The only flamboyance he'd spotted was the gold of her toe rings.

16

"Hi, Dad," the voice said, breaking into his thoughts. He looked up to see his son entering the room.

"Oh, hi, son. Hope I didn't wake you. You know me and my weird sleeping patterns."

Still only half awake, the younger man went to the coffeepot and began to make coffee. "Nah. Slept like a log. Where'd you go, out to eat?"

The small talk continued. He told him of sitting and feeding the birds, but left out the part about the woman, not knowing how his son might take it. Since the divorce years past and his growing up without him, he wasn't really sure where he stood with this boy. *Boy*? He's already in his thirties; why am I still calling him a boy? But he knew. Children would always be children to their parents, and parents always parents to their children.

The divorce had been ugly and he knew his son had been affected. Would, perhaps, always be affected. It was part of the reason for his being here in Florida now, to somehow, some way, see if he could right what had gone so wrong long ago. Yet, in the few days since his arrival, no opening seemed to present itself and he felt awkward and sensed his son did as well.

There had been the visits over the years, the birthday and Christmas gifts, the phone calls and letters. But they were always initiated by him, not the other way around, so he knew there was hurt there, and probably resentment. Still, he had to try and he didn't even know why he did, but he did.

"Working today?" he asked. He'd forgotten what day it was, but didn't want to admit it. No, he didn't like getting old, *older*, as he called it. It meant there were spaces of time, chunks, out of his life that he couldn't redo and he regretted it deeply. Time that should have spent while the boy was growing into a man.

"Uh-huh," the young man answered, "and I'll be late tonight as well. Will you be okay? Being alone in a burg like this, I mean?"

He had to laugh at his son's innocence. Alone? He'd always been alone. "Oh sure. I always find things to do. I walk the beach, go to bookstores, read, rob banks, armored cars, and old ladies' purses. You have to be careful with those purses. Most have Mace or a .45 inside."

The boy laughed and that made him happy. There was more small talk and then, like young men everywhere, he was out the door on his way to work. The closing of the door felt like the closing of a tomb.

What the hell am I trying to prove, he wondered. The kid's got his own life now, so why am I trying to get back in when I wasn't in before? Where was I when he was a teen? Off doing my thing. And when he was in his twenties? Off finding myself. What crap, he thought angrily. How much I lost out over all this . . . this shit. How I wish now I'd never gone to the Coast. How I wish I had stayed home and grown up with my son.

He thought of all the wasted years, the endless ups and downs of his life, and the god-awful people he'd met in his travels because of it. And he wondered why it had turned out this way, since it was the opposite of all his plans and dreams when his son was born.

But he knew why. Alcoholism. The same alcoholism that had ruined his parents' lives had ruined his as well. It had taken him from airline pilot to the bars and dashed all his dreams. It had taken him into divorce court and losing it all, and then sent him away, far away from his family as well. It had carried him on its broad and ugly back into the world of publishing, to fame of sorts, to Hollywood. The gold and the glitter. What bullshit.

And through it all, through the bars, the women, the endless financial and health problems, somehow he thought he was still doing the right thing. That, one day, all would be right in his world again. The Great Lie, it's called in certain circles.

But someday never came and now he was angry and disillusioned; angry at himself, disillusioned with the world. Money? What did that mean to him now compared to his

18

losses? Here he was approaching the autumn of his life sitting in a one-horse town a continent away from his home, trying to fix things with his son. To recoup some of his losses, or perhaps, to assuage his guilt. And it wasn't working. He could feel it. He'd beaten the booze, he'd managed to escape the clutches of La-La Land with some semblance of his sanity intact, but what good was it doing him?

His thoughts drifted back to the woman and why she had come into his life now, and this bothered him as well. Another groupie out for herself? Another one-night-stand? He'd come to rewrite an important chapter in his book of life, and found instead another about to open. He knew it. He knew because he knew life now and he knew himself.

Yet, there was something different about her. A sort of sadness of her own, a worldliness to her that asked what she was doing here, in this burg, instead of in one of the world's capitals. And something deeper. It was the "something deeper" that intrigued him most. No, this was no groupie, no ordinary woman, for that matter. Hell, she might be an angel for all I know. Or a demon.

Whatever she was, whoever she was, she had his attention, no doubt about it. He looked at his watch and wondered what time sundown arrived on this coast. Then he made his mind up not to meet her, picked up his new book and began to read.

CRAZY AS A LOON, HE SAID

Pouring the coffee into the thermos and remembering she had to stop for a container of vanilla cream, Amber grabbed ice from the freezer and broke it into the small Igloo cooler. She plucked a small cluster of grapes from the fruit bowl and laid them on the cubes and on impulse, tossed some cookies into a Ziploc and put them in, too. If nothing else, the gulls would enjoy them, she thought absent-mindedly.

Stuffing the thermos, cups, and spoons in her book bag, she looked around to see if she was forgetting anything. Satisfied, she changed into fresh jeans and a sweater and quickly braided her long hair. It was a beautiful evening, perfect for putting the top down and feeling the wind in her face.

The drive over was pleasant. Spotting a parking place exactly where they'd parted earlier that morning, she smiled to herself. Never a front row at sunset, why tonight? Coincidence? No, she didn't believe in coincidence. And look, a vacant picnic table sitting at the edge of the sand facing the sea. The sun was beginning its fall into the water, and suddenly, she wished she'd thought to bring a table cloth.

His voice from behind startled her. "You drive that thing or fly it?"

She turned around to see him standing there, watching her. "Fly it when I can," she answered with a smile.

She got out of the car, reached into the back seat and lifted the bag and the cooler at the same time. He made no move to help her.

Slinging her purse over her shoulder, she headed for the table not waiting to see if he followed, assuming he would as he was, after all, there. "Rude bastard," she whispered just beyond earshot, but found herself amused. She brushed the sand off the table, emptied her bag, and started to pour coffee in her cup without looking up. She felt him walk up behind her. He reached over and placed the other cup next to hers.

"Not too heavy on the vanilla," he said, moving around her.

"Vanilla? What vanilla?" She could play the game too.

"This vanilla." He grinned, opened the cooler, and removed the container.

Feigning annoyance, she grabbed the creamer from him, poured his cup a quarter full and topped it off with coffee. "Suppose you want a cookie, too?"

"Well, I sure don't want one of those grapes," he said with mock distaste.

She handed him the coffee and the Ziploc. "Help yourself," she said, moving around the table to sit facing the sun. She watched from the corner of her eye as he sipped his coffee, his eyes not on her but on the Gulf.

"So, what's brought you to our little South Florida beach town? You don't strike me as a tourist in the real sense of the word. Course, we're all tourists in that sense, the real sense."

"I'm visiting my son for a few days." The tourist remark caused him to turn toward her.

"Nice. Always nice to visit a son. I have a couple myself, sons, that is. You going to be here long?"

He thought about it longer than necessary, as if unsure. "I don't know. Couple of weeks, maybe. Depends. I don't make long range plans; kind of take it as it comes."

21

He looked back to the water and watched a flock of Pelicans sail by on an up current. After a moment, he looked back to her. "So when are you going to ask the rest of the questions?"

"The rest of what questions? Oh, you mean about rainbows?"

"Rainbows? No. Like how old I am. What I do for a living. Am I married. You know, those questions women always ask."

She felt irritation as he compared her to other women, but pushed it back. "That's none of my business. Nor, am I interested in your vital statistics or your past. I'm interested in your face, and the story it tells. I'm interested in the mystery in your eyes and the love you have for bookstores and Bach. It showed, you know." She motioned with her head toward the Gulf. "I'm interested in what you think of that sun out there, and why you feed seagulls. Your superfluous arrogance doesn't interest me at all."

At this he burst into laughter, that deep laughter that now held a sound of relief instead of imperviousness. "You know," he said, "I think I may just have one of those grapes after all."

"Good. They didn't spend all that time ripening just to be looked at or posing for an artist's brush."

"Point taken," he said, reaching for the cooler. "You talk as if the grapes are alive," he added as he popped one into his mouth.

"They are for their time," she said sipping on her coffee. "As alive as we are."

Suddenly he felt okay, felt he could talk to this woman without putting on the masquerades that had become, over the years, second nature to him.

"I wasn't going to come here tonight, you know," he said.

"No? Then why did you?"

"No. Then I read something in the book today, the new book by Bach."

"And what was that?"

22

"What the caterpillar calls the end of the world, the master calls a butterfly."

Now what is he talking about, she thought. "Well, I'm glad you did, decide to come that is."

"Yeah?"

"You seem to like the ocean. I see you looking at it a lot."

He nodded again.

"You've spent time by the water then?" It was more of a statement than a question.

"A good bit of my life, I'd say. A much angrier sea than this one, though."

There it was again. He talks in riddles. Why all the mystery?

As if reading her thoughts, he turned to face her. "What does your husband think of you packing grapes and cookies off to the beach to feed rude tourists and seagulls?" he asked, changing the subject.

"Now who's asking questions that women always ask?" She smiled at him. "My husband doesn't live here anymore, but I'd guess that he wouldn't mind at all."

"Doesn't live here?"

"No, he died two years ago. I live alone now." Now it was her that wore the face of life's agonies. "You up to a walk on the jetty? It's nice to be surrounded by water when the sun goes down." She jumped up before he could respond. "And, I have a few friends over there you may enjoy meeting."

He didn't want to meet her friends. He was content where they sat. Why did women always want you to meet their friends? he thought.

Sensing his hesitation and guessing why, she added, "Pelicans. You can learn a lot from a pelican."

Laughing now, he answered, "Why am I not surprised?"

"But, you are," she answered, and he knew she was right as she headed for the jetty without him. Taken back that she'd just move off like that, he thought, I should just sit here and let her go on alone. But something about her drew

23

him. "Yes, definitely different than I'm used to," he muttered as he began following her.

He followed slightly behind watching the way she moved, the way the wind blew her auburn hair. She took on another persona out here in the natural world, more light-hearted and free. Quite the opposite of the tense little woman he'd met yesterday in the bookstore.

She stopped at each new discovery along the sand, a shell here, a piece of wood there, studied it momentarily, and if found worthy, tossed it into her book bag. Upon reaching the rocks forming the long jetty, she found a seat on a large flat piece of concrete and sat, seemingly content, as if he wasn't there.

He climbed up on the jetty wall and lowered himself onto the seat beside her. Now he could see the pass connecting the inner coastal waterway that divided the mainland from the barrier islands and the ocean beyond. It was a boat channel, a highway of water. He found himself suddenly thinking of ships and the faraway places that had once been a part of his life in the military.

A large tri-masted schooner came along, chugging up the waterway with sails furled and fenders in, and suddenly he was happy that he'd come here, happy that he'd followed this strange woman to meet her friends after all.

They sat quietly for awhile, each breathing in the salt air and watching the waning sunlight, each looking around. And then she was up again and holding out her hand to help him stand.

"Come on, let's walk," she said, withdrawing her hand as soon as he stood, "out to the end, where the water surrounds the jetty."

She led him to another rock seat at the tip, this time facing the setting sun, taking time to introduce him to the pelicans perched here and there along the way. "This one's name is Birdfriend," she announced matter-of-factly, pointing to one of the large birds.

This crazy damn woman actually means it, he laughed to himself. They *were* her friends; no doubt. She talked to them

24

softly, and they seemed to know exactly what she was saying. Great, he thought, a woman who talks to birds. I must be with Mrs. Doolittle, losing my mind, or both. But it more than amused him, since he had bird friends, too, although he wouldn't readily admit it. Pigeons, gulls, hummingbirds, doves, anything that flew.

They watched the sun go down in silence, she intently, he occasionally watching her. They were unaware of time passing until it had and day was turning to night. Waves began to break over the rocks and he suddenly sprang to his feet and was moving back toward the beach, away from the surrounding water.

"Coming?" he asked without looking back.

She rose and followed, curious at his sudden retreat. He was walking faster than normal, but not quite running. Full darkness was approaching by the time they returned to the picnic table, and she began to gather the rest of her belongings.

"What's your hurry?" he said.

My hurry? she thought, but didn't comment. "Oh, time to be going home. I often come here to watch the sunset, but it gets chilly after dark, so best to get going."

"Let me," he said, grabbing her bag and the Igloo. They walked to her car silently and passing beneath one of the park lights, she noticed a frown on his face.

"You ever put the top up on this thing?" he asked as he loaded the car, stalling.

"Not in this kind of weather. I love the wind in my hair and the sky over my head." She put her hand out to him. "I hope you enjoyed the sunset, and I wish you a wonderful visit with your son while you're here."

"Thanks, I did and will," he said as he briefly took her hand. "Maybe you could show me a little more of your town over the next few days."

She hesitated. Oh, what the hell, she thought. "Well, I have to go to work tomorrow. You may be gone before I have time off again." Her voice was distant, as if not wanting it to be.

"You don't work twenty-four hours a day, I'm sure," he said, smiling. "At least let me return the favor. Is there a real coffee shop in this town? You know, one with exotic flavors."

"You mean like a Starbuck's or such? Yes, but it's a ways from here, up town. This is just a burg, I'm afraid. Not very convenient like in big cities." Sensing by his mannerisms that he probably came from brighter, faster places, she felt almost embarrassed at her simple life.

He thought of his son calling the town the same thing and grinned. "Burgs are okay now and then. It would be a way to give me a ride in that plane of yours," he teased, referring to her fancy convertible. "By going uptown, I mean."

"You got your co-pilot's license?" she kidded.

"As a matter of fact, I do."

"Okay. I suppose I could meet you here on Wednesday evening. If you're free then, coffee it is."

"Okay, deal. I may even give you a pointer or two."

"What?"

"About flying." He smiled and gave her a mischievous wink.

Amber got in her car, started the engine, and backed out with a toss of her hand, then sped away, spewing gravel behind her.

Ben watched her drive off, the wind already catching her hair and the music playing louder than one her age might play it.

"HEY!" he yelled after her. "WHAT TIME?" But she was gone, her music carving a trail through the humid air like the wake of a boat.

"Crazy as a loon," he said, but he was smiling as he said it.

* * * *

Pulling herself from her reverie, she hung the dish towel out of sight and turned to look at Ben, still staring at a PBS program on the television. The look on his face told her he was engrossed.

Amazing, she thought, his insatiable thirst for knowledge. His quest seemed more to figure out the why's of things than the how. She related to him, this man who shared her intensity; though in a different way. She felt the rush of compassion his inner turmoil instilled in her. It was that same unrest that often cramped her stomach in fear.

There was still a chasm between them that shouldn't be, after the special time. Since that joining together, she'd been an open book, taking him through every page, while he, it seemed, remained the dusty novel hidden on a shelf.

She joined him by the fire, plopping on the small couch across from his chair. He grunted an acknowledgment of her presence, but his eyes never left the screen. An interview of some sort was in progress, so she picked up a magazine, content just to be near him for now. He smiled slightly at her silence, her knowing that he wanted to hear the end of the discussion that had caught his interest. Yes, they'd come to know each other well.

As the program was ending Amber got up, and taking her wind breaker off the coat stand, went to sit on the porch swing. The weather had moved elsewhere now, and the moon was a crescent hanging low over the ocean among a myriad of stars. She heard him following her through the door a few minutes later.

"Nice ending to a rainy day." Handing her a cup of coffee, Ben took his seat along side her on the swing. She took the cup and sighed.

"Yes, always the calm follows a storm, doesn't it?"

Looking at her wrapped in the yellow jacket befuddled and amused him. She'd insisted on wearing it since the night he'd loaned it to her. Three times her size, she had to clutch it around her and he often thought it was her way of holding on to something tangible, something that would never leave.

"So what took you so long doing those dishes? Not much mess with a bowl of soup," he said, wrapping her hand in his.

27

"Oh, just thinking. You know me, always pondering. And now I must be like a little chipmunk, storing our memories and our moments for winter." She was talking more to herself than him as she leaned over and rested against his shoulder.

"Well, tomorrow is another day," he said, giving her a squeeze. His thoughts raced. Will I be able to walk away without telling her the truth? Must I? Which will hurt the most?"

* * * *

A PERFECT NIGHT IN APRIL

For two days, the thought of going to meet this man again nagged at her. She didn't even know his name. And since Jeff had left there was no interest in meeting other men. None, not even for coffee. No man could be what he had been to her, so why bother? She was perfectly content alone with her thoughts, her memories, and her books. She had her sons and they became the men in her life, all she needed. So why this concern over a promise to have coffee with a stranger?

She wondered even more about the strange feelings that had come over her when she'd looked at him; like a familiarity, but not. And why, when he'd accidentally brushed against her in the bookstore, did she react as if she'd been burned, but from within? It was almost as if she knew that touch.

It wasn't that she was afraid to go for a ride with him. She trusted her inner instincts that he was harmless enough. Actually, she wasn't afraid of much of anything. Feeling fear usually signaled impending danger, pain, or death. Most feared death, she supposed. But she'd already experienced death, and pain was second nature now. Fear had changed into acceptance, or maybe, tolerance.

But what was his motive? Did he even have one? He was in a strange town with nothing to do while his son worked. Was he bored? Willing to give the poor widow a tumble in her lack of physical fulfillment? Do her a favor, like so many other assholes had intended when they'd hit on her?

This man was worldly; she could tell by looking at his face, in his eyes. The arrogance was there, the impatience that matched her own at being intruded upon, the scars left by many traveled roads. Yet, a sadness and a gentleness were there, too, maybe an underlying understanding that somehow there was more to be than he'd been, or a need to experience the things that had gotten away? Who knows? She was guessing.

She remembered how he looked that morning sitting and throwing crumbs to the gulls. Almost as if he were trying to figure things out, content at the attempt even. She recalled the feeling of camaraderie she'd felt at seeing him sitting with the birds hovering all around him.

"Oh, hell. Enough of this analyzing," she snapped out loud. What possible difference could a strange man and one cup of coffee up town make in her life one way or the other? Especially one that would soon be gone.

"Damn. Where's that spirit, woman?" she asked herself. "Would Jeff have you moping about like this? Of course not. He'd have you down those stairs, and turning down a road just because it was there." Oh God, how she missed him, she thought, as she headed for the closet to grab a clean pair of jeans and a top. Soon she was out the door and down the steps to her car.

Driving to the beach, she wondered if he'd even remember that he'd invited her to go for one of those exotic coffees. Or, that she'd agreed to go, to take him for a ride in her plane, as he called it. Recalling how he'd mentioned knowing about flying and giving her a pointer or two made her laugh. Just what I need . . . more damn advice. But she liked the humor in the idea, and if he didn't show up, she'd just go inland and ride, alone and fast. She didn't really need a pointer on flying and it was a much too beautiful mid-April evening to be indoors.

He was standing in the exact spot where the car had been parked on Sunday. He was dressed casually and waved as she pulled into the parking area.

"I see you made it," he said.

Amber laughed. "Never doubt a woman promised pointers on flying. Should I park, or do you still wish to repay a cup of coffee?" Seeing the sparkle in his eyes made her feel good. Perhaps they both just needed a little lightness of heart for a change.

"Your belt isn't buckled. Pointer number one," he said, trying to be funny. "Are you sure you know how to fly this thing?"

"Oh, just get in. I never wear a belt. Too damn confining. But feel free to buckle up if you must." She motioned toward the passenger door.

He hesitated and seemed to be looking around.

"Well?" she asked.

"I'm looking for one of those machines that issue insurance. You know, like at the airports." He looked apprehensive as he started around for the passenger side.

"For Pete's sake," she answered, "What do you take me for, some kind of lunatic?"

"Of course," he answered as he got in and buckled up. "Why else would I be having a cup of coffee with you?" He looked up from his buckle and winked, "See, I kind of like lunatics."

She saw the mischievous grin just beginning to curl on his mouth. Ah-ha, she thought. Now I get it. He likes to tease. Okay, I can play that game too. "Oh, don't worry, I really am a safe driver. My license says so," she answered with an enigmatic smile. Before he could reply, she slammed the accelerator down hard and spun around in the gravel as the car fairly leaped forward.

"Holy shit!" was all he could say as she barreled out of the lot and onto the roadway.

31

Glancing over as she rounded one curve, tires whining, she couldn't tell if he was petrified or stunned, but one thing was certain; she was getting a kick out of it and kind of felt he was, too. He turned and said something, but between the wind and the music, she couldn't understand him. She turned the song down so she could hear.

"What? Did you say something?"

"I said do you always drive like this?" Now he was laughing as he leaned over and turned the CD back to loud, and then laid his head back on the seat so he could feel the wind full on his face.

For the rest of the ride they were silent, listening to the music, she watching the road, and him watching the stars. And, occasionally, her. It was a comfortable silence, though, not one of those nothing-to-say, strained, kind. Strange, she thought, peeking over at him. He looks as if he belongs sitting there, as if a peace had come over him, a feeling that he was about to be one of those things he'd rarely been. Content.

She saw the Starbuck's sign a block ahead now, and eased over into the right lane, slowing down. "Just about there," she said, hesitant to interrupt his thoughts, whatever they were. "And, it looks like it's going to be a safe landing after all, oh ye of little faith." Now it was her that winked at him.

"Never doubted you for a minute. Nope, not a minute. Have a question for you, though, if I may," he added.

She turned into the lot and a parking place. Switching the key off, she turned to face him. "And what might that be?"

"How does one who loves sunsets and rainbows, books, birds, and quiet things, also love speed, sporty convertibles, and hard rock music? Seems at odds."

She looked at him intently, suddenly serious herself. "It's a vibration of sorts. Different, yes, but vibration just the same. Anything that moves within my veins and touches my soul, that vibrates the life in me, that, I love." It was almost a whisper, she said it so softly. Then she opened the door and got out, grabbing her purse from the floor behind the seat. "Vanilla, right?"

"No, you don't," he said, climbing out the other side. "I owe you a coffee, remember? And, for the ticket to ride." He was looking at her now, really looking at her. Not moving.

Starting for the door but sensing something, she turned and looked back to where he stood, still not moving. This time their eyes locked, and neither looked down. Suddenly they were no longer strangers, never had been. They'd just been on the journey that would bring them here. To a ride for coffee under the stars. Their lives would never be void of the other again; of that she was certain. No matter what road either traveled from that point on.

Each moved around the car and they walked side by side toward the coffee shop entrance. As they did, their hands grazed gently, but there was no urgency in the moment. No desire to grab hold. No need for words about it. No electric shock as when in the bookstore. It just was.

"Yes, vanilla," he said, opening the door for her.

THE ROAD NOT TAKEN

Thoughts wound through her mind like the wind ruffling through her hair as she meandered, driving slowly now, along the curvy coast road. The music played softer, too, a calming music over an easy listening station. The sea, dark and endless in the night, was as void of form as was her understanding of the previous few hours. She pulled over to the shoulder and peered into the blackness that was the water.

That the water was there was an absolute, but where it began and how far it traveled to the horizon, was shrouded in obscurity. Much like the experience of the previous hours. It was a mystery, but one that held no fear, no tenseness; only wonderment. She was feeling a quiet acceptance for the first time in a long while.

They'd enjoyed the discovery of many mutual passions over their coffee at the shop, spent hours talking of books and bookstores, wildlife and Nature. They'd learned that they shared a mutual love of the sea and the world around them, its vastness and power. Both were intrigued by the mysteries of life, especially their own.

He'd talked of his youth, of the places he'd been, boats and ships, an island he'd lived on in Micronesia. She'd talked of her own, simple in comparison. He'd continued to tease her about her "flying machine" and she'd noticed the lines in his face softening at the very mention of flying.

He joked a lot, so she'd asked him if he wrote as he spoke, with a flair for truth that wore a bright cloak of humor. The mention of writing seemed to irritate him, if only slightly.

Shifting his eyes to his coffee cup, he'd asked, "What makes you think I write?"

"Because you look like a writer," she'd answered.

He was surprised at her response, not offended, but seemingly not pleased, either, at her guess. She didn't really understand what the big deal was and passed it off as another of his quirks.

But, it was their eyes that had spoken the most. Where, she asked herself, was this awareness coming from? She sensed they'd both felt it during the first encounter in the bookstore, then in the parking lot at the beach . . . a familiarity, some inexplicable pull across time. But, it was conveyed only when their eyes truly held, and something layered in them seemed to understand that.

Wanting to be alone with these new-found feelings, and a tired waitress informing them that it was closing time, she'd asked if he'd mind taking the long way back.

"Not at all, I rather think I'd enjoy it."

So, they'd ridden away from the water this time, inland, where the breeze and the stars were uncluttered by buildings and city lights, where the pavement was open and belonged only to them. And so she'd driven, and driven, while each wrapped themselves in the seclusion of private thoughts.

At one point they stopped at one of those small roadside picnic areas one never saw anyone using and wondered why it was even there. They sat, listening as the night sounds made a music of their own, and looking up into the star-filled sky at worlds beyond this one. She, wondering if the paths they'd previously taken, or were about to take, were up there somewhere.

It was here that he'd told her of flying, really flying, and his years spent in airplanes above the clouds and away from the noise and clutter below. Listening to him and how he spoke almost in awe of it, she'd wanted to fly with him, then, right then.

It happened as he quoted from one of her favorite poems by a young and long-dead poet named John Magee:

"Up, up the long, delirious, burning blue I've topped the wind-swept heights with easy grace. Where never lark, or even eagle flew. And, while with silent lifting mind I've trod, the high untrespassed sanctity of space, put out my hand and touched the face of God."

He'd taken her hand and they'd remained silent, occasionally looking at each other in the moonlight. It was she who had broken the spell. Impulsively, as all her movements seemed to be, she'd started the car, cranked up her music and had driven him, fast, back toward the coast and home.

When stopped in front of his son's place, she tore a page out of a notebook in her purse and quickly jotted down an address and phone number. He'd looked at it, put it into his pocket, and then got out of the car.

"Thanks for everything," he said. "I really enjoyed tonight."

"So did I, and thank you for the coffee and the pointers." She smiled up at him, but modestly.

He was staring at her again and it had made her feel awkward; why, she didn't know.

"Later, babe." He smiled as he turned to go. That was all, as if he'd somehow known her need to be away from him, or from herself. She waved goodbye as she pulled away, and so they'd parted, her driving home to her world, him climbing the stairs to his.

She pulled into her driveway, parked, and lingered in the car. Part of her was dreading going in the house. Acceptance of the emptiness of life without Jeff had come only by crawling on her knees through a desert of despair in that house. Yet, another part of her yearned for the comfort of its walls because her answers were found in that desert.

Now, her mind held a new question. This no-longer-stranger would never really leave her life again. She knew that. But, her rational mind kept asking how could he not? She lived in one world, he in another. Without it being spoken, she knew his life was different than her own. He'd have to return to it and deal with it, because a rage or a sadness, she wasn't sure which, seemed to boil within him. She'd felt it in his touch, an almost trembling inside.

She climbed the stairs, inserted the key in the lock, then looked up for a last glance at the heavens. A lone star shooting across the sky from east to west caught her attention. It seemed to hang there just above the treetops, winking brightly in the black velvet sky as if smiling at her. She smiled back, then pushed the door open and went in.

Ben slipped inside quietly. It was late and he didn't want to wake his son. Of course, he thought, he might not even be home yet, remembering his own days of partying until dawn, then going to work. Well, it's his life now, just as mine is mine. All he hoped for was that the family curse, the alcoholism, hadn't gotten to his offspring the way it had him.

He'd mentioned it when he first sobered up, and the boy seemed to understand the risks. Yet he also remembered himself saying at one time that he would never be like his own parents in that regard, and then had become them in so many ways. Would his son do the same?

At least now he could pass on what he'd learned in life, and maybe that would help keep his son aware and the mistakes from repeating themselves. It's about all he had left to give him, all things considered.

On impulse he started to check the boy's room to see if he was home, and then stopped himself. Privacy meant just that. Going into the kitchen instead, he turned on the light and made some coffee. He sat and pulled the slip of paper she'd given him from his pocket. It wasn't an address but a post office box, and he wondered why she would have that instead of a street address. Maybe because she's alone, he thought, and doesn't want people to know where she lives. And, she'd forgotten to write her first name. Only the last, an address and phone number.

The evening had been sort of strange anyway, so in a sense, the slip of paper was all part of that. How many times in the past he would've been asked to come in to spend the night, and how many times he did. Yet, this woman seemed as if she couldn't get away fast enough, and the interesting part to him was that he didn't mind.

A memory came to him then of the time he'd written a poem called *"One Night Stand"* about his misadventures, and he smiled at the recollection. When he'd read it aloud to a group, he noticed the women fidgeting in their seats, the men grinning like the hormonal fools all men are, and then the looks of disbelief, and relief in some cases, when the poem turned out to be about a night stand beside his bed, and not about sex at all. It had gotten some laughs and the usual phone numbers slipped into his hand.

Those were halcyon days at the university and on the circuit and tours, days he'd enjoyed immensely. But, he'd tired of the whole scene after awhile, as he seemed to do with all things, and had left. There were just too many crazies, too much drinking, too many desperate people as he himself had been. In the meantime years had passed; he'd been forgotten and had forgotten what he'd been.

His thoughts returned to the woman. Why had he said, *Later, babe*, as if she was just another bimbo, which she clearly wasn't? He didn't know.

"Habit, I guess," he said aloud, as if someone was across the table and listening. Which they weren't. Which they hadn't been in many a year by his own design, his own reclusiveness. Now, he mostly just watched people from afar, if he paid any attention to them at all, no longer eager to enter the mindless bantering that went on. Men were interested in sports, women were interested in men and babies, and none of them interested in life itself. No one wanted to talk about what made it work. Was there afterlife? How could God be a loving God and allow such misery? Why people hate, why they love. Do dogs smile? Why do traffic signs say *walk* when they should say *run for your life?*

That evening, he and another like himself sat in an open car and had done nothing much more than stare at the stars. Now she was gone, he was back in his son's apartment not knowing what to do about his situation, and it was getting late in more ways than one.

There was just a twinge of pain in his groin. He reached for the yellow-lined pad lying on the table that he always carried on trips, the one he'd scribbled on off and on since his arrival. He stared at it for a moment, then picked up a pencil and began to write.

Hours passed, his hand never stopping, the pencil moving effortlessly from one line, one thought, to the next. Somewhere around four or five in the morning he put the pencil down, looked around the apartment as if seeing it for the last time, got up from the table and went into the spare bedroom. He emerged a few moments later suitcase in hand, walked to the front door and left without looking back.

On the table sat the yellow pad with the words, a story, and the story was his. *My Dearest Son,* it began. It ended with *Your Loving Father.* In-between were the joys and heartaches of a lifetime, the words most men want to say to their children and never find the time, the words most can't bring themselves to say, and the feelings they keep inside. Forgotten words, lost words, estranged words. Words of endearment. Words of truth.

Below, in the semi-darkness of approaching dawn, a cab pulled up, he got in, the cab pulled away and the words were left behind. When the cabby asked where he wanted to go, he answered, "Back about thirty years." When the confused cabby asked the destination again, his answer was simpler, yet more revealing.

"Just take me to the airport, any airport," he said as he stared out the window.

Above the cab, above the town itself, rain clouds were forming. There was a crack of thunder, then falling rain as the cab carried him away from his past and into his future, revealing by its tire marks and disappearing red tail lights if but briefly, the road not taken.

* * * *

"Yes, tomorrow is another day." Amber sighed, watching the moon climbing higher among the stars now. Funny how, if you turned your head just right, a crescent moon looks like a big smile in the sky, or a frown, she thought. "But, there are only so many tomorrows left for you and I," she added, almost as an after thought.

Ben turned to her. "And, would you ever have enough yesterdays?"

"Probably not," she answered. "Does a squirrel ever gather enough nuts for winter?"

Her honesty never ceased to surprise him, this woman, who never shrank from his questions. How can I make her understand it's not her I'm leaving, but the yesterdays we aren't going to have if I don't?

"No, not many tomorrows left," he said, "and I still have some unfinished chapters in my life. I need to write the endings while I still can."

"I respect that," she answered quietly. "I know you don't really want to discuss it much either, as I'm not part of those chapters." She shifted Tag on her lap and turned to look at him in the shadows. "Yet, don't I hold a place in how those endings are written? You spoke earlier of limits, finding our limits, and accepting them; not running into rock walls at 100 miles an hour."

"I know where you're going with this, and it isn't the same thing," he snapped.

He pushed down the irritation starting to build, and why he'd avoided this talk. She didn't understand that she'd already written the endings to the open chapters. Written them with her simple way of going after what she wanted. She didn't know that, and he couldn't tell her different.

"Dammit, Ben, it *is* the same thing. It's banging your head into a wall that's not going to move because it's in the past and can't. So you had a hand in building some walls. Hasn't everyone built a few walls in their lives? My God, you can't knock them all back down. Maybe you aren't supposed to, ever think of that? Maybe climbing some of those walls is what will help another out of the same pit. Why can't you understand that?"

"Goddammit, I do understand it," he started to yell and caught himself, "but I have to make sure others understand it, too. I have to try; why can't you understand *that*?"

She was pissing him off now, and maybe that's what he needed. Anger often served him well as a tool. "I can't just spend my remaining days chasing rainbows with you, much as I might like to. They're *your* rainbows. I have no rainbows. I have only the rain."

He looked her in the eyes with this remark, and softened as he saw the wound he'd inflicted take hold of her. She looked so vulnerable at times and he couldn't go on.

"Okay, Ben. Guess I'm a dreamer," she finally said. "I chase the jewels you've already chased, the glitter you've already held that turned to dust in your hand. You feel like you've left your home port to sail yet uncharted water. You wonder when yet another gale will upset your damn boat. Yet, this time it's different and you don't quite understand it. Do you? For once, the diamond still sparkles and the dust never settles, and it scares you to a degree, I think. It scares you to just be, to forget what's past and quit beating yourself over it.

She really wasn't talking to him as much as she was thinking out loud. He just listened until she stopped. He owed her that.

"But no," she went on, "you have to figure it all out, don't you? The hows, the whys, the whats, of it all." She sighed deeply. "Oh, my dear pragmatic man, how I ache for you sometimes. I do love you so, you know."

41

Then, with all the strength he could muster, he simply told her, "I have to go. Probably the end of the month, and I need to know what you'll do."

She looked away and said no more. The argument was pointless; she was beating horses, and she'd traveled this road with him before. On a night long ago when he'd bought her coffee and held her hand as they sat under the stars. These same stars.

* * * *

THE LETTERS

The rest of the work week passed uneventfully. Amber had learned to follow her daily routines comfortably, if not happily. Thoughts of the no-longer stranger fluttered through her mind off and on, but she really didn't expect to hear from him again for the remainder of the work week. Maybe she'd never hear from him again, and that thought concerned her. She found it confusing more than anything. How could you miss someone you barely knew? Someone you'd spent only two evenings and a couple rather void mornings with? Maybe you wouldn't miss them so much as you'd question your reactions. You'd wonder at the inner rumblings you'd diligently taught yourself to listen to.

Readying herself for work on Friday morning, the thought suddenly came to her . . . *I don't even know his name.* Names didn't seem to be an issue in their short time together, and were never asked, nor mentioned. Strange. Yet, the whole series of events was strange. Perhaps she dreamed the whole thing, imagined it. Then laughing at herself, thought, no. Surely, she hadn't taken total leave of her senses!

"Well, if I don't know his name, he probably doesn't know mine either," she said out loud. "Damned if I remember if I included it when I scribbled down the address and phone number. Information that he didn't even ask for anyway, you nut." The thought amused her as she went out the door to work, deciding to put the entire matter out of her mind.

That evening driving home, top down, and the music lifting her spirits as it always did, her thoughts returned to the man and how he'd affected her with his reverie of trips above the clouds. She could still hear his words, uttered almost reverently, "Wish I could take you flying," he'd said. "It's something else going up through the clouds *where never larks, or even eagles flew.*"

He'd sounded so alive when repeating the famous poem, but even then, she'd sensed the underlying siege going on inside him. It was like flying described him. When riding above the clouds, part of him was afraid that he'd never make it back down and another part was equally afraid that he would.

She entered her driveway, then almost turned around and went back over to the beach to watch the sunset, but didn't. If by some chance he was there, it would appear as if she were chasing after him and that was the last image she wanted to portray; the damnable desperate widow thing.

Turning the key in the lock, she heard the phone ringing and her heart kind of skipped a beat. She dropped her things on the long wooden table and rushed to pick it up.

"Hi, Mom. I was beginning to wonder if you were out on the town or something," her son's voice teased.

"Not hardly. Had to drag out my big stick, but I managed to keep them all at bay," she teased back. "No, hon, just took my time riding home. I kind of went the long way around," she said, serious now.

"Well, just don't piss off the State boys by making them chase you for five miles like last time," he chided, laughing.

"Nah, only run them a couple now, and have the crying act down pat." She laughed back. "But, I'm gonna stay right here and do some reading this weekend, so don't you worry one bit about me. I'll call if I need you. Everything all right up your way?"

"Sure is. I plan a quiet weekend myself."

Suddenly, she just wanted to get off the phone. She realized she was disappointed at the call not being from him and it startled her. She exchanged a bit more light conversation with her son and then they said their good-byes, promising to be back in touch on Sunday. She hung up and waited, hoping the phone would ring again. It didn't, and she finally went to bed and a restless sleep.

Over the next couple days Amber hashed and rehashed it over in her mind. By the end of the weekend she'd reconciled it as a lesson learned. It was okay to pay attention to her inner turmoils, and not suppress them. It was okay to feel reactions she thought herself no longer capable of having, but not okay to take everything so damn seriously. This would take some doing, she was intense by nature, but do it she would. The stranger had brought her a message all right, she'd just read it wrong; read it to mean there was a connection from somewhere, sometime, when really they were but two damaged ships passing in the night.

Yes, that must be it, she decided. He obviously had a much more compelling life to return to than he could've ever found in this small town. And, he'd probably found her equally boring and dull as the town itself. Yes, that was it.

Monday dawned gray and overcast, much like her mood. Meeting the stranger had brought on a questioning of her purpose, an inner rage at the circumstances of life she, once again, seemed unable to put in a meaningful perspective.

Determined to put it all aside, for the work day anyway, she turned on the radio and busied herself getting ready for work and jotting off a few lines to her sister who was going to be royally pissed at her failing to keep in touch the past week. The thought of calling her left as soon as it came. She wasn't sure she'd be able to pull off the "everything is fine" line. But the music cheered her, and soon the sun was burning through the clouds, as well as her mood.

"Well, let's get on with it," she cajoled herself, while heading out the door. Chuckling at her penchant for talking to herself of late, she fired the engine of the convertible, backed out and turned toward the post office to mail her letter. "To hell with it all," she sang out, "Just live in the damn moment."

"Morning, Richard," she called to the postmaster upon entering the small community building. "I figured it was about time to come empty the box."

"You don't start coming a little more often you'll have to get a bigger one. Got a package for you here behind the counter too," he answered

"Okay, be there in a minute. Let's see if I need a bigger box first."

She turned the combination on the lock, then smiled at the way the mail was stuffed in neatly to accommodate her lax pick-up routine. She drug it all out and threw the ads in the can provided, silently cursing the waste of precious trees.

"You say I have a package, Richard?" she said, going up to the counter.

"Yup. Came in on Saturday. Hope it isn't something that might've improved your weekend," he kidded.

"Doubt that." Smiling at his joke, she thumbed through the stack of envelopes in her hand and exchanged a few more barbs with him as he retrieved her package.

Something caught her eye, a handwriting she didn't recognize. It was addressed to "Rides-With-the-Wind" and her heart stopped for just a second. She said her goodbyes to Richard and hurried to the car. Tossing the rest of the pile on the seat beside her, she carefully opened the letter.

Dear Rides-With-the-Wind, it began.

I call you that because I don't even know your first name; just the last that was on the paper you gave me. I call you that because I do like lunatics. I write this now because I'm leaving town and didn't want to go without saying

goodbye. Why I'm leaving has nothing to do with you, I don't think.

I came to accomplish something and didn't, it's that simple. So I left. I seem to have a need to just go when the mood is on me, when things are going wrong. Less fuss and muss that way. I don't know if I'll return. I don't even know where I will be going beyond this flight; perhaps back to the West Coast, perhaps not. I'm writing this from the airport as you can see by the stationery and post mark.

About us . . . well, it would be imprudent to say there was something there, and impudent to say not. As you must know, I feel something toward you; what, I'm not sure. I sense you do the same or I wouldn't be writing. It's an affinity of some kind, like rain to pavement, or rainbow to storm, something like that. I don't know. I do know you brought me some measure of relief, if you can imagine it. I do know we share many secrets, but what they are, I'm not sure of either. Some form of kinship.

I'm soon to be free of this earth, if but for awhile, as my plane leaves in ten minutes. Hoping this finds you well, hoping that perhaps our paths will cross again, I remain, A Stranger who really isn't.

She read the letter over again more than a few times, hands trembling, and felt a sense of awe that this strange man had aroused something in her yet again, and that he, too, felt the stirring of whatever it was buried in both of them. Words that he was able to speak with a pen, but not the voice. Writers were like that.

And just as mystical to her, was that he could walk away from it. Suddenly, she knew there would be no facing the job today. A walk by the shore and time to think was more important. She shoved the letter back in the envelope, smiling at the way it was addressed, and started the car. She turned back home to change clothes and call her employer.

The same parking place was empty; the one where he'd teased her about driving fast, and where she'd picked him up for coffee a little less than a week ago.

"Damn sentimental fool," she chided herself.

She gathered her book bag and locked the car. The top was up. For some reason, having it down today made her sad. Walking toward the water down the same path where he'd stopped her from leaving, she noticed their bench was empty as well. It looked almost lonely sitting there on the edge of the sand, void of even the gulls looking for breadcrumbs from a gullible tourist. The beach, too, was near deserted on this Monday morning, but she liked it that way.

"Still the loner," she told herself, "so why the muddling over the absence of someone who has *Stranger* for a name? Is it the traveling of a road because it's there again, or do you need someone in your life more than you care to admit?" Actually, she shunned social encounters. Until the events of the last few days, being with anyone accentuated the absence of the other half of her life. "So what is it with you?" she thought out loud.

She rounded the bench, sat and looked out over the water. A calm breeze soothed her flushed cheeks and she let her mind travel back to times long ago.

Her early years were that of an only child in a blue collar family. Patterns were in stone and conformity was expected. Life's roles were a given depending on gender, and straying from these was unacceptable. Her only sibling had not been born until she was thirteen, and she'd served as the learning tool in her folks' acquisition of parenting skills.

She'd been a pretty child, properly attired in frills and lace, but had found her real pleasure in mud puddles and Mulberry trees. She wanted to know the hows and whys of the things around her, and the shoulds and should nots of life became her nemesis.

She didn't want to learn about cooking and sewing. Instead, she yearned for books and pictures of faraway places. She didn't understand the things they'd told her about roles and purpose, God and wrath. But if she tried real hard, maybe they'd love her anyway? Just as she was . . . different. They didn't.

Over time, she found herself happiest when alone and resolute, then her life changed. She met Jeff when they were young. He was a soul like her own, adventuresome, a lover of life and simple things, yet excitement, too, and a loner like her. The marriage was instant in its way. Jeff didn't worry about things like acceptance and shoulds and should nots. He taught her to question an idea if she didn't accept it. He encouraged her to do what gave her joy, not do what didn't; to travel a road simply because it was there.

He was centered about 'self' in his way, too, demanding to be his own, while teaching her hers. About these issues, he'd been stubborn, almost to a fault. Yet, he was kind, strong, and loyal, and held an insatiable zest for new horizons. "Spirit," he'd called it . . . things bigger and beyond, things smaller and hidden in a forest. He'd taught them to her by allowing her, forcing her, to be what she was.

After many long and happy years of exploring life and raising two sons, he'd left one day. Not because he wanted to, but because he was going where she couldn't yet go. His last gift to her was a rainbow.

Rebellious, she'd fought it. Angry, she'd cursed him. Broken, she'd fallen into despair. She moved back to the small town near the sea where they'd spent a good portion of their life together, back into the little house they'd built and always kept. She worked during the days, but evenings were lost in the books that seemed to borrow other voices to speak what he would have spoken to her.

She'd known the greatest love imaginable, but had lost it to a power much greater than herself, and she feared that loss. She'd never love again; of this she was certain, unless that same power taught her how. Was this the power seen in the eyes of the stranger? Another who'd rather be alone than settle for less than the sharing of Soul?

His letter subtly uttered the same confusions, the same ponderings, and the same hopes their meeting had fostered in her. He'd hinted at feelings of loss, anger, and mistrust at the coffee shop. He'd shared the wonder felt under the stars and above the clouds, the pleasure in feeding a gull, talking to a pelican. Like mind, shared soul, entangled in opposite lives, tossed together by a wave on a sea of chance? Or ships, indeed, simply passing in the night?

"Damn. Why do you have to analyze everything to death?" Digging her heels in the sand, she forced herself back to the present. "Because that's who you are and you wouldn't want to be anyone else."

She looked up to the sky in anticipation as the last words seem to come from outside of her. No, no rainbow today. She got up and kicked off her shoes, felt the soft sand hug the bottom of her feet, and headed toward the water's edge. The wind suddenly gusted and wrapped itself around her.

"I know, I know." She laughed. "And I just need to walk with you awhile."

* * * *

An hour passed in silence, the old swing creaking softly with its slow to and fro movement. Ben made no effort to get up after telling her he'd probably have to go at the end of the month, but Amber said no more. Words weren't always a must for the two of them. Mind, between them, was near telepathic. He knew she was thinking and needed time to digest his announcement of leaving. He did himself.

The moon was high in the sky when he finally spoke again. "I really would like to know what you plan on doing when I'm gone," he said. *If only he could make her understand. Hurting this woman was the last thing he ever wanted to do.*

"I really don't know," she answered. "I may stay here another month, experience a Nor'easter or two, and then go home. Or, I may not go home until after Christmas; it's only a few weeks away now." She turned to face him, her look intent. "You just go where it is you have to go and don't

50

worry about me. I do quite well alone in case you've forgotten."

"Babe, don't tell me not to worry about you. You know that's not ever going to happen." He started to go on, but she was laughing now, and he turned to look at her, surprised by the sound. It was a laugh filled with sadness and resolution, a little anger. Sarcasm seeped through her words.

"Please, you've stated you must go. To do, to fix, to whatever, so go. I'm a big girl now."

"Abby, why— ?" She didn't let him finish his question.

"Perhaps, I read too much Bach, too much Emerson. Maybe I go about on a cloud when my feet should remain on the ground." Her voice had the sound of surrender. "Aaah, but what the hell. To me, it's kind of a polarity, degrees of the same thing. I just choose to strive for the more positive degree. Still, the pendulum does swing; it's supposed to, I guess. As you said, limits."

"Dammit, Abby, would you just—" She wasn't listening.

"So right, you go, you don't wonder about me. Your pendulum won't swing as far to the future as mine. Fear of failure, fear of your imps, as you're fond of calling them, impedes it. And, trust. While I trust in a rainbow, you trust only in the fucking rain. Maybe you fear a loss again, I don't know. Actually, I have nothing to lose. I suppose you do."

Now it was him wiping a hint of moisture from the corner of his eye. He thought of how he'd felt when he left her the first time, the letters he'd written.

* * * *

Slowly, as she began to blend back into the routine of her life, Amber was beginning to put the stranger, whoever he was, out of her mind. She'd heard no more after the initial explanation written on airport stationery. Her assessment of a special connection seemed to be errant. Two damaged ships passing after all, nothing more. It was only when she stopped

51

at the post office and found another letter that the questions stirred again.

Though stunned, she gathered up the mail nonchalantly, noticing that Richard was watching, as he always did. But, that was okay. He knew of the changes in her life since Jeff died and he'd been kind. She walked back to her car in a normal manner, pulled away from the post office in a not-so-normal manner for her, but once out of sight, sped home, eager to see what the letter contained.

Once parked in her drive, she nearly ran up the stairs, grabbed her reading glasses and sat at the table. There was no return address and she couldn't make out the post mark. She carefully opened the envelope and began to read.

Dear Rides-With-the-Wind, it started. *There's a lot more to the human, as you know, than just Biology. From birth to death, there's that plus learning plus experiences plus thinking ability plus health. The Biology, or chemicals, are the oil in the engine is all. But it does, that and genetics, kind of help explain at least some of the things we all do in life. Those in the arts, say, are almost universally a rather depressed crowd who only feel right when performing. The aggressive ones in life, they only feel right when being aggressive. Or you, who only feels right when the spirit is upon you. I paid attention, see?*

What all this awareness does, is explain things. It doesn't necessarily change anything unless we apply the knowledge. Haven't you ever wondered why just one Einstein and not us all? Why one Picasso? So does God do this, or is it just our luck in the draw of life? What it really seems to mean is that we can drop all this "you can be anything you want to be" philosophy that works for some, not for most, and get down to what we are. Those like us can't help but reach out and explore, if all this is true. Admittedly, it's a big IF.

There are those who can't help but seek safety in numbers, and there are loners. Sure, experience is the greatest teacher of all, and those who can't explore as you do, will never "get it." Yet, even if they looked as you look, seek as you seek, would they even see? Capabilities. IQ. Synapses and gray matter. Heart. Perhaps you and I are mutants to the world, but if so, it's the mutants who guide, not the masses. In that regard I guess we could call ourselves lucky, and would, were it not for this herding instinct everyone has. Instead we feel unwanted and outcasts UNTIL we find that special nook that is 'us'.

I just wanted you to know that you're not just an anybody; you are a somebody. And through all of the above you are supposed to be that somebody. So keep on keeping on, Rides-With-the-Wind. Your uniqueness may stamp you as odd among your fellows, but then a wolf stands out among the sheep, does it not? Yet both the wolf and sheep know exactly who the Master is.

The letter ended with, simply, *Yours.*

My God, she thought, what an unusual letter. More importantly, he seemed to be looking into her very depths, as if he'd been inside her all her life. Am I going crazy? Who is this man? How could he possibly know all this about my thoughts from a couple casual meetings? And it almost sounded as if he was just thinking out loud, and not really talking to me at all but himself, or as if it was me talking to myself. "Or, Jeff, himself," she cried out.

It frightened her. It made her wonder if he was even real. Had she, somehow, imagined him? Was she even reading a letter, or was it her imagination? And why now, when she was beginning to forget, or at least understand, the meeting in the first place? And still no return address on the envelope.

"Get a grip," she told herself. "It's pure coincidence." Then she remembered she didn't believe in coincidences. She started to read the letter again and then threw it angrily onto the table.

"This is a hell of a way to show me you're still around," she blurted into the quiet of the room. "Dammit, Jeff!"

She broke and let the tears come. And come they did, pent up inside all this time, a gusher of tears that flowed from her as if she couldn't stop them and didn't want to. She laid her head on the table and sobbed. Behind her in the kitchen, the clock ticked. And ticked.

Hours passed, or was it days? She didn't know. When she'd finally cried herself out, she raised her head and looked at what seemed to be a surreal setting. Somehow, her home looked different than before. It wasn't that anything had been moved. It wasn't even a different color. Her flowers were still there, and the fruit bowl on the table. Yet, somehow, things seemed different. Had she slipped into one of those twenty-three dimensions the physicists talked about and she believed in? Had she, too, died and didn't realize it? Was she in one of those Out-of-Body experiences she'd read about?

A sudden scratching at her front door brought her back to reality. She knew what the scratching meant. Wiping away her tears, she rose and walked over to the kitchen cabinets automatically.

"If I'm dreaming all this, then it's a nightmare." She reached into the cupboard and withdrew the box of cat food, emptied some into a bowl, and went to the door.

"Hello, little one. I'm definitely glad to see you," she said to the wild opossum who came to the door every night since her husband's death. She sat the bowl down for the animal and watched as it ate hungrily as it always did, wondering if it, too, felt abandoned.

But before she could give it any real thought, something in the distance caught her eye, something off across the back grass that was her yard. She stared. Nearly hidden in the palmettos and wild fronds that marked the edge of the cleared space, a fox stared silently in her direction

"Damn!" she whispered under her breath at such a rare sight. The events of the day and the letter were suddenly forgotten as she hurried back inside to see what she had that a fox might eat. She found some sausages in the refrigerator and turned back toward the door, half afraid it would be gone, and half afraid it wouldn't be. But it was still there, still watching, still waiting. She'd never seen a fox on her property before, and it mystified her as much as the letter from the stranger.

Cautiously, she stepped out onto her porch, careful not to disturb her friend still gorging on the cat food. She descended the stairs slowly, afraid that the fox would suddenly bolt. But it didn't; almost, she thought, as if it could read her mind. She walked slowly across her clearing to the thicket, and still the fox didn't move. As she moved closer she could see it was a male by its markings, and she stopped not ten feet from it, eye to eye.

Showing him the food, saying nothing, she gently tossed the sausages to within a few feet of the animal, then turned around and walked slowly back toward the house. Off in the distance a lightning bolt singed the air and its near-sonic boom of thunder echoed through the trees. Rain clouds were forming overhead.

She made her way quickly up the stairs and then turned, looking back to the thicket. The fox, but not the food, was gone. She looked toward the bowl on the porch where the possum had been eating. It, too, was gone, as was all the food in the bowl.

"A fox that isn't there, a possum that is, a letter that is but shouldn't be. Am I losing my mind?" she wailed. "Well, at least I know the 'possum is real. Now if I go inside and find that letter missing, I'm calling the hospital for check in."

With that she opened the door and stepped back inside, even as raindrops began to patter her roof. Even as her fear that the letter wouldn't be there pattered her mind. She closed the door to the rain and the outside world, then turned and stared at the table where she'd been sitting. The letter was lying where she'd left it.

IT WAS A THURSDAY

April had drifted into May, then June, and there were no more letters. But there were gardens and flowers and the new growth of spring. With it came a new growth in Amber as well. She'd always loved spring when new life pushed itself out of the earth, and the buds held within them what had already been. What had already been, she'd often thought, was only the foundation for what was to be. And what would be, itself, became the foundation for whatever followed. Yes, cycles, as in the seasons. "A time to live, a time to die, to sow, to reap."

Traveling had become her passion. It was the one thing she looked forward to since alone, seeing what she could of the beauty in nature. Deserts, mountains, prairies, and, of course, the sea. She loved it all.

Now, with friends in the west, and family in the north, summer became the time to move, and she was getting restless. Wanderlust pulsed through her veins like wind through a canyon. Thoughts of the man that had aroused such questioning in her had, once again, begun to wane.

Yes, there had been an element of destiny in her time with him, a higher thing. But, maybe it had simply been to serve as an awakening of the possibility that life does indeed go on, that feelings she'd thought impossible to feel ever again could, in fact, be felt. Kind of like spring. Kind of like a seed in the soil of earth. Now, she held a fondness for the memory, but it was no longer an obsession, no longer frightening, and she truly desired that he'd found whatever it was he'd been searching for.

She had plane tickets for a trip to the mountains, with a stopover in Chicago to spend time with her oldest son. And then perhaps a romp with an elk. Jackson Hole, Wyoming, the gateway to the majestic Tetons, would be a dream come true.

In the fall, a visit with her youngest son in Philadelphia, highlighted by a weekend of the nitro-burning funny cars at an NHRA Nationals meet, was also booked. She loved the racing, the raw power and speed, the earth trembling beneath her feet, the noise that deafened an unprotected ear. She would never outgrow it, no more than she'd outgrow her love of the rock music known as Classic Metal. Yes, the child, the innocence, the burden-free heart within her would always remain just beneath the surface, clamoring to play a little each day. She could always find her peace in that child no matter how difficult life presented itself.

Feeling light of heart with thoughts of coming plans, she joyfully greeted this Saturday morning. Taking her coffee to the gardens beneath the stilted house, she sat in the swing listening to the birds chorusing their morning repertoires. And smiled at the squirrels chasing their tails, and each other, while jumping from branch to branch in the big Oaks.

"Well, look at you all puffed up this morning," she crooned to the little lizards leaping among the Kalanchoe plants, then laughed at herself. What the neighbors must think. She had to admit that not just everyone talked to lizards and snakes . . . or themselves. Oh, but she loved them all, every one of the little creatures. The menagerie around her home had become her family and she didn't really care much what the neighbors thought. Yes, life was good.

It was a Thursday. She sat in her car outside the post office glancing through the pile of bills and junk mail just collected from her box. It was raining and had been all day. Laying the pile on the seat next to her, she started the car and turned on the wipers. She was about to shift into reverse when an envelope sticking out from the junk mail caught her eye. There was something odd about how it stuck out like that, she thought, but dismissed it and drew the gear lever into position. As she looked behind to back out of the parking space, her eye was again drawn to the envelope and she hesitated. Somehow, she knew it was from him. She shifted back into Park, turned the engine off and drew the small tan envelope from the stack.

"All right, let's see what you have to say this time," she murmured, intrigued that he'd write again. But her mood changed when she noticed the return address. It was from a hospital in Texas.

Frowning now, she looked the envelope over more carefully. She could tell by its weight and the small bulge at its base it contained something more than just a letter. The rain seemed to be falling harder as she opened it and withdrew the stationery inside.

Dear Rides, it began. *I hope this finds you well and as full of life as I remember you. I would have written sooner, but couldn't. It seems that something like a tumor got in the way. You see, I don't trust doctors all that much, having seen what I've seen in life. Oh don't misunderstand me, by thinking what you're thinking. Theirs is an honorable and difficult profession. It's just that they are human and subject to the same ignorance as the rest of us, so in difficult times it's always best to look around for alternative opinions, and that's what I've done.*

Yes, I've been all over the place you might say, and wound up here. You know, Rides, these bodies of ours are amazing things in how they're built, how they function, all the goings-on involved, all the cells having to work together to produce and keep life balanced. I guess I sort of burned

58

mine up over the years, and needed to find a first-rate mechanic to fix me. Problem so far is everyone is saying the warranty has run out.

I guess you never thought of your body being like a car or other machine, did you, or how you have to keep it maintained in order to keep it running? Well, you do. It was probably the cigarettes or the booze, but who knows? Frankly, I don't even care how it happened, only that it has, so here I am for tests, they say, to experiment, they mean. But that's all right too, because that's how we all learn, isn't it?

Do you remember in one of Richard's early books how the main character, a seagull, was determined not to be just another gull, and so, experimented? He climbed higher than the others, dove faster than the others, until he found what he was looking for. Transition. Do you remember?

I've been like that bird; I think you have as well. Always looking, rarely finding, isn't that about right? But finding what? Whatever there is to find, I guess. The bird didn't find it until it had, and when it had, it changed. Yet, it didn't know change was what it would find when it began, only that it wasn't satisfied being what it was. What made the bird so inquisitive, so unsatisfied with being just another bird? It didn't know and neither do I. It only knew it must. I only know I do.

So here I am lying in this bed miles from you, miles from anyone I really know, and writing on stationery that isn't even mine. They're still running tests, which means some lab mouse or chimp will probably die from what they took from me to inject into them. And I wonder, am I worth that chimp's life? That mouse? Are any of us, in the long run I mean? Isn't all life precious, from snail to snapdragon?

Yet, that's what medicine is all about, isn't it. And that's what humanity is all about as well, isn't it? Saving others, alleviating suffering. Prolonging life, because life is where it's at, isn't it? If you asked the chimp I'm sure it would agree, or the mouse. I'm sure they would tell you their life is as important as my own. And to them, they'd be right.

59

Thus do I question all this. I think about that mouse and that chimp. I think about you on that seawall and of the bird we both know who went beyond. I've looked back over my life and decided that I am but just part of something bigger, too big to even comprehend, perhaps. Like the rainbow, like a deer in the woods appearing out of nowhere for our human delight, or a fox.

Here she paused, startled by his mention of a fox. How did he know of her encounter with the illusive fox on the day his second letter had arrived? A chill formed at the base of her spine as she continued to read.

As for me, I don't know if this will be my final landing or if it will be just another takeoff, what pilots call a 'touch-and-go.' So I'd like to give you something, which I've enclosed. I've had it many a year and now pass it on to another 'bird in flight,' if you'll excuse the analogy. When you take it from the envelope and look at it, you'll under-stand.

My name is Ben, by the way . . . Benjamin Bishop Riley, and never mind where it came from. I'm tired now and have to rest, but if you wish to write you can find me here for the next few weeks. Or not.

The letter was signed Ben, and she was awed when she read it. How did he know about the fox? How did he know how many times she'd wondered about passing on, or where her late husband was now? How well she remembered the bird in the book he'd mentioned, and how fascinated she'd been when reading it years ago.

Lying her head on the headrest and closing her eyes, she thought how wrong she'd been about him, as he was mortal after all and not a ghost come to haunt her. And he was dying, it sounded like. Yet, mortal or not, he seemed to know things he shouldn't know, could see things she couldn't see. Some kind of gift or some kind of curse?

She remembered the envelope and what the letter had said . . . *When you take it from the envelope, you'll understand.* She opened her eyes and picked it up, turning it so that its contents slid into her hand. She stared at the object in almost shocked recognition, and as she stared, thoughts began flooding in from her memory. All the thoughts over the years, the hardships, the joys and sorrows, trials and tribulations, they paraded now across her consciousness, triggered by the simple object held in her hand.

"Oh, yes," she said.

With serenity unknown for a long, long time, she calmly clasped the object and its chain around her neck and listened to the rain outside. Her hand cupped around the gift and she let it take her into the clouds of her imagination where she, like him perhaps, belonged.

She started the car, backed out of the parking space and drove away, back to her home and the letter she would write. Back to her home where she knew the fox would be waiting, now for all time. And as she drove and turned and twisted her car on the rainy road, the object around her neck turned and twisted with her. For that was what seagulls did in the rain, even small gold and silver ones who flew not through earthly skies, but into the endless dimensions of time and space.

SNAPDRAGONS

He was just drifting off to his nap when the nurse entered the room with a vase of flowers that looked to be from a private garden, definitely not from a professional florist.

"This is a strange bouquet," she said, as if reading his thoughts. "The delivery boy said he had to go to a local grower and pick them up special. Snapdragons. Never saw anybody get Snapdragons before." She set the pastel flowers and a letter on the bed table and left the room, glancing over her shoulder and mumbling something to herself.

Ben noticed a wolf's face staring back at him from the return label, and below that, a name . . . Abigail A. Allyson. The name meant nothing to him, but the return address caught his eye. It was from her. He was suddenly wide awake, and studied the blooms next to him as he sat up and opened the envelope.

Hello Ben, it began. *'Rides-With-The-Wind,' huh? I like that. It brought a smile when I read it the first time. Yes, I am well. The wind does carry me through many a storm. I often wrestle with it in the beginning, maybe don't want to go where it's going, or don't think I can. But upon reflection, I find the ride or the destination is often better than where I am, so let it take me where it will.*

You were a storm of sorts in that respect. Tossed me around a bit when you disappeared almost as soon as you'd arrived. At one point, I actually entertained the notion that you were but a message-bearer crossing dimensions of time and space, my late husband entering and leaving my existence at will. Next, I assumed I'd been 'Touched By An Angel,' so to speak. I was starting to wonder if I hadn't imagined the whole thing.

But I thought back to the eyes I'd looked into and the hand that held mine, as if searching, reaching out, just as my own, and realized you were real after all. With time I became comfortable with the experience we'd shared, and you became kind of like spring for me. A new growth of sorts.

Your second letter was as a breeze encircling my own thoughts and questions. It was as if you were speaking truths from beyond when you told of "the wind swept heights where never lark or eagle flew," truths that resonated within me. Seems you have a way of jumping out at me from behind mysterious curtains when I'm least expecting it. So yes, you were new rain to my rather parched pavement and a rainbow that forms just where the edge becomes mist.

On this new day, I find myself writing to you with a gull of silver and gold resting just above my heart. A Birdfriend that has felt the beat of yours now shares it with the beat of mine. So let me tell you something: I don't believe in coincidences, so we're going to get you a new warranty. We're going to fly higher and dive faster than ever before. I'm now going to go talk to the pelican about it, or did you think I was going to sit idly by while you shop mechanics? Just what kind of a lunatic do you take me for? Damn. Think of me on the seawall, or in the stars, Mr. Riley. Or perhaps, as a fox that came for dinner.

The letter was signed, *Amber*. He read it over several times, then laid it down and looked at the flowers in the vase.

"I hate snapdragons," he said to no one. But he was smiling when he said it.

A week passed and Amber heard no more from Ben. She wondered if the letter and the snapdragons had reached him. That had been a feat in itself, finding a florist in the area who could supply 'specialty' items from a gardening friend. She'd been assured that the requested flowers could be procured and delivered to the hospital, which to her, was an omen.

Now, she wondered if they'd been given to someone else accidentally, or if Ben had checked out prior to their arrival. But, wouldn't the letter have been returned? A call to the hospital seemed her only answer. She hesitated. He had, after all, only told her to write him there if inclined to do so.

"No, I'll wait and see for a few more days. I just hope he is okay," she muttered out loud.

But restraint was difficult for one moved by impulsiveness. Would he understand her aggressiveness if she called? Would he think her unconcerned if no attempt was made? He'd told her the prognosis may be serious, but how long would someone remain in a hospital just for tests? She suspected it was more than tests.

"Well, damn him. Always the mystery man," she said out loud. "Pops in and out like a yo-yo. What the hell does he think I am? One to just sit and wonder?"

Glancing down at the bird in motionless flight across her chest, she walked to the phone and dialed information.

He was asleep and the phone startled him. It took all he had to answer.

"Hello? Mr. Riley?"

It was her. He could tell by the raspy voice.

"Just what do you think you're doing sitting around that comfortable room when you could be sitting on a rocky seawall?"

She was trying to sound cheerful and her voice was a tonic to his ears. He managed a weak smile. "Well, Ms. Allyson," he slowly answered. "If I remember right, I'm

64

sitting here because it's hard to move around with tubes attached to you. Besides, hospital food is excellent, in case you haven't heard."

"For Pete's sake, how'd you know it was me?"

He moved to get more comfortable. "Oh, easy. This place has videophones. One in every room so we can see who's calling. I'm looking at you as we speak," he whispered, his voice weak.

She looked around her house self-consciously. "Really?"

He managed a slight grin. "Sure."

Ever the smart ass, she thought, but his slurred speech bothered her. "So, how are you doing, Ben?" There was a pause, too long a pause.

"I'm not doing worth a shit if you really want to know. They're using some new kind of drug on me, and I don't like it," He spoke softly trying to sound normal, and winced as he said it.

Her frown deepened. "What kind of drug? Are you all alone there? How much longer do you have to stay?"

He was touched by her concern. "Like I said, they've got me in here to experiment on. Trying to see what's what. Something about peptides, whatever those are."

There was another long pause and she listened to his labored breathing. "Should know in a few more days. If yes, I'll leave. If no, I'll leave anyway, you could say. Yes, I'm alone, Abby. What of it?"

She was momentarily stunned at his calling her Abby, but recovered quickly. "What of it, did you say? Hey, you write, you don't write. Then you write again. You share with me, tell me of hospitals. You send me a Birdfriend part of you and ask me to respond if inclined." She paused. "What the hell kind of a question is that? Damn," she said, more frustrated than angry.

"Sorry," he managed weakly.

"Why did you call me Abby?" she asked quietly, her emotions welling up inside.

He didn't answer, maybe couldn't answer.

"I'll be there in a couple days." It was a matter of fact statement. "Bye for now," she said as she replaced the phone in its cradle.

He listened to the dial tone for a moment, then using what energy he had left, dropped the phone on its base and lay back, looking at the vase of flowers she'd sent.

There was a knock at the door and his doctor walked in, along with three others, none smiling. Their visit was brief and to the point. The experiment had failed. They were sorry. How much time? They didn't know, but they'd discuss check out in a few days if he regained his strength, or attempt more treatment. Either way didn't seem to matter.

After they'd gone, he lay alone with his thoughts, not knowing whether to be mad or sad. *What should I do?* Make arrangements with the attorney, of course. Should I notify my son? The few friends I have left? Or should I let them find out through the paper? He hated funerals and doubted anyone would show up anyway.

What if he told his son and the doctors were wrong? Wouldn't that burden him, unnecessarily? Secretly he was afraid the boy wouldn't care, and that would hurt even more than the final agony. And what of her? Abby? She's only been widowed a short time, and to have to go through it again? Nothing seemed fair. Why hadn't the doctors arrived earlier so he could have told her the facts, kept her from making a long trip for nothing?

It's not that he feared death itself, for he'd seen plenty. It was that he'd be leaving things undone like always, and this bothered him most. No, he reasoned, he must do what needed to be done to tie up any loose ends while he still could. There were letters to write, people to say goodbye to, and that's what he'd do. He'd write them all letters, farewell letters, give them to his attorney and have them mailed after he was gone. He'd make final arrangements to pass on his possessions to his son. Then, if he didn't die anytime soon, the letters would always be waiting.

"What am I saying? If I don't die anytime soon?" He sighed heavily. "The doctors just told me there's hardly any time left."

His thoughts raced. He had to get out of here, get things going. He tried to get out of bed and couldn't. Too weak. "Fuck!" he yelled, but the yell was only a whisper. He tried again and it was as if some force held him there. He had to call her, stop her from coming. Again he attempted to move, and again was stopped by his weakness or whatever was holding him. As he struggled, his mind flashed to another time when he'd been paralyzed, but that time from fear.

He's twenty-three and afloat in an orange lifejacket on the ocean, bobbing and riding the swells that took him up, then down, washing over and making him sick. It was raining and a gray, somber day.

He was asleep when the shark came. His eyes flew open at the touch as the shark's dorsal scraped his dangling legs and feet. Instinctively, he tucked his feet up close and tried to see in the emerald green of the ocean beneath him. Panicking, he looked everywhere around him as another swell carried him up. Nothing. His teeth began to chatter. The shark's dorsal broke surface not twenty feet away and cruised by, like in the movie "Jaws" and he saw it plainly. A twelve-foot hammerhead. The fin turned toward him and sank beneath the surface.

He reached out to the phone, shaking. Somehow he must reach her. Three feet. Two feet. One foot. His hand reached the receiver, then knocked it off the table to the floor. Frustrated, angry, tormented, he yelled out.

The nurse came in and found him lying on the floor trying to reach the phone, now dangling from its cord.

"Mr. Riley! Now look what you've done."

He stared at her wild-eyed, as if not knowing where he was.

"I'll have to get some help to lift you, so don't move."

She reached for the call button on his bed as he laid his head down and imagined the sound of large engines coming closer . . . the water gurgling the tune of a turning propeller in the distance.

Men's voices somewhere above him. There was a sixty-foot shrimp boat just feet away with its black wooden hull and stench, its chugging engines. The smell of diesel invaded his nostrils. A burly, foreign-looking man was climbing down and getting a rope around him. "He's still alive," he heard the man yell in broken English-Jamaican. "Help me get him up, mon."

The orderlies lifted him back into his bed, one of whom looked like the man in his dream.

"Yeah, mon, you'll be all right now," he heard the man say.

The nurse and orderlies tucked him in, restrained him with straps, then left. The Jamaican stopped at the door as he was leaving and looked back at him for a second, then let the door close behind him.

NURSES THAT SMILED TOO SWEETLY

Amber walked to the stove and turned the heat on under the coffee pot. Moving to the cupboard where she kept the phone directory, she reached in and lifted the book off the shelf. Her mind was spinning, both at what she knew she must do, and at the conversation that had just taken place with Ben.

"Why did he call me Abby?" she asked the yellow-eyed wolf poster hanging on the wall by the cabinet. Only one person had ever called her Abby, and hearing it had jolted her. Even her family called her Abigail. But, she'd taken on her middle name years ago and few knew her by any name other than Amber.

She assumed he'd spotted her legal name on the return label of her letter. In fact, in their opening words he'd called her Ms. Allyson, but then he'd called her Abby.

"Oh, damn," she brought herself out of her musing. More important matters presented themselves now than a name. This man had suddenly become a key point in her life yet again, even though she didn't understand exactly why.

"Enough of this trying to figure things out," she chided herself. "This is something I feel a need to do and I'll do it.

Who's to ask why?" She opened the directory to the listing of airlines.

She booked a flight for the following afternoon, made arrangements for a rental car at the airport, then called her employer to let them know she had to leave town for a few days; an emergency had come up. That done, the most difficult task lay before her; calling her sons and explaining why she was picking up and going off to visit a near stranger in a stranger, yet, city. Once more she picked up the phone, her hand shaking as she dialed.

"Hello, that you?" she attempted a jolly tone when the familiar masculine voice answered. "It's mom and I have something to tell you."

"Who did you say this was?" he teased.

"Me. Who'd you think it was?" She laughed into the phone.

"Hi, Me. Everything okay down there? Not like you to call twice in one week." His voice turned serious, a slight concern in his question.

"Oh yes, everything's fine. I'm just going to take a little trip to visit a friend and I wanted you to know I'd be away from home for a few days in case you called."

"Sounds like fun. Anyone I know? Where are you going?"

"Actually no, you don't know them, and I'm going to Texas."

"Texas?"

"Yes, I've just gotten news that someone I've come to know in a way I cannot explain right now is gravely ill and I feel like I must go there. He's all alone."

"What do you mean, you can't explain? Since when can't you explain something? Usually, you offer more details than I want to know." He chuckled to abate his sarcasm.

She pretended not to hear. "I'll call you when I arrive and explain when I know more myself. I just don't want you to worry, and I know this sounds mysterious."

"Did you say *he*?" he asked.

70

She ignored the question. "I need you to trust me on this one, hon. I'll call your brother as soon as he gets in from work and tell him, too." She left no room for argument, and now he offered none.

"Mom, you know I trust your judgment, but don't you think you should at least provide me with a name and where you'll be staying? In case I have to rush off and rescue you from your latest adventure?" Sensing his mother's nervousness, he tried to lift the mood.

"Oh, of course. Sorry. I'm afraid I'm not thinking quite straight as this has come up rather suddenly, and it's certainly not an adventure. My friend's name is Ben Riley and he's in a hospital near Houston. I have to go help him, son."

"Yes, I suppose you do," he agreed, sounding resigned now. "Knowing you, it doesn't surprise me, really."

"I've rented a car at the airport; I'll find a motel close by and call you as soon as I arrive. My flight is at one thirty tomorrow afternoon."

"Okay, Ma. It'll do no good to argue if you've gone so far as to make reservations and rent a car, so I'll just say have a good trip and check in as soon as you can." He tried to sound light, but she could sense his hesitation.

"Everything's fine. I'll talk to you tomorrow afternoon, and now I have to pack. I love you, and don't be concerned. I'm a big girl, you know." She forced a laugh and said goodbye.

"I love you, too, Ma."

She took a deep breath and hung up. Exhaling sharply, she blew the hair off her sweating forehead and wondered, again, if she wasn't taking leave of her senses.

Sitting now, looking out the window of the big jet as they taxied toward the runway, her thoughts drifted back to Ben. She sensed the fear in him, the anger. She'd seen the same anger and fear before in her husband. The agitation was often simply the result of the drugs and violation of the body with tubes and needles.

Her decision to go to his side was automatic. No one should be alone at such a time, and especially not one who had spoken to her inner recesses as only one before had been able to do. It was as if Ben was calling out to her, and she him, across a gap of an unfulfilled time. As if at some starting point they had just missed each other and took a different route to the same place . . . a bookstore by the sea.

Yet, her mind couldn't fathom regret for the detour, as that had been her life. And Ben's. But now their paths had intersected, and it seemed as if this may be one of those roads Jeff had taught her to follow just because it was *there*.

A smile came at the thought of Jeff. No, she'd made no wrong turns on life's journey. Her end destination just hadn't been reached. Now, maybe she was enroute to that end, she thought as the plane hurled itself skyward into the western sun.

The flight was smooth and she gazed at the billows of clouds below her. Unconsciously caressing the bird on a chain around her neck, she thought of larks and eagles, and gulls that could fly higher. Suddenly, she gasped at the sight before her. As the receding sunlight caught on the droplets of moisture at the edge of a huge, cottony cloud, she saw it! Its arc reached up beneath her, and its span stretched from the cloud below toward her destination off in the distance, as if guiding her.

She stared, stunned, as it expanded and split into a double arc of glistening colors, almost too vibrant to be real. A most beautiful double rainbow was showing itself again. Tears spilled down her cheeks and dropped on the golden gull around her neck.

Yes, she cried silently. We travel together again, briefly, you and I. Thank you for showing me the way, my love.

She hurried through the airport, collected her luggage, and asked an attendant for directions to the car rental. In what seemed hours, she was driving away while studying the rudimentary map sketched by the clerk at the rental desk.

The traffic, the bustle around her, seemed like a fog as her mind focused on signs and highway numbers. Unconsciously, she pressed buttons on the tuner in the dashboard until she heard the sound that would make her one with the car, the music that made her forget she was small, frail, and alone. That made her invincible for just a while.

Inching her way along the map, while in reality speeding along the busy freeways, she finally saw the exit sign to the hospital. Easing over for the ramp, the thought struck her: what if they won't let me in? What if visiting hours are over? She glanced at her watch, remembering she'd gained an hour of time in the air. She wondered if that was the same as going back through years of time spent elsewhere?

At the entrance to the hospital, she turned into a large facility and took a ticket for the visitor parking area. Pulling into the first available space, she took a moment to collect herself. Taking a deep breath, she closed her eyes and concentrated on just relaxing. She counted to ten, then grabbed her purse and keys and got out, locking the car behind her. She looked around, located the entrance, and began walking toward the big door far across the lot.

The receptionist at the Information Desk was pleasant and directed her to the wing where one could find Benjamin Riley. She found the elevators and pressed Six. The nurse at the station directly across from the elevators looked up and smiled as she exited.

"Hi. I'm here to see Ben Riley. Is it possible to see him now?"

"Why, of course," the nurse replied. "He's at the end of this hall in room 613. He may be sleeping though, and I have to warn you, he's weak. Don't expect a great welcome."

"Weak?"

"Yes, dear," the nurse said quietly, her eyes answering Amber's fears.

She fairly ran down the hall, looking at the numbers posted above the doors. It was quiet, too quiet, in this wing. No sounds of TVs, radios, or talking with visitors. As she approached the door of his room, she composed herself,

73

eased the door open, and looked in. Her legs weakened at what she saw. The color of the man asleep in the bed was that of ash, and he'd lost so much weight since the night he'd flippantly told her, "Later, Babe."

She tiptoed to his bedside and looked down into his face, taking hold of his hand gently so as not to wake him. Then, emotion enveloping her, she squeezed his hand with all her strength, and laid her head on his chest. His heart beat faintly and then the anger burst out of her very depths.

"Damn you, Ben! What are you doing? Lying here giving up?" she cried. "Didn't I tell you I'd be here to get you? Wake Up! How dare you ignore me when I—when we have come so far!"

She dissolved into him, letting go of his hand and wrapping her arms around his neck, resting her cheek against his. "We have to leave this place," she murmured in his ear.

His eyes opened as if coming from a dream.

"Abby?" his weak voice whispered. "It *is* you, isn't it." It was not a question.

"Yes, Ben, of course it's me. I've come to take you out of this place, this horrible place. You're going home with me, to the seawall and the Birdfriends, and we'll ride again under the stars, and you'll take me flying above the clouds, and I'll take care of you until we can." The words came in a continual flow now, and her tears flowed with them, bathing his ashen cheek.

She felt him stir beneath her and then the weight of his arm across her back. With what strength he could muster, he softly patted her comfortingly. "I don't . . . think so, babe. Doctors told me it's . . . ."

Rising up just enough to look into his eyes, Amber spoke as forcefully as she dared.

"You just never mind what the doctors told you. I'll speak to the doctors. You ARE going to get up out of this bed in a few days, and you ARE going to walk out of here at my side. Do you understand? Do you? For now, you're going to rest, and I'm going to get you something warm to drink, and you're going to start thinking about what I've told you. Do you understand me, Ben? You just put everything else out of your mind. I'll sit here with you for a few minutes while you go back to sleep."

Amazed at her own outburst, she took his hand in her own again and held it tight, as tight as she could without hurting him.

Looking up at her, his eyes brightened just a little. It was as if he could almost feel her strength slowly beginning to enter him through his hand. He didn't have the heart to argue with this woman, nor the energy. Best she hears the news from the doctors, he thought, but deep in the recesses of his still-drugged mind, the fragments of a new hope were beginning to form.

A small smile pulled at the corner of his mouth, and in a gallant attempt at cheering her, he whispered, "You really are a lunatic, you know." He was getting sleepy again, and afraid that maybe he was dreaming all this, too. "Abby?" He looked into her eyes. "Will you be here when I wake up?"

"You can count on it, Ben. I'm not going anywhere without you. Sleep now. I'll just be going to see the nurse about getting you some supper."

She released him and sat quietly on the side of his bed, listening for the relaxed breathing that would indicate sleep. A thousand thoughts were rushing through her mind as to just what she'd have to do as a means to her end. The first thing was to find out exactly what was going on, what they'd been giving him, and why. So far, all she knew was something about experiments on tumors and killing chimps. And, nurses that smiled too sweetly.

Once sure Ben was sleeping, she rose and walked softly from the room. Outside the door, she leaned against the wall and tried to clear her mind. She dug the name and number of the hotel out of her purse, looked up and down the hallway for a public phone, and spotted one in the nearby lounge. She straightened, gathered her resolve and walked in that direction, opening her change purse along the way and wishing she'd not fought the idea of a cell phone.

"Best Western, Medical Plaza," the refined Texas accent came over the wire.

"Hello. My name is Abigail Allyson. I have a reservation, but I'm going to be held up at the hospital. Would it be possible to check in by phone and pick up my room key at the desk when I can get there?"

"Well, it's customary to register in person, ma'am," the accent came back.

Amber bristled. "Listen, I'm involved in a less than *customary* situation here. You have my credit card number and will have no problem charging me if I fail to appear. I cannot believe, considering your location, that my request is out of the ordinary. Now please, check your records and tell me if I'll have a room waiting upon my arrival or not. If need be, I'll call elsewhere as I will require accommodations for at least a week."

Doing some quick figuring, the voice drawled back, "Oh yes, Ms. Allyson. I have it in front of me now. Yes, of course, you may pick up your key at the desk whenever you're able to get here. Is there anything you'll need in your room?"

"Thank you, no. Just hot water and a bed will do." She hung up the phone.

Now, to let her sons know she was safe and reasonably sound. Sighing, she again removed the phone from the receiver and dialed. Her conversations were brief. That done, she turned and approached the high counter separating her from the nurse who'd warned her of Ben's condition.

"Good evening, and excuse me. I want to thank you for preparing me for Ben's, Mr. Riley's, condition. He sounded so much stronger on the phone just a couple days ago. I wasn't prepared for the rapid deterioration to his present state," she said, softly.

"I'm sorry to have been the one to tell you, dear. Mr. Riley was in much better circumstances just a few days ago. Tell me, are you the one who sent the Snapdragons?

"Yes, I am. Ben really has no close family, and I'm just a special friend, you might say. My concern is finding out when I can take him home, Miss Reynolds." Her gaze rose from the nurse's identification tag up to meet her eyes. Peering intently into them, she smiled politely.

Miss Reynolds hesitated. "I'm sorry, dear. The doctors were around earlier and have left for the day. I'm afraid you won't be able to talk to them until morning. Will you be staying close by?"

"Yes, I'm booked at the Medical Plaza across the street, and I do appreciate your concern. I've come a long way to get here. I called and checked in at the hotel, but I think I'll go and sit with Ben a while longer before I go there, if it's okay. In the meantime, would it be possible to get him some warm green tea? I'll wait right here by the phones and take it to him myself since I know you're busy."

"I'll see what I can do." The nurse reached for her phone while smiling at the tiny woman standing in front of her. I hope she's a gutsy little thing, she thought, picturing Dr. Millstone in her mind. "Would you like a cup for yourself, Miss—?"

"Allyson. Abigail Allyson, but please call me Amber, and thank you. I'll wait in the lounge." She smiled gratefully, and then walked across the hall.

Sitting in the big chair, she felt the weariness take over. Her mind was tired and it was almost as if the scene around her was a recurring nightmare, hurling her back into the past. So many times she'd paced hospital corridors; so many times she'd sat in Wing lounges. The voice of Nurse Reynolds brought her back to the present.

"Ms. Allyson? I have the tea you asked for, enough for you both."

She stood and reached to take the tray from her. "Thanks so much, Miss Reynolds. I really appreciate your help."

"After you've had your tea, why not go to your room and get some rest. I'll look in on Mr. Riley through the night," the nurse offered.

"Yes. Yes, I think I will. And, thank you again for your trouble." She turned and headed back to room 613.

Ben was sleeping when she re-entered the room. She sat the tea tray down on the bedside table, then gently sat on the edge of the bed next to him. He stirred slightly with the movement. Looking down into his now peaceful face, she no longer questioned what had compelled her to rush to this man's side. She knew it was the only place for her to be. The room was cold and she gently tucked the blanket around his shoulders.

Noticing the IV pole by his bed, she walked around to check the bags hanging there. Glucose, potassium, some antibiotic, the usual you'd expect to find. She saw no indication of chemical compounds that would indicate a chemo-therapeutic. Evidently, the experimental drug had been withdrawn and they were administering only nutrients and precaution against infection. Moving back around to her seat beside him, she smiled as she noticed his open eyes watching her.

"You really did come, Abby," he rasped, still weak.

"Why, you didn't doubt I would, did you?" She brushed his cheek gently with the back of her hand. "And, since you're awake, how about a sip of warm tea? It's good for what ails you."

"I don't like tea," he muttered, but it was less than a refusal.

Helping him rise just enough to lean against her, she tossed the covers back to free his arms and noticed the bruises above his wrists, as if he'd struggled with restraint straps.

"Oh my dear Ben, what have you been through here?" she uttered almost inaudibly. Reaching for the teapot with her left hand, she poured a small amount of the liquid into a cup, supporting him with her right arm around his back.

"Here, have just a sip." She placed the small cup into his hands. "When did you last have some food?"

He sipped the tea slowly, surprised at how good it tasted, how it warmed him as he swallowed. "Ate pretty good at first, but then it started making me ill. Not sure now how many days have passed. What day did we speak on the

78

phone? What day is it now? Was a day or so before that, I think."

He squeezed his eyes shut, and open again, trying to clear his head. "This tea isn't bad but I want to lie down again now. I'm getting kind of dizzy."

"Sure, let me help you." She took the cup from his hands and helped ease him back to the pillow. "Try to sleep again if you'd like. Sleep heals. Maybe in the morning you'll want some breakfast. Oatmeal maybe?"

"Don't like oatmeal. Thanks for coming, Abby." He was already closing his eyes.

She brushed a light kiss on his forehead causing him to stir, but only slightly. She sat quietly, watching his chest rise and fall, breathing in life, and a love he'd yet to know.

WHERE'S YOUR AIRPLANE?

A kaleidoscope of colorful hues trapped in crystalline bubbles lapped at the wings of the seagull, resting now on the sun-browned skin of her chest. She studied the froth twinkling in the reflected light from over the vanity and let the hot water soothe her tired body. It cleared her mind and relaxed the tempest brewing just beneath her surface calm. Serenity. She'd always been able to tap into it in her bubble baths.

Recollecting the day, she knew she'd done the right thing in coming here. Any doubts vanished the minute she saw Ben lying in such a cold, antiseptic, environment. In their brief times together, she'd seen the pain, the hopes and dreams of a lifetime, in his eyes. She'd heard the joy at simple things in his laughter. He wouldn't die without flying above the clouds again. She simply wouldn't allow it. He'd appeared in her world for a reason. Perhaps he'd always been there, lingering in unstaged plays, behind curtains just beyond the horizon.

"Damn. Damn. Damn!" She pushed herself down and laid flat under the water, her auburn hair billowing out amidst the bubbly foam.

Sitting now, yoga style in the center of the king-sized bed, she dialed the hospital. "Nurse Reynolds, sixth floor nurses station please," she answered the operator. She wanted to make sure Ben was sleeping soundly so she, too, could get some much needed rest. Tomorrow was going to be a busy day.

"Sixth floor Nurses' Desk, may I help you?" came the now familiar voice.

"Hello, Miss Reynolds. This is Amber . . . I mean, Abigail Allyson. I wanted to make sure Ben was all right before I go to bed myself."

"Yes, he's fine, Amber. I just checked on him. You rest now as I'm sure Mr. Riley will sleep until your return."

She hesitated. *How do I say this?* "Nurse Reynolds, may I ask you an off-the-record question?"

"Certainly, dear, what is it?"

"What's wrong with Ben?"

This time it was the nurse who paused before answering. "Cancer dear, I thought you knew."

"No, I don't mean that, and yes I did know. I mean, what have they done to him? Why is he so terribly ill?"

"Oh," the nurse said, "treatment for cancer can be pretty debilitating, I'm afraid."

"That's still not what I mean. I mean, what kind of treatment did they give him? He told me it was experimental."

"Why not talk to his doctors, dear. They should be here around eight AM. I can leave a note for the doctor about your concerns, if you like."

"Yes, please do, but what I want to know, they won't tell me. I already know that as I've had experiences in something like this. I'd just like to know the truth, Miss Reynolds."

"My shift ends at five, but I'll leave word with my relief of your unease and I've already written a note to Dr. Millstone, the one in charge, on Mr. Riley's chart."

"Nurse Reynolds—?"

"This is a research hospital, dear, if you didn't know," the nurse interrupted. "Patients come here when they have nowhere else to go. Nowhere else to turn."

"I see." The dread washed over her. *The last resort*, she means. "Thank you, Miss Reynolds." She hung up and nearly bawled. "Not again, dammit! Not Again!"

The shrill ring sat her straight up and for a brief moment she couldn't remember where she was. Then awareness returned and she reached for the phone in the gloom of dawn peeking through the vertical blinds on the window. "Good morning. This is your automated wake-up call. It is now Six AM. A continental breakfast will be served on the mezzanine level starting at six-thirty." The recorded message droned her into a semblance of wakefulness.

An hour later she pulled into the parking area. Eager to see if a night of sleep and added hours off the drug had improved Ben's lucidity, she walked briskly toward the entrance. Noticing the gift shop was already open for early morning visitors, she impulsively entered; the ringing of the bell reminding her of another door, another bell, only a few short months ago.

She purchased a single yellow rose, a small bag of gumdrops, and then hurried to the elevators. Exiting on the sixth floor, she nodded to the group of nurses readying for the day shift and swiftly made her way to Ben's room.

His eyes were closed, but she did detect a hint of color in the cheeks so ashen the previous afternoon. Passing the breakfast cart in the hallway, she was glad that she'd be able to encourage him to eat. She hadn't thought of a vase for the rose and looked around the room. All that was available were the plastic drinking cups by the water pitcher.

"Well," she mumbled, "it holds water," and bit off the long stem so it wouldn't be top heavy. Hearing a slight chuckle, she turned in reflex, the rose still in her teeth.

"So, you gonna dance for me, or what?" He was smiling, not broadly, but really smiling this time.

Amber brightened, instantly. "Maybe. Depends on your oatmeal," she teased, placing the rose on his bed tray.

"Oatmeal? I hate oatmeal, and what's that got to do with dancing?" he asked, raising an eyebrow at her while looking at the yellow rose in a silly plastic cup. "Is that supposed to be my breakfast?"

"And, I see you're still the smart ass," she said, laughing and bending over to kiss his forehead. "No, your breakfast is coming.

"I'm not hungry, but some coffee may taste good." Tiredness remained in his voice.

"Coffee it is then, and maybe a bite or two just for me, okay?" She sat on the edge of the bed and took his hand, serious now. "Are you feeling a little better today, Ben?"

"Maybe. You being here helps, I think." His voice trailed off as his thoughts returned to how he didn't want to hurt this woman.

As if reading his mind, she spoke softly, "Ben, don't worry about a thing except regaining your strength. I'm going to take you from this place. I promise."

He felt hope beginning to rise again. "Yes, get me out of here, Abby. I can't stay here now; I have things to do. And quickly."

She squeezed his hand as the orderly entered the room with his breakfast tray. Thanking him, she took the tray and placed it on the table and lifted the stainless steel lid, relieved to see a small container of fruit alongside the rubbery-looking scrambled eggs and oatmeal. Something he might eat that was light and wouldn't upset his stomach.

"Here's some coffee, Ben. Let's prop you up a bit." She fluffed his pillow and handed him the cup. "Sorry, no vanilla this time, but the milk will be good for you. How about some toast and a little fruit?"

"I don't like fruit." He wasn't smiling when he said it.

She stiffened. "No you don't. And, you don't like tea, oatmeal, or much of anything I suggest. I know that already. Do you like lying there and wasting away better?" She'd lost her patience. "I'm going to do everything in my power to get

83

you out of this place, Mr. Riley, but I'm going to fail miserably if you don't at least try to cooperate. Now eat some damn toast and some damn fruit because I'm NOT big enough to carry your ass out of here." She wasn't kidding now.

Sighing, Ben nibbled on a small corner of wheat toast, but only because he realized she was right. He'd have to regain strength if he was ever going to leave. And, the coffee was good.

She opened her purse and brought out some vitamins. "Here," she said, shoving one into his mouth. "Won't hurt, will help."

"Argggh. Goddamnit, first fruit, now pills." He coughed.

"Yes, and lots of them," she added, relieved at his anger. A healthy sign for sure. "I'm going to aggravate the crap out of you until you can't stand it, and then we'll leave."

He started to protest, but smiled instead. "Damn lunatic," he said weakly, still smiling.

"Yeah," she said. "And aren't you glad I am."

There was a loud knock on the door and it immediately swung open.

"Excuse me. Good morning. You look much livelier today, Mr. Riley. And you must be Ms. Allyson," a stern voice announced all in one breath.

Amber turned to see a rather tall, attractive woman brusquely entering the room as if she owned it, and the entire hospital. She was impeccably dressed under her starched white lab coat. Her dark hair was styled in the latest coiffure, and she reeked of snobbery.

"Yes, I'm Abigail Allyson, a close friend of Ben's." She met the woman's eyes.

"Nurse Reynolds left me a note that you had arrived late yesterday. My name is Dr. Millstone," she said, turning back to Ben and leaving Amber feeling dismissed.

"When do you think it might be possible for Ben to leave, Doctor? I've come to take him home." She tried to sound congenial.

The doctor turned and answered coldly. "Ms. Allyson, I'm afraid Mr. Riley isn't leaving." Turning back to Ben, she continued. "Have you filled your friend in on the results of your treatment, Mr. Riley? If not, you might consider it. I hardly think you'll be waltzing out of here just yet."

"Can it, doc. I want out of here, and now. Just bring the papers; I'll sign them. I want to leave no later than the day after tomorrow. By then I'll be strong enough, Abby will see to it. I want out of this mortuary while I can still walk."

"Mr. Riley," the doctor began, "you came in here voluntarily. You signed an agreement, remember? I thought you understood that when volunteering for experimental treatment as you did, the final decision of your leaving rests with your doctor so we can monitor your progress or the effects. You can't blame me—us that your treatment didn't work. But, I'll determine when you're strong enough to leave."

Amber interrupted. "Doctor Millstone, was it? I beg to differ. Ben came to you for help, which you obviously couldn't provide. When I arrived he was nearly dead. And now you're suggesting he stay? For what purpose?"

"Kindly stay out of this, Ms. Allyson. You're not even family."

"Not family?" She came around the bed and got right in the doctor's face, clinching her fists. "No, I'm *not* family, but neither are you. You're the one who damn near killed him."

"Who do you think you're talking—," the doctor began but was cut off.

"Listen, *doctor*, I'm proof of the fact, *doctor*, that when I arrived Ben was at death's door and little, if anything, was being done about it. You'd already written him off. Do I make myself clear? Or would you rather talk to an attorney about your callous *research* program?" Her words dripped with venom. "Your patient says he wants to be discharged; he's here voluntarily. I'm a witness; so you'd better get your starched and insufferably smug ass to wherever you have to go to get those discharge papers. And I suggest you do it within the time frame Mr. Riley requested."

Doctor Millstone's face flushed from shock and wounded pride, but nothing compared to Amber's face, which was the color of angry strawberries.

"We'll see about that Ms. Allyson." Without another word she twirled around Amber and out the door.

"Bitch," Amber mumbled, watching her go.

"Ha-ha," Ben's laugh came from behind.

She whirled around, still clinching her fists. "What's so damn funny?" she snapped.

"Why, you! You must have grown a foot while chewing her ass out." His face was full of admiration.

All the nurses smiled when she finally left to get something from the commissary. She sensed by their knowing looks that she'd taken on the terror of the floor and won, and this made her happy.

Still, the medical issues loomed as somewhat of a closed door to her now, after the confrontation and not being a family member, so she turned her full attention to nurturing Ben's return to strength. At least to the point of getting him to the hotel. There, she'd care for him for a day or two more if necessary, and then they'd decide in which direction to go. Where the road led beyond that curve, perhaps only the seagull, from his lofty perspective, knew.

Doctor Millstone turned the case over to the medical Interns on staff, a more caring group than the Research team, and didn't return.

Three days later, with Ben holding on to Amber's arm, they walked out of the hospital together. All the nurses came over to say goodbye and Nurse Reynolds gave her a hug.

"Good luck, dear. Never underestimate the power of love, I always say. Maybe the doctors should research love instead of drugs." Then added with a wink, "or Snapdragons."

Love? That's something Amber hadn't allowed herself to consider for a long time. She returned Nurse Reynolds' hug and thanked them all, and then they were at the front door.

When Ben saw the sunlight beyond, he gently but firmly, removed her arm from his and took her hand instead. His grip was weak, but he was so improved over what he'd been when she arrived, she knew he was on his way back.

"Where's your airplane?" he joked weakly.

COOL BLUE, OLD WOOD, AND
TEDDY BEARS IN CHAIRS

Ben stared out the window at the clouds and earth below. He was amazed at how fast he'd regained strength under Abby's care and some decent food. He'd tossed and turned a lot in the motel bed while she'd slept mostly in the chair, but in two days he was nearly back to his old self, in disposition at least.

Amber was mostly pleased with Ben's progress. She noticed that he seemed to have something on his mind he didn't want to discuss, but didn't ask. Her intuition told her to take one day at a time.

Now they were on an airplane bound for Florida, and although he still tired easily, his personality had returned and he was more like when they'd first met. She guessed the restlessness while he slept was due to his treatment while in the hospital, the drug or whatever it was, leaving his body. But, some of the things he mumbled while sleeping disturbed her, and she realized he'd seen more in life than she'd even imagined; things that had left permanent scars.

Yet, when not fretful and in a deep sleep, his face turned almost angelic. It seemed as if there was a peace beneath his hard veneer that he kept hidden from the world, or simply couldn't reach when awake. She ached to know what that peace was and how it could become a permanent part of him again, as it must have been long ago.

At the motel, he'd insisted on going back to his home on the West Coast, adamant that he had urgent things to do. But she'd convinced him he'd be better off going home with her until he was stronger. Besides, she'd reminded him, there's always a telephone, faxes, the Internet. Reluctantly, he'd relented, but not before attempting to walk out and falling. He was indeed stubborn, but so was she, and her logic prevailed. After the fall, he'd told her that he'd go with her for a short while, a week or two at best, and then he'd have to return home.

It was agreed, and now they were six miles above the earth flying at just below the speed of sound, and heading not to his home, but hers. She wondered how she'd manage it. The thought hadn't crossed her mind before due to Ben's emergency, but it dawned on her now that since her late husband's death, there'd never been another man in her home. Where would he sleep? In *their* bed? How would her sons take it, knowing a man was in their late father's house? Her family? The neighbors? To hell with the neighbors, she didn't care about them. But she did her sons and family, and she did her memories. She began to wonder if maybe she'd made a mistake by forcing the issue.

"Look there." Ben's voice startled her and brought her from her thoughts. He was pointing out the window at something, so she leaned across to see. She hoped to see the double rainbow as a sign she was doing right. But it wasn't a rainbow that had grabbed his attention. It was a huge thunderhead, a cloud towering above all the rest and shaped like an anvil at the top.

"Beautiful, isn't it?" he marveled. "Yet beneath all that majesty is fury so intense it's wrecking havoc on those below. Rain, wind, hail and lightning, maybe tornados. People and animals are running for shelter or hiding from that cloud. Rivers may be rising, things drowning, homes being destroyed. While up here it's all sunshine and serenity. Quite the paradox, wouldn't you say?"

She settled into her seat. His face had an odd look to it, as if he was trying to tell her something without telling her, letting her figure it out.

"Yes. Yes, it is. So, what are you saying?"

But he didn't answer. Instead, he continued to stare at the cloud, at the sky, at whatever he was staring at in his own mind. She left him to his musings, and then felt his hand close around hers.

"What am I saying?" he suddenly continued. "That every cloud has a silver lining only if one can get above the storm. That's what I'm saying." He looked away. "Just talking, I guess. I'm tired. Do you mind if I doze off? We still have an hour or so before we land."

Without waiting for her answer he laid his head back and closed his eyes. The dreams would come as they always did.

He's in his late twenties and flying alone in a small single engine airplane high above the clouds. The airplane is an older one with a wooden prop and overhead wing. He is doing Lazy-Eights in the sky, climbing up, then turning into a dive. The old engine drones and whines under its labor, its simplified instruments a reflection of a bygone era. At the top of one climb, he rolls it onto its back and into another dive, this time inverted. He's a dolphin playing in the ocean, an eagle in flight, thoroughly enjoying himself. The engine sputters and quits but he isn't concerned, as that's what this kind of engine does when upside down.

At the bottom of the loop he's back upright and the engine, its prop still wind milling, fires back up and he adds throttle, coaxing the J-3 into another climb. Off to the right is the top of a thunderhead towering far above him, its anvil top pointing west. On impulse he checks his climb and rolls in the direction of the huge cloud, the wind from the windowless plane blowing his hair.

Looking at him now, sleeping with a small smile at the corner of his mouth, her thoughts returned to how she might explain suddenly bringing a man into her home. A friend, she'd say if pressed, for now. There was an element of truth in that. An eyebrow may raise, but the boys knew her principles. And, they probably wished she would consider a new relationship in her life. There had more than a few comments about her being holed up with a book and a plant. She smiled at the thought.

Ben stirred next to her, his face showing strain again. She was always tempted to wake him when his sleep became agitated, but it was as if he was doing a sorting out, an examination of things he had to meet over and over again until he could let them go into the past where they belonged.

He's in his thirties and at the control of an airliner bouncing wildly inside a storm. Lightning is flashing almost constantly, accompanied by thunder as loud as a cannon beyond the iced windshield. A bell is clanging and an instrument panel light glows red, indicating an engine out. The younger co-pilot is sweating profusely, as is he, as he reaches for the bell switch to silence the alarm.

"Center, this is 637," he calls on the radio. "We're iced up and have lost an engine, can't hold altitude. We need an immediate vector to Sioux Falls, do you read?" No reply. He repeats his call as the aircraft's stall warning horn sounds.

The bluish-green of the Gulf shimmered below the wing as the airplane banked. The Barrier islands with their white sugar-sand beaches appeared as the big plane continued its turn and began its descent. They'd be landing shortly, and she took Ben's hand, hoping to wake him naturally rather than startling him by calling out his name.

Once on the ground, she'd take him home, surround him in an oasis of simple things, and help him heal by leaving him to himself. Nature would do it, she was positive. And, if need be, they'd go to a *real* doctor. Lifting his hand in hers, she entwined their fingers and applied just enough pressure to wake him.

"We're almost there," she whispered. "The pilot said we'll be landing in five minutes."

"Did I sleep that long?" He had a confused look as his eyes fully opened.

The landing was uneventful, except for Ben mumbling "amateur" under his breath, and soon they were walking hand in hand along the glass-framed corridor that led from the boarding gates to the main terminal.

Seeing the corridor again, his mind ran to the night, not so long ago, he'd walked this same aisle when leaving this town and the woman who now walked beside him. He remembered the letters he'd written that night, one to his son and one to her, and wondered if it was those letters that had changed their lives, not his visit. If I'd left without a word, he thought, as I have so many times in the past, by now they probably would've forgotten me. What the hell am I doing here?

Amber broke into his reflection. "Tell you what. Why don't you rest while I get our luggage and then we can walk to my car together?"

"No, Abby. I'll get the luggage while you get the car. I'll stay in the air-conditioning while you melt into a pool of sweat in the parking lot." He grinned at her.

She hesitated, sensing he was trying to help, no matter his joking, but, could he handle it, even two small bags?

"All right, but if you have trouble, call an assistant to help you. That's what they're here for," she cautioned.

"Ha!" he retorted, but Amber had turned and was headed for the parking lot. He walked on to the baggage carousel which was already unloading. Snatching their bags as it came around, he found it was true. He was still weak and struggled with their luggage as he turned toward the same doors he'd seen her leave through. Again his thoughts ran to why he was there, but not for long.

He heard her coming before he saw her, or rather the music, and couldn't help but laugh out loud. She came to an abrupt stop outside the door and he was almost surprised to see that she'd left the top up, remembering how she loved the open air. He walked out the door toward the car waiting at the curb, and thought of parking lots by seawalls.

Opening the door, he maneuvered the bags into the back seat, being careful not to let her see he was out of breath. "Home, woman," he quipped, and slid in beside her.

Amber pulled the car out into the exit lanes and shot out into the traffic. She really did drive to her music, he noticed as the speed increased or decreased to the beat. Still, he felt relaxed riding with her again and it seemed almost too soon that they were wheeling into a driveway leading directly under a house nestled in the trees. He couldn't help but smile again.

"Damn lunatic hasn't changed a bit," he mumbled as he looked around, intrigued. The last remaining rays of pink were streaming through the big Oaks to the west casting a special glow to the place. Suddenly Amber stopped short, sliding in the crushed shell of her drive.

"Oh, Ben! Look! Straight out from the back of the house," she whispered turning the music off and pointing. "There he is!"

It stood in the shadows watching them, its eyes reflecting in the running lights on the front of the car. It hesitated, then disappeared into the undergrowth. She felt a calm come over her. The fox, like the rainbows, gave his approval of this new venture she was about to begin, she was certain. It had come to say everything would be all right. Ben said nothing. She parked beneath the tree house, as she called it, curious at his silence.

"Come on, Ben. Come on in," she said climbing out of the low-slung car. She walked around and took his hand, led him up the steps and opened the door. He paused, looking up at the canopy of green over his head, and then stepped cautiously into a world of cool blue, old wood, and teddy bears in chairs.

GLASS BUTTON EYES

Sensing Ben's hesitation, she walked across the room toward the glass door wall where a huge stuffed Polar bear nearly as large as she sat in a velvet rocking chair looking out onto the deck beyond. She scooped him up into her arms and informed him they had a house guest and he'd have to move to the couch where another menagerie of sorts was spread about.

"Sit here, Ben," she said patting the crème-colored rocker. "You must be tired from the trip and probably thirsty, too. I'll make lemonade while you rest and get comfortable."

She turned to the kitchen, hesitated, and then looked back. "And, if you're having second thoughts about coming here, I assure you everything is going to be fine. For now, just enjoy my infernal pampering. Okay? It's been awhile."

"All right, Abby," he answered, looking at her and wondering if she had any idea what she may be opening herself up to.

He crossed the room and sat in the chair vacated by the bear, who now sat on the long sofa watching him through glass button eyes. "And yes, I am kind of thirsty," he added as he rotated the chair to look outside.

The house was on stilts and almost shrouded by large oaks dripping with gossamer moss. The arms of the trees embraced railings and corners that had been carefully fit into their space. Across an expanse of mown grass a near jungle stretched behind. Beyond to the sides, laid openness with tropical gardens and Palms. The space of it compared to what he was used to in Los Angeles, the crisp, smogless blue above . . . he liked it and quickly understood why she called it her oasis.

"It'll just take a minute to make some lemonade. Grow my own citrus, you know, and I still have some juice from the last crop in the freezer," she called to him.

Glancing into the living room and seeing Ben sitting in Jeff's chair gave rise to some emotions she wasn't expecting, but that was normal, she told herself. In what little previous time they'd spent together the territory had been neutral, home to neither of them. What she couldn't tell him was that if not for foxes and rainbows, the bear would have stayed in the chair and he would've been shown to the couch. She chuckled quietly at the thought.

"Take your time, Abby. I'm fine," he answered, winking at the bear with button eyes of glass, still watching him as he looked around.

The house was mostly open and he watched Amber as she moved around the kitchen making drinks. Few walls and high ceilings gave it, though small, the illusion of being larger. A long wooden table served as a divider between the living room and kitchen, and the furnishings were mostly of old wood and crème colored velvet with blue roses; a strange combination, he thought. A table made from the base of a tree trunk caught his eye, and there were carved walking sticks, dried flowers, and wood shelves holding a variety of birdhouses, cats, and other collectibles.

The cupboard doors held posters of wolves, bears and mountain lions, and over the long, low sofa was a large seascape. Oil lamps and candles were on every table and lighting was subtle. A large aquarium with a carefully arranged sea floor served for a more conventional lamp. Yes, the home spoke of her, this woman who had captured him in one sense and made him want to run in another.

"Here you are," she said, breaking into his reverie and handing him a frosty glass of lemonade. "This will hold you until I get supper. I'm going to bring our things up from the car and then run to the store, unless you don't mind from cans or the freezer."

"That'll be fine, Abby. Cans or from the freezer will be fine."

"You're welcome to watch TV or just look around," she went on, handing him the remote and pointing to another door opening. "There's a bathroom right off the hallway."

With the effort she was taking to make him feel welcome, he suddenly felt a relaxation of sorts. Instead of his normal quip, all he could manage to say was, "Thanks." How strange his lack of words felt, as if he'd left his sword someplace and couldn't remember where.

Amber went about preparing supper relieved to hear the TV go on. Now he'll relax, she thought. She heard the sound of applause coming from the set, and a quick peek revealed him now dozing and fidgeting in yet another dream. "Damn," she muttered to no one.

A forty-ish Ben is in a tuxedo and on a stage, accepting some kind of award. It is a small auditorium, and on the back wall, a banner proclaiming 'Pacificus Foundation' hangs. He speaks sheepishly into the microphone.

"Ready," she said as she brought the food to the table and lighted the candles. He flicked off the TV set and came to join her.

"Looks good, Abby." He smiled up at her as he sat. Sitting across from each other in the flickering candlelight, they ate their meal and spoke little. It was as if they'd always been together, even when they weren't. She looked at him intently, and as if feeling it, he looked up. There eyes met and the silence spoke their words for them. Just let it be.

When he started picking at his food, she rose and went to the stove. "Vanilla or milk in your coffee, Ben?"

"Neither, really. I'm so tired I can't stay awake much longer. Must be the long day and the flight and all. Would you mind if I went on to bed?"

"Why no, I don't mind. I realize you must be beat," she assured him. "Here, let me get you a towel and you can shower or just wash up while I open the bed." She turned off the coffee pot and headed toward the linen closet in the hallway.

"Ah, don't bother, Abby. Think I'll wait until morning to shower," he said rising from the table and then slowly following.

"Okay, but here's what you'll need whenever you're ready." She handed him a towel and face cloth, then turned on the light in the small bathroom that would be his. He shrugged and took the towel, stepped inside and closed the door.

She went to the bedroom and pulled back the spread on the bed used only when her sons came to visit. She made sure the sheets were fresh, fluffed the pillows, and turned around to find him behind her.

"There's a TV on the dresser," she began, but he reached out and lifted her face to meet his own, her long hair falling over his hands. He stared at her for a moment, then pulling her to him, softly kissed her eyelids. She let herself lean into him, the gull on its chain hearing the beat of the only two hearts it had known. After what seemed a long moment, she straightened and kissed his chest where the gull had lain ever so briefly, then walked from the room.

"Good night," she heard him say.

She finished in the kitchen, then strolled to the living room and plopped on the sofa. "So, what do you think of Ben?" she whispered to Bear as she hugged him close. "Why yes, I like him, too." She giggled in his big, bear ear. Then fluffing Bear's pillows, too, she decided to wait for morning before going to the store. "I've got coffee and whatever else we'll need for breakfast, and the tiredness is catching up with me, too, Bear," she told him. She hugged the animal, placed him among the pillows, and headed to the small den where she'd been sleeping on the couch for so many months.

She changed into her nightclothes and stretched out on the couch but was restless as soon as she turned off the light. Another presence in the house permeated the usual emptiness, disquieting any sleep that might come. It was an emptiness she'd grown accustomed to, felt safe in. Now, the soft drone of the television in the next room, quiet for so long, invaded her silent world making her wary.

Were the nurturing instincts, so strong in her, simply reaching out for relief from the drought? Did she see in Ben what she felt in herself? She tossed and turned, her thoughts racing. Had past and present collided?

"No," she whispered into the dim shadows cast on the walls by the moonlight. "Doubts are born out of the shoulds and should nots drilled into me for so long. I'm different, I've always been different." Then, anger overwhelmed her yet again.

"Damn you! Oh, damn you, Jeff, for leaving me when I wasn't strong enough to remain behind," she whispered through gritted teeth. You were the wind that kept me in flight, let me . . . no, made me, be what I was. And now, you slink around as a fox in the underbrush and paint rainbows in the sky. And, Ben? What am I to do? Dammit, what am I supposed to do?" Literally shaking, she bit her fist to keep from crying out.

Wide awake and afraid of disturbing Ben by moving around in the house, she quietly slid open the glass doors leading to the deck outside her room. Moonrays filtering through the big old trees lighted the yard below, and the night sounds soothed her mood. She leaned over the railing searching the grounds hoping to see the fox foraging in the cover of darkness. But she heard only the chattering of the raccoons playing beyond her vision. Inhaling the night air, she let nature work its miracle on her. She exhaled slowly, the anger and confusion leaving as abruptly as it had come. She felt him behind her even before she heard him.

"You okay, Abby?"

"I'm fine, Ben." She smiled into the darkness without turning. "I wasn't sleepy and didn't want to disturb you. I forgot to tell you I'm kind of a night person. I love the night. Things are quieter then; less noise of the world rushing about and swallowing you up." There was no answer.

"I have so many things to say to you," she went on, "but I have to kind of sort them out first, if you know what I mean." Still he didn't answer, as if encouraging her to talk her way through her thoughts. "We really need to rest some, both of us. The last few days are catching up with me, too, I'm afraid."

She turned around to face him. "Is there something I can get you before I lay back down?"

She found herself staring into the gloom of the house with no one there. Surprised, wondering if she'd imagined his voice, she slipped quietly inside and peeked into the bedroom. He was there, sound asleep, and by the sound of his light snoring, had been there all along.

She closed his door, returned to the couch and lay back down, pondering the mystery of it all. The voice hadn't frightened her and it had definitely been Ben's, or so she thought. But she let it go, let it float away into the realm of clouds and bows, and closed her eyes. She knew then Jeff had never left her at all, and never would. Just let it be.

She woke with the sun bathing her face and sat up with a start. Glancing at the clock and relieved to see that it was still early, she stepped into her jeans and went quietly into her bathroom hoping Ben was still sleeping. She pushed down the urge to peek in the room as she was passing into the kitchen. Instead, she busied herself pouring juice, making coffee, toast, and oatmeal.

On impulse, she grabbed her garden scissors and ran down the steps, snipped a bright yellow Day Lily and bounded back up. She found a vase in the cupboard and set the table with the flower as its centerpiece.

Going to the door of the bedroom to wake him, she saw that it was standing open. The room was empty. How had he gotten past her without her hearing him, she wondered. She checked the bathroom only to see it was empty as well. She turned back around expecting to see him at the table having come from the other direction. The hallway connected both ends of the house; there were no dead ends. Not there either.

"Ben?" No answer.

A small panic began to rise in her throat. If he wasn't in the house, where was he? She hurried to the front door and out onto the porch. She looked down at the chairs in the yard. Not there. She half ran down the stairs and looked around the grounds. Nothing, and she would have seen him when she went for the flower anyway.

A nagging fear was beginning to replace the immediate panic. Had he decided, again, to leave in the night? There was one more place to look . . . the thicket out back leading into the jungle beyond. Could he have wandered in there unaware of the rattlesnakes and other critters she loved and who trusted her, but might be wary of a stranger in their midst?

She ran to the back of the house to where she could see the thicket and stopped. There at the edge, his back to her, Ben was squatting down. She felt a rush of relief come over her. He was all right. But what was he doing, almost sitting like that?

"Ben?" He seemed not to hear her as she called out in a low voice.

She walked slowly toward him and when within a few feet, saw what held him trance-like. Sitting just inside the growth was the fox, staring at him, just as it had once stared at her. She stopped, almost afraid to move for fear she'd scare it. The fox glanced in her direction. Their eyes caught for just a moment, then with one long look back at Ben, it backed into the underbrush and was gone.

"Beautiful, isn't he?" he said as she came over and bent down beside him.

"Oh my, yes," She was smiling now. "But, how? I mean when?"

"I don't really know. I was having a dream about you, and I woke up with a strong urge to come outside. I can't explain it as anything but that, just some kind of urge. So I tiptoed past where you were sleeping and let myself out onto the porch. Then it was as if I just found myself walking out here, and there he was, sitting and watching me. As if, well, welcoming me."

"I've never been able to get that close to him," she said, still stunned. "He's always backed off if I approached."

Ben didn't answer, just continued staring into the undergrowth.

"You said you had a dream about me?" she asked.

"Imm-hmm. You were standing on a porch or something overlooking a bluff. Beyond was this wild sea, and you were talking, I guess to me. You had your back to me so I don't really know. But you were talking to someone, so I assumed it was me."

She felt the goose bumps prick her skin. "Can you remember what I was saying? In the dream, I mean."

He thought about it for a moment. "I think I asked you if you were all right, and you said something about being tired."

Turning to look at her, he pushed a strand of hair off her almost pale face. "Why? Is something wrong? You look like you've seen a ghost."

"No, nothing's wrong," she lied.

It had been Jeff behind her, she was certain now. She hadn't imagined it. Maybe not him in person, maybe something else, but him nonetheless. She dismissed the bluff in Ben's dream as symbolic, it being her porch and the wild sea being her wild yard. She shook it off and changed the subject.

"Why do you suppose the fox is here, Ben? There aren't any foxes anywhere around that I know of. There's hardly any wildlife left around here but for my small oasis. The developers are taking all their space."

101

"I don't know, Abby, but I'll tell you something," he said, looking away. "I've seen that fox before, or rather, its eyes." He looked into her face, as if searching for an answer. "I recognized those eyes when we pulled into your driveway. That's why I got quiet. Spirit Eyes, Abby." He turned away and stood up, pulling her up with him. "Sorry," he mumbled, embarrassed.

She squeezed his arm. "Don't be. Who can say, but we both know there's more to life than what we see. Come on, let's go back to the house and I'll finish making breakfast." She tugged him around and they walked back to the house arm in arm.

"Do you suppose that the fox has something to do with us? He's always run off before. Do you suppose now he'll stay?" she asked.

He shrugged and undid her arm from his as they reached the steps. "I don't know," he said, as he looked back over his shoulder to where the fox had been, and then smiled at her. "Maybe."

She finished putting the dishes away, her heart glad again. Ben had eaten ravenously, a good sign he was improving.

"If you feel up to it," she said over her shoulder, "I've taken a couple more days off work and we could go feed the seagulls and say hello to Birdfriend again. Or, if there's something else you'd like to do, just say so." She wondered if he'd thought of his son, being so close and all, yet how to explain that he was in town and staying with a woman.

Again, as if knowing what she was thinking, he smiled that little corner smile of his. "Bet those gulls are hungry, Abby."

They sat now on the same bench they'd shared the first time, another ravenous flock fluttering above their heads as they tossed crumbs. The day was warm but the breeze off the water was cooling. Ben was laughing at the antics of the birds as they swooped and tried to out-maneuver each other for the food, and the salt air brought sparkles to his eyes again. Already she noticed a hint of pink painting over the paleness of his cheeks. The ashen color was gone.

She wanted him to tell her of the health issues that had sent him away, and then her to him. But now wasn't the time to ask. He'd tell her when he was ready. Today they would just enjoy the beauty around them. And each other.

WARM SIDEWALKS AND DOGS NAMED KING

They walked along the shore as his strength allowed, feet shuffling to avoid the rolling surf. At times, with just the little fingers of their hands entwined, they'd share tales of childhood and youth, simple things, and laugh about them. Other times, she ran ahead, pausing to scoop up some new treasure from the sand and then back with hand outstretched to show it off. He watched her and chuckled at her childlike qualities. She, when turning back, was happy just in seeing him following at his leisure and smiling at her. Someone, again, to share with.

Returning to the benches, she found a picnic table near a huge old Slash Pine filled with squawking parrots. Ben seemed amused with the birds and the tree offered shade, so she left him to guard it while going to the concession to get sandwiches and sodas for lunch.

They swapped more anecdotes as they ate, and laughed at the squabbling in the bird colony. But he was looking tired again and she thought of using the shopping, yet to do, as an excuse for him to rest.

"How about if I take you back to the house and you take a nap while I make that trip to the grocery store?" she said while picking up the wrappings from the table.

"Yes, Abby, I think all the fresh air, and now lunch, has me sleepy. Would you mind?"

"Actually, I insist." She tried to look serious. "I have no intention of dragging you everywhere with me."

Inside, she was thinking of the obvious questions that would be asked if people she knew saw them together at the store, and she wasn't sure if she was ready to answer them, or worse yet, make up fibs about an old friend visiting. He grinned at her as if reading her mind again.

Carrying the grocery bags up the stairs, she hoped to get supper started without waking Ben. She unlocked the door and quietly piled the food on the table after taking a moment to walk to the bedroom and check on him, glad to see him sleeping peacefully for a change.

She put the food away, washed vegetables for supper, then took coffee out to the deck to relax a moment and think. All was quiet out toward the thicket. It was late afternoon and the life in her little jungle seemed to be napping, too, waiting for dusk to begin scurrying about. She thought of the fox and of the things shared today with the man sleeping in her bedroom.

As children, both had an insatiable curiosity and lust for adventure. In game playing, he was Robinson Crusoe, while she built explorer forts in the snow with discarded Christmas trees. Both had experienced, or endured, a less than ideal relationship with parents. Both had a love of being in touch with nature and animals. She'd told him of her dog named King only to find he, too, had had a dog named King. Hers a shepherd, his a collie.

She'd laughed when he told of lying on warm sidewalks during summer rain, or after the setting sun to watch the stars appear, only to find she'd loved the same thing. They'd told of catching fireflies, honey bees in jars, snakes and spiders, and grasshoppers spitting tobacco juice. And roller skating, both had taken lessons, both had become proficient on the wooden floors of skating rinks. Each was moved by music and dance and so much more. Both had been, basically, loners. It was uncanny, and the *chance* connection was becoming more mind boggling for her with each revelation. It was more a reunion than a meeting.

Movement inside the house, alerted her that Ben had gotten up. She hesitated just a few minutes, wanting to give him some privacy before going in to start their meal. He appeared at the glass door, pulled it aside and joined her on the deck.

"Nice out here," he said, walking to the rail and peering into the woods, as she'd done moments before. Still looking ahead, he asked, "Would you like to go out somewhere for dinner? It would save you cooking."

"I don't mind cooking, and we ate enough restaurant food at the hotel to last a year," she said, rolling her eyes. "Unless, you prefer something I don't have."

"No, it's not that at all. I was just thinking you've done enough waiting on me hand and foot already." His look showed a mix of gratitude and independence.

"Tell you what. Why don't you just make yourself at home, go walk around the yard a bit, enjoy the swing and the gardens. I'll put on some music and have supper on the table in no time. Then you can watch TV while I do the dishes and we can take a ride afterwards, if you'd like, or just sit here and relax." Not giving him a chance to protest further, she stood and moved toward the door.

"Okay, Abby. Think I'll just sit out here for awhile. You have any more of that coffee?"

"Sure. You want vanilla or milk?"

"Milk before dinner, vanilla after," he answered as he heard the telephone ring inside the house.

A few minutes later Amber returned with his coffee. She appeared a little strained, so he asked. "Trouble on the phone? I heard it ringing."

No, not trouble. It was just my son making sure I'd arrived home safely. I should've called them both. It was inconsiderate of me. I just wasn't thinking. But hey, we can talk of sons tomorrow. Tonight, let's just enjoy the ending of a beautiful day."

Taking his coffee, and seeing she didn't wish to discuss it further, he smiled at her. "Yes, a beautiful day."

After dinner, they decided to take a ride by the water. Amber parked the car near the seawall and they walked out to the spot near the end, where she'd first introduced him to Birdfriend. As darkness approached Ben wanted to find the benches so they could sit awhile.

The sea was mysterious at night. You could hear it and smell it, more than see it. They listened to the waves lapping at the shore and searched the stars overhead. Taking her hand, Ben felt her slight shivering and realized she was chilled. He took off his yellow windbreaker and draped it around her shoulders. "Here take this. You're cold."

"Thanks," she said, pulling the jacket tight around her. "Gets chilly by this water at night. You think we should head back? I don't want you coming down with a chill yourself. Especially after being in the sun all day."

"Maybe so," he answered, taking her hand again.

Back home, Amber made fresh coffee while Ben remained outside poking around the yard by the light of the floods. She wondered if he was looking for the elusive fox. She lit the oil lamps in the living room and informed Bear he could have his chair back. She was sitting on the sofa when he came in the door and was almost startled at how easy it was seeing him enter her world.

"I made coffee," she said, surprised at the calm in her own voice.

When he sat beside her, she leaned over and rested her head on his shoulder as if it was the most natural thing in the world.

"Penny for your thoughts, Abby."

"Oh I don't know how to put it in words, Ben. I was just thinking how natural it looked to see you come through the door of my home."

He leaned forward and picked up his cup saying nothing.

"We part for a day and find we aren't really away," she went on. "Why? Who would know? There are things I can't explain; things I just feel. Times when I shut my mind off and just listen to my soul."

He sat his coffee down, reached around and pulled her close. He held her tightly for a few moments, then gently raised her face to meet his own.

"Abby," he said softly, "I have to tell you something."

Sensing something foreboding in his voice, she drew back to look into his eyes. "What? What could you tell me after such a perfect day? What's troubling you?"

"This," he said, gesturing around the house.

"What do you mean? My house is bothering you? Don't you like it, or—"

"No," he answered softly. "Not the house; I love the house."

"Well what then?" She didn't understand him.

He looked away, then at the floor, then back at her. "I don't know exactly. That phone call from your son made me realize that even though we share much, there's things we don't and never will. You have a family. I have the remains of one, sort of."

Where was he going with this? "I don't understand, Ben. What has that to do with us?"

He took her hand in his and looked down at them.

"Everything. You can't let go of your family and neither can I, nor should we. What with my health situation and all."

She was stunned by his remarks. "Well, who said anything about giving up family?" She withdrew her hand and raised his face up to meet hers. "I found you, you found me. Whichever. You're going to get well again, you already are, and the past is the past."

"Oh, Abby, playing house is nice, but do you really think I could ever replace your late husband to your sons? To you, even? No. They'd always resent me being in your life. When with me, you'd be thinking of them. When in the stores you'd be feeling foolish if I were by your side. Then, before long, you'd resent me, too."

108

"Ben—"

"Sooner or later," he went on, "to give what we have merit, you'd want to get married, and I'd have to say no. Where would that leave you?"

Staring at him now, she was, momentarily, speechless.

"This house, these grounds, they're all you, Abby." He pointed to the pictures of Jeff and the kids on the wall. "And they're all him, and they're all your sons. I'm like the intruding fox. If I brought something home I liked, a picture, perhaps, then it wouldn't belong, would it? My clothes on hangers, or in drawers, wouldn't belong, would they? And alone in bed at night, my body next to yours, whose breathing would you hear? Do you see what I mean?"

He rose and paced about while his words rang in her ears. Words she didn't like, but words that he seemed to have to say. "Abby, I've only known security a few times, and that was long ago. The rest of my life has been like a suitcase with rumpled clothing. Some memories here, some there, but always on the move in some way, shape, or form." He gestured around the room again. "Now this . . . and you. You deserve so much more than I can give."

He turned and stared at her. Sighing, he sat back down beside her dreading what he figured would be yet more tears. But there were none. She was just staring at him.

"Abby, why are you looking at me like that?" he almost blurted at her.

She turned toward the wobbling flame in the oil lamp, its light making strange figures on the wall. She was trying to decide if she was feeling irritation, compassion, or a sense of amusement at his concerns.

"You're scared, that's all, scared of being trapped. Maybe more scared of caring about someone again." Then, as his words sunk in, she felt a furor rising and couldn't push it down.

"Playing house, did you say? You think I want to play house? I don't know whether to laugh or get really, really mad. You sure know how to throw an insult, don't you? After hearing nothing for weeks, I go all the way to Texas to be with you when you're alone and near death the result of some guinea pig experiment. I bring you home with me so you can rest and heal, and you call that *playing* fucking house? Suddenly I know what I'm feeling, and I can tell you it isn't damn amusement." She moved to the edge of her seat and turned to him.

"Abby, I—"

"You had your turn, now let me finish," she almost shouted, her temper building. "What? You think you'll become like that . . . that damn bear in the chair there, some kind of possession of mine? Is that it? A fixture, or a toy, to place where and how I want to?" She tossed her hand in the direction of the bear, who seemed to be watching them intently, the flame from the lamp dancing in his glass eyes.

"I can't explain the feelings rising up within me, Ben. It's like from some deep well of . . . of destiny, for lack of a better word." She watched his face but it told her nothing. "God knows, I've tried to push them away. So hell no, this isn't *playing house*. It's bigger, much bigger. I don't feel things deeply unless they ARE deep."

Now she rose and paced, collecting her thoughts, gathering the storm to her. She swiped at the hair falling around her eyes and looked to the ceiling.

"Damn you, Ben! That doesn't mean I'm trying to have you replace my dead husband in my life, my home, or anything else. You're right about one thing. You couldn't."

He tried to interrupt, "That's not—"

"Worse still, to even think it! It would be an insult to both of you to imply that maybe you could, or should, walk around in another man's shadow. Or, that Jeff would want you to." She turned to face him, but he was now staring at the floor.

"But, married? I would have to have you marry me to give my love MERIT? Sign some license to frame and hang on the fucking wall like a . . . a damn Certificate of Ownership? A proclamation that we're deemed acceptable in the eyes of the world? Damn! Damn you! That really pisses me off!"

She almost threw herself against the back of the sofa as she sat back down, the anger fading. "Damn!"

He glanced up, stared off across the room for a moment, and then turned to her.

"Bad choice of words on my part. I didn't mean it as it sounded," he said.

For what seemed an awfully long moment neither spoke, each wrapped in their own thoughts. Amber finally broke the silence, carefully. Measured.

"Do you remember the first day we talked at the beach and you asked when I was going to ask the questions all women asked?"

He nodded, but said nothing.

"And, all I wanted to know was if you believed in rainbows?"

This made him smile. "Why did you ask me that, by the way?"

She ignored him.

"All right, Abby, so you don't want to play house and you don't want to get married. Maybe that wasn't the right thing to say, but what about the other things? Me being the intruder in this house, the sons, the rest of your family and friends? My own son right here in this town?"

She relaxed a little and rested her head against his shoulder again.

"My sons know me. They respect my decisions. Oh, they might question me, caution me, think me a bit nuts even, but they'd never mistreat you, if that's what you mean. The rest? What rest? Neighbors? Family and friends?" She paused, letting it sink in. "I'm more concerned now with you, and what you want from life. What do you want from life, Ben? What is it you haven't done that you want to do? What are you searching for?"

His eyes turned almost cold blue as he answered. "I don't know. I've never known."

There was silence now, deep foreboding silence.

"When you feel up to it," she eventually said, "you should go home and take care of the business you work so hard at keeping private, make your decisions. I'll go on as before. If you come back, we'll go or do what we must to have *our* life. If you don't, I'll respect that, too. I'm used to traveling rough road, and I'm used to doing it alone. You owe me nothing."

She took his hand and placed it on her chest over the gull pendant. "You fly free, Ben. Go above your clouds, your storms. There'll be time to fight your battles when you're strong again."

He felt the beat of her heart in his fingers. Again, he wondered, marveled, at this woman, the tenacity in her. He wanted to feel the abandon again, just forget everything else and ride in the pipeline of this wave about to crest on yet another sea. Her skin was warm and the glow from the flame of the lamps softened the harsh corners of his landlocked world.

"Amber," he softly whispered. *Yes, Amber was a good name for her*. He pulled the yellow windbreaker down off her shoulders and lifted her up onto him. She buried her face between his neck and where his shoulder circled around her. He held her close for a few moments then gently raised her face to meet his own.

"Abby, I . . . ."

Then his words were muffled as their lips brushed for the first time. Tentatively at first, then surrendering to all the underlying emotions, the fight, in both of them. Holding her to him, they met as one, and this time it was their world for as long as it could be. It was only his breathing she heard.

YOU LUST, YOU LOVE, SO WHAT?

The following day he was left alone while Abby went to work. He watched the news, then a program or two on the tube, but his mind was elsewhere, as it always seemed to be. He laid his head back and closed his eyes, hoping the flashbacks wouldn't come, but they did.

In a series of kaleidoscope images that flashed across his mind, he saw himself moving from one scene into another, as if they'd never end. He was in a seedy bar in Mexico, passed out. He was in a glitzy nightclub, out on the dance floor. He was alone in a room late at night, typing away on first a typewriter, then a Word Processor. A stack of paper sat nearby, then another, and another, like the Sorcerer's Apprentice. Outside, the seasons changed from one to another to another.

He was in Hollywood, making the rounds of the studios, and in New York. He was at an angry Author's Guild meeting, then at an even angrier one at the Screenwriter's Guild. He was signing autographs for the groupies in a coffeehouse.

Just as suddenly, he was back in childhood in his middle class neighborhood, then in his car as a teen. His parents fought, the whisky flowed, and he lost himself in books and one misadventure after another. His collie dog, King, was there, then a monkey on his shoulder while in Micronesia. He saw his marriage, the birth of his son, and the night he had come home, drunk again, to an empty house. The loneliness swallowed him and he sobbed in the vastness.

He was driving fast in his Austin Healey on a two-lane, the pipes reverberating off the blacktop. He was in college, dozing at his desk as the prof droned on and on. There were sea waves blocking out the sky from the ship he was on, and a machine gun firing as the ship turned into a patrol boat with blood, lots of blood, carnage, and puke. His puke.

And the clouds floating high above it all, and him above them while the music played. Played all the tortured songs of the changing times and the lyrics of his tortured life.

His eyes blinked open, startled at his surroundings. He got out of the chair, still dazed, and wandered toward the sliding glass door. The air hung heavy outside and he began sweating as soon as he stepped onto the wood deck. Nothing was moving off in the woods beyond the spacious yard. No one was driving along the road beyond her jungle. He might as well have been on another planet. The pain seared his groin. He came back into the coolness of the house and went to the phone. He pulled a card from his wallet, sat down and dialed.

The voice answered, "Law Offices, how may I help you?"

The crowd of customers seemed to swarm in on her like angry bees and she fought the claustrophobic feeling of being trapped. Crowds did that to her. She didn't want to be here. She wanted to be home with Ben, hated having to return to work, but she'd missed nearly three weeks and felt she needed to put in an appearance. Yet with things still so unsettled between them, she was having difficulty remaining focused.

"Excuse me!" The impatient voice brought her back from her day dreaming.

"Oh . . . sorry, I'm afraid I was in my own little world for a moment," she apologized to the annoyed customer. "What can I help you with?"

"First, you can give me the attention you are being paid to provide," the sarcastic woman said.

She suppressed an overwhelming urge to tell the woman to fuck off. Instead, she ignored her and simply filled her order.

She hated her job in the retail business, hated the snobby attitude of the rich women from the Keys, but it provided the more mundane needs of life like cash flow and health insurance. But, mostly she stayed because she had an agreement that time off would be no problem as long as she gave ample notice. With her penchant for traveling, a family spread out over the Country, and an impulsive nature, this was the biggest draw of her job. She'd learned that life is too unpredictable to always be moved to the back burner known as the future.

She managed to get through the rest of her shift by pushing thoughts of Ben to the background of her mind. There were still a few days to approach the nagging issues, his health and hospital stay being her biggest concern. She'd purposely avoided bringing it up, wanting him only to rest and recuperate. A peaceful mind was a tonic to the body.

Now, leaving the store and walking to her car, she smiled at the thought of having him there to greet her upon her return. But, she also worried how he'd made out in the house alone after his uneasiness the evening before.

When she walked in, he was waiting for her.

"I have news," he said. "I called my lawyer back home and have an appointment on Monday."

She felt a chill come over her. Lawyer? On Monday? "I see. Going to go back home, then? Take care of those mysterious items, are you? And, so soon?"

He nodded. "Well, I'm going to try. It's a bit of a mess and time I straightened it all out." He looked at her. "As best I can, anyway."

She feigned indifference, although his words cut deep. "Good then," she answered as she laid her purse down and went into the kitchen to pour some lemonade, more to keep busy than because she was thirsty.

Why was she uneasy? Hadn't she been the one to tell him to go take care of things? Why did she doubt herself now that he'd followed her suggestion? She knew why. She was afraid, and she wasn't expecting him to go for at least a couple weeks.

She reached into the cabinet for a glass, attempting to gain control of her reactions before she spoke again. Ben came into the kitchen and put his arms around her from behind.

"Hotter than hell today. How about some lemonade from that tree of yours?"

"Oh, no hotter than usual," she answered, nonchalant. "You're just not used to it, like a lot of things you aren't used to." She poured him a glass and handed it to him.

He took the glass and her other hand, then walked her back into the living room and sat down on the couch, pulling her down with him.

"I don't know how long I'll be gone," he began as she silently stiffened. "Maybe a couple weeks, maybe more. I have to arrange for things to be taken care of after . . ." He stopped, unable to say the words.

"After what?" she asked, although she already knew. "Go on, say it out loud. After you die, you mean."

He nodded. "Yeah, something like that. I've kind of let things go over the years, never got really ready, like most do. I suppose I thought it would never come, but I had to face it at the hospital and it made me realize how much needs to be arranged."

"I see," she said, sipping her drink. "So let me ask you, are you going home to die? Is that it?"

Her words caught him off guard. "Well, no, not exactly. I'm going home to make arrangements, like I said. Who to call when it happens. Who gets what, a Will and all that. When it happens. No, Abby, I'm not going home to die."

She leaned against him, suddenly tired. "Ben, you've never really told me exactly what went on at that hospital. I only know you were given an experimental drug for reducing a tumor of some kind, and that the drug itself damn near killed you. Now I think you could tell me exactly what they told you and what you believe is happening, or is going to happen to you." She took his hand in hers, not looking at him, dreading his response.

"He sighed. I suppose I should tell you. You have every reason to know." He hesitated, as if not knowing where to begin. "Cancer is in my family tree. It killed my sister at an early age, killed an aunt, and almost killed my mother."

"Almost?" she asked.

He nodded. "It was a long time ago, of course, and they know more now than they did then. In those days they mainly did surgery, and chemotherapy was new. So, on my sister, they operated and she died. She was forty-two. On my aunt, they operated and she lived, but only a few months. With my mother, they couldn't operate and she lived several more years."

"Why couldn't they operate on your mom?"

"Mom had advanced osteoporosis, as many older women get. They tried for a lung biopsy, and in maneuvering her around I guess, they broke her back."

"Damn!" was all she could think to say.

"Yeah, pretty bad alright, but it might have saved her life."

"Because they couldn't operate? I don't understand."

He leaned back into the couch, his mind far away. "By breaking her back, they couldn't remove her lung, which was the normal operation then. They couldn't remove the lung because the other lung would have developed pneumonia, since she wouldn't have been able to move around on the bed. Change positions. So they didn't feel they could operate."

"So what happened? You said she lived for a few more years?"

"We were at our wits end, my dad, brother and I. There were new drugs going around, many experimental, and my dad asked the family doctor to use one. I don't remember its name anymore, but it worked. She eventually walked out of the hospital cancer free and died several years later the same way."

Now it was becoming clear to her why he'd gone to the hospital in Texas. It was a research hospital. He, too, was looking for the same magic bullet. "Damn," she said softly.

He looked strained, as if explaining all this was wearing him down. "A few years back I went for a routine physical and was diagnosed with cancer myself. I wasn't even surprised, considering how much harm I'd done my body over my lifetime. But the specialist I went to wanted to operate and I balked. Instead I began to research the illness myself and started trying the alternatives. I think that's the only reason I'm here with you now."

This would explain some of the nightmares he'd had in the motel, the restlessness in sleep, she thought. Things were beginning to make more sense now.

"For awhile now I've been having pain," he went on, "and so knew it was time to look into this more deeply, or rather, get back into some kind of regimen. Then I found that hospital on the Internet, and the rest you know."

She was silent for a moment, thinking it over. "Well, no I don't, Ben. Not exactly. When I got to the hospital you were almost dead, and you've recovered from that, so I don't see the big rush to get your affairs in order. Why not just stay here and continue recuperating for at least a couple weeks? Get on the alternative regimen again."

"Because," he began, "I don't know whether I have another day, another week, another year left. That's why. They gave me a drug. It didn't work, as you say. But what you don't know is that they gave up on me and told me my time was short, the tumor wasn't minimized. How short, they couldn't predict. I wanted to call you back and stop you from coming. I tried, but I was too weak. Once you were there, I was glad that I was. You've given me this time, Abby. You've given me happiness, and I'd forgotten the feeling."

Her mind raced. None of this actually surprised her, but hearing him say it was unsettling. No longer able to sit still, she got up and walked to the sliding glass doors that led to the deck. Looking out toward the spot they'd last viewed the fox, her voice came out in a raspy tone as she fought yet more tears.

"So, you're just going to take their prognosis and run with it, huh?" She turned to face him. "Time is short and you must prepare your final arrangements. You go to some experimental research center and let them half-ass kill you with some poison, and then accept their death sentence when the results weren't as they hoped for. Some miracle, overnight cure that would make big headlines and insure them more funding. And you found this facility on the damn Internet?" Suddenly, she was angry. How dare he give up!

"You don't understand," he said, flatly.

"I understand more than you think I do. What do you think I am, some dumb-ass lunatic, as you're so fond of calling me? Groveling around in my grief and chasing first encounters around the fucking country? Enticing them to my lair to play house with me?" She was trembling with near rage again, all sign of tears gone.

"Hey! Wait a minute." he got to his feet, irritation rising in him, too.

"No! You wait a minute. I've been at your side for nearly three weeks, spent several days watching you toss and turn, have nightmares and cold sweats getting that poison out of you in some damn motel. In the three days here, I've seen you go from pale gray to a healthy glow again. I've seen you actually enjoy a grape."

"Yeah, but—"

"But nothing! You let me have my say. You owe me that much." She rushed up to him and pushed him back toward the couch.

Shocked, he didn't know whether to sit back down or push past her and leave. He moved around her toward the front door, and then turned back, deciding to see this through. Strangely, he was moved by her volatility, her passion. And, she was right, he did owe her that much.

She stood there watching his next move. Her eyes were spitting fire. Finally, he sat back down, but couldn't help adding sarcastically, "All right. Have your say. Clue me in on how you'd save me from my appointed doom, Miss Nightingale. Miss Bird Lady."

He might as well have slapped her face.

"Fuck you, Ben. Just, fuck you! Go do what you must. Go prepare to die. Have you called for a plane reservation? Would you like me to do that one last thing for you? I make a good secretary, too, you know. Probably get one out of here tonight if you say it's an emergency. There's no sense wasting anymore of our time." She went to the glass doors and slid them open, almost violently, slamming them shut behind her.

He watched her for a moment and then got up and went to the phone. Perhaps she was right, he thought. Best to get out of here as soon as possible. He dialed Information.

"Reservations," the bored voice answered after he'd pushed all the appropriate buttons.

"Well, shit. You mean there are actually live people on this line?" he snapped, his anger coming out at the person on the other end. "Oh never mind." He hung up the phone.

"I can't leave her under these circumstances," he said out loud. And that surprised him, too. He, who'd always been so adept at leaving when the situation became uncomfortable. This damn woman was beginning to have a much bigger impact on him than even he'd realized. Her and her damn fox, her damnable rainbows. Rainbows that he'd yet to tell her he kind of believed in, too. Shit. Now what do

120

I say to her, he thought as he got the cold water pitcher from the fridge. He poured two glasses full.

She was leaning over the railing staring off into the yard as he opened the doors and walked out on the deck behind her.

"I brought you some water because that lemonade was making you bitter as hell," he attempted to joke.

"I'm not bitter. Quite the contrary," she answered, turning to take the water from him. "Thanks."

"Well you could've fooled me." He smiled at her. "You kind of surprised me turning angry so fast."

"I'm sorry. Truly, I am. I just fail to see how anyone could give up so easily based on some dumb prognosis that wasn't even concrete," she said quietly, her anger spent.

"Who said I was giving up, for Chrissakes? I said I was going to make arrangements. Just in case."

"Can't you see?" she said, turning to look in his eyes. "That *is* giving up. Oh, not going home and getting your affairs in order, not that. But, the reason you feel so compelled to do it so fast, before you've even recovered all your strength back, is because you're convinced you have a short time to live. In case, you say? Oh Ben, you're not going to die one day before your time, or live one day longer, and dammit, you have some control over how you spend the time in-between." She turned back to the railing.

"You don't even know if the drug they gave you worked or not, hon. Just because they didn't see instant results, doesn't mean there won't be long term results. They may have arrested the growth of the tumor. Killed it even. God! They monitored you for a lousy few days, and probably got scared when you had such a bad reaction to the drug."

"Always the eternal optimist, Abby. Listen, you could be wrong. Dead wrong." He turned her around to face him again. "And if you *are* wrong, then the lawyer and the State will get everything. Everything I've done or tried to do gets thrown in the trash. The son gets nothing, my friends . . ." He paused. "And there's you. I don't want you to get your hopes up and be left alone again in a matter of months."

"So that's it? You're worried for me too?" She smiled and he nodded.

"Ben, let me tell you something about me. I don't deny anatomy and physiology, illness or death, heredity or genetics. I honor common sense, and I honor a degree of pragmatism. I may be a whacko tree hugger to some, but I'm not an idiot who'd sit and bleed to death while attempting to chant closure to a gash in my flesh. But, I also know we're not just lumps of flesh and bone. I know we're multi-dimensional beings with a powerful Force behind us."

He leaned back into the railing and crossed his arms. "So?"

"So, what I'm saying is, if you give up, you are indeed lost."

"Aw hell, Abby. Don't you realize it's better safe than sorry? I've spent most of my life being sorry for things I left undone. But not this. It's too late."

"I don't realize any such thing, Ben Riley. Not in the way you are using it. I can sit and flip-side every premise you raise. The bottom line is maintaining a balance. I believe in polarity, different degrees of the same thing. I just choose to strive for the more positive degree is all. Don't you get it? I live! And you? You're dead just because *they* say you are."

She saw something flicker in his eyes, anger or resentment, she wasn't sure which, but he didn't move and he didn't answer.

"I'm finished now." She turned back to the railing.

"You speak," he began softly, "as someone who has never been to the edge. You lust, you love, yes. So what? Everyone does. But not everyone survives reckless abandon as you have. Not everyone cares to risk it all every fucking moment."

At the edge of the low-slung Palmetto branches, something grabbed her attention, a flash of light. "I've been to the edge many times," she answered. "That I'm still here at all often amazes me." She looked closer into the dusky edge of the jungle.

122

"And what's more," he went on, "I've lived that life of reckless abandon that you speak of and where has it gotten me? Nowhere. For every thrill, I found a loss. For all excitement, I found wanting. You have no idea; you only think you do because you've never come close. Not yet anyway. You've skirted the edge and called it living. But if and when you ever do see the edge up close and personal, you'll change your mind."

She searched the Palmettos, but the light was gone. "Ben, you have absolutely no idea what edges I've looked over. Not a clue what losses I've experienced. Yet, while you looked for thrills and excitement to hide behind, I simply looked for life and committed to it. With all its risks. No, I didn't live a life of reckless abandon; I lived a life of love, and a love of life."

Then she saw him. The setting sun reflected in the yellow eyes of the fox, sitting there, staring at her. Suddenly, she understood. Understood what had to be done. "Thank you," she said, smiling.

"What? What are you talking about? Thank you? I'm not finished," he answered, his voice rising.

She looked at him then, still smiling. "Not you." She turned back toward the thicket. "Him."

Ben turned and stared, following her gaze, but saw nothing. "Him? What him? Who's out there?"

She didn't answer, instead kissed his cheek and moved to the glass doors, sliding them open.

"Where are you going?" he asked, exasperated at both her argument and her sudden serenity. "Goddamnit, we're not through with this conversation."

She stopped midway through the door and looked back at him. "Where am I going? To help you pack. That's where I'm going." She stepped inside the house and closed the doors behind her.

"Jesus Christ!" he railed. "Lunatic! Goddamn-can't-argue-with-a-woman fucking lunatic," He swore as he, too, opened the doors and stepped into the house.

At the edge of the clearing, the fox rose from his haunches and started to back-step into the Palmettos. Turning, he disappeared in the approaching darkness, but not before a glance back at the doors Ben and Amber had just walked through.

REMEMBER THE RAINBOW

Inside, Amber was throwing clothes into the washing machine. Ben, still riled, stood in the doorway of the laundry room.

"What are you doing?" he demanded. "I said this conversation wasn't finished yet."

"I'm doing what little laundry you have, and I suggest you get on the phone and make or change your reservations. Unless, of course, you want to stand there and talk to yourself because as far as I'm concerned, this conversation is definitely finished." She poured a capful of detergent into the machine. "You say you need to go home and take care of unfinished business and now I'm agreeing with you."

She closed the lid on the washer and turned to face him before he could speak. The last red tint of the setting sun was reaching through the window and painting highlights in her hair.

"Ben? Do you remember in the hospital when I said we were going to fly higher?"

"What's that got to do with any of this?" he snapped.

"It has everything to do with this. At the time, I thought all that was stopping us was you being so ill. But now, I see that we can never fly higher as long as your feet are mired in the loose ends of the past. If I'm going to fly with you, I need you free to soar with me. If you're looking back over your shoulder at every headwind, every turn, we'll both crash land. Why even launch a doomed flight?" She walked to him and put her arms around his waist.

His anger melted away. What is it about this woman, he thought, that makes me want to run so fast one second, and unable to imagine life without her the next? He was asking himself this question more and more frequently.

"Okay, Abby. There are legal things that I really do need to address; a few people I must contact and let know what's going on. But yes, let's get it done and behind us and then we can see where our lives go. It may be somewhere higher, may just be a short commute, but we won't know until we have lift off, will we?" He smiled at the top of her head. "Since I'm the pilot, I better go start on the flight plan." He held her tightly for a moment, then disengaged her arms from his waist and moved toward the telephone.

She heard him talking in the other room where he'd taken the portable phone. Calm now, she went on about the business of readying his few things, again enjoying simply caring for him. A few minutes later he reappeared in the doorway and announced he'd be on a flight late the next afternoon.

"Now, I think I need to clear my head, or as you say, 'feel the wind in my face', Abby. What would you say to another ride out that same road we took weeks back?"

"Oh yes, lets," she agreed instantly. "And Ben, I've asked this before, but why do you call me Abby?"

"Oh, I don't know. Seems like that's what I've always called you. Seems right."

"You want to drive, hon?" she asked, walking down the steps to the car.

"No, you drive, we'll get there faster." He winked at her and headed to the passenger door.

They picked up coffee and fish sandwiches at the edge of town and headed east, with a rising moon in front of them

126

and a dark scarlet sky, brushed by the residue of the setting sun, behind. The Metal played, not so loudly now, but enough that she drove fast and it was as if they were leaving one world and entering a new one.

He leaned his head back and looked up at the stars growing ever more brilliant as the dusk grew darker and settled in around them. His thoughts trailed back to a night not so long ago, a rainy night, when a taxi had carried him over a road not taken. This time he'd follow where it led, like her, just because it was there.

Upon approaching the little picnic area where they'd stopped before, she slowed, pulled in, and turned the engine off. The radio went silent and the night sounds permeated the stillness of dark.

"Abby, twice you've asked me if I believed in rainbows, but you've never said why it was so important. What do you mean by believe in them? Sure, there are rainbows, everyone knows that. What is it, this thing you have for rainbows?"

"It's a rather long story. May bore you," she replied.

"I'll risk it. It seems a part of you that I'd like to know, maybe need to know, this curiosity about rainbows."

"Okay. I'll try to be concise, but yes, it is a part of me. Although, I don't think I'd call it curiosity."

"Whatever. And don't worry, if you bore me, I'll let you know." He smiled and took her hand.

"When we first moved to the mountains," she began, "I'd been a city girl all my life. A flower garden in front, a vegetable patch in back, a small park, a vacant lot, maybe a trip to the zoo, which I didn't like, was all the Nature I knew.

"Why did you hate zoos?"

"Because I hated seeing animals in cages. They always looked sad to me."

"Okay. Sorry to interrupt. I should've known that already."

She smiled. "Anyway, after his open-heart surgery, Jeff and I decided to move back to the country where he was raised. What's the old saying . . . 'You can take the boy out of the country, but not the country out of the boy.' Jeff wanted to go back to a simpler time, the boys were grown and on their own, so off we went on a new adventure.

"We rented a big white farm house with a swing on the porch in a small town nestled in the Appalachians." Her voice lowered as she lapsed into her memories. "We'd often sit on the swing after supper taking in the sunset, sometimes the moonrise, over the mountains.

"One afternoon a huge thunderstorm came through. I'd just gotten home from work and we were cooking supper when we heard a clash of thunder. We ran out to the swing to just listen and watch the sky. Mountain thunder is an incredible sound. It echoes and reverberates like a Cosmic symphony.

"Sounds like a beautiful place, babe. Then what?" He found himself going into her memories with her.

"The storm passed as quickly as it came and the sun returned, bringing with it, the faint hues of a rainbow. We sat there taking it all in and the bow grew larger and larger and more vivid. One end fell into the floor of the valley meadow just north of the house, and it appeared as a stairway to heaven, truly."

He sensed her face light up in the telling.

"And then, suddenly, a second arc began to form. They bathed the valley in wonderful colors and made things shimmer as if alive. The air crackled with Energy and . . . oh, I can't describe it with just due."

He squeezed her hand, but said nothing.

"From ground level, the arcs appeared to be about fifty feet apart, but so close it was as if a canopy had been placed over our heads. I'd never seen a double rainbow in all my life. You don't see many rainbows in the city. Even if one forms, you might see bits and pieces but they're always obscured by structures of some sort. Anyway, we were spellbound, and just sat and stared until it began to dissipate. I was ecstatic and went on about it for days. Weeks. Something about that bow registered in me.

"So, that's your fascination with rainbows then. Now I see." He turned to her in the darkness.

"I told you it's a long story, hon. There's more."

"Oh, sorry. Yes, go on."

"When Jeff lay dying, he mentioned that bow. He said to me, 'remember the rainbow . . . remember the rainbow and never give up'. Those were the last words I heard him utter."

Another understanding washed over him. So that's why she rails about not giving up, he thought.

"Jeff died around ten in the morning and that afternoon, after necessary arrangements were taken care of, I told my family I had to go to the farm. It wasn't far from Atlanta where Jeff had been taken by Medivac.

"Once there, I went to our swing. I was angry and bewildered. My right side, my very life, had just been taken from me, or left me, I wasn't sure which. I yelled at them from that swing, Jeff and God both, demanding to know why any of this had to happen. Why'd he have to get sick so young? Our lives were just beginning it seemed, the family raised and all. Then it began to appear in the sky, the same sky as before. A double rainbow. I hadn't seen one since the first one, but I'd been told just that morning by a dying man, 'remember the rainbow'.

He sat watching her, now taken in by the depth of her story.

"Coincidence?" she went on. "Possibly, but the next week back home in the treehouse, I had to return to work. I pretended it was all just a bad dream and Jeff had gone back to work over the road. Did I tell you he drove a rig? I talked to him, begged him, 'please help me do this, help me keep going'.

"I came from work one afternoon sure that I was dying myself, and convinced I wasn't going to be able to go on as if things were the same. Something made me look up. In the sky, a rainbow was developing before my eyes. Then, incredibly, a double rainbow. Stunned, I asked my friend walking with me, 'would you look at that bow and tell me I'm not seeing things'. I wasn't. She saw it too."

Emotional now, she took a breath and continued. "That evening my phone rang and it was my sister, who adored Jeff and was stricken by his loss, too. She was excited. She knew about the rainbows. That afternoon about the same time I was leaving work, a double rainbow had formed over her house, north of me over a thousand miles. It was so brilliant and sighted by so many there, it made the broadcast news. So it really did happen! I wasn't imagining, or having visions, as others were seeing them, too."

"Is that the last you saw them, or do you still see them?"

"Oh, now and then I do if I'm faced with a dilemma or even just unsure of things. That's why they're so special. Last summer I flew to the west coast to visit friends, and I was more than a little frightened. I'd never traveled that far without Jeff. And they were new friends that he didn't know, that I'd never met in person myself! They were from an Internet group I'd gotten involved with. As the airplane was nearing San Francisco, I thought . . . Jeff, am I totally nuts here? This is scary, maybe I should've stayed home.

"I was staring out the window at the white, puffy cloud tops beneath my feet, and, suddenly I saw it. I was looking *down* on the most vibrant double rainbow of all! I found myself in a world of colored cotton candy, like a child again. It was as if that bow was guiding me to the ground, telling me, no you're not nuts. You're alive, so live. The road is still there for you. I'm not gone, I'm not far away, and I can be whatever I need to be . . . a double rainbow, a breath of wind, a shooting star, or anything else to guide and to love you.

"So now you know my *thing* for rainbows." She sighed audibly. "I feel a rainbow brought you into my life as well. You see, it appeared again when I was coming to Texas to see you." She looked over at him. His eyes were closed but she thought she saw a hint of moisture at the corners, glistening in the moonlight.

Standing now, watching Ben move through Security to board his plane, she felt calm. He'd promised to call when his affairs were in order. The fear that they might not include her had vanished when another favorite quote had come to mind . . . "If you love something, let it go. If it loves you, it will come back to you. If it doesn't, it didn't love you anyway." She knew in her heart, she could accept no less.

She tossed him one last wave as he walked through the gates, then turned toward the parking area.

The headlights chased the pavement in the tunnel of dusk stretched out before her. Out from under Ben's slightly disapproving glance, she could now drive really fast again. The comforting bass thump of AC/DC reverberated against her back on the seat. It opened a valve that released all the thoughts and cares of the last few weeks. It was as if they drifted out the windows on the twangs of the lead guitar to be carried away by the wind and sewn into the piecework of the future. When Ben returned, if he returned. For now he was safe, and she was doing what she loved more than anything.

The car took on a life of its own as she fed it power through the pedal beneath her foot, and she pushed down hard, feeding it like a hungry beast. She was a passenger along for the ride as the car streaked through her life. Tail lights in the distance brought her back to reality and she slowed her speed slightly.

"Damn. Just once I'd love an empty highway to nowhere and everywhere," she grumbled.

The red lights pulled away as she slowed. Realizing the vehicle ahead was moving nearly as fast as she was, she again fed the engine. Closing the distance, she spotted the second tier of lights and realized it was an eighteen wheeler, probably monitoring the CB radio and hauling ass to make a middle of the night delivery. It was full dark now and she'd just been given a ticket to ride. An ass-hauling trucker with a CB and a schedule to keep.

She fell in behind, but far enough back so the driver could see her head lights in his mirrors. She flashed the signal telling him she wanted to ride his draft, and got the answering 'okay' flutter of the red tail lights.

The next forty miles were pure pleasure as the big truck seemed to pull the silver car along. Laughing at the thought that maybe vehicles had connections, too, she almost felt disappointment when the big green sign announcing her exit loomed ahead. She flashed her 'thanks' to the driver, who soundly blew a 'have a safe ride' on his air horn, then signaled and pulled off to the right.

The clock on the dash told her she'd made record time coming home from the airport, and she silently saluted the trucker as she pulled into her drive. Now all she wanted was sleep. It was time to put this chapter of her life to bed.

She climbed the steps, unlocked the door, and tossed her purse and keys on the wooden table as she entered. A flip of the light switch brought a smile to her face as she noticed they'd landed on top of Ben's half-eaten bag of Cheetos.

BOOK TWO

AMBER COMES HOME

The rhythmic cadence of tires against pavement lulled her into reverie. The ever-present music was silent now, turned off, as she wanted only to lapse into the world stretching out in front of her. The ribbon of highway ambled over the flatland and was beginning to furl into the gentle rises and turns of the foothills. The verdant hue nestling on the horizon ahead hinted of the Appalachians that would soon pierce the landscape. Amber was going to the farm.

A few weeks had passed since Ben had called to let her know how *things* were progressing with his affairs. He'd offered no number to reach him, and she didn't ask. A gut feeling told her this was a world in which she wasn't welcome. The long drought in their communication had taken its toll. Too much time to ponder had her questioning previous conclusions yet again. Funny how a curious mind could be a source of frustration as well as wisdom. And, the fox had disappeared.

On impulse, she decided to take a week off and head to the mountains, a simpler time, and a much needed rest. She yearned to sit again in a quiet grove of trees by a waterfall. She wanted to hear the cows bellowing in the rolling pasture valley, to clear her mind of everything but how a flower grows and how a calf is born.

133

She called her boss and informed that she'd be away for a few days. It didn't matter if she still had a job on her return or not. It didn't seem important at the moment. She could get another job; she couldn't get another life. It was time to live this one. She'd waited for Ben long enough.

Now she was heading north, away from the sea and the little house in the trees to another house, and another time where she'd learned so much about life. And so much about death.

"Hey, Silver Lady. Got your back door here. You got a weaver coming up with a pedal on the metal. Hop in the Granny lane and ease her up a notch," the deep voice came over the radio. Instantly, she was alert.

She grabbed the mic from the seat beside her and flipped the turn signal lever with the little finger of her left hand. "Copy that," she replied.

She quickly scanned her mirrors and surveyed behind her. Before she completed the lane change, an old pick up spewing gravel and grass from the median careened by on the left, more off the road than on.

"Dumbass!" she spat out, braking to let him get as far ahead of her as possible.

"Where's the Bears when you need them?" She laughed into the mic. "Thanks, driver. I was in my own little world for a minute there. You quite possibly saved my ass end."

"That's a ten-four, Silver Lady. Bear den at the one-three-seven. Going over to nine and try to save that guy from himself."

"Yup. That one needs a spell in the cooler. Thanks again."

She turned the channel indicator to nine and listened in as the driver reported the weaver, and once again a deep respect for the truckers filled her heart. They had a rough life, but most had a love for the road. It was their second home, in some cases their only one, and they took damn good care of it for the most part.

She flipped back to nineteen. "Ok, Lady, they'll get him. Hope he lasts another ten sticks without killing himself, or somebody. Been watching you since I pulled out of the "J" back a ways. Saw you had your ears on."

She smiled at the observation. Any trucker worth his salt could tell the portable antenna attached to her right side window was connected to a CB. She wouldn't think of getting on the highway without the Cobra; best escort going for a woman on the road alone. You could have your cell phones and their roaming charges. Even when a CD was in the player, an occasional glance at the transmission light alerted her to any excessive radio traffic signifying possible dangers ahead, or in this case, behind.

"Appreciate the cover, driver. Got my head back where it belongs now. Nice rig, by the way."

With the crisis past, she noticed the familiar slant-nose of the black Kenworth behind her. It was a 600, probably with an old Cat that had seen many a mile. It almost shouted TLC from its sparkling chrome.

"Yes, ma'am. Another hundred thou and it'll be all mine. Got an eye for the rigs, I see."

She smiled. She had an eye for the rigs all right, and she knew the driver was referring to miles, not money, before the shiny black tractor would be debt free.

"Sure do," she answered. A big soft spot in the heart, too. Spent some time out here on the road with you guys. Racked up a few coast to coast runs in a KW much like yours. Candy Apple Red, she was."

"It shows. Like I said, been watching you a while. I can spot a driver."

"I rode shotgun mostly. But, I did it with one of the best drivers out here."

"No matter," the chuckle came over the speaker. "You know how to behave in the living room. Be careful now and have a safe ride."

"And, you. Keep on keeping on, and take good care of that rig."

"That's a big ten-four, ma'am. A big ten-four."

She saw the driver's hand salute in her mirror and gave the standard 'so long' signal tap with her brake lights, then resumed her speed. She pushed the CD back in the player as she pulled away. Now she was ready to put the miles, and the reflective mood, behind her.

The scene outside her windows was turning green now, the city left behind in its maze of glass and metallic activity. She made the turn off the main highway and entered a different realm. The mountains, where old timber reached to tickle the hawks languishing on currents in a cerulean sky, stretched out before her. Where roots, like gnarled fingers, grasped the rocks protruding the earth and sucked life-giving water out of the little streams trickling over them. Roots that dug deep into the soil of times before.

She lowered the windows but for the one supporting the antenna. Again, the CD was ejected so she could hear the chorus of wild sounds around her. It was late afternoon and the songbirds, up from their naps, were performing their arias to whatever it was songbirds sang to, other songbirds or the forest itself. Little choristers, they were, whose melodies were conducted by the wind whistling through treetops and mimicked by Mockingbirds that could sing any song they chose.

The raucous calls of crows cackled through the higher limbs as they shouted warnings of territory invasions or danger below. If you listened, really listened, you could hear the squirrels scampering around the forest floor in a nut-gathering frenzy as late summer thought about autumn.

Slowing, she looked for a place to pull off the road. Spotting a wide shoulder on the next curve, she eased the car to a stop, got out, stretched her legs, and reached toward the treetops. The remaining miles to the farm were a series of hairpin turns and a respite was in order.

She walked a few feet into the woods and leaned against an old Poplar, breathing in the scent of a world spared progress and all its frustrations. Shadowy corridors between the trees beckoned like the hallways in a huge mansion, and she peered into the little clearings, like rooms, for the movement of a deer or a fox.

The aroma of foliage, tree bark, and rich black earth was like fine cologne to her, the echoes of the calling birds was an age old symphony unrivaled by the compositions of man. Feeling rejuvenated, she returned to the car suddenly wanting to reach her destination. The farm that had taught her so much.

Twenty miles of winding road later, Amber came around the last bend on her journey. A lump formed in her throat at seeing the farmhouse. Like a weary old sentinel, its whitewash grayed and scarred now by the seasons, its tired wood pillars yet proud, it stood overlooking the valley. The long front porch still invited passers by to come sit a spell and hear the stories of simpler times, but harder, too. Times when a man worked the land and lived with it, but never took it for granted.

She pulled into the long driveway still guarded by the huge Maple, and followed it up the hill to the house that had been home for so long. As her strange car ascended the rise, the sound of barking dogs quickened her heart. Would they know her? She parked alongside the barn behind the house.

"Now, Sara! Is that any way to greet me after all this time? Carrying on like I was a stranger or something? And, look at you, Muffy. Skittish as ever. Is that any way for a coyote dog to act?" she called to them through the open window.

She climbed out of the car and the two dogs, momentarily stunned at the sound of her voice, suddenly leaped all over her. Sara, the German shepherd, yipping and jumping, was so excited she nearly knocked her down. Muff, the half-coyote, whimpered and licked and then just threw her head back and howled. All three of them fell into the soft clovered grass and wrestled like kids, laughing and crying and yipping and howling. Amber had come home.

The commotion, probably Muff's howls, brought young Beth out to see what was going on. Upon seeing the three of them rolling in the grass, she squealed in delight.

"Well, I'll just be. That you, Amber? That really you! Muffy, will y'all just quiet down so I can hear what your mom is saying? Durn old dogs are acting pure crazy."

"Yes, dear Beth, it's really me." Amber picked herself up from the ground and pleaded with the dogs to settle down a bit. She laughed and hugged Beth while the dogs continued their dance.

"You're just in time for supper and I bet you planned it that way." Beth gave her a wink. "Just wait until I tell the rest you're here. Now shed yourself of those dogs and get on in the house."

Beth, the lady of the house now, bounded up the steps to the porch not waiting for her to follow. Shedding the dogs would take a while and Beth probably knew it.

Beth was now the wife of the farm owner's son, but she and Jeff had watched her grow from a bubbling teenager of fourteen to the blushing bride she'd become. Many an evening, she had come to visit and they'd sat on the swing and discussed the perils of a young girl in love. Her husband, Chet, was like one of their own sons, and Beth became like a daughter.

"Amber, you coming in here or what?" she was calling out the screen door. "You can play with those durn fool dogs after supper, and you can bet they aren't leaving the porch knowing you're inside this house. Time to wash up, everyone's coming to see you, girl!"

"Did y'all hear that, girls? Why you've went and got me in trouble already and I just got here. Now go and lay yourselves down." Amber laughed, as she lapsed into her exaggerated Southern drawl. Oh, it was good to be home.

MIRACLE

Beth had called the rest of the family scattered around the four hundred acre farm, and hours later after explanations, good food, laughter, and a sharing of memories, she excused herself and took a cup of coffee out to the swing to be alone. The dogs curled at her feet as she sipped her coffee and looked into the night. It was like sitting in an incredible outdoor amphitheater and it made her feel so alive.

Above, millions, even billions, of stars illuminated in a fairy light. An almost-full moon served as a spotlight for the stage show being put on across the road, fireflies dancing in the trees accompanied by an orchestra of crickets and the occasional hoot of an owl. So different from the concrete jungles and the bustle of the city, she thought.

The distant sound of a heifer bawling in the back pasture for its calf, apparently lost in the dark, brought a smile to her face. She thought of the days when she'd wandered through the cow pastures calling each in the fifty-plus herd by name. And, they'd come to know and accept her as one of their own. A sigh escaped her lips as she thought of Miracle and another night under these same stars . . . .

* * * *

She sat on the knoll above the barn and watched the old cow in the enclosure below. It was limping around slowly, nipping purple flowers from the clover. She swiped at the tears streaming down her face at the obvious pain the old mama was enduring in her hip. It was swollen and the bone protruded grotesquely.

She'd been caring for the animal for several days now, as her milk was running and she was ready to give birth. Her burgeoning belly warned that the calf was going to be a large one, and Amber shuddered at the animal having to bear yet more agony than she was already experiencing in her arthritic joints. She worried if the old girl would have the strength to deliver. There was nothing more to be done but wait and try to make the heifer comfortable. Her own helplessness made her angry.

"Dammit, hasn't this poor old creature been through enough?" she cried out to whatever Power had control of these affairs. "It's up to you to do something! There's no more I can do," she implored. "If you care for a fallen sparrow, why aren't you helping this poor cow? She's a good cow and much too gentle to bear this suffering any longer."

No answer came and finally in full darkness Amber trudged, totally dejected, into the house. An hour later after a hot bath, fatigue overwhelmed her.

"Still no baby coming, huh?" Jeff asked as she crawled into bed beside him. "You're going to make yourself sick over that cow, you know."

"Am not, and I don't care anyway. I can't just leave her all alone down there," she retorted.

Jeff hugged her close. "It'll be okay, Abby. Nature will do what it must. Now try and get some sleep."

"Easy for you to say. Everything is always going to be all right with you. Dammit, Jeff, it isn't *all right*. She's hurting and there's nothing I can do." She rolled over and punched her pillow, hard.

Jeff said no more. It would be futile and only upset her further. He knew that some of the country ways were hard on her.

140

She sat up with a start. A fear she couldn't explain was stuck in her throat. Jumping up, she grabbed her jeans and shirt and struggled into them while running to the door. It was just pre-dawn and the cool grass was wet under her feet. She backtracked and grabbed her old boots from inside the enclosed back porch.

At the barn, she fumbled for the light switch and nearly fainted at what she saw. There, on the hay she'd piled up, the old heifer lay panting and the hay beneath her was turning crimson red.

"My God," she gasped. "Jeff. Help! Jeff!" she yelled as she fell on her knees beside the heaving cow. Then she saw it.

"Oh my God, the baby! The baby's going to suffocate. Damn! Jeff!" she wailed.

She jumped up and yelled again out the door. "Jeff! Oh, won't somebody come help me!" Frantic now, she rushed back to the heifer's side, terrified at what was happening.

The calf was a large one, indeed, and seemed to be lodged in the birth canal. All that was visible were its head, shoulders, and one leg. Then some Force took her over. She grabbed and ripped the membrane away from the baby's face, furiously wiping the mucous from its nostrils.

"Oh, God, it isn't breathing! Jeff!" she yelled again.

She jumped up and threw herself on the cow's bulging sides and pushed as hard as she could. The baby didn't move and the old cow groaned in its agony.

"I've got to get it out! Somehow . . . oh God, help me, please. Jeff! Where in the hell are you? Damn! Why isn't he coming?"

She grabbed the baby's head and pulled. She pulled and pulled with every ounce of her strength, but the calf didn't budge. She positioned herself with her feet against the old cow's rump, hugged the baby's shoulders and pulled again.

"Jeff! Dammit! Somebody, anybody, help me!" Her screams were barely audible raspings now. She was becoming hysterical. No one was coming and the baby wasn't moving! Then in horror, she saw that the old cow's sides were no longer heaving.

"No! NO! You can't die on me! Wake up!" she cried. "I need your help here. Wake up! Oh damn, you have to wake up!" She kicked the rump of the cow wildly and the baby suddenly inched toward her. "Oh my God, it's moving. That's it, come on. Come on!"

She pulled again as hard as she could, and a strength came from somewhere other than her. "Just a little more!" she urged. "Yes, that's it, yes. Come on, dammit, don't you quit on me, too!" she pleaded.

Then it was free. She fell backward and the calf came with her, pinning her under it. Pushing it off, she scrambled back to her knees and tore the sack off as far down its body as she could. Then she pressed on its sides. She pressed and pressed as hard as she'd pulled. For how long, she didn't know.

"Baaaahhh . . . ." The most beautiful sound she'd ever heard cut through to her frenzied mind. The calf was breathing and suddenly struggling to free itself.

She ran to the house as fast as she'd ever run in her life. Inside, she grabbed towels, sheets, anything she could get a hold of, and ran back to the barn. She didn't even bother to wake Jeff now.

She wiped and cleaned the baby, crooning to it softly, then remembering it had to eat, had to have mother's milk, she bolted again. She grabbed a bucket from the feed stall and laid it on its side under the swollen milk sack of the mother. She pulled on the teats clumsily, but the precious milk began to collect in the pail. It wouldn't take much. That, she knew. When there seemed to be enough, she kneeled by the calf and forced it on its side. She yanked its head back and pried its mouth open with her fingers.

"Come on, open up. That's it, open up. Don't get stubborn on me now!"

She cupped her hand in the warm milk then slathered it all over the baby's mouth, forcing some in the sides. Instinctively it opened its mouth to lick, and she poured the

142

contents of the bucket down its throat. Seeing that the baby took to the milk, she did it over and over again. Squeeze the teats. Collect the milk. Pour it down. She took on the regimen of a machine, crawling on her knees between mother and baby, watching the calf's throat for movement and continuing until she was sure it had swallowed enough, crooning to it all the while.

The baby was quiet now, breathing effortlessly, and she was exhausted. Her clothes were covered in blood stains and wisps of hay tangled her hair. Milk droplets had dried on her hands and face in sticky little circles, and she had no idea how much time had passed. She sat down and pulled the calf close to her, cuddled his head in her lap and stroked his body. Oh yes, he was a beautiful bull, the color of fresh-pulled Taffy.

"You're going to be just fine, little guy," she crooned. "You surely are a miracle. And, look there at your mama." She pointed to the big heifer free of her pain at last. "She's sleeping now, but a fine mama she was. Oh yes, a fine mama she was . . . ."

* * * *

Amber sipped the last of her coffee. The cow in the pasture was quiet now; she'd found her baby. Somewhere, a big old taffy-colored bull was lying in a field of clover. Somehow, she knew it. She rose from her seat, took one last look at the moon over the ridge top, bent and patted the dogs lying at her feet, and smiled as she turned to enter the house.

"Yes, Jeff. Everything is going to be okay," she said to the night, and Jeff was listening and smiling with her. Somehow, she knew that, too.

THEY'RE MOWING HAY TODAY

The fog, a gray pall trapped between the ridges, was slowly dissipating in the burning rays of the rising sun. On her side and perched on an elbow, Amber watched the transcendence of night into day through the window by the bed. The view from the upper story window of the old farmhouse was almost primordial. What a disparate world this was, she thought, mysterious, yet so simple. Eerie, but so peaceful.

The house was still quiet but it wouldn't be long before the others would be up. She wanted to get an early morning walk in before the day's activity so she rolled away from the window, rose, noiselessly bathed, and put on jeans and a long-sleeved shirt.

She checked her closet and the old farm boots stood there waiting as if they'd just done duty the day before. A close inspection revealed bits of mud and hay preserved from happier times. She brushed at them gently, almost lovingly, for they knew and had served an era in her life.

"Yup, you're loosing it, woman," she kidded herself. "Talking to trees is one thing, but fondling a boot is pushing it. Better get this bod moving before the whole valley shows up and you end up on breakfast detail." She giggled quietly.

144

It was announced at supper that they would be mowing hay this weekend and that meant about twenty neighbors showing up as soon as the fields shed their morning dew. A walk would be out of the question if she didn't get going. A few brush strokes and practiced hands produced a long braid in minutes. Tiptoeing down the stairs, she grabbed the thermos of coffee made the night before, and quietly let herself out the back door. Immediately, the dogs were leaping on her.

"Come on, girls. Let's go to the woods. Where's Papa?"

She realized what she'd said when the dogs stopped short and looked around, then charged for the gate beyond the barn. An overwhelming sadness seized her for just a moment, but she followed the dogs to the gate that opened to the path through the pasture, and on to the trail up the mountain. It was a country kind of day. Just a hint of approaching fall in the air, and a crystal sky overhead that promised many bales of hay would be in the barns by nightfall.

Sara and Muffy ran ahead now, stirring the herd grazing in the bottom. Usually the cows paid no attention to the dogs ambling through, but this morning they were running so the calves, not to be outdone, began to chase them. This drew the mamas' attention and the bawling began. The resultant bovine chorale was music, familiar and sweet, to Amber's ears.

"How're you doing, my old friends?" she called to them as she drew near.

The dogs and the calves were running in big circles and she called the dogs to her so the calves would settle down. At the sound of her voice, Buttercup, a dear old friend, came lumbering up to her. She was a pretty cow, all red and white speckles and a nature as gentle as a butterfly on a petal. She lowered her massive head to receive a pat, and time suddenly stood still for Amber. It was as if she'd never left this place.

* * * *

145

"That bull of yours is eating the peas again." Jeff tried to look exasperated but the twinkle in his eye belied his disdain. "You really should keep him out in the pasture with the others now. He's nearly three months old and should be weaned off that dumb bottle you lug around. I think you keep him sucking on that thing on purpose."

She smiled at the eggs in the pan. "I do not. And I told you not to plant your dumb peas by the barn. He likes his bottle and he doesn't know how to drink water out of the creek yet. I tried to put him in the pasture and he came right back up here."

"Abby, he's never going to learn to drink water out of the creek if you keep shoving that stupid bottle in his mouth," Jeff countered.

"And how do you propose I teach him to drink water like other cows? They learn by watching their mama, you know."

At this, Jeff burst into laughter. "Well, I suppose you're going to have to show him then. I can just see it now."

"Oh, shut up, darn you." But she was laughing, too. "I have an idea on how to teach him when the time is right. But, he still needs milk and I can't fill a watering trough with milk. Here's your breakfast and I'll go get Miracle out of your silly pea patch." She grinned at him as she headed for the door.

Out in the yard, she called "Miracle" in the sing-song voice she always used. In seconds the frisky little bull came bounding around the corner of the barn, his taffy coat gleaming in the morning sun. He kind of half-hopped and half-ran up to her, head lowered to deliver his greeting, a vigorous head butt. She stumbled backwards despite the fact the calf still only weighed just over a hundred pounds. What he'd not yet achieved in size, he made up for with enthusiasm.

"Are you in Papa's peas again? What am I going to do with you, Miracle?" She hugged him as best she could before he was off.

Following behind, she decided to open the gate and walk him out to the pasture again. He really did need to play with the other calves and learn how to be a cow. She caught up with him and maneuvered him into the barn where his harness and leash hung on the stall door. One shake of the harness and its attached bell was all it took for the little bull to stop short in front of her, head erect. In moments they were headed to the herd.

"Come on, little fella," she cooed at him when he moved behind her. "You're going to grow into a fine bull and what're the girls going to think if you must have your mama with you all the time?"

Miracle really didn't understand that he was a bull, and he hid behind her like any child in the presence of the large heifers. Their size frightened him. Only the young calves lured him away from her. It was something she knew she was going to have to do, break ties with this animal. He, like every living creature, needed to be what, and all, he was and could be. But there would be time to worry about that later. For now, he still needed her care.

Seeing the other calves, Miracle started to run to join in the fun, pulling her along like a rag doll. "Okay. Okay! Stop a minute." Laughing, she pulled hard on the leash and he leaped back to her so she could take the harness off his head and let him run free. He raced down the hill, but not before turning to look back to make sure she was following.

She sat on a big rock along the path and watched him play. Often, she was overcome with love for him and the knowing she'd have to eventually let him go. And, the day would come that he wanted to. Perhaps, that was the hardest part of all.

* * * *

"Okay, girls. Let's go to the woods," she called to the dogs, now sprawled under the Hemlocks at the edge of the pasture. At her call, the dogs bounded up the trail and disappeared into the forest bordering the high mountain meadow. Entering the grove of tall pines along the rushing creek, she felt like she was entering a cathedral.

The trail was more rigorous as it began it ascent up the mountain. She followed the creek banks, noticing a hint of vermilion hues on the wild blackberry bushes. Soon they'd be dropping their leaves in preparation for the winter hiatus when roots rested and stored their energy for the spring blossoms that would become the tangy fruit. She and Jeff had spent many hours scaling the rocks and gathering the precious berries for jelly and cobblers.

Smiling, she watched the dogs run ahead of her, occasionally stopping to bury their noses into a smell only they could smell. Muff took off in pursuit of a rabbit, as the coyote hunter in her demanded.

"Hey, you! Get back here and leave that rabbit in peace," she called her back.

The predator instincts still roused mixed emotions in her. Acknowledge them she did, but found herself always rooting for the underdog, or in this case, bunny. Would she do the same if the coyote dog had been hungry? No. She accepted the balancing acts of nature; but didn't want to be a spectator to the hunt and the kill.

The rushing creek slowed as the trio approached the trail's summit. The headwater, fed by an underground spring, pooled in the small clearing near the base of the rock cliff that was the mountain's peak. Embraced by a ring of Mountain Laurel and Wild Azalea, it begged a seat be taken on one of its rock pews. She lowered herself onto a flat circle of slate that angled into the water and pulled off her old boots. The crystal tarn was icy cold, lapping at her toes as it swirled around before embarking on the long cascade to the flatland.

The dogs drank deeply from the water and then stretched out, one on each side of her, panting from the long climb. They, too, sensed the wonder of this place, she thought, and wondered if they could smell the permeating essence that had been committed to it not so long ago. Sara and Muffy were Jeff's best friends and it was here that his remains were returned back to the Earth, as he'd wanted.

She spoke softly, a tremble in her voice. "Me and the dogs thought we'd come sit with you a while. I know you'd like that. I've had a lot on my mind lately so figured it was time to come up to the farm and spend a little time remembering the things you taught me, Jeff. I still kind of struggle with my priority settings. But, you know that too, don't you?" She could almost hear his gentle laughter rustling in the pines above her.

"They're mowing hay today. You know, I see you yet in my mind's eye, off on the high knoll mowing the Purple Tops. Sailing your tractor on a lavender sea, content in your solitude with your God all around you. It's not easy for me to understand that where you are now could be better than that." Sighing, she brushed away a tear.

She laid back on the rock and searched the azure sky encasing the forest. Her movement drew a slurping lick from Muff, and she resisted the petty urge to wipe her face. Instead, marveled at the communication possible between a half-wild dog and herself. As the sun dried the moisture on her cheek, she absorbed again the sense of unity between all living things. The dog, the forest, the water, the sun, the quiet laughter rustling in the pine needles, and her. The same Energy vibrated in all of them. A poem she'd written long ago drifted back into her mind.

Aaah, for thou, With ears that hear,
A chorus surrounds.
For thou, with eyes that see,
A ballet abounds.
For thou, with flesh that feels,
Mighty forests tremor their secrets,
Whispering low.
And as you lay, gently pressing
Your ear to Earth
Heart of flesh 'gainst heart of Soul,
Symphonies of truth gently flow.

"Thanks, Jeff. Thanks for bringing me to a place that could help you teach me of life, and for sharing yours with mine. Thank you for teaching me to travel a road because it's there in front of me with all its mysterious twists and turns. The road without you has been an arduous trek to say the least, but I'm finally beginning to understand that I can crest new hills, live and love another without lessening my love for you. That, that love is its own and only enhanced by ours. Love could never be a lessening, I don't think.

"Well hon, I suppose I'd better get these dogs back down to the house now. Help out with the Kool-Aid making for the mowing crew. By the look of the fields, it'll be a big crop. But you know that too, don't you? If I listen real, real hard I can hear your tractor running up there on the knoll. Up there in the Purple Tops."

She forced herself to her feet. "Come on, girls. We should be getting back now. There's hay to bring in," she said to the dogs.

The dogs rose a little more reluctantly this time, not so eager to leave this place either. They took another long drink of the cold mountain water, and then Sara, leaving Muff behind, strolled to catch up with Amber already moving down the hill. The dog walked closely by her side this time. A chill ran up Amber's spine as Muffy's howl echoed through the quiet of the forest.

WHAT? YOU WANT WHAT?

Amber spent another week on the farm. She spent lazy days exploring the old barns, again marveling at their treasures of times past. She cried when uncovering her old wagon wheel, overgrown in weeds in the now untended remains of her country garden by the canning shed. The shed was gone now, too, victim of a tornado that had twisted its way through the mountains on an angry spring night. Only the weathered clapboard floor was left to tell its tale to future generations.

But, she'd smiled when discovering a late summer poppy bloom thriving in the brush several yards away. The seeds she'd planted so long ago had created more seeds and scattered by the winds, they'd taken root to sprout a new flower. The bloom told of her own hands tilling this country earth and giving some small something back to what had given her so much.

Beth had sat with her on the swing in the evenings and they'd laughed and cried as many stories were re-lived in the telling. Friends and neighbors had come to see her and still teased about the bull with the wide red ribbon around his neck who'd taken to being shampooed daily. They'd shared their concerns for how she was doing alone without Jeff and she assured them that she was managing okay.

The week's end came with a cool front and she and Beth sat on the swing bundled in sweaters. "This'll put frost on the pumpkins for sure," Beth said with a shiver. "I can remember lots of frosts in late August, early September."

She was shivering, too, and thoughts of warmer climes and sea fog pushed their way into her mind. "Beth, the past few days here have been wonderful. I thank you so much for letting me barge in like this."

"I don't want to hear that kind of talk from you, girl. You know this will always be your home too. Told you that when I moved in the house after you left here. If I had my way, you'd be selling that place down there and getting yourself back up here where you belong. What do you think about that, silly dogs?" She leaned over and patted Sara's head where she laid at Amber's feet. "These darn dogs been acting strange again this evening," Beth added in a low voice. "You got something to tell me, Amber?"

She looked down at the dogs. They'd traced many trails back into time and memories over the past few days, even the high trail where she and Jeff had followed the bear tracks and found the cave. The cave had been abandoned, and she hoped the bear hadn't fallen victim to a hunter.

"Yes, hon. I wanted to tell you that I'll be leaving to go home in the morning. I really should be getting back to my job, and I don't like to leave my house sitting empty for too long."

Beth seemed to expect this but clearly wasn't happy. "I suppose there's no talking you out of it. I know it's hard on you being here with all your memories, and sharing a house that was your own and Jeff's. I'm glad you came and got to spend some time reflecting and walking with these durn crazy dogs. They've been so happy since you're here. I wish you'd stay longer, but I do understand. I really do."

"I know you do, Beth. And, thank you for taking such good care of these 'durn crazy dogs'. I'd love to take them home with me but it would be cruel to take them from this farm where they can run free and be what they are. At home, they'd have to go on a chain and be deafened with sirens going all the time. I'm afraid the city would break their hearts worse than missing me. For sure it would break their spirit and that would be tragic." She sighed heavily.

"Oh, the dogs are fine here. No trouble at all," Beth assured her. "When you aren't here they spend most of their time up in the woods by the headwater. Come down to eat and guard the house if we go off. Every now and then you can hear Muff a howling up there. Guess it's the coyote in her."

"Yes, guess it is." But she knew better.

The next morning as she was putting her things in the car the two dogs sat watching her, no longer dancing.

"Aw, don't you two be sad. I'll be back to see you again real soon, I promise," she crooned to them. "I depend on you two to take good care of my memories while I'm gone. Okay? And, how would Papa feel if you just went off and left him?" The tears burned her eyes as she kneeled on the ground and hugged the animals close to her. "God, how I love you both."

She pulled herself up and pointed to the gate. "Now do something for me, will you? Get yourselves up to those woods. Go on, get up there and make sure everything is as it should be." The dogs hesitated but she pointed again and spoke more sternly. "Go on now, go see Papa."

Muffy first, then Sara, moved half-heartedly toward the gate. She sobbed audibly, and they turned and looked at her, but she pointed again to the woods, the trail, and the headwater. This time they took off running and she watched them cross the pasture and disappear into the forest out of sight.

The music was loud. She was watching the light on the CB radio and traveling fast, the brown haze in the distance telling her she wasn't far from the flats and Atlanta. The cool green of the forest was behind her as she glanced in her

153

rearview mirror at a cherished time in her life that had taught her real gut-wrenching truths. Truths of the seasons of birth, life, love, and death. Of revering and sharing what time you had and letting go when it was up. She thought again of the bull she'd birthed and raised and had to give up because he didn't know he was able to hurt her. Maybe Jeff didn't know that either.

Now she was coming home to the present. She thought of Ben and a new road, wherever it led. Perhaps it wasn't there at all, but she wanted to be home if it was and pushed the pedal harder. She had miles to go before the salt air would fill her lungs once more.

It was nearing dusk when she pulled into the driveway and was surprised to see a strange car parked there. Probably one of the neighbors had company and didn't think she'd be home so soon, she thought.

"Yes, that's it," she mumbled when she saw the familiar logo of a car rental company on the rear bumper.

She parked behind it and got out, stretching her arms over her head to straighten her back after the long ride. Bending to reach inside for her purse, she noticed something out by the thicket. She grabbed the purse and went into the yard, her eyes never leaving the edge of the jungle where he sat staring. Moving quietly across the grass, she came up behind him.

"Hello, Ben. What are you looking at anyway?"

Startled, he flinched. "Just looking for the fox, I guess." He rose and smiled at her. "I see you've been away."

"Yes. I took a trip down Memory Lane, you could say. How was the flight?"

"Okay. I called, got no answer, so decided to come on anyway. Been here two days, staying at the Ramada up town."

"Oh. Well, wish I would've known. I've been to the farm."

"I see," he answered, as if lost for words. "Now you're back."

"Immm-hmn, back." This wasn't like him, she thought. He was too non-committal, almost shy. "Let's go in out of the heat. You must be thirsty."

She turned and went back to the car, got her suitcase out of the trunk, and headed toward the stairs. He followed, catching up and taking her bag.

The house was stuffy, as it should be in her absence, so she quickly lowered the thermostat for the A/C. She heard him behind her running water from the sink and getting out a glass. Stepping out onto the open porch to check her plants, an almost liquid breeze thick with smells from the humidity in the air engulfed her. The constant reminder that she was no longer at the farm and that Jeff was gone. Everything seemed in order so she re-entered the living room, closing the sliding door behind her.

He was sitting on the couch, a glass of water in hand.

"So?"

"So?" he answered back.

"Did you get things taken care of?" She crossed the room and took some juice out of the freezer, settling for some water herself while it thawed. He was watching her as she turned to look at him, still waiting for his reply.

"Yes, I think so. For now," he added.

There it was again. The same reluctance in his voice as in his manner in the yard. Something wasn't right. And why had he stayed at a hotel and not with his son?

"You seem distant, Abby. Are you upset that I was gone longer than you'd expected?"

"Not really. I was concerned for you is all. You hadn't totally gained your strength back when you left. But, I needed the time, too. Time to think."

"Yeah, I suppose so," he mumbled.

She finished her drink and came to him on the couch. "Okay, tell me what's wrong. And before you try and alibi and say there isn't, I already know there is. I'm the bird lady, remember, and birds know things." She smiled, but he just continued to stare ahead.

155

"Hey! Are you with me here, or what?" She was beginning to get really concerned. Had he been ill again?

He leaned back into the couch. "Well, things didn't work out as I'd hoped. How's that for starters?"

"Meaning?"

"Meaning . . . I didn't have as much as I thought. Some copyrights had been mishandled, some things I had done as work-for-hire, and didn't know I had. The house was a mess. A close friend had died and I didn't even know it, didn't go to the funeral." He looked at her. "See, Abby, I didn't even realize it, but I hadn't been home in over six months."

His eyes were moist as he spoke and, again, she could feel his angst. *Why was he so lost? How could someone just go away for half a year and not even know it?*

"So I made what arrangements I could, wrote some letters, had the attorney file them for safekeeping, all that. Made a will, put the house with a realtor." He looked down. "And, thought about you. I mean us."

God, the anguish in him, she thought as she took his hand, almost clutching it in her want to understand and be there for him.

"And so, I've reached a decision." His voice fell to just a whisper.

She tightened. *This is why he's being so remote, so distracted. Is he going to end it right here and now, and he's fighting telling me? Could I have been so wrong? Was the fox just a fox, nothing more?*

"And that is, I want us to live together. I mean, if you want to."

Her breath caught in her throat. "What? You want *what?*" Her voice was a whisper.

He looked up and their eyes caught, locked, in that inexplicable way they'd done before in bookstores, parking lots, and under stars.

"I want us to live together," he said again.

"You mean now? Here? In this house? You want to stay with me in this house?" Hearing the opposite of what she was expecting, she was caught off-guard, her thoughts spinning.

"Well yes, now. Here for now. I know you'd have to have time to tend to things, the house and all. But I was thinking maybe we could take a trip, a vacation of sorts, and see if there's a place somewhere. A place we might find our own house, have our own life for as long as we can."

She was stunned. She hadn't heard a word in weeks and now this. Holding his hand tightly, she forced herself to look away, out through the glass doors, out into the semi-darkness. Was the fox out there looking in at them? Was she dreaming this? The seagull around her neck lay heavy on her chest, just over her pounding heart.

He sensed her hesitation. "But only if you want to. I know these last weeks have been hard for you, and I'm sorry for that. But I had to come to grips with some things. I couldn't offer you anything of myself until I knew what I had to offer. If you've had a change of heart, I understand."

She looked back to him. "Ben, I've had no change of heart. Not now. Not ever."

He leaned forward and brought her to him, kissing her deeply, and now, longingly. She responded equally, and they held onto each other as if about to go over a falls or a chasm of some kind.

While out in the yard, out in the wilderness of her acreage, perhaps up in the branches of the big oak where the squirrels played and a hot yellow moon was rising, a breeze came up and stirred it all. But still, no fox appeared. And still, he hadn't told her everything.

ODE TO SOLOMON

It hadn't taken him long to move in. Traveling as he did he required little, and what he didn't have, they bought at the local stores. Ben's needs, it seemed to Amber, were simple indeed.

The one thing he did buy was a laptop computer, and with that, pencils and a yellow notepad. He bought walking shorts and summer shirts, but no underwear. This amused her, that a man his age would be so bold, or so absent-minded, or both. She chuckled silently, but not so silently that he turned and looked at her as they were going through the line.

"It's nothing," she said, barely able to contain herself. He thought she was laughing at his outrageous shirt, a god-awful flowery thing guaranteed to get looks, and jests, among the more staid populace. *A walking petunia*, she thought, but said nothing.

Once home they changed into the cooler clothes and headed for the beach. The smiles she expected at his attire didn't come. It was, after all, a town of hardy fishermen, retirees, tourists and beach bar folk. Most were too tired, too old, too fun loving, too *something* to much care what other

158

people wore. A standard joke in Florida was that formal meant white shorts.

To her surprise and amazement, once at the shore, he mentioned how cool the water looked and handed her his wallet. Without another word, he dove in, clothes, shoes, and all. When he surfaced not ten yards out in the gentle green swell he was smiling. *And, he calls me a lunatic. Damn!*

The next thing that happened, happened quickly, too quickly to anticipate, for she then did exactly the same thing, clothes and all. Oh, she'd had the sense to drop her purse and his wallet first, but it was as if something had taken her and thrown her into the water, too, some benevolent force pulling them back into childhood.

Yes, she was wild and impulsive in her own way, but being a woman, tempered it somewhat. But not now. Now it was him and her and the waves, and the beachgoers, an older lot for the most part, could be hanged.

She surfaced in front of him, and her first reaction was to laugh out loud at both her impetuousness and his face. His glasses were all watery, his thin hair appeared pasted to his forehead, and the petunia shirt was rapidly losing its color in the salt water, surrounding him with dye. The thought struck her that he'd killed the shirt, and this made her burst out laughing.

"You didn't really think I was gonna wear that monstrosity anywhere, did you?"

But she was laughing too hard to even realize what he'd done, his little trick having fooled her yet again.

A wave lifted him and pushed him into her, knocking her back, carrying them into the shoreline wrapped together like so much seaweed. The beachgoers, if anything, looked on in idle curiosity and nothing more, then resumed their newspaper reading under their beach umbrellas.

And none, not a one, it seemed, sensed what had happened. But he did. And she did. And perhaps the wave did as it became, in a way, a baptismal fount that shed the old them and birthed the new there in plain sight of their past, their present, and their future. It curled itself up and crested under a perfect sky on a perfect day, when nothing else seemed important but the cycling of water droplets and the melding of their souls.

They took the long road to the north bridge home, and both were wet, tired, and content. He stopped at a gas station to buy cigarettes, and the clerk, a young man in perhaps his twenties, said nothing about his appearance. The shirt was white now with what seemed to be drawn flowers on it.

Ben was singing as he approached the car, switching tunes as he opened the driver's door and got back in, giving her a wink as he turned the key in the ignition. She, again, marveled at his knowledge of song and poem lyrics and shook her head in mock wonder at his mood, showering him with a mist from her wet, matted, hair.

Now he drove slowly along the winding shell back roads, looking at the homes nestled close to water's edge on both sides of the key, occasionally commenting about them. They crossed a drawbridge or two and he drew in a long breath.

"Creosote." He smiled. "Haven't smelled that in a long, long time. LA is all concrete, no distinguishable smells at all. I grew up on tar and creosote, muddy backwater, oily barges and tugboats that smelled like old socks, near the Texas Gulf coast. The ocean just doesn't seem like the ocean if it doesn't smell."

"You *like* that?" she asked, wrinkling her nose.

"Sure. Reminds me of home. Boats. Ships. Ever been on a ship?"

She shook her head. "I've been on boats, pretty big ones, but ships, no. Unless you count a cruise ship. I've been on those."

The gravel crunched beneath the tires. "I like that sound, too," he added. "Cuts hell out of tires and bare feet, even shoes, but has a magic to it, don't you think?"

She thought that what she preferred was the smooth sound of tires on a highway at eighty or more, but she only smiled, encouraging him to continue.

160

"Can't say I'd want to walk on it anymore, but did as a kid. We'd go crabbing, my folks, their friends, and I. Take horsemeat, long-handled nets, tie a thick string around the meat, toss it in. The crabs would latch on and nibble, we'd bring the meat and crabs up slowly, get the net under them, then into a burlap sack. Went on most of the day, until we had fifty or so. All Blue Shell." He paused, as his mind wandered back.

She was hearing about his childhood again, but this time a different part than what she already knew. "Then what?" she asked, wanting him to continue.

"Huh?"

"Then what? What'd you do with the crabs after you caught them?"

"You'd eat them of course." He seemed surprised at the question. "We'd take them home put them in a pot of boiling water until done, and they're delicious right out of the shell. Of course . . . ."

He paused again and she saw his face change from light to somber. "Of course, then the adults would all get shit-faced, and more often then not, wind up in an argument." He glanced at her. "Know what it's like to see your parents make fools of themselves? Best thing in the world for making a kid inhibited the rest of his life."

She didn't have an answer, but yes, she kind of knew.

When Ben hit the main highway he floored the accelerator, and the car shot down the road as if on grease. He had a strange look on his face, as if expecting lift off. Was he unconsciously pulling back on the steering wheel, like a pilot in an airplane? When the speedometer reached ninety, he relaxed and let the car have its 'head.' For a moment she visualized them in an airplane, both wearing leather helmets and goggles in their open cockpit.

She loved the pace and gave in to the force of the wind, resting her head against the seat back. The raw power of speed and wind, were near orgasmic, an escape from her often harsh reality. But not this time. This time she wanted to

161

pinch her flesh to insure the last twenty-four hours had not been a dream.

Sensing a slowing, she turned to see him deliberately easing off the pedal and applying light pressure on the brakes as if suddenly aware of his lapse into days of piloting a plane.

"Hey, that's okay. She doesn't smooth out until she hits 100."

"It's not okay, Abby. You shouldn't even know that 'she' smoothes out at 100. I don't know what came over me. Only an idiot would drive so fast on tires weakened from driving on shell roads a lot of the time."

She wanted to laugh but the serious look on his face stopped her. She reached over and laid her hand on his leg, saying nothing, smiling instead. She pushed a CD into the player and let the music take her up, even as the car was slowing to the speed limit. The Aerosmith CD was playing one off her favorite songs about wanting to spend her life in a sweet surrender to the moment forever. She squeezed his knee and sang along, loud, over the noise of the wind.

Then they were leaving the highway and turning onto the road that led to her treehouse. Her treehouse? For a moment it seemed like *their* treehouse, but only for a moment. In a flash she realized what he'd said was true. They could never really be themselves as a pair unless they started over again somewhere else. But where? That was the question.

"Have to get that back so they don't charge me for another day," he said, as they pulled in the drive behind his rental car.

"Oh, what's another day," she teased, "when we have the rest of our lives?"

But instead of making him smile, he said nothing and sent a little prayer of gratitude to someone or something, somewhere, that the pains in his groin had been absent since his return.

"You ready for a shower?" she asked as she got out. They had dried off on the long, slow and fast return from the beach, and felt sticky from the salt water.

"Yeah," he said, suddenly resuming his previous jovial mood. "Then a change of clothes, something to eat, return the rental, then back here for the ceremony."

"Ceremony?" she asked.

"Sure," he sort of grinned. "Burial by torchlight. Out there." He pointed to the yard.

"I don't understand. What burial?"

"Why, this, of course," he said pointing to his shirt. "This thing's ugly dead, so might as well bury it," he snickered, tickled at his own joke.

Again, she laughed at his foolishness, but damn, if that isn't exactly what he did later on when the moon was up, the mosquitoes out, and the Tiki was smoking away as if celebrating some sacrifice on some lava-laden crest in another time, another place.

She'd realized for some time that her neighbors thought her somewhat crazy, but this, and Ben dancing around the torch, would confirm any doubts they might have had. In other words, it was a glorious end to an incredible day.

The following morning she woke to an empty bed and the smells of brewing coffee and bacon frying. Ben's voice filtered through the closed door so she took her time rising to give him some privacy with whoever he was talking to, perhaps his son, on the phone.

She lay there half-way listening to the muted conversation and breathing in the scent of him where he'd lain next to her. When it was quiet but for the rattling of utensils she got up, silently brushed her teeth, and then joined him in the kitchen.

"Immm . . . coffee," she droned.

"I was just about to call you. Scrambled or over easy? Sit down, this will only take a minute," he said without turning from the stove.

"Breakfast, too? Aren't you just full of surprises? Scrambled will be fine." Then she saw the bear and burst out laughing. "Is that who you were talking to?"

"Why, of course," he answered. "I had to cut a deal for the evening use of the rocking chair and it cost me a bacon sandwich."

The stuffed bear was propped up on the wooden bench, glass eyes staring at an empty plate on the table in front of him. She took her place across from him, touched at the gesture.

"Well, big fella," she said to her friend, "looks like we're being spoiled rotten this morning."

"Don't get used to it, it'll be your turn tomorrow," he said, placing the food on their plates. "Now, eat."

She looked at all the food and frowned. She rarely ate breakfast, living alone as she did. In fact, she rarely ate at all.

"Surely you don't expect me to eat all this food first thing in the morning?" she said as he took his seat beside Bear.

"Yes I do. I expect you to try anyway. You're like a rail, Abby."

"Oh, pppffffftt. Am not."

But, looking at Ben, and the bear sitting across from her, she realized she was hungry. It was good to have someone to share the table with again. She stifled another giggle at the sight of them and picked up her fork.

After breakfast they went to the local mall and walked around, doing nothing, doing everything. It seemed as natural to her as when Jeff was alive. They had lunch at an outdoor café, and then went for a drive into the country again, away from town. The road wandered along as if built to inspire nothing more than dreaminess.

She laid her head back while he drove, watching the clouds above, the top being down, of course. She drifted into the childhood fantasies of cloud faces and found herself thinking of Bach's "Illusions" and the moving of clouds at will to form whatever you wished.

164

Looking out across the flat terrain of sawgrass and pastures dotted with cows, a pond here and a pond there, she smiled. Not like the farm in the mountains, but quaint and peaceful in its own way.

"Penny for your thoughts," he said above the wind roar, but she just lazily shook her head.

They pulled into a country gas station and got out to stretch their legs. She bought a soda from one of those old red lift-top coolers full of ice and water, and Ben bought a road map.

"Are you lost?" she asked, kidding.

"No, just thinking about where we can move to." Then questioning his statement, "When we move, I mean."

"Oh, okay." She smiled, but said no more.

When they were moving again, her thoughts turned to decisions that were going to have to be made, and fairly soon. There was no doubt in her mind that finding a place of their own making was meant to be. Her only questioning in regards to Ben had been his own questioning, his hesitation. Not everyone listened to the 'Soul' voice as she did, and you can't force it. Nor, can you write another's music. The song must come from within.

"Yes, hon, it's time to make some plans," she said, breaking her silence. "I'll start addressing it first thing in the morning."

"I'm not rushing you, Abby. Take the time you need."

Her thoughts started wandering again, only this time seriously. She'd inquire about taking an indefinite leave at her job, check her finances, she had no idea of his, do what was necessary to close the house up, and somehow find the right words to write to her sons. She'd break the news by letter and give them time to digest it before a call.

She reached over the console and took Ben's free hand into her own, squeezing it just enough to say what words could not. He said nothing in reply, but returned the pressure, saying that he understood.

Later, lying next to him and listening to the rhythmic breathing of his sleep, she smiled her gratitude into the darkened room. Time had negated the more bestial groping of youthful flesh, but the passion between them was no less in its gentleness. She thought of the Ode of Solomon she'd read once and never forgotten . . .

> *"You split me, and tore my heart open.*
> *You filled me with love.*
> *You poured your spirit into mine.*
> *Now I know you as I know myself."*

Outside the window the night sounds chirped approval, and wrapped their peace around her. And she could swear she heard a fox yipping, almost whimpering, ever so softly.

MAINE? DID YOU SAY MAINE?

Amber woke early. She'd felt Ben get up in the night, heard the soft rumblings of the TV in the living room, but had drifted back to sleep remembering his odd sleep patterns in the hotel in Texas. He wasn't talking about his illness and she wanted the roots of positive thinking to take hold before she brought it up. He was now sleeping peacefully at her side so she rose quietly, gathered her clothes from the closet, and quietly shut the bedroom door behind her.

A few minutes later she was washed, dressed, and out the door, hoping to catch her boss early before the store opened. She started the car, careful to turn the music down, took a deep breath and backed out.

Ginny, her manager, was stunned. "You're going to do *what*?"

"I'm quitting," she repeated.

"I know that's what you said, Amber, but surely you're not serious. Who in the hell has pissed you off now? Tell me, we'll work it out. I know you're over burdened at times and that fiery side of you does a slow burn now and then, but quitting?"

"No, Ginny, I'm not pissed off about anything and you've been good to me, letting me take off whenever I wanted. It's not that at all. But things are changing in my life and it's time to move on. I'll give you the customary two week notice in writing, but I felt I owed it to you to tell you personally, as a friend."

Ginny's eyes narrowed. "Hmmm, have you met someone? No dependable woman like you just up and quits on her own. And, what do you mean by move on? Are you moving away? What about your house?" She smiled in that only-a-woman-knows smile all women possess. "You've got a new man in your life, haven't you?"

Amber bristled slightly at the question. *Why is it you had to have a man in your life to make a decision or move on,* she thought. But, she returned Ginny's knowing smile.

"Let's just say some new opportunities have come my way and I'm at a point where time is moving fast. There are things I want to see and do, and it's not fair to always be coming to you expecting leaves of absence. I have a new friend, yes, and I'm going to shut my house up for a few months and do some traveling. I haven't thought beyond that. I just know I want to do this and I'm going to follow my heart."

Ginny saw the resignation on Amber's face and knew her well enough to guess there would be no talking her out of this. She also realized no more information was going to be offered. Amber was different than most of her employees. Actually, Ginny thought, she was rather mysterious. Her silver convertible, the rock music blaring through the parking lot belied her age, and caused many heads to turn and wonder just what kind of life she did lead in private. The younger employees loved her and would make comments like, "Amber just arrived; we hear her coming."

In a resolute and sad sort of way, Ginny quietly agreed, "Okay, hon. I'll get you the necessary forms."

"Thanks," was all she could say.

The manager stalled just a bit. "I have to say I do so with hesitation, you know."

"I know. You've been a good friend, Ginny, and a good boss, too."

On impulse, Ginny suddenly hugged her, and then held her at arm's length. "Well, you deserve some happiness after all you've been through, so can't say as I blame you. I'll have the papers for you by next shift, how's that?"

"Thanks. I knew you'd understand."

Ginny turned and walked away. Staying, she'd lose her managerial resolve in front of the other employees. Secretly, she envied Amber and her abrupt walking away was to stop the tears already forming.

Watching Ginny go, she felt a slight pang herself. Here, she'd made friends. She hated her job, but not the people. She had mixed feelings about it all, but knew deep down it had to be. As she turned to leave, she noticed some of the other employees watching, probably hearing the boss's loud, "You're going to do what?" She forced a grin and waved at the crew behind the counter.

"See y'all tomorrow," she said cheerily, as she walked to the front doors, leaving the rest to whisper behind her.

Once outside she sighed heavily, feeling relief at getting that part over. Her boss was right. It wasn't like her to just up and quit a job, but Ginny didn't know about Ben. Now she was eager to get home and tell him that they could make their plans and get on with their lives.

She walked in the door, grateful for the cool air that washed over her. The coffee maker on the countertop told her he was up and about, but he wasn't in view.

"What did you do with Ben?" she asked the bear still perched on the wooden seat. "Bargained for another bacon sandwich, I bet." She picked him up and twirled around the kitchen, holding the almost-as-big-as-her fuzzy bear close.

"Can I have one of those hugs?"

She turned to see him standing in the doorway with his glasses perched on the end of his nose and the recently purchased road map open in his hand.

"I thought you'd never ask," she said putting the stuffed bear back on his bench and going to his outstretched arms.

"Well, you certainly are in a vibrant mood this morning. Where've you been off to so early?" He grinned as he whirled her around the kitchen, too.

"Quitting my job." She looked up at him. "I did agree to a two-week notice, though. Is that all right?"

"Sure. You'll need some time to make arrangements around here. You don't close a house up overnight," he said, then added, "You sure you're okay with this, Abby?"

"I see you have the map out." She ignored his question and stepped away from him toward the coffee pot. "Any ideas where you'd like to go?"

"No place in particular, unknown places in general. Somewhere neither of us has been before."

"Sounds good to me," she said. "We'll just start out and see where the road leads. One day at a time. Say, are you going to see your son, tell him what you're doing?"

That was the next hurdle she faced. Telling her own sons that she was about to close up and go tooling off across the country with a man they'd never met, or even knew about, other than a few suspicions following the trip to Texas.

"I'm thinking about that, Abby. There's not been much communication in recent years. Last he heard from me was on a yellow pad on a rainy night, the heart of a dad poured out. But, you have a point; I suppose I should make contact. It was a rather odd way for me to leave."

She didn't need to turn to see the hurt in his eyes; it was apparent in his voice.

"You do what you think best, hon. But, if you left your heart on a yellow pad, don't you think you should go see how he's taking care of it? You may find that you get it back whole and healthy again."

"You don't understand," he started to say as she turned to face him. She didn't let him finish.

"No, perhaps not. But at this point, you don't understand either. Your son may have two hearts to give back to you, yours and his own. If not, you'll have done all you could to tear down the wall that rose between you. He's grown now. If he chooses to rebuild it, it will be his wall, not yours.

170

Then, maybe you'll understand what he couldn't. At least you'd be free in the knowing."

"Abby, your relationship with your sons is entirely different than mine. I told you I'd think about it; now let's drop it."

She heard the finality in his voice. "Okay, I shouldn't interfere, sorry. Now, let's have some coffee and take a look at the map, or should we just throw it away? We'll have to head north first and I don't need a map for that." She smiled at him wanting the shadow crossing his face to pass as rapidly as it had appeared.

The following week was a flurry of activity as Ben poured over many maps and they made preparations for closing up. She'd have to shut off phone and cable, decide arrangements for her mail. Her mail? What would she do about her mail? Richard would hold it up to a month, but she didn't know when she'd be coming back. And since she didn't as yet have a forwarding address, what was she to do? By month's end, though, she may have one and could call him then. Bills weren't a problem as she did most of that by Internet and there were always places to get Ben's laptop online.

Personal contacts, too, were mostly done by email, so she messaged cyber friends about her upcoming trip and not to worry if she disappeared for long intervals. How odd they would think her. But no, she told herself, they already thought she was odd, so this wouldn't surprise them. The thought caused her to smile.

Her family, her sons especially, she'd call by phone. But the rest? What rest? Oh, there were one or two close friends in town, and those on the farm, but mostly, she was a loner.

Should she rent the house out? The thought passed quickly. She and Jeff had built this house, so no, there would be no strangers in it. The fight between her and Ben came to her, when he'd mentioned playing house. Although his comment had angered her at the time, now, she could see his point. He'd always feel like a stranger invading a territory not his own if she'd insisted on staying here.

No, she'd lock the house, give her neighbor a key and enough money to take care of the property for three months. That's what she'd do, and if this all worked out, then her sons could come occasionally, during the months when icy winds wrapped their own homes in winter. In a way, the house was already theirs; she'd made the legal arrangements. And other family members, too, her and Ben included, may enjoy having a tropical getaway in the midst of the January through March doldrums. She'd not trouble herself with details too far in the future to warrant concern.

Her days were spent at work and her nights in deciding what to take along on their trip. The car didn't allow for much but clothes and necessities. And, what was really necessary in today's world of shopping malls and Wal-Mart Supercenters in every nook and cranny?

She didn't interfere with Ben and had decided that wherever he wanted to go, she would, too. Her only stipulation to him was that it be near the ocean, which he readily agreed to. But when he finally told her where he thought they should look for a place, it surprised her.

"Maine," he said one evening over supper. "I think we should go to Maine."

For a moment it didn't register. Both were hot climate people, didn't really like the cold, so when he suggested one of the coldest places in the states, it caught her off-guard.

"Maine? Did you say *Maine?* Are you nuts?" she asked, unsure if he was teasing. His face said no, he wasn't teasing at all.

"Maine is still wild, still untamed in spots. Kind of like you." He grinned when he said it.

"It's also colder than hell," she retorted, running the thought across her mind.

"Sure it is, but just think of the isolation. The rocky coastlines, the four seasons, the beauty of the woods, the—

"The icy roads, frostbite," she interrupted.

"Wood burning stoves, water from a well," he went on.

"Are you planning on becoming Mr. Greenjeans or something?"

He laughed aloud and threw a grape at her from across the table. "Yeah, maybe."

He rose from the bench and nudged her shoulder. "Look," he said grabbing the map off the kitchen table and going to the sofa. Pushing the candles aside, he laid the map out on the coffee table, smoothing the folds with his open hands as he grinned up at her.

"Come here," he said.

God, she thought. Maine? But she went to his side and looked at the map spread out in front of him.

"I figure we'll just drive like this, see. He pointed to a line drawn on the map that took them mostly through small towns and back roads. "We can stop as we need and want to. Not knowing when, or where, and caring less, just following the moods as they strike us." He looked at her, eyes sparkling, almost mischievous.

His enthusiasm was infectious, and she found herself being drawn into it like kindling to a fire.

"Maine?" she persisted.

"What, you'd prefer the Dakotas? The Black Hills? The Great Plains? Trout fishing in icy water, wind that picks you up and carries you along like a leaf? Hell, woman, where's your spirit? Want to try Seattle? Fog? Rain? A closet full of raincoats and a backyard full of water most of the year?

The thought of him in Maine brought a picture to her mind and she wondered what he'd look like in bib overalls tilling rocky soil. She laughed.

"What's so funny?"

"Nothing," she answered, trying to suppress her grin.

"Maine it is, then," he said. "We'll have our own orchard out back. The wild critters will eat supper with us each night. Why, it'll be paradise."

Colder'n hell, she thought. "Okay, OKAY, so you want to go to Maine and play Paul Bunyan. Fine. Just don't beg off on me when you're freezing your ass off."

He turned and grabbed her in his own version of a bear hug. "Oh, I won't freeze. Not when I've got your skinny ass to keep me warm at night. Well, you and a couple of quilts, anyway. And just think. You cutting the wood, working in the garden, making our food, bringing water from the well, doing the sewing."

"Oh, no," she blurted out, unsure if he was serious or not. He burst into laughter and began tickling her.

"Stop it, damn you. Stop it!" she cried, trying to wiggle free of his grasp. But he kept tickling and laughing and she soon was nearly in tears from the merriment, the stupidity of it all. For sure, she thought, he's lost his damn mind, and the thought absolutely delighted her.

"Huzzah," he said, releasing her long enough for her to jump up and run to the kitchen. She grabbed a banana from the fruit basket and turned in a mock attack stance. He, arming himself with an umbrella from the stand at the same time, struck a fencing pose from some old movie.

"En Garde, Damsel, you've met your match," he said while advancing on her with the outstretched umbrella.

She nearly collapsed with laughter at his absurdity, and at her own. Talk about second childhood. But when he reached her and opened the umbrella over the both of them with a dramatic flair, she melted against him.

He lowered the umbrella until they were both cocooned inside it, and she saw the laughter in his eyes and the seriousness on his face, and she knew she'd be going to Maine, or anywhere else he wanted to go.

MOM, HAVE YOU GONE CRAZY?

The sun shone opalescent through the morning mist as she sipped on a second cup of coffee. She'd risen before dawn, silently brewed coffee and carried it to the deck.

She looked at the portable phone, silent now on the table beside her, then at her watch in the faint light. Still early, she thought. Better wait a few more minutes. Her last shift at the store would be completed today and it was time to face the one thing she'd been hesitant to do. Calling her sons.

There was rustling in the low-slung Palmettos and she stared into the vegetation, hoping to see whatever was scurrying on a hunt for breakfast, but nothing showed itself. Just as well, she thought, I don't need distractions now. She dialed the number slowly.

"Hello?"

"Sounds like I woke you. I'm sorry. Thought you'd be up for work by now."

"Mom? That you?" the sleepy voice asked.

"It's me, alright." She tried to hide her nerves with a cheery agreement.

"What's the matter? Why are you calling so early?"

"Nothing's the matter. Quite the opposite, in fact. I'm about to begin a new adventure and I'll be leaving in a couple days, so thought you needed to know. That's all."

"Another vacation?" Her oldest son chuckled. "Wish I had your job. Where you off to this time?"

"Well, it's not exactly a vacation, son." She could feel his confusion through the brief silence that followed, and struggled for words.

"Not a vacation?" he finally asked.

"No, and I've quit my job as well. Last shift is today." *Damn, talk about blunt.* She took a deep breath in reply to another pause. "I was going to write you first, but decided that wasn't fair. Ben and I are taking a trip and we aren't sure where we're going or how long we'll stay." *This wasn't going to be easy no matter what she said.*

"Ben? Who's Ben? Oh, wait a minute. That the guy in Texas? Are you going to Texas again?"

"Yes, Ben is the guy in Texas, but he's not in Texas now. He's here with me. It's complicated and I should've told you both before, but Ben is the man I think I want to spend my life with. At least, what life we have left. We—"

"Wait just a minute!" Her son's tone was no longer tinged with the softness of sleep. "You've quit your job and now you're taking a trip to *you don't know where* for *you don't know how long* with some guy that showed up from Texas. Do I have that right?"

Now, it was her that hesitated before answering. She realized how this must sound to him.

"You don't have it exactly right, hon, but most of it. Ben is not *just* some guy who showed up from Texas. We've known each other for several months now." She inhaled again. "I'm shutting the house up for a couple months until I know more of what—"

"Mom, have you gone crazy?" he cut her off again. "This isn't like you! To run off on impulse to travel and see places, yes, that's you. And, I've been glad to see that. Even running off to Texas to help one who's sick and alone, that's you. But Christ, to quit your job, abandon the house and go

176

flitting off to God knows where with God knows who is a bit much! What would dad think anyway? Christ, Mom!"

She heard him sigh heavily before going on. "I'm coming down there to meet this man! Don't you dare leave until I get there!"

She felt her own anger triggered, but held it down. "Excuse me? Your father would want me to be happy, first of all. He'd want me to live and be all the things he believed in and taught me were important. And you know I just don't *flit* about anything. I never have and I'm not going to start now." Sensing that her voice was rising, she paused.

"Yes mother, but . . . ." His voice trailed off.

Mother? "But nothing, hon," she said gently. "I know this comes as a surprise to you, and it will to your brother, but I do have my own life to think about now, just as the both of you have yours. We plan on leaving in a day or two so there isn't time for you to come and meet Ben right now. Besides, he doesn't require your approval, nor do I."

She bit her lip, realizing he was right in a way about this not being like her, at least to them. But it was like her to her. Exactly like her.

"But, I promise, I'll call you every couple days, even if just to check in and let you know where we are and I'm all right."

"But, mom, listen—"

"At this point, all I'm asking for is your support and your trust. All I'm asking, hon. I think I deserve that from you."

"Damn, I need to chew on this for awhile," he finally said. "I'll call back later. At least promise me you won't take off before we talk again."

She heard the concern in his voice and smiled. "No, I won't leave without talking to you again. I promise. And, I still have to call your brother. I'd appreciate it if you'd allow me to tell him myself, before you talk to him." She could visualize the flurry of phone calls between the two boys, well, men, now.

177

"Have you heard? Mom's finally gone off the edge. She's about to run off with some guy from Texas," the one would say.

"No!" would come the shocked reply from his brother.

"Yep, just gonna close up the house and hit the road with this nut, whoever he is."

"No!" the other would say. "Should we call the cops? Fly down there? Throw his ass out?"

It touched her, actually. They were caring and protective kids and she was grateful to have them.

She said goodbye and sighed as she clicked off. Gazing out over the railing into the lush green, again a rush of sentiment took hold. She loved this place. It was her home. It had wrapped itself around her like a blanket in the last months alone, releasing Jeff's part in it and becoming hers. Just hers. Yet, she knew Ben would never understand that. He'd always feel like an intruder inside these walls, so she'd have to leave it for a time. But she'd never give it up entirely. She just couldn't.

The phone was quiet in his hand now and he tried to absorb what his mother had just told him. One thing she'd said managed to make its mark. Dad had always been one to follow a dream, chase a challenge, so she was just doing the same.

Why should I be shocked that my mother would continue the 'spirit'? And, she was right that dad would want her to. Awww, hell, we'll still be a family; nothing would, or could, ever change that. Yeah, what am I worried about? This Ben guy must be okay or Mom wouldn't even entertain such a notion. Besides, she's been alone since dad left, and we've been after her to meet someone.

Because of the suddenness of it, that's why. And why all the mystery? Why do they have to go off to parts unknown? Leave the house standing empty? No address, no way to contact her. And, she never questions those 'inner' things she talks about all the time. Whatever they are. Why not? Dad didn't question either. What's wrong with me? Hell, I

178

question everything. Damn! I better call my brother right this minute.

Laying the phone down for the second time, she noticed movement inside the house through the glass doors but felt no need to get up. He would want a few minutes to himself to wake up and gather his wits before getting into a conversation. Especially one about her phone calls.

The call to her youngest had pretty much followed the course of the first, as she'd known it would, and now her thoughts returned to Ben. She'd just sit and sip her coffee and wait until he found her.

Moments later he appeared at the door, his own mug in hand. She moved to the farthest chair so he could sit by the plant table with his coffee. *Funny how things around here were now set up for one.*

"Nickel for your thoughts," he said, taking the seat she'd opened up for him.

"Nickel? What happened to pennies?" She smiled at him. "Good morning, by the way."

"Okay, penny then. It's too early to argue, and besides it looks like it's going to be a nice day."

She nodded and looked away, hiding the slight sadness in her heart.

"Today's the day, isn't it," he said, "Your last shift at work?"

"Yes, sure is."

"Not having second thoughts about all this are you, Abby?" He noticed the phone lying on the table, but waited for her answer.

"Not at all. I'm dreading going in to work, even today, but I will. I do want to leave on good terms. Never burn a bridge and all that, you know," she said. "Besides, it's Friday. We'll have all weekend to tie up loose ends and we can leave Monday if you like. The only service I'm stopping is the phone and cable TV, and they can be turned off from their offices on Tuesday morning. I'll call this afternoon

179

before work if you think you'll be ready to go by then." She didn't mention his son and what he planned to do about that.

"Oh," she went on, "and I just talked to both the kids and they're aware of our plans. Not thrilled, as I suspected, but at least I've told them."

"I figured that might be what you were doing out here when I saw the phone lying there. Are they going to be okay with this? I imagine they think you've popped a cork or something. Coming out of the blue like that."

"Well, yes." She laughed at his remark. "They questioned the degree of my sanity for a few minutes there, but after the initial shock they'll be fine."

"It's a wonder they aren't heading this way as we speak to throw my ass out of here. Should I keep an eye on my back today while you're at work?"

She laughed as he said exactly what she'd been thinking, and what was probably being said between the brothers right about now. "Nah, don't worry about your back. You might be careful who you open the door to, though." She played along with his mood, but he turned serious.

"You can't really blame them, babe. Might be a little different if they'd met me or something, but not even knowing who their mother is about to run off around the country with is a bit much."

"They trust me, Ben. Once the idea sets a bit everything will be fine. Besides, I told them I'd keep in touch often. You let me worry about them, and you concentrate on getting ready. I'm ready to take off to . . . where was that again? Maine? Oh God, Maine." She stood and approached the door. "I'm ready for more coffee. You?"

"No, I have plenty. You coming back out here with it?"

"Yeah, I'll be back in a minute, but not for long. I've got things to do before work. I need to clean out that fridge for one thing. And go shopping for woolen underwear, snowshoes, and an electric blanket." She winked over her shoulder, then stepped back to kiss the top of his forehead. "Maine? Damn!"

"You might want to go by the pet store and check out the supply of sled dogs, too." He chuckled as she left, but once she was inside, he sighed. He sensed she was trying hard to sound cheerful, but her eyes whispered sadness. Leaving this place wasn't going to be easy for her at first and he realized that. But once on their way, she'd be fine. Or, he hoped so anyway.

He wondered more how he was going to be with all this. He'd had second thoughts again and again. But shit, he wanted this time with her and he'd just have to take his chances that the pain wouldn't return, that the damn treatment had knocked the tumor into recession, or eliminated it altogether. It might be his last chance to experience this strange new love he felt, and just maybe, the happiness that had always eluded him. He peered out over the yard below and thought about their future.

Inside, she poured her coffee and wondered about the idea forming in her mind. It bothered her that Ben hadn't made an effort to contact his own son. She disliked the idea of doing anything sly to interfere, but her mentioning it had gotten no results. I just don't see how we'll achieve our own dreams when he, obviously, lives with all these past regrets, she thought.

"Okay you, ten minutes is all you get, then I must get busy," she quipped as she carried her coffee to the chair across from him. "And speaking of pocket change, you look as if I need to offer dimes for your thoughts. Anything I should know?"

"What?" He returned from his daydream at the sound of her voice. "Oh. No, just thinking I need to check the car for emergency equipment while you're at work. Maybe go to the hardware store and get whatever we need. Knowing you, that will require a list," he said, returning to the previous humor.

"Well, I suppose it's the pilot in you. Can't be helped, all this pre-flight safety business. Me, I just hook up the old CB, check the tires, fill the tank, hit the road and take off."

"Yes, and with your methods we might just make it to the state line even." He laughed. "You leave this up to me

181

and concern yourself with getting all your clothes in one overnight bag. Now, I'll let you get on with your chores and I'm going to get started on mine." He rose from his chair and looked at her over the top of his glasses with a smile of anticipation.

She muttered some kind of agreement, but she wasn't looking at him. He followed her eyes to the tree branch overhead. Two squirrels sat there watching them almost as if they understood what was being said.

"I'll get your breakfast right away, little fellas," he heard her say and then he knew why her hesitation at leaving. These were the only friends she had now, the squirrels and all the other critters, as she called them.

Gathering their mugs and the phone, she moved toward the door with him. He hugged her close as they entered the house together, but said no more.

Amber finished scrubbing out the refrigerator then, on impulse, reached up in the cabinet above it and pulled out the phone directory. Ben had gone to the hardware store and now would be a good time to follow up on her idea. Turning the pages toward the back of the book she stopped in the R's. "Ri . . . Riley. Damn, there's quite a few," she said out loud. "But only one on Channel Drive; that must be him."

She remembered the name of the street where she'd dropped Ben off the night after coffee months ago. Dialing the number, and wishing the knot in her stomach would go away, she was about to give up after the fifth ring when another sleepy voice came over the wire.

"Hello?"

"Hello. I'm sorry to wake you, and you don't know me, but I'm a friend of your father's." *It dawned on her she didn't know the young man's name. Ben, like her, had always referred to him as son.*

After a brief pause, the voice said, "My father doesn't live here. In fact, I don't know where my father is. You must have the wrong number."

"Is your father's name Ben Riley?"

Silence, then, "I'm sorry, but you have the wrong number."

"Well, if your father's name is Ben Riley and he stayed with you a few months back on Channel Drive, I don't have the wrong number."

"Wait. Is my dad okay? Who'd you say this was again?" His voice was alert now, and concerned.

"Yes, your dad is okay. He's here in town. My name is Amber Allyson, and we met when he was here visiting you last spring. We've become close friends, you could say, and we're planning a trip together. So, I thought you might like to come by and see him before we leave on Monday."

She was beginning to think she'd made a big mistake, but it was too late to worry about it now. She couldn't hang up or he'd be worried, if not down right angry.

"You're saying, Ms. Allyson, that my dad is in town, the two of you are taking off somewhere, yet I'm hearing from you, not him? Did it occur to you that if my dad wanted to see me he would've called himself?" The irritation had returned to his voice.

"Well, that's just it," she answered. "He thinks you don't want to see him, so I'm calling without him knowing."

There was no response.

"Listen, let me tell you where I live and you come by, or call him even," she went on. "I have to leave for work soon and you could have some time alone together. I'm sorry, I know this is a strange call and I don't mean to upset you. I'd like to see your dad at ease, and you as well. He loves you, you know." She managed to rattle off her address and phone number before she heard the *click.*

"Well, at least I tried," she said to the wolf poster looking down at her from the cabinet door. Apparently Ben had been right about his son after all. How, she thought, could a father and son end up like that? It just doesn't make sense at all.

She was gathering up her extra uniforms that needed returning as Ben came through the door laden with purchases.

"Well, for Pete's sake. What'd you do, buy out the store?"

"Nope, but we'll damn sure make Maine," he announced.

He looked so darn cute standing there, a long flashlight protruding out of one of the bundles, she couldn't help herself. She went to him and wrapped her arms around him, bags and all. He didn't see the moisture escaping her eyes as she laid her head on his chest. *I wish his son could see him now, she thought.*

"Hey. Isn't it about time for you to get that last shift in?"

"I've things to do. Now on with you, you're holding me up from my appointed tasks," he said, disengaging himself from her hug.

Amber walked into the store in uniform for the last time. The girls up front smiled at her as she headed back to her department, and she gave them an uneasy smile back. When she got to the end of the aisle, she saw the balloons and the big grease-painted banner. *Good Luck, Amber. We'll Miss You* stood out in bright blue. A fairly large circle of employees and customers alike stood clapping as she approached. This time her tears fell openly.

NO REGRETS?

The weekend was spent trying to decide what to take and what not. Everything held a memory, everything was precious. Yet, none of it, or very little, could fit into the car. Ben's suitcase was already in the trunk, and, for the first time, she realized just how small her car was, space-wise.

"Are you about finished with closing up inside? Pulling appliance plugs and all?" he asked.

But she didn't hear him. It suddenly dawned on her that she'd be leaving everything behind. Everything. All her memories, her furniture, her paintings and photographs, the chairs, the coffee table Jeff made from an old Apple tree trunk . . . and Jeff . . . *everything!* She felt more vulnerable than she ever had in her whole life. *I must be crazy, like they say. How can I do this? How can I go off and just . . . .*

"Babe?"

She looked up at him staring at her, as if he understood. "Listen, Abby, once we get settled, we'll come back with a trailer.

"No, it's all right. I just got caught off guard, that's all. I'll be fine." She forced a smile. "You'll see."

"Okay, but, you know, why not take one or two small things? Little things from the past. Mementos. You want to?"

By late afternoon her car looked like something from a yard sale. The back seat was crammed full of anything and everything, from dishes to dish soap, towels, a stand-up lamp that stuck out from one window, collectibles, clothes, the laptop, two plants, a wall clock, a box of photos and posters. And, of course, the huge bear.

"Jesus Christ!" he yelled when surveying the car. "We'll look like gypsies on the road. A couple of hunkies just off the goddamn boat. Hell, I said a few things, not half the damn house!"

"Oh, be quiet," she snapped back. "These few things won't get in the way, and besides, a woman needs certain things in her life to feel comfortable."

"Comfortable? Damn good thing you aren't planning on taking the animals, too." He paused, looking at her. "You aren't? Planning on taking the wildlife, too?"

"Don't be silly. Of course not. Besides, this is their home. Why would I want to uproot them from their home?" Her voice lowered into a sad tone.

He missed the point. "Good. I don't need some squirrel gnawing on my foot while I drive, or some . . ." He stopped, because she'd turned away and he could tell she was about to cry again.

What an ass I am, he thought. Here she is, giving up everything that means anything to her anymore, and I'm complaining about the few things she's packed into the car.

"Listen," he started to say, "I didn't mean it that way." But she was gone up the stairs, leaving him, again, to his own thoughts.

Man-o-man, he thought. I sure as hell hope we both know what we're doing.

Inside the house, Amber was thinking the same thing.

The following morning Ben was up at four am, making coffee and filling the thermos, while Amber attended to the final shutdown of the house. All windows Locked? Yes. Plugs unplugged. Yes. The sliding doors locked, too? Yes, that, too. And then it was time and they both walked down the stairs to her car, which now looked like a pick-up. Sort of.

"No regrets?" he asked her.

She shook her head no, but hesitated. "There is one last thing I have to do. Won't take long."

She disappeared around the side of the house, and he put the thermos into the car and fiddled around, waiting for her. Dawn was just approaching, its light working wonder on the moss and tree lichen, turning the darkness into color.

He wondered what could be taking her so long and quietly moved under the house looking for her. He saw her then, squatting down by a fern patch, talking quietly to someone or some thing. And then it dawned on him that she was talking to Fred, the big Black Indigo snake that lived in the pit.

Slowly, he moved to where he could get a better view, and *JESUS!* He'd never seen Fred before, and it startled him. The snake was at least five feet long and purplish blue in the morning light, perhaps as big around as a half dollar. It had curled itself near her ankle and was lying there while she talked to it in quiet, soothing tones. She was crooning to it as one might a cat, and damn if it didn't seem to understand that she was saying goodbye. At one point it even raised its head to look at her, and to him it seemed it might strike.

But it didn't, and as he would later learn from her, wouldn't. She gently nudged it away, said something to it, and Fred uncoiled and slid slowly back into the ferns. When she stood and turned, tears were streaking down her face and he felt a tug at his own heartstrings.

This is no ordinary woman, he thought. She has some kind of gift, some kind of understanding that the rest of humanity has forgotten, or never had. Whatever it is, it's special.

She approached the car along the path and he came up from behind.

"Where've you been?" she asked, rubbing her eyes, pretending it was the sunlight making her squint.

"Had to pee," he said non-comittally. "You ready?"

She looked around one more time, then turned and smiled. "Ready." With that they got into the car and he drove away.

As they rounded the corner, a car came down the street slowly. The young man inside strained to see house numbers, and then stopped in front of the house on stilts. After a pause, he got out and walked slowly up the drive, looking around. He checked the address on a slip of paper then went up the stairs to the front door and knocked. He waited and then knocked again. Getting no answer, he crumpled the paper into his pocket, returned to his car, got in, and pulled away.

Out on the main highway, he reached over and patted Amber's knee, very conscious, after what he'd just witnessed in the garden, the lengths she'd go in the following of her intuition.

"Ben?" she spoke softly.

"Mmm-hmm?" He smiled, without looking at her.

"I know you said you wanted to take the main interstate to the line, but I'd like to follow the coast road out on the keys. We can pick it up over the intracoastal bridge when we get downtown. It goes to the Skyway Bridge over Tampa Bay, and once north of Tampa we can take Old Nineteen. That runs closer to the water and goes up through the Sawgrass swamps and the old towns not affected by development. It's relaxing and different than around here."

"Well, we're not supposed to be in a rush, so that's fine with me," he answered. "Point me in the right direction."

"Just keep heading straight on this highway. Once we get downtown, I'll tell you the turn."

"Okay, noted," he said.

"Good." She smiled at him. "The Gulf is soothing first thing in the morning. You can almost see the colors change with the rising sun. We can have lunch at a place I know of just south of the swamps, and there are a couple good state roads that connect back to I-75 south of the state line."

"Did you roger that, Tail?" he asked over his shoulder with authority.

"Tail? Who's tail?" she questioned with eyes widening.

"That's why you brought the bear, isn't it? To ride tail gunner and watch for Papa Bear? You know. Smokey."

"Oh." She laughed, turning to see Bear sitting behind them, his glass eyes sparkling in the morning light.

"Yes, ma'am, ol' Tail Gunner, there, can keep an eye out for his own," he said again.

"Why? I'm not driving," she answered in all seriousness. "It's unlikely they'll pull you over, unless it's for going too slow."

He burst out laughing, and then relaxed against the seat with an audible sigh. Aaah, he thought, she's gonna be fine. Yes, this is going be a wonderful day after all . . . the first day of the rest of our lives. Whatever time we have.

Amber lapsed into silence as he drove north through the city, speaking only to direct the turn west out to the coast road. As they topped the intracoastal bridge she inhaled deeply as the sea, wearing its early morning sheen came into view. Funny what the ocean did to her. Seeing it made her think of endless; smelling it made her think of life. Now, she thought of a new life about to begin.

Glancing at Ben, who seemed taken with the view himself, the doubts of leaving home ebbed. For this moment, this day, home meant this car, and the man beside her driving it. Once clear of the bridge, he eased into the right turn lane, onto the road that would follow the coast north. North to where, she wasn't sure, but somewhere up there was Maine. In between were miles of road, experiences, and time. All of a sudden, she'd never felt more at home in her life.

"Coffee?" she asked, reaching down for the thermos on the floor.

"Yes, and breakfast if you spot a place."

"I know just the place for that, too. It's just south of the Skyway Bridge and has tables outside right by the water. Can you wait about thirty minutes?"

"Don't know. It'll be close," he said, feigning weakness.

"Well, then, pull over and let me drive and we'll be there in fifteen," she replied, matter of factly.

"Uh-uh." He winked at her. "No crash helmet."

"Suit yourself. There's a cookie in the back if you get desperate."

They sat side by side at the small table, eating their breakfast and making small-talk about the day and the trip. An incredible day had dawned, and the sea spray billowing over the seawall shimmered in the sun. Then in unison they stopped talking and looked at each other, sharing a silent thought.

She stood first and threw her toast crumbs to the gulls already lined up on the seawall.

"We have to go now, little birdfriends. Today, me and Ben are living the first day of the rest of our lives," she cooed to them. She bent over and kissed the top of his head. "Ready to head north, driver?"

He rose and followed her toward the silver car, its iridescent finish like the sea mist, sparkling in the sun. It too, seemed full of energy and sweat like a thoroughbred ready to run. He couldn't remember the last time he'd felt this free.

They'd continued north along the water to the Bridge, hooked up with Old 19, and left the density behind. The road began to curve inland now, away from the sea and into swamp country. With hardly any traffic and Amber staring dreamily at the surroundings, he relaxed and looked around at the primeval sawgrass swamp. He imagined how this land must have looked millions of years ago before the encroachment of humans and their settlements.

"Abby?" he asked, breaking into her reverie.

"Yes, hon? Want me to drive a while?"

"In a bit. I'm fine for now. But I have a question for you."

"What?"

"Do you believe in telepathy?"

"You mean reading people's minds? Sending and receiving messages?"

190

A flock of herons crossed the road above and in front of them, their large white wings beating effortlessly. "Well, yes, kind of like that. But more like sharing thoughts, sharing minds even." He watched the herons as they uniformly set into a glide.

"Hmmm, I do between certain forces, certain people. But no, I don't think we can just walk up to any stranger and read what's going on in their head. That would be a terrible thing! The one place you should be able to go, with no worry of intrusion by another, is your mind. Why do you ask such a thing anyway?"

He shrugged. "Oh, I don't know. Watching you with the animals, the nature around you, and always going on about things being connected in some higher kind of way." He looked over at her. "Like us even."

She smiled. "Oh, I know. You're one of those brain versus mind types. The must have a grip on everything, kind. Mystery for you has to be explained. For me, that spoils the magic."

He grinned. "Magic? You're a witch, too?"

"By all means. Put a pretty good spell on you, didn't I?" She turned and winked at him.

"No, seriously," he went on, "for you it's a mind-over-matter kind of thing, I guess. You seem to think you can just fly off on a magic carpet ride above it all, that insights come to you through the eyes of a bird or that fox of yours. You think you can imagine yourself into a creation of some sort. Heal yourself even. If you can, I want to know how you can, that's all."

She pondered for a minute. "Well, let me see if I can explain to you how I think. Physically, can my body ride an asteroid, say? No. Can a hand, by itself, pick up a pen and write a word on a sheet of paper? No. But, the mind can create the book and create the movement of the hand that writes it, and all while riding an asteroid. Get it?"

"If you say so." He grinned.

"I believe in a Spirit and oneness with the Universe, many Universes even," she continued. "You love the idea

191

but don't quite buy it. Yet, your very curiosity is spiritual. Didn't know that, did you?"

"Well, no, I never thought of it like that."

"You're pragmatic and I'm adventuresome. You think like a Scientist, and I like a Spiritualist. I believe your Science *is* Nature, Creation, or God, whatever you wish to call it. We travel identical paths, but you with a flashlight, and me not needing one. Don't you see? We both love many of the same things, yes? We both feel a kinship with nature, all creatures, and that there's something special about stars dancing across the sky, even though they dance only in our minds. And we share with oceans, with wind and sky, and everything else, a connection of sorts, yes?"

"Well . . . ."

"Well? Well? And there's more, lots more examples. But Ben, can we talk about this another time? I'd really rather just enjoy the day."

Holy shit, he thought. Remind me not to ask again.

She turned to look out the window at two Blue Herons wading in a water-filled ditch near the edge of the road. "Look. See that?" She pointed. "See those birds? You think they worry about why they're birds? Or if they should be birds? No, they just are what they are. And, so are we."

He reached over the console and took her hand. *How could he argue with that, he wondered?*

TAG-ALONG

The mid-day sun filtered down through the pines in the hammock where Amber spread out sandwiches, chips, and drinks. They'd spotted a ramshackle country store in Otter Creek where an antique Coca Cola sign hanging in a rusty frame announced: *Now Serving Lunch.* She'd smiled to herself when "lunch" consisted of the pre-packaged variety housed in an equally old Pepsi cooler.

Yet, the store had character with its creaking old boards, and the hollow slap of the screen door, its holes failing to keep the flies at bay, shutting behind them as they entered. A rather lazy ceiling fan barely interrupted the heat inside, and burlap bags holding seeds for the area farmers seemed more the intent of the place than lunch or tourists.

The globes of glass containers spread out along the counter now held dust instead of penny candy, but there was a plethora of utensil knick-knacks and the odds and end staples that may be discovered missing in some farm kitchen in between Saturday trips to market.

"City folk, I see." The toothless old fellow behind the counter grinned, looking over Amber's head at the convertible parked on the gravel. "Afraid, we ain't got no fancy stuff here, but y'all help yourselves."

"Thank you." She smiled back at him. "I'm not looking for anything fancy, just a snack. But perhaps you can tell me if there is a roadside park near by?"

"Sure is, ma'am. Couple old eating tables just down the road a piece. That is, if you don't mind sharing your lunch with a gator or two. Got them tables sitting right by the river, they do. Sometimes a big one will haul itself right up on the bank, I'm told." He grinned, waiting for her face to show shock at the thought.

"Oh, I don't mind a lazy gator, or two." She played along knowing the man was trying to scare her in a teasing way. "You see," she quipped, "I'm half gator myself. One of them might even be a nephew."

The shopkeeper grinned, delighted at the jousting, or maybe just any conversation at all. "Hee, hee, yes ma'am. Maybe you are at that. Y'all just passing through?"

"Yes we are, and I want to thank you for your hospitality and for having this wonderful store here. We city folks have lost all our heart, you know, and seeing a real store with a real person is charming." Her smile was genuine.

The old man continued to grin, and even blushed at her compliments. "Well, you and the mister over there," he gestured at Ben poking around in a row of barrels holding nails and chicken wire, "just enjoy yourselves. Oh, and we're durn glad to have some city folks with manners stop by for a change. Y'all just enjoy your lunch, too, and let me know if I can be of any help." He took her money and punched the keys on the old cash register, making change right in his head. A lost art.

"We sure will, sir, and thank you again. Have a wonderful day."

Back outside she'd laughed to herself at how often people forget that the small towns in north Florida are about as deep south "Cracker" as you can get. Sad, too, that their old-fashioned charm was missed now that everyone traveled the interstates and Florida itself had since been wrapped in the glitz of tourism and developers. Somehow, to her, a gator "hauled up on a creek bank" was more appealing.

194

Ben approached the table just as she was finishing laying it out and burst out laughing. Surprised, she looked up to see him looking at the bear sitting up at the table.

"Well, don't you think he needs a break from his post, too?" she asked. "He'll be going on duty when we leave because I'm ready to drive for awhile. Besides, knowing you, after lunch you'll be needing a nap."

"Right, you are," he admitted, "especially after that gator hunt I've just been on."

"You don't look as if you've been mud wrestling. Didn't you find one?" She attempted a look of disappointment.

"Nope, must have scared him off," Ben quipped back, then added, almost reverently, "This is a wonderful place, Abby."

"Yes, it is," she said, taking a panoramic view of the area surrounding the dilapidated old table. "Those huge Live Oaks with their wisps of Spanish Moss are probably older than you and I put together. Now come eat your lunch before it's carried off by that gator behind you."

"WHAT? Holy shit . . . !" Ben paled and jerked around to see.

She almost fell over the bench laughing as the color returned to his face. And he laughed, too, realizing it was her that had played the joke this time.

"And, after lunch we can pick up Highway 47," she continued, trying to regain her composure, "and that'll bring us into I-75 at Lake City. Maybe we can find a place to spend the night this side of the line, a quiet place where we can take a walk or something."

Ben agreed, munching his sandwich and occasionally looking over his shoulder.

The sun was tinting the tree tops crimson when an old motor lodge greeted them around a curve.

"Look, Ben, how quaint. Let's stop now." Amber was fidgeting excitedly in her seat and pointing to a row of free standing cottages nestled under a row of Carrotwood trees. A sign reading "V-can-y" was winking in old pale neon. "And, look at that!" she squealed. "There's a swing! Not a damn swimming pool, a damn swing! Stop, Ben."

"Okay, okay. Relax, will you? I'm stopping. Look you're loosing your grapes all over the floor." He tried to sound perturbed, but was grinning at her exuberance.

She gathered the grapes she'd found at a roadside fruit stand and shoved them back in the bag. "Never mind the grapes. I love this place. There's a real honest-to-goodness *swing*! It's been a long day and we're tired. Please, Ben, can we stay here?"

"Yes, Abby. Calm down. I'm stopping."

It had been a long day. The roads had been bumpy from under-use, their tar and pitch rising up to the pull of the weeds in the cracks and the weight of the John Deere tractors of the locals. Yet the sights had been incredible, a step back in time. Where a city-on-my-cell-phone yuppie might have seen decay and ruin, they'd seen wholesomeness and a simpler time, marveling that places like this still existed. The paint may have faded, those who took care of them the same, but the spirit still lived in each, and they'd felt a rejuvenation. A giddiness. A connection.

She'd said, "look at this" and "look at that" so many times he'd lost count. They were almost kids again, eager to ride their first roller coaster, try out new skates, eat their first red snow cone or pink cotton candy. How many miles they'd gone, they didn't know, didn't care. They had the rest of their lives, so why worry about miles? And here Amber was, again, fairly jumping in her seat over the spotting of a rotted old swing.

He pulled up to the middle building declaring itself to be the office with a hand-painted sign in the window. Amber pulled herself from the car and walked hastily toward the swing, leaving him to go inside and arrange for a cottage. His thoughts, watching her as he walked to the office, wandered back to the first day they'd walked a shore and she kept bounding ahead to check out a treasure on the sand. Moments later he reappeared and called to her as he headed for the door to Number Six. He opened the door for her and then went to retrieve their suitcases from the trunk.

She stepped inside and turned on the light in the tiny room. It reminded her of days when she and Jeff were on the road.

"Excuse me," he said, half-way pushing around her and dropping the bags onto the bed. "Oh boy," he muttered, surveying the room. "Not exactly the Taj Mahal, is it?"

"Oh pish," she scoffed. "It's clean and right now that bed looks like it was made for a queen, I'm so tired. What a day."

"Yeah, sure was," he agreed.

He moved their luggage onto the fold-up cot provided for families, and just fell into bed. "I think we overdid it, babe. I feel like I've been riding Brahma bulls.

"Yes, a little stiff myself. I'm going to take a hot shower," she called from a check of the bathroom. There was no reply and when she peeked around, Ben was dozing off where he'd fallen, still in his clothes. "Damn, Mr. Excitement," she muttered, but grinned at the sight of him.

She drew back the shower curtain, turned the hot faucet on, undressed and slipped inside the recently tiled shower. How divine the hot water felt, its steam rising around her in a haze. Standing there letting it run over her, her thoughts again turned to other rented rooms, other showers, and road trips. She loved the traveling, the seeing things new and different, and was content that Ben, too, had really enjoyed the day. *He's special in his own way, Jeff. And he's good to me, really. You'd like him, I know you would.*

When she came out of the bathroom, Ben was sound asleep, so she rolled him aside and slipped under the covers.

"Goodnight, gentle Ben," she whispered, and then turned the bedside lamp off. And just as suddenly, turned it back on and sat bolt upright.

"Ohmigod. I almost forgot."

Jumping out of bed and grabbing her bathrobe, she ran out to the car. Within a minute or so she reappeared, but this time with her standup lamp in one hand and the big bear

197

clenched tight against her with the other while struggling to get them both through the doorway into the room.

"There," she said, placing the lamp at the foot of the bed and tucking the bear securely in the middle, before sliding back under the covers.

Outside, two eyes glowed yellow in the old yard lamp as the motel cat watched Amber disappear through the door, and then ran off into the night with a slight meowing.

She woke with a start, unsure of where she was. There was no familiarity in the gloom, only a yellowish cast on a strange wall. Raising on one elbow to see better, recognition returned as she came face-to-face with the bear and heard Ben's breathing alongside.

Falling back down on the pillow, she wondered what had awakened her so suddenly as there'd been no dream. Lying motionless for a moment, listening to Ben's even breathing, she wondered what time it was. Had she slept long? The light coming through the green drape over the single sash window was not enough to read her watch by, and was barely enough to light the yard outside.

She kicked the covers, now a wad at her feet, away and sat up, swinging her legs off the bed and searching out her thongs with her foot. Slipping her feet into them, she sort of stumbled to the bathroom, shut the door, and fumbled for the light switch.

"Damn, it's only 5:15," she moaned in the glare of the bathroom light. "Oh well, might as well get up."

She splashed water on her face and dug her toothbrush out of the travel case. "Maybe I can get some coffee at that gas station across the road," she said quietly. Then looking at herself in the mirror, thought, *Amber, you're really going to have to stop talking to yourself, you've got company now,* and then laughed at her own foolishness.

Suddenly, there it was again. That sound. I knew something woke me up, she thought. What was that sound?

She turned the water off and listened intently. All was quiet. She hurried then, finished brushing her teeth and

198

wiped her face. Turning the light back off, she slipped silently back into the room and grabbed clean jeans and a top from her suitcase. Half-way back to the bathroom, there it was again. It was like a little squeak, but she knew that sound, knew it well. Where was it coming from? Not in the room. Outside? Well, there's only one way to find out.

She quickly dressed, ran a brush through her hair, then moved quietly out the door, pulling it to but not locked, behind her. The faint light in the east cast an eerie glow, and the morning dew was heavy in the yellow pall of the yard light. Walking to the corner of the cottage, she peered into the darkness between the buildings.

There it was again, coming from the back. She inched her way along the wall and knelt at the rear corner of their unit, waiting, letting her eyes adjust to the darkness. And then she saw the cat coming out from the narrow crawl space beneath their room.

"So you're the one I heard," she whispered. "I knew I wasn't imagining things." At the sound of her voice the cat hurried away, ducking around the corner of the neighboring cabin.

"Well, that's okay, little guy. I didn't mean to scare you. Heard you out here and just wanted to make sure you were all right." She stood back up and started for the door to the room. As she rounded the corner, the lights came on in the gas station and small store across the road. "Hmmm, bet I could get coffee there."

In the room, she grabbed her purse and walked across the street. A bell over the door reminded her of bookstores. A heavy-set woman was making coffee in an old Bunn machine and spreading out donuts on a tray.

"Good morning," Amber called cheerily. "I sure am glad you open early."

"Morning to you, too, Missy. Yes'm, bet you're staying across the street at the motel, that right? Most of them comes here for their morning coffee." The woman smiled. "You're up mighty early. Just now six."

She got two large coffees, a donut for Ben and a small bottle of orange juice from the cooler while chatting amicably with the woman, who like everyone everywhere they'd stopped, seemed glad for the conversation.

"When we leave, I'll come back and fill up with gas," she said gathering her things in a carry tray. She suddenly felt as if she needed to, no, *wanted* to, patronize these small places that struggled in the competition with the chains on the interstate exits.

"Well, we'd appreciate your business, ma'am. Sure would. See y'all a little later on. Now don't forget."

"Oh, I won't," Amber promised with the tinkling of the bell.

It was lighter now as she retraced her steps back to their cottage. Ben should be waking soon, but he didn't mind if his coffee wasn't real hot anyway. She'd check on him and if he was still sleeping she'd take hers to the swing. The table light was on when she entered, and the bed was empty except for Bear. The water was running in the bathroom and the other suitcase was now open. She set Ben's coffee and donut on the dresser and turned to the abandoned bear.

"Come on with me, Bear," she said gathering the stuffed animal into her arms. "We'll have coffee and orange juice out on the swing while Ben finishes his shower. Sun will be above the treetops soon and it's going to be a beautiful morning." Stopping at the car, she set her coffee on the hood, put the bear behind the wheel and reached in and got some paper towels off the roll in the back seat. "You wait here until I get my coffee and wipe us off a spot on the swing; I know that dew has it drenched. Won't take a minute."

At last they were situated on the swing, and she inhaled the morning air deeply. It smelled of pine needles and wet sand. The old swing sang a sing song of un-oiled chains as she moved it gently to and fro with her feet.

"How do you like that, huh?" she cooed to the bear.

Movement in the corner of her eye made her turn her head in time to see the motel cat coming from between the buildings with something in its mouth.

"Caught your breakfast, I see. But if you don't mind, I'd prefer if you didn't join us." She chuckled softly expecting to see the cat dart out of sight with its prize. Instead, it kept walking steadily toward her. "Now don't be bringing that over here. I know you're just being a cat, but I really don't care to witness you eating your catch. Go on. Shoosh."

Now in full daylight, she could see the cat had been nursing kittens by the swell under its belly. "Oh, so *that's* what you're doing under the cabin, huh? Raising a family." The cat kept right on coming toward her, seeming unafraid of her now. "Oh damn, you insist upon company for breakfast, do you?"

Hearing this, the mama cat broke into a trot. She came as close as she dared, then dropped her 'catch' about ten feet from Amber's foot. She nudged it gently, once, and then took off like the proverbial "bat out of hell." Amber stared wide-eyed. "Oh, my god," she whispered, realizing what it was.

Ben exited the room a few moments later, coffee in hand, and looked around. Spotting Amber on the swing, he walked over.

"Why am I not surprised?" he muttered as he saw the bear with her on the swing. "Got room for me on that contraption?" But she didn't answer, just seemed to go on whispering to the bear.

"Damn bear gets more attention than I do," he half-grumbled. "Say! I said do you have room for one more in your little gathering?" He raised his voice just below a yell.

Amber jumped up and whirled around. "Oh, Ben! Hurry. Look! Will you look at this precious baby? She just brought it right out here and dropped it at my feet. And he's scared and he's trembling. And what am I going to do? And . . . oh, Ben, can we keep it? Can we? Please? It won't be any trouble, I promise. And Bear will help. Why, it'll think the bear's its mom. All soft and furry just like her."

"Abby, what *are* you going on about? I don't understand a word you're babbling. What have you got there anyway?"

"Can't you see? It's a kitten, a little orange kitten. It's just a baby, hardly a month old, I'd guess. Its mama just brought it to me and then ran off just like she wanted me to take care of it. Dammit, Ben, will you just look!" She moved close to him, cuddling a tiny ball of orange-striped fur.

"Abby, its mother will come back for it. You can't keep it. What in the hell are you going to do with it?" he protested.

"She brought it to me, I tell you, and she isn't coming back for it. She ran away! What do you mean, what am I going to do with it? I'm going to take care of it. What do you think I'm going to do with it? In fact, you're going to hold it right now while I go get it some milk. *Please,* Ben."

Before he could object further, Amber thrust the kitten in his arms and was running to the cottage to grab her purse. A full ten seconds later, she was running across the road to the gas station on the other side.

"Hell of a way to say good morning, I'd say. Do you always make such a flamboyant entrance into one's day?" he grumbled, looking down at the little ball of fur not much bigger than his cupped hands. "Damned if you ain't a cute little thing, and by the looks of the way that damned lunatic I'm hooked up with is carrying on, I guess I'm going to be stuck with you for awhile."

He rubbed the kitten gently with one finger trying to give it warmth, and felt it stir in his hands. He looked down at it and smiled, as he thought of Amber leaving all the critters who'd been her friends behind. "Ahhh," he lamented, "what's the point of arguing? Meant to be, maybe, that you just tag along."

He looked up to see if she was coming back. Not seeing her, he went on soothing the kitten, which yawned, even while still trembling, and his heart softened more by the second. "Just dropped off were you? Yes, I know that feeling. But hey, this is your lucky day, little guy." He paused. "Oh yes, you're a little guy. Okay." He grinned, upon the inspection. "You see, that damned lunatic . . . well, let's just say she's going to take good care of you. She's kind of like that."

202

A COUPLE OF NUTS

Amber held the speed steady at eighty despite the urge to press harder on the accelerator. The concrete gray of Interstate 75 stretched out ahead of them as the Sawgrass gave in to the red dirt farm land of southern Georgia. She turned and glanced at Ben. The tiny orange puff of their tag-along was balled in his lap, oblivious to his part in their adventure. The drone of the engine, like a mother's purr perhaps, had lulled him to sleep.

Ben seemed at ease as he gazed lazily at the passing scenery. Looking in the rearview mirror, she noted that even Bear in his rear seat lookout post seemed to be enjoying the ride, his button eyes looking back at her in a contented sort of stare.

What a sight we must make, she thought, a family of sorts in a temporary home on wheels and a limitless expanse for a yard. Even the silly lamp, now repacked, added its charm as it stuck out from the side.

Unlike the excitement of the previous day, today they'd limited their sightseeing to roadside rest stops, satisfied now to move on and see what lay before them. And wasn't that what they were supposed to do anyway? Whatever moved them at the moment? The world ahead was beckoning, and today they wanted to gather a chunk of it in.

Ben closed his eyes and listened to the road beneath them, how the tires sang, how the wind roared past, a melody all its own. He suddenly wanted to be a kid again, riding in the family car with no more concern than where the next hot dog stand would be, and did it have Kool-Aid.

The horn blast from a big rig passing in the other direction startled him, and he opened his eyes to see the driver wave. Amber must have flashed him some kind of signal with her lights. He smiled, knowing about her experiences on the road, and imagined how such a little thing like her must have looked in the cab of a giant eighteen wheeler.

The pop like a gunshot brought him from his thoughts and to full alert as the tire blew and the car swerved slightly.

"Damn!" he heard Amber swear as she took her foot off the pedal and let the car slow naturally, while quickly pushing the emergency flasher button to alert those behind. Thank God for tubeless, thank God for power steering, he thought as he sat up glimpsing at the speedometer leaving eighty. The car rolled, with a thumping sound, over to the shoulder, and he didn't know whether to smile or act nonchalant. "Well?" he said, looking over at her.

"Well, what?" she scowled back. "The stupid-ass tire blew, so what?" She knew what would be coming next.

He was stifling a laugh, watching her anger. "Well, can't say I didn't tell you not to drive so fast. Could've flipped us, you know."

"What? What are you talking about, flipped us? I've seen dragsters at two-fifty get into trouble, so what's the big deal?" She attempted to hide her own relief at the safe stop.

"All right, have it your way," he chortled. He leaned back into the seat, re-positioned the kitten in his lap and closed his eyes. "Let me know when you've changed the tire."

"What? *Me* change the tire?"

He opened one eye and looked at her. "Well, you were the one driving."

"Oh, bullshit, so what? I'm not changing the damn tire alone. You're gonna help." She paused, eyes widening. "You are going to help, aren't you?"

"Nope. I wasn't driving. You were. Driver changes the tire. Rules of the road, you know."

"To hell with that! I'll sit here until hell freezes over before I change the damn tire alone."

"Oh, really?" he answered, eyes still closed but barely able to contain the laughter within. "Then I guess here we'll sit until some poor fool comes along to do it, because I'm not changing the tire. That'll teach you to drive like a maniac."

"I don't believe you, Ben Riley!" She folded her arms across her chest and stared out the windshield. "Fine," she said.

"Fine," he said.

A car or two passed, then a big rig, then another car. The sun climbed high in the sky, birds flew, clouds passed, as Ben kept his eyes closed and Amber stared out the windshield.

"Fine," she said.

"Okay with me," he said.

More cars passed, more rigs, the bear stared with glass eyes and the kitten began to squirm in Ben's lap, probably getting hungry.

"Going to get a ticket sitting here, you know," he said.

"Fine," she said, her arms still folded.

"Mighty fine with me," he said, eyes still closed.

"Neither saw the police cruiser pulling slowly up behind them, nor the perplexed look on the trooper's face as he saw the lamp sticking out and the top of the bear's head.

"Howdy, ma'am, sir," the State Trooper nodded to them both, catching them by surprise. "What seems to be the trouble?"

"Trouble?" Ben asked.

"Yes sir, you're pulled over on the shoulder and just sitting here."

"Ohhh, that. No trouble, officer. We've got a flat tire is all," Ben said amicably.

The trooper looked. "So I see. So, don't you have a jack?"

"Of course we have a jack," Amber blurted out while turning to the officer. "What we're missing is chivalry."

The trooper looked to Ben who was making a circling motion with his finger and pointing at his head, as if to say she's crazy.

"Well, you can't just sit here on the shoulder, you know. You're creating a traffic hazard. If you need a tow truck, I'll call one for you."

"No, no, that won't be necessary, officer, but thank you," Ben answered. "We'll be on our way as soon as she changes the tire."

"See?" Amber blurted out again. "That's what I mean. Now I ask you, officer, what kind of a man would sit there and let a woman change a tire?"

Ben had lighted a cigarette and was blowing smoke rings.

The trooper looked at the two of them, at the bear, the kitten, and the lamp sticking out. *Oh, man. And I always think I've seen it all out here.* "Tell y'all what. I'll give you about ten minutes to be on your way, how's that?"

Amber looked at the smiling Ben and he looked back as they both got out of the car. He passed Tag-along to Amber then opened the trunk and got out a can of FIX-A-FLAT. With the trooper watching, he inflated the tire, kicked it once, and with a satisfied look pointed Amber to the passenger seat of the car. "I'll drive now, Abby. Thank you, Officer," he said turning to the trooper. "We'll be on our way and you have a good day." He swiped his hands together in a brushing motion and turned toward the car.

"I think we'd better get the hell out of here while we still can," he whispered as they got in. He started the car and drove slowly off, waving over his shoulder to the trooper.

The trooper stared at their departing car, shaking his head, and then turned back to his cruiser. "Next thing I'll

206

probably get is somebody from California, or worse, New York," he said out loud.

The road peeled away as they drove along, Ben still smiling and humming a tune.

"You mean," Amber began, "that we sat there for nearly two hours, and you had that can of stuff all along?"

"Of course. I told you I go prepared, but I also told you this was going to be an adventure."

"Going to jail is an adventure?"

He grinned but didn't answer.

"You know what?" she said. "You're the lunatic, not me." She smiled, too, in spite of herself.

"Yeah." He patted her knee, still grinning. "And I think it's time we stopped for lunch."

"You're certifiable, you know that?" She laughed.

"Yeah, that too." He glanced at the kitten balled up in her lap. "What do you think, Tag? You hungry too? Bet I could eat the hide off a buffalo about now."

She stared at him in disbelief. He really was enjoying this silly caper and, suddenly, she was too. Shaking her head, she got the *Atlas and Exit Guide* from beneath the seat and began to study it.

"Abby, are you looking for a place to have lunch or perusing mileage charts? I'm Hungry. Hunnn-gry!"

"Oh, be patient. You're not going to waste away in a matter of minutes. I'm trying to find an exit that will give us a back road up to the north Georgia mountains." She looked up hoping to see a mile marker. "We're coming up on Exit 66 and there's a Flying J truck stop there. According to this, it's the exit that will take us up to the lake country just south of Gainesville. Maybe we could stop for the night there."

"Well, if I don't get nourishment soon, I won't make it to nightfall, and that cat will be turning ferocious, and the bear may decide to eat us."

"Don't be so dramatic. Tag is sleeping like a baby, and besides, you just had donuts for breakfast." She reached over and gave his belly a poke. "Don't look like you're starving to me."

"What? Donuts for breakfast! That was five hours ago. Just because you can survive on a grape a day doesn't mean the rest of this menagerie should go on a fast along with you. And, don't be poking my belly. I'm liable to deflate any minute."

"Oh, God forbid. Here's the sign now, Exit 66 two miles. Take it and the J will be to your left."

"Do they have grits? I'm not eating in Georgia unless they have grits."

"Oh, who knows, dammit. We'll find out when we get there. And stop your complaining. Sheesh! It's your own fault for sitting on the side of the road for two hours being stubborn. Weren't worried about food then." She laughed as she poked his belly again. At which, he made some noise that sounded like the Pillsbury Dough Boy.

They found a parking place by the door of the Flying J restaurant and Ben didn't bother to wait, hopping out as soon as the car had stopped.

"I'll order you coffee," he called back as he went through the door.

She gently placed the kitten into her purse. "Yes," she whispered to the topaz eyes now staring out of her oversized bag, "chivalry is dead. Come on Tag, we'll get you some fish. Or, would you rather have chicken?"

She felt waves of nostalgia come over her as she entered the truck stop, and was almost drawn toward the Driver's Lounge. She'd spent many hours in such places, and had a feeling of instant rapport with the drivers at the wall of pay phones who were calling home, calling drop points, checking with brokers. It wasn't an easy life, and she had an admiration for those able to do it.

A faint "mewing" sound coming from her shoulder bag brought her back to the present. She spotted Ben sitting at a table by the far window, two coffee mugs in front of him.

"What took you?" he asked as she sat across from him. "I've already ordered ham and eggs with double grits so you can have some." He grinned at his own joke.

208

"Thanks, but no thanks. By the looks of you, I think you can handle it by yourself. All that's missing is a fire, a spit, and a wild boar roasting to complete the picture." She poured cream into her coffee and took up a menu. "Did you order for me, too?"

"Course not. How would I even know what you want? It's only been a day or two since you devoured a bag of grapes, so you're probably good for at least another week."

"Very funny."

"Yeah." He smiled, eyes sparkling.

"Hi, there," The waitress smiled at Amber. "Have you decided on anything, yet?" she asked while refilling both cups. "Your husband wasn't sure if you'd be eating."

"Immm, I think I'll have the melon fruit cup and a grilled chicken sandwich, but don't hold up my husband's meal. He's close to expiring, as you can see."

The waitress laughed and cracked her gum while scribbling on her pad. "Got it." Amber smiled and struggled not to laugh out loud at the *husband* remark.

The waitress left and Ben attempted a look of shock. "*You're* having a sandwich? Will wonders never cease?"

"No. I'm having a fruit cup. Tag is having a chicken sandwich, half of which I'm sure you'll eat later." She turned and looked out the window at the rows of rigs parked outside.

He followed her stare and suddenly remembered some of this had to be difficult for her.

"You okay?"

She nodded.

"Guess this does bring back lots of memories for you."

"Yes, it does, but they're pleasant memories, not sad at all." She took his hand in her own and gave it a squeeze, fork and all. "And here comes your food now."

The waitress set a huge plate of eggs and grits down in front of him and returned to the kitchen.

"I thought you wanted lunch. You weren't kidding about those damn grits, were you?"

"Lo--hmph--ve grits," he said with a mouthful.

209

"God." She rolled her eyes.

Shortly, she had her fruit and was cutting small hunks of chicken, which she inserted inside her purse and then felt the scratchy little tongue of Tag as he licked them from her hand.

"Hey."

She looked up.

"You've got me thinking about that fire and spit," he said wiping his mouth. "What would we need that we don't already have to camp out for the night?"

"You serious?"

CAMPFIRES, BEAR CUBS, AND ROAD FLARES

They'd shopped locally, Amber on a mission to patronize small and struggling shops, and had found two lightweight sleeping bags and a small cooler. A shopkeeper had told them of a secluded campground by a lake, and now they were sitting before a small fire Ben, feeling quite proud of himself, had built. Tag was curled in Amber's lap, eyes wide and looking around.

"Quarter for your thoughts," she said as they both stared into the flames.

"Hmmm? Oh, just wondering what the fascination is with fire, how you just automatically stare into one, as if you can't help yourself," he answered.

"Yeah, the inner beast in us, I guess. Right, Tag?" She nuzzled the kitten with her nose.

It was quiet and dark, but for what looked like a full moon. Ben cocked his head and listened. "Hear that?"

She listened intently. "What?"

"Nothing, that's what. No humans, no cell phones ringing, no radios, television, car alarms, sirens, arguments. No airplanes, polluting buses, cars and trucks honking at each other, no gunshots, babies crying."

"No society, you mean. Just a melody of quiet in a cathedral of trees and skylights."

He nodded. "You wax Shakespearian."

"Uh-uh, more Bach and Emerson. Shakespeare? Well, he was more interested in the human condition. But Bach, Emerson, Thoreau, too, they were interested in the intangibles. What we don't see that makes up all we do see."

Both sat quietly, him thinking about what she'd said. A crackling of brush got his attention.

"Company? Did you see anyone else pulling in here, babe?"

"No, most were going to the main grounds by the camp store." They both focused toward the sound, just out of the firelight in the woods.

"Raccoon or possum, I'd bet. Maybe smelling our—" She didn't finish as a small brown bear cub suddenly appeared from the brush on the other side of the fire, sniffing.

"Shitttt. Don't move, Abby."

"Shhh, don't scare him," she whispered. "It's just exploring, I bet. Maybe hungry."

"Yeah, and I don't want to be its supper. Can you make it to the car on the count of three? At least we'd have *some* protection."

"No, hon, don't run. Here, take Tag and move slowly toward the car. It might smell the cat, in addition to the food. Here, take him and go. But slowly."

He gingerly took the kitten from her, stood and moved off toward the car. "Come on, Abby. What are you doing, for Christ's sake?"

"I'll be along. Go ahead, get in and be ready to drive off, but don't start the engine."

"Damned lunatic! That's a baby! The mother isn't far away. Get your ass in the car!" His attempt at a harsh whisper got the cub's attention. It stopped short and looked up at them.

"Well, look at you," she cooed to the bear. And to Ben, in the same voice, "Keep your voice down and get in the car, please, hon. You're going to scare the little guy. Try to shut the door quietly and put Tag in the console. Relax and don't worry. I know what I'm doing."

"Goddamn crazy woman," she heard him muttering as the car door clicked shut quietly.

She turned her attention to the cub, now sitting on plump little haunches staring at her curiously. Careful to make no sudden movements, she continued her croon.

"So, you decided to wander off and explore a little on your own, did you? Your mom is probably not going to be real pleased about this, you know. By the looks of you, food is not the priority here. Just a little mischief, maybe?"

Sensing no danger from Amber, the baby again started poking around in the clearing lighted by the fire. Amber took the opportunity to stand up and move slowly toward the spot where he'd emerged. The moonlight now picked up where the glow of the fire left off, and she could see the seldom used path. *Ben's right. The mama is not far. The main thing is not to have the baby cry out in any way and alarm her.*

She turned to see the cub working his way back to where she was standing. She glanced back towards the car, and could see that Ben was watching her and the bear intently. The power window was still down and she had to laugh to herself that, in spite of himself, Ben had followed her suggestion not to start the engine to raise it. She raised her voice just enough be heard, but kept the melodic tone.

"Ben, listen. I'm going to try to get the cub to go back to its mother. She's probably already missed him and will be looking, so whatever you do, don't panic and make any loud noises. I'm going to try to entice him down that path."

"You're WHAT?" He stopped when the cub turned to look toward the car at his outburst.

"Ben, please. Trust me. Unless you want a real angry mom ripping right through that convertible top, you best let me do what I have to do. Please."

"Shit, Abby. Will you just get in the damn car and let's get out of here." He really was scared now. He knew Abby had an uncanny affinity with the wild creatures, but this was

213

pushing it. The cub was near as big as her, and its mother would probably be twice that.

"We can't leave a fire burning in these woods. I'll be along. Just be ready to start up and drive off if we have to."

Her mind was racing, her eyes searching for something to lure the bear into following her. The first notion of it being hungry was dispelled. The baby was new to fire, its heat, possibly, keeping it from discovering their human food on the coals. It seemed more interested in her than anything else. She spotted the unopened bag of marshmallows and thought of using them for bait, but decided against it. Introducing a wild bear to human food was issuing it a death warrant. *No, she had to think of something else, and quick.*

Then it came to her. "Okay, Little One, let's see what I've got for you."

She inched in the direction of the car, the cub again stopping at her movement. She kept in her direction and it side-stepped as she approached. Beyond, she could see Ben's face, almost mesmerized now by what he was watching unfold.

"Ben, will you reach behind and get Bear out of the back seat? If he won't go through the window, open the door slowly and pass him out to me."

"Jesus . . . what?"

"Ben, just do it. Please?"

She was almost to the car, keeping her eye on the baby who was circling back around her with each step she made, his eyes still just curious. She kept up her soft talking to him and he showed no sign of aggression, or leaving for that matter.

She saw Bear being pushed out the window, momentarily hiding Ben's face. Grasping him, she hugged it close to her, its furry white body, now free, almost hiding her. The cub cocked his head in question at the sight.

"I'm going to attempt to get it to follow me, hon. Please just stay in the car with Tag until I get back. Everything is going to be fine. The last thing I need right now is to worry about you."

"Abby, you're nuts," he whispered. "You've got to get in this goddamn car now so we can get the hell out of here."

"What? And, leave our food?" she whispered back. "It's fine, Ben. Once I get this bear back to his mother, the danger is past. These animals won't hurt me. I promise."

"Abby, goddammit!"

"Right now all I have to do is reunite a mom and her baby. I'll be the least of her concerns, so calm down.

"I fucking give up. You're completely mad!"

Ignoring him, she once again turned her attention to the cub now sniffing the air in the direction of her own Bear.

"Come on, young one. We're gonna take you back to your mother. She must be worried sick by now."

She started slow steps toward the path, giving thanks for the cloudless night. She paused at the opening in the brush, lowered her stuffed animal close to the ground, and let the cub get a good look, grateful, too, for the innate curiosity in all babies everywhere. She waited while her eyes adjusted to the darkness inside the woods, then began inching down the trail, the cub at her heels.

In the car Ben sat with his mouth open. "I fucking don't believe it. If I wasn't seeing this right in front of my eyes, I just fucking would not believe it!"

She heard the mother before she saw it, and stopped short, holding her stuffed bear in front of her. The cub plopped right beside her.

"Go on, little guy. There's your mom. Oh, *please* go now."

As much as she loved and understood the animals, she wasn't anxious to have an irate mama bear, who may not listen to reason, pissed off at her for what she might consider kidnapping.

"Damn!" She took a deep breath, forced her mind to be methodical, and re-focused her eyes in the night light that was the moon. She didn't want the bear to mistake her submission as fear. The smell of fear incensed the wild creatures, as it often meant death for them.

The adult bear was lumbering now, right for the spot she stood her ground. The branches and twigs along the path snapped beneath her weight; it was maybe fifteen feet away. She wondered how she was going to appear to the mother, lugging a huge white Polar bear under her arm, and the subject of the agitated search sitting beside her like a pup.

She quickly looked around for a way of escape if it became necessary to use one. A huge old White Pine just off the trail would be the closest barrier, and then just as quickly, she dismissed the thought. Nothing escaped an angry or frightened mother bear. Nothing.

"Go, little guy. Go now! To your mother." She said the words softly but firmly while nudging the cub's rump with her foot. The bear didn't move. And now it didn't matter.

The mother bear stopped abruptly, no more than six feet away, at seeing the trio in front of her. The mist of her exhaled breath was made an ominous glow by the pale moon. She tensed and for just a moment examined her adversary. Amber could almost hear the rapid beating of her heart in the massive chest.

Then, suddenly, the adult rose on her hind paws, revealing her intent. To do what most mothers would do to retrieve their child from danger, kill if necessary. Amber was stunned at her size, the magnitude of the powerful paws as the ivory of the tearing claws were caught in the moonlight. The sheer bulk and majesty of the creature reduced her to but a wisp in the other's presence.

For what seemed an eternity, nothing moved. Only the heavy breathing of the mother bear filled the night. She looked at her cub, then at Amber. Amber stared right back, frozen in her spot.

"I think I have something that belongs to you," she barely whispered.

At the sound of her trembling voice, the huge animal let out what must have been a low growl, but sounded to Amber like an earth-shattering roar. She hugged the furry body of her own bear as tightly as she could in reaction. The roar startled her more than the enormous size, but she knew she couldn't, mustn't, show it.

"Oh he's fine, I assure you. He just wanted to play with my baby. See?"

Tentatively, she held the white stuffed animal out for the mother's inspection. The adult sniffed the air, unsure, and then everything happened at once. The cub scampered to his mama, who forgot all about Amber. She lowered back to all fours, checking it out thoroughly with a series of sniffs and snorts, before giving it a swift cuff for its mischief. The cub yelped more in despair at his mother's discipline than pain from the blow, but Amber still didn't move. It was as if she'd become entranced by the joining with the world she so revered.

She had no idea how long the three of them stood there all looking at each other in the glow of the full moon, but finally, as if deciding no harm had been done, the mother pushed the cub behind her and started backing away, her eyes still locked into Amber's own.

A trust, an understanding passed between them in those brief seconds. Just before she blended back into the darkness, the mama turned around to go on her way, but not before pausing to look over her shoulder at, what must have been to her, a strange pair of creatures. A tiny 'human' with an extremely odd looking baby.

"Was nice meeting you. Take good care of the baby. It's going to grow into a fine young bear some day," Amber called out softly. Then relieved, but almost wistful at seeing them go, she turned to retrace her steps. Poor Ben must be near a stroke by now.

As she started back toward the fire, he suddenly stepped from behind a tree, causing her to gasp.

"Oh!"

He frantically motioned *come here* and turned, heading in the direction of the firelight. She could see that he was holding something in one hand as they made their way back to the camp. Something long, like a stick. Once off the path and back in the clearing he turned to face her again. He threw the "stick" down and firmly gripped her shoulders and was almost shaking her.

"You're okay? You really are okay?"

"Y-yes. Yes, I'm fine." She glanced at the ground and saw what he'd been carrying wasn't a stick at all but an ordinary road flare. "Everything is just fine. What an incredible experience."

Suddenly, the anxiety of the last half hour or so dissolved into a fury. Ben released his grip on her shoulders and stood back from her.

"INCREDIBLE EXPERIENCE? Are you insane? You risk all our lives and it's a fucking incredible experience!"

"Ben. Wait a minute."

"NO! *You* wait," he yelled, as he immediately began throwing more brush and twigs on the fire making it flame up, adding light to their surroundings. "Instead of getting your ass in the car and getting the hell out of here for our lives, even that of the damn kitten, you have to play Miss Jane of the Jungle! What in the hell are you trying to prove to me anyway? How powerful you are, and controlling, even over a goddamn wild BEAR! Do you want me and the whole world beneath your thumb of mystic powers? Just what the hell is it with you anyway?"

She was shocked into silence, and sat down, thinking about the encounter, and now Ben's rage. When the fire was large, he came up and sat on the bag beside her, anger spent, his face serious.

"That was the dumbest thing I've ever seen," he said, more softly now.

"No. It wasn't dumb at all, Ben. I told you they wouldn't harm me. The animals know me and I know them."

"You do, huh?" He stirred the fire with a long branch, still not looking at her.

"Yes."

"Then, why are you shaking?"

She looked at her hands. "Because . . . ."

"Because just for a moment, you realized you'd bitten off more than you could chew, that's why. The size of that

218

thing scared the shit out of you, as it should have." He turned to look at her.

She flushed, upset at his words. "That's not true. I was only concerned that the mama might misunderstand. I knew that animal wouldn't hurt me once she knew what I was doing. But what about you? Did you think you were going to save me with that stupid flare there? If the mama had spotted you, sensed your aggression, it might have been over for all of us."

"Oh she knew I was there. She smelled me, right along with you. Bears can smell like you wouldn't believe, but you're right in a way. Because she couldn't see me it made her suspect a trap, maybe. And that might be what saved your crazy ass."

She thought about it before answering. *How could she explain it to him?* "Ben, listen. I admit I didn't really think we were in danger all that much because I've had these encounters with large animals before. An elk, for example. A bull I raised from a calf. I know the animals won't hurt me because they know I won't hurt them. That bear was only interested in getting her cub back."

"Yeah, unless threatened. Then it doesn't matter and you walking alongside her cub meant you were a threat. You risked all our lives needlessly, but especially your own." He turned back to stare into the fire as he spoke.

"You just don't understand."

"I've seen them tear the doors off refrigerators, so even the car wouldn't have helped had it come after us."

"But it didn't, did it? And speaking of that, just what good do you think that silly flare would have done?"

"A distraction, Abby. It would've been a momentary distraction to get it off you and toward me if it had attacked. That's phosphorous in that flare, and phosphorous will burn through almost anything." He looked at her. "Even bears."

She was touched, and she didn't know what to say. Here was a man she still didn't really know, still couldn't figure out, a jester most of the time, dead serious when he wanted to be. And he'd just risked his life for her, or so he thought.

It didn't matter if he was right or wrong about what had transpired between her and the animals. What did matter was that he'd been there for her all along, and she hadn't even known it.

"See, Abby, it wasn't the bear that was out of sync with Nature. You were. Even with your extraordinary gift, you were trespassing in the bear's world and had it killed you, it would have only done what was right. Just as I would've had it attacked and I'd have had to kill it, if I could. Law of the Jungle, Abby. Gift or no gift."

She reached out and put her hand on his. "But I wasn't trespassing, hon. That's the point. I was helping, and the bear, both bears, could sense it." She stood and went to the cooler. "Now we better settle down and get something to eat."

"Eat? Hell no, we're not gonna eat; we need to get out of here. Haven't you listened to a word I've said? I'm supposed to settle down and eat when there's a thousand pound mother bear probably just out of sight who may decide at any moment she forgot to have dinner?"

"The bear is long gone, trust me. It's been reunited with its baby and they're both happily getting as far away from us as they can." She took out the franks, putting them on sticks. "Here," she said handing him his. "At least get some food in your stomach and then we'll decide what's best to do."

He stopped and stared at her for a moment, and then as if just accepting what made no sense to him, took his frank and placed it over the embers away from the flames. "I give up. You're, without a doubt, the most stubborn individual I've ever encountered in all my years on the planet."

"I know." She smiled and took her place beside him, holding her frank next to his.

After they'd eaten, Ben poured coffee from the thermos in ceramic cups and she packed the food away in the cooler, closing the lid tight. She carried it towards the car and noticed the windows were now up.

"Oh, God." She sat the cooler down and looked inside. Tag was sitting on the seat, staring up at her; his wide kitten eyes glimmering in the dim light.

"Awww," she said as she opened the door. "I bet you're starving. In all this excitement, I forgot your dinner."

She picked the kitten up and crooned to it as she got some cat food from a bag, then carried both Tag and the food back to the fire which was again getting low. She looked at Ben who was still sipping from his cup. He looked tired, strained even. It worried her.

"Guess we better build that fire up and get some sleep. I'll help just as soon as I feed poor Tag here."

Later, when they'd crawled into their sleeping bags and Tag was again sleeping soundly in the console, she lay staring at an especially bright star. The night was again silent but for a few cicadas singing whatever it was cicadas sang as the summer waned. It would be getting colder the farther north they traveled and she could almost smell frozen pumpkins on brown vines. Somewhere a bear and her cub were thinking over what they'd learned that day, and a few nocturnes were scurrying about the forest floor. She thought of the man beside her, the evening they'd just spent, the way, she noticed, he'd again secured the road flare just in reach of his bag.

"Ben? You awake?" she whispered. Softly, in case he wasn't.

"Imm . . . mmm," he answered. "Just barely."

"Ben, I think I love you."

He opened his eyes and followed the trail of smoke on its ascent upward, beyond the glow, into the night. How long had it been since he'd heard those words, spoken simply just like that? Out of the blue. He couldn't remember. He noticed the quickening in his heart, yet, he didn't know what to say. He said nothing.

She woke to the smell of bubbling coffee. Ben had found the old camping percolator and some coffee she'd stuck in with it. She stretched in her bag and watched him stoke the coals back to life, laughing silently as he muttered something about the ash turning the old pot black.

"Don't get it burning too high, hon," she mumbled in a sleepy voice. "I'll pack up so we can get on the road. I know you're ready for breakfast and maybe there's a Denny's in Gainesville. We aren't far from there. How'd you sleep?"

"Not too bad, I suppose, considering I had to keep one eye open all night in case your brood decided to return and join us." His tone told her he still wasn't right with the events of the night before.

"Well, you can sleep in the car after breakfast. I'll brush my teeth right away and have my coffee while I put things in the car, while you make sure the fire is out. Probably should get some water from the creek and pour on it, then cover it with dirt." She struggled into her jeans and sweater as she spoke.

"I do know how to extinguish a fire, ma'am. You may be the Jungle Queen, but I have ventured out of the city a time or two in my life, you know."

His sarcasm was real. He was quite close to being weary of the entire scene, she could tell, and he probably hadn't slept much at all. He looked tired, haggard even. Thoughts of the hospital entered her mind.

"Sorry, of course you do. It's me. I worry so about fires in the forests. They get out of control so quickly, and often get started by a campfire that wasn't really out."

"Okay, here's your coffee and let's get going. You're right, I'm starving."

He handed her a mug and she wrapped her hands around it warming her fingers. He re-filled his own and then headed for the creek to fill the pot with water, the road flare protruding from his back pocket. *This can't stay between us. How can I make him understand, she thought.*

Gathering their bags and the cooler, she stuffed them back into the over-filled trunk. She positioned Bear and the lamp back into the rear seat, then called Tag to "wake up" while shaking the yellow box of Meow Mix. Pouring a little of the dry food into the palm of her hand, she reached in to get the kitten out of the console. Once on the ground, he scratched at the earth, squatted, and then busily covered his 'business' with grass and fallen leaves. He nibbled at the nuggets in her hand, but was more interested in a green beetle out on his morning stroll.

"Oh no, you don't. That little bug isn't bothering you a bit," she chided, scooping him back up and into the car. "Get yourself in there and we'll get you some milk at breakfast."

"You ready?" Ben was approaching the car from behind her, turning to look around to make sure they'd not forgotten anything.

"I'm ready. Let's get on and see what this day holds." She smiled up at him.

They got in the car and she turned the key bringing the engine to life. The wipers cleared the morning dew from the windshield, and slowly they started weaving through the trees on the narrow road.

On a small rise, a few hundred feet away, a large brown bear and her cub watched the silver car slowly make its way out of the forest and back to the highway.

THE ARTERY OF A BEAST

Breakfast had been uneventful at Denny's. Ben was talkative enough, but it was distant conversation and not his usual light bantering. As he'd suggested, she continued to drive the next leg while he slept. She could tell he was still tired because even her music didn't wake him. Odd, she thought, how refreshed she felt, even after the encounter with the bears. It had thrilled her to get that close to something wild, as wild as she was in her own way, but it saddened her, too, to see Ben's reaction. His fear, his pragmatism, whatever it was that held him back, she was sure he'd overcome in time, for deep down she felt he did understand these things. He had to, she'd see to it, for it was the power behind his healing.

After lunch, she decided to bring the subject up again, to see his reaction. He was wide awake now, so the time seemed right.

"Remember our talk under the stars when we first met?"

He looked at her.

"You told me about flying, remember? Well, you were out of your element then because you don't belong in the sky. Just as you think I'm out of mine with the animals. And we don't belong on the water, either. Yet we go into the sky, and we go on and under the water all the time, don't we?"

"What are you getting at?"

"It's one and the same, don't you see? Life is full of danger, but only because we don't understand it, maybe haven't discovered the way to mesh with it. Once we do, we can overcome the danger, can't we?"

He paused, thinking it over before he answered. "Abby, listen. We survive the elements, as you say, because we avoid what can kill us. Pilots don't fly through tornadoes, sailors don't purposely sail into storms, and divers avoid the dangerous sea creatures. Sane people don't tempt fate as you did with the bear."

"Sure, Ben, but I'm to the animals as you are to the sky. You've learned what to do and what not to do in order to fly a plane. And I've done the same by my instinct with the wild things. It's why they come to me. They trust me."

He was shaking his head. "No, Abby. There are creatures of the wild that no one can tame; no one can get close to because they don't have the brains the others do. Sharks, for example, spiders, snakes. They're pure instinct."

"Well, a bear isn't. A bear is a highly intelligent animal."

"I don't care how intelligent it is. It's a bear, goddammit."

"So you would run from it, kill it, because you don't understand it? And even if it was just instinct, it knew I wasn't going to harm it. It *knew*, that's the difference. You don't see me swimming with sharks, fondling Tarantulas, whatever. I'm not talking about taming. I'm talking about giving and sharing space. Respect. Same you'd do with any living creature, man or beast. That's all."

Both fell silent then, each thinking their own thoughts and she didn't press it further. *In time, she thought.*

They continued on Highway 129 until they'd left Georgia and entered North Carolina, the sports car straightening out the miles of mountain curves as if designed only for that. How she loved the car, how it was, like her, so full

225

of its own spirit. At Ben's insistence she was wearing her seat belt, and it bothered her, but she humored him rather than start another fight.

They stopped for gas and let Tag run around some at a park. The kitten seemed to be taking to the trip quite well. She pointed out the different mountain ridges and Ben, more like his old self now that they were moving again, had nodded his agreement. There was so much to see, so much beauty along the roadside and off in the distance, it was hard to imagine how any ugliness could exist in the world.

"How'd you like to watch the sun fall into the trees and dabble your feet in a waterfall?" she asked.

"Dabble my feet in a waterfall? Any I've seen had to be viewed from a bit of a distance, Abby."

"I know of a special waterfall not far from here and we should be able to make it there before sunset. Maybe we can get a place to stay in a small town nearby. Tonight, I think I need a hot bath and a soft bed."

"Sounds good to me, too. As long as there aren't any bears around this waterfall you're planning on me dabbling my feet in, that is. Don't know if I'm up to saving your ass two nights in a row."

"Why not?" She turned and winked at him.

He sensed it wasn't a question. He shook his head in reply to her damnable innocence, and sighed. He couldn't stay angry at this woman.

As they approached an intersection, she veered into the left turn lane. This road would take them west about ten miles into Tennessee and Route 68, north. About three miles west, she asked Ben if he minded if they stopped on a pullover so she could take Tag for a little walk in the woods before continuing. A small country store sat perched on a knoll on the opposite side of the roadway, and he agreed that he'd wander over and get them a soda while she took the kitten.

She stood at the forest's edge watching Ben cross the lanes to the store. He hadn't questioned her familiarity with the area, assuming, she supposed, that she was merely reading maps. What she hadn't told him was they were only about three miles from the farm she'd lived on so long. She wanted just a few moments to reflect on her life here, and she wanted to spend a few minutes with Jeff. Turning, she cuddled the kitten and strolled about fifty feet into the emerald world of pine.

"Here you go, Tag. Get down and smell the earth of these mountains." She stooped and put the kitten in a patch of lacy fern. "Now you listen to what I'm going to tell you about this place," she whispered. "A real special Spirit sort of lives in the mountains around here, and I think he'd like to meet you. Course, I think he already has, but he'd like you to know the smell . . . the taste, of this special place."

Tag, as if understanding what she said to him, looked for a moment at her face, then began to roll around and play in the fern patch, leaping on and under the fronds, then peeking at her from his hidden place. She sat on the cool earth and smiled at him.

"Wonderful place to play, little friend, and if you listen real, real close, you may even hear a coyote howl a welcome to you." She closed her eyes, breathed deeply, and thought of Sara and Muffy. Thought of a time when she sat in a similar fern patch petting and soothing a wounded half-coyote pup, while a German Shepherd dog looked over her shoulder at the discovery. Tag crawled up into her lap and returned her to the present.

"Okay, we'd better get back now. Ben is going to think I'm out bear hunting again. Come on, little guy," she said, as she scooped him up and with a last look into the deep green, said her goodbyes and headed back to the car.

Ben was leaning against the fender and taking in the view of the mountain chain rising into the horizon, its late afternoon smoke beginning to hug the taller elevations. He turned to greet her as she approached.

"This sure is pretty country, Abby. I'm glad we came."

"Yes, it's a special place, the foothills of the Great Smokey Mountains. Now, we have a waterfall to visit for sunset and we better get moving." She hoped he hadn't noticed the moisture in her eyes.

She gave Tag a drink of water and a Pounce treat and placed him back in his console bed. Ben buckled up and she pulled onto the highway. The next turn veered off to the right and a sign announcing NC294 grabbed her attention, but she ignored the oft taken turn and continued on the road west.

Not far down into the valley beyond that right turn, on a hill behind an aging old Sentry standing proud in its peeling paint, a German Shepherd dog sat with ears suddenly erect. The half-coyote dog sitting next to her threw back her head and howled a mournful cry.

"Welcome to Tennessee," she read out loud as they passed the rather rusty sign, its buckshot holes the result of a kid with a new shotgun, or a hunter testing his range. "So much for your visit to North Carolina, Ben." she said in a mock tour guide voice. "What you say we put the top down so you can smell the air and feel the breath of mountains on your face? Touch the sky if you want?"

"Yeah, and it'd be nice if you slow down a bit, too, so I don't feel as if I'm being fast-forwarded through *A Day In The Appalachians* starring Sheena of the Bear Clan," he quipped.

"Oh, I'll be slowing down when we turn on 68. Can't go fast on that road, nor would you want to." She patted his knee with a reassuring tap. Inside, she bubbled with excitement at what she was about to show him, and at his return to his teasing ways.

She pulled off onto the shoulder, and in seconds the convertible hooks were released, the top was lowering into its cradle, and she was fumbling through the cases looking for Ben's Bocelli CD. Perfect for Ben's entry into Cherokee country, she thought.

"Ready?"

"Proceed, Sheena," he joked as she checked her side mirror and pulled back onto the road as the strains of "A

Time To Say Goodbye" escaped on the contrails of wind behind them.

Ben looked over at her as Amber blended with the road, the wind, and the music. Her auburn hair whipped around her face as if the wind was claiming her for its own. *If true freedom could really be achieved, this was a portrait of it, he thought.* He smiled at her, a smile she didn't see, and thought back to the night before when she'd said I think I love you.

They turned north on Route 68. A couple miles more and he saw an old timbered railroad trestle arced over the winding road like a gateway. He loved old things and thoughts of a coal burning engine, its smokestack belching, wafted through his mind as he laid his head back and looked at the belly of it as they passed under. Then he was taken into a realm unlike any he'd ever experienced. Oh, he'd seen mountains off in the distance, walling in a western desert, just treeless mounds of rock, really. He'd crossed over passes on concrete ribbons of highway that invaded the intermittent valleys with their endless cargo of people, but this was different. Here, the mass, the strength of the mountain, absorbed you into itself on a road so narrow it was as a wound in its side.

Water, the lifeblood of it, trickled down its rock wall bones, seeping out of the cracks in its moss flesh. He was slowly beginning to understand the woman next to him, how she flowed through this nature, becoming but another fiber in its web. The Life Web, he'd heard her call it, and now he was beginning to realize what she meant. This mountain was a living, breathing entity and he suddenly felt very small and, equally, privileged in its presence.

They traveled the next ten miles in silence. What could be said to express this world better than the world itself? The forest, its pine, majestic old oaks, and red maple, their green giving way to the tinge of autumn, was the lungs of it. The air hung heavy with its breaths, a mix of earth smells, compost, and wild flowers.

The road wound through it all like an artery through the heart of a beast. Above, the endless blue was as a bonnet, its ribbons, the waning sun rays, drifting down among the arms of the trees and nestling on the ground where scurrying squirrels gathered nuts for winter.

Bocelli sang out to the calls of jays, and the shriek of a hawk circling over a distant meadow. Ben felt a tension leaving him, replaced by a calm long since forgotten. For a split second, he felt he'd entered Eden once more. He suddenly flinched, as the remembering seemed to come from his depths.

She glanced over at him. His expression told her he was finally beginning to "get it." This time it was she who smiled a smile he didn't see, as she took his hand in her own. *Welcome to my world, Ben . . . welcome to 'our' world, now.*

The asphalt beneath them began a different tune as it began an ascent up the rising mound of rock, each note a tale of a freeze and a thaw at the upper levels of the mountain's torso. The winter winds could be brutal here, forming huge icicles in the humid lungs of the forest, and hurling them to earth like daggers. Attacking the roadway put down by man for his intruding machines.

Through the gnarled skeletons of dead trees, victims of the killer ice of winters past, Ben caught glimpses of the valleys below, dressed in the patterned swirls of cultivated corn fields. He heard Amber saying something about her affinity for the skeleton trees. How their roots still clung to the earth that bore them, while their dried and twisted fingers clawed at the sky, as if imploring someone, some *thing*, for life once more. Not seeing the tiny progeny of their seeds peeking out at their feet.

"The circle of life is so simply explained by observing a tree," she was saying, and he was taking it all in, faint answers to questions he'd asked for so long. This place didn't need words to write its book. The pages spread out before them said it all.

WATERFALLS, REVERIES, AND A LADY IN RED

Now the road was falling again, back into the thick trees where gravel roads led to old country cabins that stood in clearings sawed out of the woods. Only the mailboxes driven into the rocky clay shoulder gave hint of their existence.

"We're coming in to Coker Creek, hon. We can find a room for the night, grab some sandwiches, and have a picnic by the falls. How does that sound? We've about three hours before dusk, so that will allow plenty of time to get back out before dark." She smiled at him with a look of anticipation, excitement, dancing in her eyes.

"Back out? What are we going in?" His eyes widened at her choice of words.

"Oh, a deep, dark cavern far beneath the mountain where legend has it that the ghosts of all evil deeds reside." She scrunched up her face and did her best witch cackle. "And no one is allowed there after the rising of the sixth star, or they can never return to the surface again."

"Babe, you are most certainly a total nut. There's no doubt." He couldn't help grinning at her antics. "Let's get the room and then see these waterfalls you're yammering about. My feet are so hot they could use a dabbling about now."

"There it is on the left. See the old country inn with the big water wheel in front? Oh, I hope they have a vacancy." She pointed to a two story building pressed between the trees with a rock garden crawling down to meet the road. She slowed and turned up a gravel drive that led to the office.

They were able to book a room on the ground floor just behind the water wheel. Ben was fascinated, and she delighted, at the small lanterns hanging inside the large wheel causing the drops to sparkle as it turned. They unloaded their suitcases and readied for the falls, Amber digging out a red sweater for herself and a jacket for Ben. At a small grocery, they refilled the coffee thermos, bought sandwiches, and then headed down the narrow gravel road into the park itself. At the bottom was a small parking area, a mowed grove, picnic tables and rest room facilities.

He was surprised to see such a well-kept park at the end of such a treacherous entrance road. There were other vehicles there, and a family gathering of fifteen or so was preparing supper on the fire grills. The sound of children's laughter echoed from beyond the trees.

"What a pleasant little park," he said as they pulled in a parking slot. He got out, stretched, and inhaled the fresh air deeply. "Yeah, I like this."

"Here, hon. Will you take the thermos and the sandwiches while I get Tag?" She reached in the back, handed the food out to Ben, who was still doing a panoramic view of things, and plucked Tag out of the console.

"Okay, Taggie boy, finally time to let you look around a bit," she said, hugging the kitten and placing him in her bag. "Come on, Ben, you're in for a wonderful surprise."

They headed for the small wooden sign marking the walk to the falls. The path, barely wide enough for two, was lined with the hearty purple clover of fall and a lingering stalk of Goldenrod. It wound around rocks and fallen tree stumps on its slight decline. The roar of rushing water was closer now, and she quickened her pace, half-dragging Ben along as he tried to look at everything at once.

The waning sunlight caught the churning water of the river, setting it aglow like a rushing liquid fire. As it came into sight, she ran ahead in her own joy at returning to this miraculous place. At its rocky edge, she turned and looked up at the wall of water descending upon her, her breath catching in her throat. She turned, literally dancing on her toes, to call Ben to hurry, but he was already there behind her, mouth slightly agape at the scene before him.

"Jesus" was all he could manage to get out.

"Isn't it magnificent! Have you ever seen anything quite like this?"

But he didn't answer. What lay before him wasn't just a waterfall; it was a series of waterfalls like a giant staircase descending from the sky. Twenty or so levels of varying heights, thirty feet, fifteen feet, five feet, then thirty again, each with a wide ledge before the next. The entire setting, maybe a quarter of a mile of falling, roaring water, was held in its channel by huge layers of black slate rocks on either side. Towering trees held the rocks themselves in place. It was, as she said, magnificent.

"Come on, take your shoes off," she called over the crash of water as she climbed out onto the nearest rocky ledge.

He watched as she kicked off her thongs and rolled up her pant legs, and then gasped as she ran out into the water on the shelf just in front of them. To his surprise, the water only reached her mid-calf. She held her shoulder bag with the kitten inside close to her with one arm, but the other was outstretched in a salute to the cascade in front of her, this one about twenty feet tall. That Amber was in her glory was obvious.

He walked out onto the rock, sat, and pulled off his own shoes. Gingerly, he stuck a toe in the foamy green water. It was cold but refreshingly so, and clean, oh, so crystal clean. Now with a better angle he looked up again and saw children splashing and laughing four "shelves" up, the source of the laughter they'd heard when leaving the car. He allowed his mind to wander to another time.

He could still smell the river; see its muddy current as if yesterday. And Churchill Bridge where his parents and their friends went to the beer joint. The juke box. Wooden, unfinished and dusty floors. A grown woman who had asked him, a boy, to dance and his mother had said "no." What was the song on the juke playing? "Wheel of Fortune", something about it coming his way.

He was twelve. He was in love with the woman who asked him to dance, and the river, and the fish in the river, and the sky, and his .22 rifle and he never wanted to grow up. Not ever.

Damn, he mused, where has the time gone? And yet . . . and yet, although he never danced with the woman at Churchill Bridge, he was in a dance with this one and he briefly wondered, hoped, he had enough nickels left to hear all the songs on the box.

What a place this is, he thought, coming back to the present. Almost beyond description. The "shelves" continued down for another five hundred feet or so before leveling out into the flow of the river below that meandered through the heart of the forest. He glanced out at Amber, who was now holding the kitten up so it could see the world around him. She was nearly to the other side of the gorge now, lost in her Natural world, momentarily forgetting him.

He waded out into the shelf and felt the smooth slate bottom on his feet. At the middle, he turned to look up at the torrents of flowing water rushing down toward him.

"Jesus," he said, almost in reverence. Amber, grinning and splashing like the children above, joined him as he reached the center and their eyes met.

"Didn't I tell you?"

He pulled her close to him and together they looked up into the water, the lifeblood, of the mountain. "You told me but no words can describe this," he said kissing her forehead.

"Yeah, I know," she said, still grinning.

They found a flat, dry saucer of slate inches above the swirling current and ate their sandwiches there, cross-legged, while Amber braided a leash for Tag with twine she'd bought earlier. Sharing coffee out of the thermos cup, dabbling their feet in the bubbles, they watched the sun turn the color of the kitten balled in her lap. It was falling slowly into the forest around them.

"Well?" she asked. "Dollar for your thoughts."

He stared at her, his eyes reflecting the sun on the water, but didn't answer.

"Ben?"

"It's nothing, Abby. I was just somewhere else for a moment. Sorry." He couldn't tell her how he suddenly hated the thing growing inside him. The thing that would ultimately take him away from her and the love he was feeling in her presence.

"Oh, nothing to be sorry about, silly. This place affects everyone that way their first time. You know, kind of speechless."

He nodded. "We'd better start back. It'll be chilly here soon if we don't with the mist and all."

Yes, let's go back and get settled in. I want to see how Tag takes to his leash. The lanterns in the water wheel should look pretty at night.

"Yes," he said, but his mind was somewhere else.

Back at the inn, Amber put Tag on his leash and let him romp in the cool grass while they sat in the rocking chairs by the wheel. She was gazing up at the night sky as if mesmerized. He watched her in silence, drinking his coffee, a slight smile on his face. Now, he would answer her. Here among the trees and her Nature. Here, where she was at home as if a nymph of the woods herself.

He rose and walked to the car, taking his set of keys from his pocket. He reached inside, lowered the windows, put a CD he'd bought on the road into the player, and walked back toward her as the music came drifting across the expanse of lawn.

Caught off guard by the sound, she turned just as he was approaching. *Why in the world is he playing music out here?*

235

He stopped and held out his hand to her, the same enigmatic smile on his face as before. At first she didn't catch on, but he kept standing there smiling, his hand outstretched, and then it made sense. She almost blushed, and looked toward the inn to see if anyone was watching. They were. First one person appeared on the veranda, followed by another, they, too, curious as to the music. A couple strolling not far away stopped to stare as well. *And he calls me a lunatic, she thought, happily.*

Though a bit embarrassed at this public display, she wound Tag's leash around the chair arm, and rose to meet his hand with her own. They began to dance across the lawn of the inn as if the only people on earth as "Lady In Red" played on. Ben sang softly along. They twirled right, then left, right again, in a sort of waltz as the lawn became their ballroom. The lyrics of the song fleeted through her mind about looking lovely in red, and she was happy she'd worn her red sweater if that's what had spurred his romantic display.

A small crowd of guests had gathered now on the veranda, silently watching this odd couple seemingly lost unto themselves. The people looked both curious and delighted at the same time. But, neither Ben nor Amber seemed to notice, as each was caught up in the moment by the same inexplicable force that had drawn them together in the first place. The music came to an end, and they stopped their dance and stared into each other's eyes. The people all applauded.

Now was the time, he thought. Now was the time to say what he couldn't say before, never thought he'd say again to anyone. With a swelling heart as big as the full moon above, he whispered so only she could hear, "I think I love you, too."

A COUPLE HOURS FROM ROANOKE

First light saturated the mountains in a gray vapor the consistency of soup. She woke early, the numbers 5:30 glowing orange-red on the clock. Staying still, hoping to fall back asleep, her mind wandered somewhere between total contentment and what would be next with this man lying close and breathing softly in her ear.

Wide awake now, she got up quietly, peeked out the window, and saw the tiny yard lights by the water wheel casting an iridescent glow of flaxen yellow through the billowing fog. This was definitely not mist.

"It'll be awhile before this fog lifts," she whispered in Tag's ear, scooping the kitten from the nest he'd molded at the top of her pillow. "Guess I'll try out that coffeemaker and get you a bite of breakfast. There certainly won't be anything open on this curvy road for a while."

She made coffee as noiselessly as possible, opened Tag a can of food, and pulled his aluminum litter pan out of the bathroom. Closing the door tightly to keep Tag out and heat in, she turned on the ceiling heat lamp and started running the hot water in the shower. She stepped under the stream and let it warm her. The morning air was cold and she lingered there, almost wishing she'd scrubbed the tub and drawn a bath instead. If she missed anything about being home, it was her daily bubble bath.

The room went suddenly black but for the red haze cast by the heat lamp mingling with steam. "Damn," she grumbled, opening the door on the shower just wide enough to fumble for a towel on the rack. "They should have track lighting in these places so if a bulb burns out you're not thrust into darkness."

"They should also have timers on the plumbing. You going to stay in there all morning? Man has to relieve himself now and then, you know," Ben teased.

"Oh!" she jumped, startled. "Will you stop? You're supposed to be sleeping, not sneaking in here and scaring me half to death. Hand me a towel and I'll get out."

"Sleeping? How can a body sleep with all this racket going on? Coffee pots gurgling, water running, and a cat scratching in a roasting pan as if it were a sand dune. Why, it's enough to wake the dead," he retorted, as he shoved a towel through the door opening.

"Time for you to get up anyway. There's places to go, and things to see. If this fog ever lifts, that is." She wrapped the towel around her and paraded out of the room, slapping him on the rear as she passed.

"Oh, the maids are going to love you for that one, Abby." He chuckled, as she shut the door on him. "Crazy damn woman. If only I'd met her thirty years ago."

He poured himself coffee at the vanity and turned to see Amber encased in a blanket and the towel now wound around her head like a turban. Maps and books were spread out before her, and she held her empty coffee cup out to him without looking up. Tag was leaping and tunneling under the open road map at her knees, now crossed in a yoga-like position.

"By all means, Your Highness. Would that be one lump or two? Or would you prefer it black this morning?" he taunted, taking her empty mug with an exaggerated bow.

"Black will be fine," she replied, her eyes never leaving the charts in front of her, his humor escaping her.

"Say, Ben, how about we take I-40 east out of Knoxville and hook up with I-81 north through Virginia? Pretty country up that way but the interstate makes for easy traveling. We should try to cover some ground today, I suppose. I'd like to see Maine before the next ice age, and this mild weather is going to be coming to an end up north pretty darn soon. What do you think?" Finally, she looked up into his smiling eyes, oblivious to the picture she presented perched in the center of the bed like some Buddha incense burner.

"Whatever you say, Abby. I know as much about the eastern half of this country as Columbus did upon running the Pinta aground in the fog. Or, whatever the hell boat he was on." He handed her the coffee.

"Okay, Virginia it is. I'll get dressed and we can be ready to leave as soon as it clears a bit."

"Leave? Hell, when do we eat? I'm starving." He feigned collapse.

"You're always starving." She looked at him intently for just a moment, then away. "Ben? You never really answered me when I've asked. Why do you call me Abby?"

He thought for a second. "Oh, I don't know. Thought I did tell you. First time I ever saw your name on the return label when you wrote back to me I had a feeling. Almost like I kind of knew it before I even saw it. Abigale. But, you just seem more like an Abby. Why? Don't you like me calling you that?"

"Oh, I like it fine. Just curious is all." She didn't tell him that Jeff was the only person ever to call her Abby before.

The sun was clearing the summit of the eastern mountain range when they pulled out of the parking lot. Morning dew covered the grass and bushes in diamonds as the droplets caught the sunrays. It was as if the magic of the night before still lingered there on the lawn.

"It's going to be a spectacular day, guys," she fairly gushed at the three of them, Ben already looking around,

Bear back in his duty post, and Tag, now swatting at the Indian dream catcher dangling from the rearview mirror.

Traffic was heavy and slowing as they approached the ramps that flowed into I-40 East. She thought of how Knoxville had bulged into a major metropolis out of the vegetable farms she'd seen on her initial visit here so many years ago, but this bottleneck was the result of something more than the normal urban bustle.

"What the hell is this?" Ben wondered out loud.

"I don't know, but I'll find out." She turned on the CB and listened to the conversations of the truckers intermixed with the usual sarcasm and sporadic profanity as frustrated drivers complained of being late.

Ben was obviously entertained at the 'guy talk' coming over the Cobra's speaker. "They do get kind of pissed off, don't they?" He grinned while watching Amber surveying the rigs close by.

"Yes, it's wearing on the nerves sometimes, especially when tired," she answered. But her attention was more on the chatter on the radio than on his comments as she maneuvered in behind a candy-apple red Kenworth inching toward the same lane as her. She waited for a break in the prattle before removing the mic from its holder.

"Break Nineteen. Mr. Red KW, I've got your back door at the three-eighty-five heading east. Just turned the ears on. Could you tell me if this tie-up gets better or worse going to I-81? Come back."

"What're you driving, Little Lady? I don't see no rig at my back door."

"That's because what I'm driving would fit inside your rig, Mr. K. The little silver car that'll be in your left view in about five feet."

"That be a ten, Little Lady. Saw you pass back a ways. Sounds to me like a four wheeler thought he could move a Big Truck heading west. This side should smooth out once the neck stretchers get their fill."

"Heard that," she responded.

"Supposed to be a bad one, I hear. They just won't ever learn you can't stop a hundred on a nickel," he added.

"A dollar is stretchin' it," she agreed. "Best to stay put, or vacate?"

"I'd hang with my flaps back there because the alternates are already jammed. Ain't gonna get through here no faster unless that car can beam you up." The driver chuckled at his own joke.

"Thanks for the info, driver. We'll just stick to your back door then. Hope this doesn't ruin your day."

"Nah, I'm one of the lucky ones. Did my drop early and heading home for Mama's biscuits now."

"That's a big ten for sure." She genuinely smiled at the voice as she returned the mic to its clamp. She remembered the feeling all too well, a long haul driver with "home" in his sites.

Ben was smiling too. "How'd he know you weren't some woman just chiming in on the guy talk anyway?"

"Oh they know, believe me. Truck drivers are like cops. They know their own and stick together like glue, for the most part. It only takes about thirty seconds on a radio for them to know who's one of them and who isn't. I think I've told you before, on the open road give me a CB and a community of rigs and you can take all the cell phones and toss them in a can."

Although her voice was cheerful, Amber seemed nervous. "I can drive if you want," he offered.

"No. I'm okay, hon."

Three miles and a good half-hour later she saw the flashing lights of several State Patrol cruisers, various emergency equipment, and three ambulances. A pit formed in her stomach and she forced herself to keep her eyes on the Kenworth in front of her.

"Yeah, a bad one alright," Ben was saying. "Not a whole lot left of the four-wheeler, as they call it, but a bunch of twisted metal."

Beads of cold sweat formed on her back and seemed to settle in a pool at the base of her spine. She tried to inhale a

241

deep breath, but it stuck in her throat and a throbbing pain invaded her chest. The six westbound lanes of I-40 were completely closed down and the oncoming traffic was deadlocked, going nowhere. People were out of their vehicles milling around, probably speculating on how long they'd be delayed before getting on with their life. For a couple, under blankets on the pavement, that was no longer a concern.

The pit in her stomach grew into a rock. The radio crackled incessantly, and she squelched it to only the closest transmission. In what seemed like hours but was in reality only minutes, the voice of the driver ahead came over again.

"It's clearing ahead, Little Lady. We'll be back to speed in about a mile."

She took the mic in her trembling hand. "Thanks, KW. You have a good ride and enjoy your home time."

"Handle's Rawhide, ma'am. And, you and the hubby there keep that car on the ground, you hear? Be safe."

"Ten-four, Rawhide. We'll keep her on the ground and I'll be coming around you in about two." She felt the vise on her insides loosen just a little.

"You okay, Abby? You seem edgy all of a sudden." Ben was looking at the perspiration on her forehead.

"What? Oh, yes, I'm fine."

But she wasn't. He could tell something was bothering her. She merged into the left lane and ran side by side with the rig until the traffic started to move. The driver waved out the window, he waved back, and Amber spoke into the radio once more as they accelerated into the lead.

"Sure is a pretty 'Lady in Red' you got there, Rawhide. You take care now." Rawhide answered with a flash of his headlights and Ben saw Amber do something with the brake pedal to make a signal of her own as she gained speed and extended the distance between them.

"Ben, I'll take you up on that driving offer now. I need to relax for a couple hours. I think there's a rest area ahead and we could stretch our legs and change places."

"Sure, no problem," he answered. "You've been doing most of the driving since we left anyway. In fact, I'd enjoy piloting for awhile." He kept his tone light-hearted, sensing that something had upset her and he was sure it had to do with the accident.

At the rest stop, she'd gotten a Coke out of the vending machine and now pressed the cold, smooth surface of the can against her cheek and temple. She stared out the side window as the last vestiges of urban sprawl returned to farmland and thought back in time. Tag was attempting to squat on her shoulder so he, too, could get a better view as they moved along with Ben at the wheel. She'd dragged the stuffed bear into her lap and was clutching him close with her free arm.

How many times she'd gotten comfort from hugging Bear after the accident, his soft furry body gentle to her cracked bones, bruised and burned skin. His size comforting in a time of despair.

Ben remained quiet, glancing at her now and then out of the corner of his eye. He dialed the car radio to an easy listening station, lowered the volume, and concentrated on the panorama wrapped around the windshield.

"There's the sign for the I-81 Junction ahead," he said. "That's what I'm supposed to take, right? Sure came up fast."

Amber had just closed her eyes and was beginning to drift off. "Immm? Yes, just follow I-81 north to Roanoke. You don't mind if I rest awhile, do you? It's Blue Ridge country through here and you'll enjoy the vistas, I'm sure."

"I already am, babe. You relax and don't worry about me; I'll wake you if need be." He reached over and nudged Bear into her. "Or have this guy do it. Oh, and, maybe you should put Tag back in the console. I should keep my eyes on the road and he may decide to get frisky."

She opened her eyes as if coming from a dream. "Oh, yeah. Come on Tag, enough sightseeing for now."

She gently plucked the kitten off her shoulder and placed him back in his bed, covering him with Bear's bulky paw, while lying her own head on his pudgy chest for a

243

pillow. Ben glanced over and smiled at his trio. The kitten going in circles trying to find the very best curling position, the big white bear with his living glass eyes, and Abby, almost asleep now. She appeared angelic. Her halo, the auburn hair now fanned out across Bear's chest.

The whine of the engine propelled the sleek machine forward. The wind, shattered by its intrusion, slid over and under, the metal nose. The silver fuselage shimmered in the sun and the vibration of thrust.

She laid her head back and melted into the seat, letting the spirit of it have its head, take her wherever it wanted to go. The fuel to its heart increased by the pressure of her need to fly. Then it was free, the wheels giving in, releasing their grasp on the surface. It soared upward, a streak of silver becoming one with the sky, causing hawks to swerve and billowy clouds to open channels into their inner sanctums. She languished there as in a vacuum, cataleptic, not there, but nowhere else. A clandestine place. Was it time giving her years in but a second, lifetimes in a minute?

Suddenly the sun was devoured by a black eruption of smoke as something collided with her craft. Light disintegrated into blackness and she was falling, no plummeting, downward. A cacophony of twisting metal engulfed her, and the pain exploded in her chest. No Jeff! No!

"Abby! Abby, wake up!" Ben was vigorously pushing her shoulder.

She jolted straight up to the edge of her seat. "Stop!" she gasped. Rivulets of sweat rolled from her temples.

He turned the flashers on and veered to the shoulder of the highway. "I'm stopping. What is it? You've had a nightmare. Everything is fine, Abby. Fine."

"Don't call me that! My name is Amber!" Then, blinking, becoming aware of her surroundings again, she realized what she'd said. "Oh, Ben, I'm sorry. You're right. I had a nightmare. It must have been the accident. I thought I'd overcome that, but maybe not."

"What? Overcome what?"

She buried her face in her hands, then almost savagely released her seatbelt, throwing it free. "I can't stand that thing another minute!"

"Okay. OKAY, hold on. Jesus! We'll just sit here for a minute until you can calm down, alright?" He put his hand on her back, gently. "What is it because of that wreck? What?"

She shook her head and looked up. "It's all right, Ben, I'm okay now. Let's keep moving."

"But . . . ."

"Really, it's okay. We're only a couple hours from Roanoke and we can have lunch there. I'll just watch the scenery and be fine in a few minutes."

She was looking out the windshield, not at him, and he sensed that whatever had triggered the reaction might better be left alone for the moment. It was obvious she didn't want to talk about it, at least now. Reluctantly, he eased back onto the highway.

SPIRIT CARS, LUNAR LANDERS, AND LUNCH

The vibrant colors of autumn along the ridge tops teased the blue sky as the midday sun rose high. She felt relaxed again just looking at the landscape. Bear was back in his rear post, and Tag was making it clear that it was, indeed, time for lunch. Ben was singing along with the songs on an "Oldies" station he'd found, and she marveled at his knowledge of lyrics.

"Is there any song you don't know?"

"Hmmm? Nope. I'm a frustrated rock star, I guess. Love music."

"You don't like my Metal."

"Some I do, some I don't. Depends on my mood. Seems like a lot of hollering and hand waving with no substance. No heart. No soul. Hell, you hardly ever hear a harmonica in Metal. Do you? Huh?"

This brought a laugh out of her. "But, the heart and soul of Metal is in the vibration, hon. The beat is the substance."

"Well, yeah, the one's with a harmonica, I guess."

"Oh, there's a Shoney's sign. They have a great salad bar for lunch. Want to stop?"

"Sure, you know me. Always ready to eat," he said as he patted his stomach. He croaked out a Little Richard tune, winking at her as he turned off on the exit.

"Oh, for Pete's sake! That's terrible!"

"Yeah." He grinned. "Why I'm not a rock star."

They ate lunch surrounded by the scarlet chrysanthemums of the season. The day was as crystal, warm, with only a hint of fall in the air, and they'd taken their food outside to the patio tables. Amber seemed back to her usual self and he'd asked if she wanted to drive again, a test of her mood more than anything, but she'd declined and he was again behind the wheel while she scanned the road Atlas.

The miles dissolved into the afternoon as they continued north to the I-66 junction. There was little talk, both reflecting on their own thoughts, he enjoying the softer music, she lost in the movement. At the junction, he pulled into a rest area saying he was ready to stretch his legs and take a break. He asked where they were headed next, enjoying the impulse of it all.

"Over to hook up with I-95 North, the road to Maine," she answered.

Now they were moving east again, Amber back behind the wheel, and he was observing how she handled the car, almost reverently.

"How'd you get so attached to this car anyway?" he asked.

"Huh?" she answered above the wind roar, surprised at the question.

"Well, lots of folks like their cars, babe, but you seem almost part of this one, as if it was alive, or something."

She laughed. "I suppose it is kind of alive to me, especially this one."

"This one?"

"I've never really told you the story behind it, have I?"

"No."

"This is my second silver car, hon. The first one was totaled out in a bad accident not too long before I met you."

247

Aaah, so that's the reason she was so affected by the wreck this morning, he thought. "Accident? Were you hurt?"

"Yeah, kind of. A few cracked bones, some bruises and chemical burns from the airbag release, but nothing terribly serious. Other than the loss of my spirit, that is."

"The loss of your spirit? I don't get it. You mean depressed?"

"No, well, yes, but some things are hard to explain."

"Try me," he said.

She thought for a minute. "Spirit. What holds it, what gives it back? Like can an object, a thing, actually house a spirit? I don't know for sure, but I do know that for three weeks after I wrecked my car, I was empty. Everything just kind of lay dead in me, hopeless, as if my life was meaningless again. I felt like everything I'd overcome, any progress I'd made after Jeff died was all gone again."

"I see," he said, but really didn't.

"Oh, again, I went on with life, went back to work, tried to function normally. But I kept asking myself for what because it seemed I'd lost all sense of purpose for the second time. I thought I was losing my mind. All this misery over a damn car? I was alive; I should've been grateful. It seemed so mercenary, even to me."

"Go on," he said, determined to understand this weird way of thinking that so dominated her. Maybe because of what he hadn't told her about the cancer eating at his own spirit.

"Well, it wasn't just the car, I discovered. It was the spirit the car embodied, what it stood for, the getting beyond the loss of all I'd known in my life."

"You mean Jeff?"

"Yeah. The car had become symbolic of new life, new achievements, and especially new dreams. All those things rode in that silly car with me. It became a living, breathing thing to me, my soul expressing itself, getting back to life after Jeff died. And it had taken me two years."

He started to interrupt, question her philosophy, then stopped. Seeing her reaction earlier, she needed to get this out. And maybe he needed to know and understand it.

"I told myself there'd be another spirit car," she went on. "It was out there somewhere; I just had to find it. That helped, for a while anyway, but still, each day when I'd go downstairs and it wasn't there . . . I just can't describe the feeling of loss all over again."

"I can see that," he said, half talking to himself.

"I made email searches, phone calls, poured over the classifieds, but none were out there. It had to be an exact replica, and every door was slamming shut again."

She suddenly stopped. They were passing through the remnants of an old Appalachian farming hamlet. The hard pavement beneath them was the gravestone over what once was a fertile field. *Tobacco probably, she thought.*

A small group of shabbily dressed men were just beyond the guard rail pulling dried field corn off twisted stalks. She guessed they were gleaning the shriveled cobs missed by the picking machines before the cultivators came to turn the soil over for its winter rest. So many small family farms were succumbing to buyouts, fields on both sides of the highway showed the signs of conglomerate farming methods now.

These few workers, left in poverty, would scavenge enough grain to feed a bony old milk cow, or a pig or two, perhaps. Supplement for the welfare payments that never quite fed their families. These were the rural poor, victims of the machines and corporate farming that made sharecropping obsolete. *They'd know of lost and broken spirit, she thought.*

Ben's voice brought her back. "Go on with the story of your car, babe. What did you do when doors shut?"

"Got lost in feeling sorry for myself, I guess. You know, the why me syndrome." She rolled her eyes in mimic.

"I know that feeling, for sure." He laughed.

"Then one afternoon the phone rang. It was the dealer where I'd gotten the first car. They thought they had what I was looking for. Off I went, a flicker of hope starting to burn."

"I pulled my old sputtering, borrowed car into the lot and drove around to the side of the building, and there she sat, her silver gleaming almost electric, in the sun. My heart jumped into my throat when I spotted her even in the sea of cars parked around. She seemed to shout at me, and Ben, somehow I just knew."

"Knew? Knew what?"

"That's the hard to explain part. I walked over and as I did, I felt it. I felt something shudder in the very depths of me and go into her, like some kind of magnetized energy. It was a real physical feeling, like exhaling breath, like a connection of something within and without."

"What? Within and without?" His eyebrows rose in question.

She nodded. "All I could think of was that I'd absorbed the energy back out of the first car that day in the body shop when they told me it was totaled, but it needed another car, the connection, to come back to life."

"So, what are you saying here? You're saying that the spirit wasn't the car, but something within you that needed the car?"

She looked away. "No. What I'm trying to say is the energy in the car lived on even when the car didn't. Some-how, through me, it lived on."

He shook his head. "Abby—"

"Why it lay dormant within me I don't know. Maybe it had to go away for awhile, I don't know that either, maybe never will.

"Abby, look. It's . . . ." But she wasn't hearing him.

"Nothing ever dies," she blurted. "It can't. It can only change form because all form is only energy vibrating at different rates. But the energy, the Spirit, can go anywhere and be anything it wants. It's not bound by physical limits. And this particular Energy connected to me. This isn't just a car, Ben, but a part of me, or me of it." She turned to him and smiled. "And maybe why you happen to be sharing her with me now. It's part of you too."

"You're serious, aren't you?" He stared at her, wide-eyed.

250

"I've never been more serious in my life," she stated flatly.

There was a long pause between them, then he said, "I want to show you something. Since we'll be close to Washington D.C., let's spend a day there. But first, I need to find a rest stop with facilities."

"This is fantastic," she said.

"Yeah. It is, isn't it?" he agreed.

"When were you here before, hon?" she asked.

"Years and years ago. Come on, let's go to the Space Museum. It's over there, by that tall needle."

He took her hand and pulled her with him. They'd parked on the Mall, the vast expanse of lawn and trees that separated the two sides of the street, and had been going through the various buildings of the Smithsonian. Now inside the Space Museum, he pointed out the various airplanes hanging from the ceiling, the rocket plane that broke the sound barrier, the nose cone of the Spirit of St. Louis. Amber was fascinated.

"My God, people actually flew those things?" she asked, while pointing to one made from corrugated tin.

"And died in them. Air history is full of disasters as we learned a step at a time what it took to conquer the air. But, that's not why I brought you here. It's down this way. Come on, I'll show you." They walked along a corridor which opened up into an anti-room. "This is what I want to show you," he said.

She could see a machine of some kind above the heads of the crowd. It seemed totally unlike any of the airplanes they'd been looking at, and it wasn't until she got close that she guessed what it was.

"Is that—" She couldn't finish before he answered.

"Yes, ma'am. The Lunar Lander. Seems impossible that thing flew to the moon's surface and then back to the mother ship, doesn't it?" he answered, grinning.

"Yeah, what's all the gold foil on it for?"

251

"Protection from radiation, I suppose. Here, push on through. Let's get a closer look."

They maneuvered their way through the crowd up close to the module, and she was surprised at how big it was. "Sure is bigger than those little capsules they first used," she mumbled.

"Oh, yeah," he answered. "And to look at it, it seems impossible, doesn't it? That the thing actually was on another planet. Off-world."

"Yes, it sure does," she agreed.

"And this is what I wanted to show you, and why I asked to detour."

"Just this?" she asked.

"Yes, this." She wasn't catching on. "You were talking about spirits and cars and whatnot, remember? Well, this is an example of the human spirit and mind. It has no esoteric value at all, just plain old hard work and lots and lots of sacrifice. Desire, brain power, devotion. All human traits. Not a single, solitary spiritual thing involved whatsoever. No mysticism. Math is what took this thing to the moon, not myth. And courage. Same for those airplanes back there. Same for your car, silver or not." He looked into her eyes sternly.

She frowned. "It's not the same, Ben. How do I make you see that this, all this, is but the tip of the iceberg? There's so much more. Damn, why do you have to be so pragmatic?

"I don't know, babe. My brain, I guess. My genes. Something. Maybe my experiences in life, maybe everything I am."

"Do you mind if we move on?" she asked. "The crowd is starting to bother me." She wanted to change the subject. It wasn't something she felt the need to fight about.

"Sure, babe. Follow me," he answered. He took her hand and pushed their way through the crowd, back to the corridor. "How about if we go to the prehistoric part next?"

"Fine." She wondered how he'd try to use fossils to prove her wrong.

They crossed the Mall to another building, he excitedly pointing out things along the way, she nodding agreement.

He showed her the Hope Diamond, but that didn't impress her either. "Just another shiny rock," she said.

"Yeah, true enough, but that rock has cost several their lives."

"It's still just coal, same as you'd find in any coal bin until it goes through the needed processes. And people died over it out of their greed for wealth."

"Well, maybe that's the point. That it isn't necessarily what's here on earth, but what we make of it that makes all the difference."

"Yes. It was just coal until man attached his values to it. It already had its own value whether a hunk of coal or a diamond. It's just varying forms of the same thing." She was being stubborn now, too.

"Yes, it is, and maybe that's the other point." He looked deeply into her eyes. "Just coal. No spirits, no myths. Just coal."

"Okay, Ben, just coal. But here's a point for you to ponder. You talk of no mysticism, no higher concepts, no Spirit behind all this wonder. Just simple old math and human ingenuity. So you tell me. What human ingenuity created that beautiful Hope Diamond out of a lump of coal?"

"Pure and simple physics, Abby. No magic."

"All right, just simple physics. So, did human ingenuity construct, invent, this simple physics, or did they merely discover what was already there? Did magic cease to be magic just because humans finally understood it?"

"Well, not exactly."

"Does the fact that human ingenuity made it possible to land that funny-looking thing on the moon negate the magic of the moon? Or, again, the physics that made it possible to pull off the feat once it was discovered and understood? Does that eliminate the Spirit behind it all?"

"Well . . . ."

"Could it be that magic is only magic when we fail to grasp the concept, and that really nothing is magic at all? The supernatural is as natural as we allow it to be in our ingenious brains. That's what put that landing craft on the moon, Ben, not physics, but magic which was already there." She put her arm around him and looked up at him.

"What put it there were creative and imaginative minds that refused to be limited by lumps of coal. Minds that will allow a spirit to dwell in a silver car, or calm a distressed bear. It's the limiting mind of this-is-all-there-is that's caused so many to lose their lives over the diamond. Now let's not argue about it anymore, okay?"

He shrugged. He'd hoped that what he was showing her would, somehow, get her off this Mystery Tour she seemed to be on. Back to earth. He didn't even know why he was making the attempt, as he'd certainly seen enough strange things in his own life to wonder about. And, now her questions had him wondering again because what she said did make sense, even if he wouldn't admit it.

It was when they were moving back to the car that he seemed to get an urge. "What is it?" she asked, seeing his face.

"I don't know. Just something is pulling me toward the Space Museum again." He looked at his watch. "Do you mind if we go back to it for a while?"

"Hon, at this rate, it'll take fifty years to get to Maine," she grumbled.

"Oh, babe, come on. Where's your adventurous spirit? No pun intended." He grinned. "Besides, it's time to eat and they have a lunch counter."

She checked her watch. "It's past lunch. It's three o'clock."

"Yeah." He grinned that mischievous grin of his. "Come on."

"Oh, all right. But just to eat, okay? I need to see about Tag, and . . . ."

"Tag's okay. Come on." He took her hand as they crossed the Mall yet again, pointing out the Washington Monument in the distance, and checking his watch. "Hurry."

"Hurry? What for? If it's closed, there are lots of other places to eat."

254

He didn't answer but almost dragged her along, his face both intent and half-smiling.

They were back in the museum wading their way through the crowds toward the lunch counter, when she heard a familiar voice call out to her.

"Mom? Hey, Mom, over here!"

Recognizing the voice instantly, she spun around to see her two sons standing by the lunch counter waving at her.

"So that's why you wanted me to stop at a rest stop with a phone." She was waving back and dancing on her toes.

He smiled. "I thought it was probably time to check in with your kids and introduce myself as well. So, I got the number from your address book when you were asleep, and when we got within range, I called and set this up."

"Damn!" she said, as she rushed off to greet them.

"Yeah." He grinned at her back as if he'd just pulled off the greatest surprise. Which to her, he had.

The meeting with her sons went smoothly. They all ordered sandwiches and attention was turned to him, them sizing him up, he answering their questions and such. They seemed impressed with his sincerity, and especially his knowledge of airplanes and flight. But the fact that he'd gone to such extremes to meet them and have them see their mother was the most telling of all.

Amber wanted an update of how things were going with them, and chattered of Ben's and her adventures when she could get a word in. Yet, it was obvious for this time they were more interested in who she was traveling the country with, than where they'd traveled.

Mentioning the traffic in the city and lack of time to plan, they left soon afterward. In a flurry of hugs and promises to be in touch, they headed to the door, leaving Amber a bit tearful and Ben stoic.

"They seem like good kids," he said quietly, watching them walk away. "You're lucky to have such closeness."

She wiped away a tear and took his hand. "Yes, they're good boys. I've been truly blessed in so many ways." *So very many ways, she thought.* "Thank you for doing such a thoughtful thing, hon."

"Well, Bro, what do you think?" the younger asked.

The two brothers ambled across the parking lot toward their car, the first fallen leaves chattering at their ankles.

"Oh, I don't know. He seems like a nice enough guy and Mom seems kind of taken with him. What did you make of him?" the oldest responded.

"Well, he isn't dad."

"No, he's not. Is that what you expected, to have dad suddenly reappear? No one Mom ever meets is going to replace dad, you know. Not for her either. But she's too young to spend the rest of her life alone, and dad wouldn't want her to."

They'd reached their vehicle and the youngest didn't reply right away as he unlocked the doors and climbed in. He was the deep thinker of the two and tended not to be swayed by appearances. "I suppose you're right, but she was perfectly content being alone, or so she said," he continued once they were moving out of the lot. "She never held back her adventuresome ways either. Always off in that damn car of hers going somewhere or hopping a plane around the country."

"Something is bothering you. What is it?" The older brother turned to look at his sibling.

"Oh, not really bothering me. I think Mom is safe enough with the guy. He does seem to be caring of her. Pretty cool, too, that he thought enough to call and set this up. She definitely wasn't expecting it. I understand he has a son of his own."

"What's that got to do with anything?"

"Nothing. I just thought of it is all. Mom mentioned something about it once."

They pulled onto the beltway and ground in to the last remnants of rush hour traffic leaving the city.

"Help me watch for the Philly signs, will you? I don't come over here that often."

They rode in silence out of the urban congestion, the oldest straining to see what he could of the DC landmarks. It was his first visit to the Capitol. Once beyond and moving in the direction of home, the youngest spoke again.

"Mom always says there's no such thing as coincidence and it's odd that you just happened to be here when the call came to meet up with her and this Ben. Did she know you were coming from Chicago this week?"

"Nope. I haven't talked to her since she left home. She called a couple times and left a message on my machine but I missed the calls, and with them on the road there was never a return number. I figured she might call you while I was here." He laughed then.

"What's so funny?"

"Nothing really. It does appear as one of those unexplained things she always goes on about, as if destined or something, but she was obviously surprised at seeing us. Almost nervous."

"Yes. That's what was bothering me. She seemed preoccupied about something.

"Oh, she was just worried we wouldn't like the guy, or he wouldn't get on with us. That's all."

"I hope so. Damn! Look. There on the side of the road." He slowed down so they could better see the wood line along the side of the highway. The sun was just above the horizon, and the scarlet tinge cast a pinkish glow on the shoulder grass. There at the edge of the forest, the sleek body of a fox scampered in front and along side the car.

"Yeah, I see it! Cool!"

"Odd to see a fox here, just outside the city. Deer, yeah, but not a fox. Haven't seen one in years."

They slowed and pulled off onto the shoulder out of the moving traffic to get a better look. The animal hesitated then stopped, its breath creating a slight mist as it panted from the run. It stood there, for a brief moment, intently watching the now stopped car and its occupants, and then slowly backed into the cover of the forest.

FOUR DAYS NORTH

The clarity of the early fall skies, and the tepid days of Indian summer continued north. Vivid forests had lured them into bypassing the big east coast cities, and they stuck to the back roads up through Connecticut, Massachusetts, and on into New Hampshire.

Ben was enthralled with the rural settings after so many years of being ensconced in the hustle of what he called "West Coast Glitz," among a few other choice pseudonyms. He couldn't get his fill of the old and weathered clapboard structures and the quaint stores they'd rummaged in the sleepy towns. Every small shop was laden with treasures of times past in this, an antique buff's paradise. And it had brought forth a deluge of reminiscent stories told him by his grandfather.

For her, the shops now adorned with mottled ears of Indian corn, weird shaped squash, and wind chimes, held endless hours of amusement. The hand-carved wood workings of the local craftsmen, awe. She was as a kid in any penny candy store, and "Oooh, Ben, look at this" seemed to be the only words she could utter.

The car was packed tight in every available cubit, affording Tag endless entertainment, and Bear now sported a wardrobe of various straw hats and Indian trinkets. Ben had shaken his head in bewilderment when she'd bartered an exchange with a vendor, her precious lamp for a Birch bark bird house and a whittled owl.

"It takes less room," she'd explained, "and the lady said the lamp reminded her of her mother."

They'd spent four glorious days exploring the towns and shops, the hiking trails in the forests, and each other. At night, they'd rented quiet and simple cottages; one by a trout stream where Ben had caught a fish with a makeshift pole and a safety pin with only a breakfast Cheeto for bait.

"Now what are you doing?" she'd asked, seeing him tying a string to a limb he'd found along the walking path.

"What am I doing?" he grinned, as the line floated out over the water and landed with a plop. "Something as old as life itself, babe."

She smiled, doubting he'd ever catch anything with a Cheeto and a safety pin. She sat on a nearby stump just enjoying watching him, and it wasn't five minutes before the string was taut, and he was trying to land whatever he'd caught.

"Ha! See? See!" He was backing up, dragging whatever it was toward the bank. Surprised, she hurried to see.

"Get the net!" he yelled.

"Net? We don't have a net."

"Oh, yeah. Forgot. Not to worry." And he was right. He quickly and carefully dragged a small trout onto the land, and just as quickly ran to grab it before it slipped off the makeshift hook and slid back into the stream.

"Ta-daaa!" he exclaimed, as he held the fish up for her inspection.

"Oh, Ben, it's beautiful. Look at all those colors."

"Yeah, it's a beauty, all right." He was smiling broadly.

They inspected the minimal hold of the pin a larger fish would have had no problem escaping, amazed that it had held at all. The fish was gasping and struggling, trying to get free from his hand, and Ben's joy suddenly turned serious.

"What do you say we let it go?" he said.

259

"Oh, yes. He's so young and he deserves his time, too."

She wrapped her arms around his waist as he tossed the fish back into the water, and smiled up at him lovingly when he followed it with the remains in the Cheetos bag.

"Here, don't forget your supper," he called to the departing fish. "Don't be so gullible next time, either," he said as he turned to her, still smiling. "I like to catch them. Just don't like to kill them."

She marveled again at his gentle side, gentleness he often worked at concealing. And she wondered why. They fell silent, listening to the rising crescendo of twilight sounds as the sun set and the stars began to light up the night. Only the chill in the air drove them back inside the cabin.

In the four days traveling north through New England, they'd discovered treasures, built fires, and cooked simple meals over the flames. They'd read the towns' ten-page newspapers by the light of an oil lamp she had found in a junk store, and watched a Harvest Moon rise over the White Mountains while sitting on a boulder that jutted out of the hill behind their cottage.

She watched Ben's skin take on a healthy glow, lines soften, and a long searched-for peace come into his eyes. She felt sure the healing powers were taking the last vestiges of his cancer away. Likewise for her, each day, each moment, took on a joy long since felt. Even Tag seemed immersed in the various adventures, gleefully happy to ride in the over sized pocket of the yellow windbreaker she now wore everywhere on the crisp fall days. His little face and two paws peeking out the opening had gotten the attention of many a shopkeeper, and giggles from many a child.

Evenings were spent sharing dreams and philosophies while they watched the flames of tall, multicolored tapers melt their wax down the sides of an old wine bottle found in a Collectibles boutique.

"I'm going to create our very own rainbow," she'd said, caressing the bottle. "The colors of *our* life, and *our* time to be. They're going to be colors of bright and vibrant hue.

Reds of scarlet, forest greens, and yellow, too. Violet, earth tones, and shades of blue." Then, she'd tossed her head back and laughed, suddenly realizing her words had taken on the poetry she felt in her heart.

The following morning she'd awakened with a bit of a start, and found the other side of the bed empty. Ben's sleep habits left room to be desired, and it was not uncommon for him to wake up in the middle of the night, even to take a walk outside to keep from disturbing her. But he was always at her side come daylight, and now she felt a sharp pang of concern.

Rising quickly, she wrapped herself in a blanket to go investigate his whereabouts. He wasn't inside the cabin, and she pulled the denim drape away from the small window to look outside. She spotted him then, sitting on the old porch chair, his yellow writing pad propped on his crossed knee.

Smiling as Tag leaped on the contrails of blanket on the floor at her feet, she strolled back to the tiny bedroom off the main room of the cottage, the kitten in pursuit.

"Maybe Ben's getting a muse, Taggie. He's a writer you know," she informed him. The kitten was half way up the blanket now and not in the least impressed at this latest revelation. "Let's lie back down for awhile and leave him be. Writers need their space." She didn't know how much time had passed when Ben gently nudged her shoulder.

"Going to sleep all day, Abby? Here, I brought you something."

Rising on one elbow, she took the mug of coffee he was holding out to her. "Thanks, hon. You always know exactly what I need."

"Brought you something else, too." He grinned sheepishly and handed her a piece of yellow paper off his pad.

"What's this?" She took it and saw the scrawl of his writing across the page.

"Why don't you read it and see?"

Across the top was a title . . . "The Bow." She started to read out loud . . . *"Long ago, an angel sat around with nothing to do. So God gave it a paintbrush . . . ."*

She read on in silence as the power of his words impacted her instantly. Near the end and wiping tears away, she cleared her throat and continued out loud . . . *"Thus did the angel get its clue, and to the earth below it flew. It painted red, it painted blue, purple, yellow, indigo too. It shaped the colors into form, and hooked them onto tail of storm. It made them liquid so they'd show, it made them sparkle so we'd know, then threw the brush into the sky as if to say 'The You is I.'*

"And God was pleased and made it so, and that's how rain became rainbow. For to each, and all of us, we can always see that brush. It tells us all just not to fear, for when it rains, the It is near. We know It by its graceful curve, that what it represents is love. Perfection on a higher scale, be we Angel, Man, or Snail. There is no loss, there is no found, but only rainbows, all around."

"Oh Ben! Did you write this? How did you write this?" she cried.

"Well, sure I wrote it, Abby. I wrote it for you. It sort of came to me thinking of your little rhyme last night, and your rainbow bottle candle, and the story you told me of your double rainbow taking care of you."

She fairly leaped into his lap, throwing her arms around his neck. "Ben, this is the most beautiful thing I've ever read in my entire life! And you wrote it just for me? Damn! Thank you! Thank you, so very much."

Her tears wetted his cheeks, and he was a bit taken aback by her intense reaction to his simple ramblings. But a warm knot began to swell in his chest, and he was suddenly shocked to realize that his own tears mingled with hers. Almost simultaneously, they realized. No longer any doubt, any questioning, a greater love had found them both again. Perhaps, it had never left . . . *"there is no loss, there is no found . . . ."*

Each morning the burgeoning candle of many colors was packed with care in the trunk safely away from Tag's curiosity.

"Ben?" She leaned in to him. They were standing waiting their turn for a breakfast table in a packed little diner at the junction of Highway 16 and US2. He had draped his arms over her shoulders and was resting his chin on the top of her head.

"Immm-hmm."

"Maybe we should just sit at the counter. Can you eat grits at a counter?" she joked.

"Can eat grits standing up if I have to. Why? You in a hurry?"

"Oh, not really in a hurry, but I sure don't want to spend the morning here. I wonder why this place is so busy. We're practically in the wilderness, for Pete's sake."

"Well, woodsmen have to eat, too, you know. Looks like a logging crew to me. They'll be on their way quick enough," he answered, sensing her impatience.

"You're right, of course. I'm just antsy to get on with the day." She cupped his hands with her own, pressing them against her.

"Seat over in the corner if you want it," a harried waitress announced as she rushed by, her tray holding heaping stacks of pancakes. "I'll be there in a minute to clean it."

"Thanks, take your time," Amber said, feeling empathy for the girl. "And look, hon, at least the table is by the window."

"Sure is. You send up a thought wave or something?" He was teasing her, but it did seem as if *something* watched over her.

Though the place was busy, it was efficient, and in no time they had their breakfast plates in front of them. Ben wolfed down his eggs and grits with as much gusto as any logger while she dabbled in her fruit cup and broke tiny pieces off the bacon she'd ordered for Tag. No one seemed

263

to notice the bulge in her pocket, and she grinned down at the kitten munching on the bacon bits.

"He thinks he's a baby kangaroo, I think," she mumbled, "perfectly content in his little pouch."

"Better not let him see those birds or he'll be leaping all over the place." Ben nodded toward a pair of Blue Jays having breakfast at the bird feeder just outside the window.

"Oooh. Aren't they just beautiful? The morning sun paints radiance into the blue of their feathers like an artist's brush. I can't wait to get on the road. You just about done?" She wiggled in her seat, wrapped the remaining bacon in a napkin and signaled for the waitress.

"Yeah, I'm done and the day is beckoning out there, I must admit." He drained the last of his coffee from the mug and smiled at her enthusiasm. "Where are we anyway?"

"The first day of the rest of our lives." She grinned at him and winked.

"There it is! Stop the car." She was frantically digging in the dash compartment. "Pull off. I've got to get out."

"Good God, what's the matter now?"

Her sudden outburst startled him as they'd driven the last ten miles silently, absorbing the world of green rushing past the windows. He veered to the shoulder, and before he could bring the car to a complete stop Amber had the door open and was jumping out into a sea of Goldenrod that bordered the gravel easement. Then he saw what had sent her digging for the camera and trotting down the side of the road.

She turned back to face him and he heard her yelling, "Come on, Ben. Get out. I want to take a picture of you by it!"

There, just forty or fifty feet ahead of them, almost hidden in the wildflowers, a faded carved-wood sign announced . . . *Welcome to Maine.*

264

BOOK THREE

UP THE LONG, DELIRIOUS BURNING BLUE

Ben had spotted a small grass landing strip just after crossing into Maine and turned in. The air was crisp and clean, nary a cloud in the sky.

"What are you doing now?" she asked.

He winked at her. "You said you wanted to go flying with me some day, didn't you?"

"What? We're going flying? Now? Here?"

"Why not? Look at that sky. Doesn't it just call out to you?"

She looked. "Well, yes, it's a wonderful sky, and yes, I said I wanted to fly with you, but this place is almost deserted. Is it safe? What about Tag? What will we do with him?"

"Why, hell, babe, take him along, of course. But not Bear. He's too fat to fit," he joked.

"Oh, Ben, cats can't fly in a plane without a pressurized cabin. Won't he get a nosebleed or something?" she protested.

But he was already pulling up next to what seemed to be an office of some sort. She saw no runway, but rather, what appeared to be a slightly worn grass strip.

"Stay here," he said as he got out and headed for the small building.

She looked around. There weren't any airplanes in view and she was kind of relieved. She patted the kitten and cooed to it. "It's all right, Taggie. I don't think we have to worry."

Her thoughts changed when Ben came back smiling. "All set?"

"All set for what? There aren't even any airplanes here. And besides, I thought you said you didn't have a license anymore."

"I don't. But some things you never forget, like riding a bike. Plus I already gave the guy a hundred bucks, so we're stuck."

"Stuck? Hon, I don't think any plane they have around here is very safe. Look at this place." She waved her arm in a half circle. "It doesn't even look used."

"Bull. Now come on, we're wasting the day." With that he was sprinting around to the back of the office. Reluctantly, she and Tag got out and followed.

"Don't worry," she cooed again to the kitten. "He'll change his mind when he sees we're nervous about this." Tag peered over the edge of her pocket and didn't appear worried at all.

"Oh, my God!" She stared, dumbfounded, as a little red and white fabric-covered high wing appeared from beneath the cover Ben was pulling away. "You can't be serious," she called to him. "We're not going up in *that!*"

He laughed. "Ah, babe, don't be like that. Why, this little cub will give you more thrills than a dozen other airplanes. You'll see."

"See? Not me. We'll just watch today. Maybe next time."

"Get in," he said as he went around the airplane checking it out. "The front."

"Oh, God. We'll be killed for sure, Tag."

She had to bend under the wing to even approach what seemed to her a flimsy fuselage. She looked into the cockpit at the crude instruments, the stick control, the little pedals on the floor and the smell of gasoline and grease. Small as she was, it would be a feat even getting into the plane.

"Oh, no," she said, backing out.

"Oh, yes," he said from behind, opening the tiny door and fairly lifting her and the kitten into the front seat. "Put the stick between your knees." He guided her as she tried to settle in. "And put your seatbelt on."

"But, where will you sit?" she objected. "And what'll I do with Tag? This isn't going to work, Ben." She started struggling to get out.

"Right behind ya, babe, and yes, it will work. You just hold on to Tag and everything will be fine once we're in the air."

"But . . . ." She felt him climb into the rear seat and holler at her to close her door. The next thing she knew the little engine coughed, smoked, and kind of belched into life. Tag was trying to get away from the noise, the smell, and probably, the insanity of it all.

"Ben, NO!" she yelled, but the plane began moving even as she said it. She looked back over her shoulder and Ben was grinning ear to ear as they bounced along the grass. He motioned for her to put on the earphones hanging beside her, and she frantically did.

"How do you like it so far?" she heard him say through the earphones.

"Maybe we should go back," she yelled. "Tag is scared and so am I." But he didn't answer.

"Ben? BEN! You hear me?" She looked again over her shoulder and he pointed to a microphone, also beside her. She could swear he was enjoying scaring the life out of her.

She grabbed the mic and yelled into it. "Ben, damn you, take us back, please!" But the little plane lifted off at the same time she was cursing him, and now she really was stuck.

"Damn you, Ben!"

"Okay, Abby, now you just relax. I'll take us up nice and easy and I bet even Tag will enjoy it," he said through her earphones.

"I think I'm going to kill you," she said, but she somehow knew he was right as the small airplane slowly climbed skyward. Within a minute, even the kitten was poking his head out of her pocket, looking around through the Plexiglas windows, seemingly enchanted.

As she relaxed, suddenly she knew what he'd been trying to tell her about the sky. This . . . this was absolutely glorious. She'd never been in a small plane before, much less an open one, and what a difference it made. The air smelled as clean as she'd ever smelled it, the sky bluer than she'd ever seen it, even the movement of the plane seemed impossible to believe.

"Told you." Ben's voice teased.

For the next hour, they flew in gentle circles, one into another. He took them down close to the ground, so close they went around isolated trees, not over them, close enough to see the expression on the cows' faces, and the running of rabbits.

How much you can see up here, she thought. It's like another world.

He showed her how the controls worked and let her fly some, and the more she did it, the more she wanted to. Stick over right, pull back at the same time, and push the pedal gently, too. Suddenly, the sky and the planes that trespassed there were nothing to be afraid of. Flocks of birds passed beneath them, and they spotted a hawk making lazy circles until scared off by the airplane. Off in the distance, you could see smoke from chimneys, and roads below that looked like flowing ribbons.

He told her how the instruments worked and what they were for, and she was a rapt student. They banked right, then left, and he did a gentle stall so she could hear the Stall Warning Horn. It frightened Tag so he didn't do it again. They flew and flew, and she was totally enthralled by it all.

"Oh, hon, you were right. This is just captivating."

"Glad you like it, babe. But I knew you would."

She did a pirouette around a point on the ground, climbed the airplane, wiggled the tail with her foot pedals, and flew sideways. She was thrilled at what a machine, freed from constraints, could do. What a human free of the earth, could do.

Then they were coming down, gliding to the ground below, and she did what he told her. Any fear she'd brought along, gone. She was at full attention as he guided her in, and stayed on the controls with her, working the throttle.

"Let it crab into the wind," he said. She did.

"Keep the nose up." She did.

The prop was windmilling, turning so slowly she could almost see it, and the strip was coming up beneath them. She did as he said and didn't look at it, but ahead and off to the side instead. One hundred feet . . . fifty . . . twenty . . . half of twenty . . . five.

She felt him making small corrections to the controls as he talked to her over the headset, and she was flaring, holding the plane off the ground just inches above the grass without even realizing it, and then they felt the soft *thud-thud* as the wheels gently touched the ground.

By God, she thought. I just landed an airplane! Damn! "BEN! I JUST LANDED AN AIRPLANE!" She yelled out in her excitement.

Tag, in his pocket seat, meowed his approval.

"Ha, ha." She heard him laugh over her earphones.

Driving away, Ben seemed totally content, even smug. She was dazed, as if she still couldn't believe what they'd just done.

"What are you grinning about?" she asked, poking him.

"You. I haven't seen you that excited, ever."

"Well, it isn't everyday I fly airplanes, or land them."

"Liked it, huh?"

"Are you kidding? I *loved* it! When can we do it again? Let's get a room nearby and go again tomorrow."

"Not here, I don't think." He laughed.

"Why not? What's so funny?"

"That shack wasn't an office. It was a shed full of gasoline, oil and some tools, that's all."

She didn't get it at first. "What are you saying?"

269

He laughed. "We kind of borrowed the airplane. But it's all right, because we brought it back. And, I left a hundred on the seat to pay for the gas like I said."

"My God! She gasped. "You mean we were flying around in a stolen airplane?"

He grinned and nodded. "Yeah. No one in their right mind would rent out their plane to an unlicensed pilot. Nobody."

"Oh, for Pete's sake! You mean we could've been arrested? We could've gone to jail? I don't believe this," she stammered. "I can't believe you! Are you nuts?"

He laughed. "Yeah. Ain't it grand?"

"Damn! But, yes, I suppose it is." She laughed then, too, a hearty laugh. "It sure is."

That evening having supper at a roadside café, a candle on the table their only light, she noticed him watching her, smiling in sort of Cheshire cat way.

"Now what?"

"I was just thinking about how you took to that airplane, like it was the natural thing to do."

"Hmmm . . . it did seem natural, I guess. I mean, once I got over being afraid of it. I was the same way the first time I was on the ocean, too. I've always found nature so extraordinary. The living things. You know, the critters and the flowers, stuff like that. But the sheer enormity of the ocean and the sky, made me feel so fragile, so helpless in comparison; I simply revered them, as if to invade would be to scorn."

"That's understandable. They're forces to be reckoned with for sure. Many have died for taking them lightly."

"Oh, yes. My fear was, is, of my own smallness, I suppose. But once up there today, I felt like I'd been taken out of the ordinary and made huge. It's as if you become one with it, and then it welcomes you, caresses you. The sea did that, too."

"You must become one with it," Ben agreed. "Secret is to ride with it, work with it not against it. Let the plane ride the air instead of fighting it."

"Yeah. Like a butterfly riding a tsunami wave. It won't be hurt at all if just flows with the water."

He took her hand in his, gave it a gentle squeeze, and smiled at her in the candle glow. He said no more but his expression spoke volumes.

"Thanks, hon." She smiled sweetly. Thanks for stealing that airplane and introducing me to the sky. For all my trips on big jets, I'd never really met the sky before."

"Believe me, babe, the pleasure was all mine. And now we better think about finding a place to spend the night before it gets much later. You must be tired, and Tag is probably ripping up your console by now."

"You're right. I am weary after all the excitement." She hesitated to break the spell cast by the recollection and the candle, but she really wanted to be alone with him now, away from waiters, busboys, and rattling dinner plates.

They found a small motel just on the outskirts of town. Nothing fancy, rather old, but charming and apparently clean. The vacancy sign weakly announced an available room in a flickering green. They turned in and Ben emerged from the office moments later with a key attached to a long wooden stick.

"Number thirteen at the very end," he said, pointing to the left. "Thought they didn't use that number in buildings."

"Thirteen is a fine number, hon. My lucky number in fact." She grinned at him.

"Why am I not surprised?"

"Oh, you always say that, but you are really." She laughed.

Inside, she was downright thrilled at the discovery of a small veranda through an old French-paned door leading off the one room. Peering out the tucked and drawn lace curtain, she noticed it was furnished with a wicker loveseat.

"Oh, Ben, look what's out here."

271

"Don't tell me it has a damn swing," he teased, as he peeked out with her.

Ben fed Tag while she made coffee and carried the Styrofoam cups out to a small table by the wicker seat. The stars shone superb over the tree tops, and the night air, although nippy, held on to Indian summer. The rattan creaked under her weight, and gazing upward, she imagined what it would be like to fly at night among the jewels of the sky.

"Taking a night flight are you?" He sat down beside her, picked up his coffee, and draped his arm casually across her shoulders.

"Mmmm. How'd you know?" She snuggled against him and laid her head back on his shoulder, never taking her eyes away from the mural sprawled above her.

"Lucky guess, I guess." He hugged her gently. She turned to look up at him. Cupping her chin with his free hand, he lowered his face to hers. Her eyes closed with the taste of him, but the stars never left her view.

He felt a small twinge of pain in his depths and a cold chill began inching up his spine. He held her tighter, almost desperately, and it passed as quickly as it had come.

THE SEA, BEN, THE SEA

"Ben, can you smell that?" The question came out as a whisper.

"Smell what?" he said, but was instantly alert, thinking something amiss with the car. "I don't smell anything out of the ordinary. What are you talking about?"

She inhaled deeply. "The sea, Ben. The sea. I can smell it."

For all her kinship with the mountains and the forests that dressed them, it was the sea that pulsed through her veins. The one thing that both calmed and riled her, that taught her the sheer magnitude of the forces lying just beyond understanding.

They'd risen early that morning, packed, and were on the road before full daylight, spurred somewhat by Ben's less than ethical acquisition of the airplane. Throughout the day they'd meandered across the back roads of Maine, an easterly direction their only goal, and guided by the state roadmap in her *Trucker's Atlas*. By late afternoon, they'd chosen a peninsula jutting out into the ocean as the best place to begin their exploration of the coast. They'd picked up Coast Highway 1 at Belfast and veered north, and now she could smell their destination.

"What say we find a place to stay and start fresh in the morning, hon? It's getting kind of late, and by the time we get you and Tag supper I think you'll be ready to call it a day."

He looked at her almost gratefully. "Sounds good to me. We've covered just about the width of this state today and I'm ready to eat."

"You'd be ready to eat if we'd covered ten miles." Grinning, she leaned over and poked him.

"Not everyone is able to subsist on grapes, fruit cups, and green tea, you know," he chided. "And Tag told me he's about ready to consume the Idaho page out of your map book there."

"Okay, okay! I can take a hint. The next place we see, we'll stop."

A few miles farther Ben spotted a faded sign advertising a "Traveler's Rest" three miles ahead. It was good he'd seen the sign for they almost passed up the rickety old cabins that looked like something out of a Hitchcock thriller. At first glance it seemed deserted, but a dim light in the building nearest the road beckoned her to slow and turn in.

"Geeze, Abby, it's so quaint, it's almost eerie. Maybe we should go on and see what else we find?"

"We might as well check since we're already here. Maybe whoever's inside can tell us where to eat if nothing else." What she didn't tell him, or couldn't, was the sudden pull she felt in some deep corridor of her mind as she'd neared the dim glow shed from the window.

She parked in front of the little cabin and Ben got out to knock on the door, motioning her to follow. On the third attempt, a dog barking inside told them it was occupied. He raised his hand to knock again as the door opened. A bent-over, elderly woman with flowing hair peeked around the door.

"Suppose your lost and needing directions?" It was more of a statement than a question.

"Why no, ma'am, we're inquiring about your cabins and a place to find some supper around here." He smiled at the old woman now in full view in the doorway.

"There's four cabins here but not much call for them now," she answered in a resigned voice. "The big hotels have spattered up the coast. These aren't up to date with cable TV and all that, but they're clean, and I pay a boy to keep wood chopped for the stove. You know how to work a wood burning stove?" She was looking past them at the silver sports car. Like the old man in the country store, everyone seemed to assume the car indicated spoiled occupants.

"I can handle that part of it as long as I can get some food first." He turned to look at Amber as he spoke.

"Got a small family eating place about two miles down." The woman pointed. "If you like clam chowder, best around. Some good codfish and lobster, too, I hear. I don't get out to meals much myself, so don't know first-hand."

Suddenly Amber's heart swelled for the old lady and she stepped closer. "We'd like one of your cabins for one night if it's available, and we'd be happy to bring you back supper if you haven't eaten yet. Maybe, you'd even like to ride along with us, Ms. . . . ."

"Ingram. The name is Ingram. Alice, if you'd like."

"Why, yes, Alice. My name is Amber and this is Ben." She locked her arm through his. "Would you mind that we have a kitten with us? He'll cause no damage, I assure you. Hardly leaves my side."

"That'd be fine, but better keep it indoors. Big coons running round here at night. I'll get the key and show you around."

They heard her talking to the dog as she disappeared into the shadowy interior of her own cabin. "The poor thing looks so fragile and weary, Ben. Let's stay, regardless. So what if the cabin isn't modern? We can rough it for one night and the restaurant isn't far. Can we?"

"Fine with me, babe. Might be kind of fun to throw a log in an old pot-bellied wood stove and watch the fire inside. Used to do that when I was a kid."

Ms. Ingram, Alice, reappeared with an old-fashioned skeleton key on a metal ring. An age-yellowed tag, tied on, bore a large number 2. She passed between them and started across the small yard to the cabin adjacent to her own. The door groaned as it was pushed open, and Alice gestured Ben and Amber to follow. Inside, a flick of a switch bathed the room in a soft ruddiness, and Amber found herself almost surprised that it had electricity.

She was instantly taken with the dwelling. A rustic dresser in the corner held a cracked ceramic wash bowl and pitcher with hand-painted sunflowers and chipped green leaves. Attached to the dresser was an equally old mirror that tilted to and fro. It was black around the edges, its silver backing eroding with time. Next to that sat a hot plate with a tin percolator and two tin mugs, each bearing a small yellow bloom that she was sure must have been sunflowers as well. Her heart warmed at how Alice had attempted to keep up with the times and the competition. Maybe it was all she could afford to do.

Just to the right, in the corner, stood a metal shower stall with a plastic yellow curtain, and next to it, a tiny hot water heater that fit snugly under a small hand sink on the back wall. A small, free-standing closet stood in the opposite corner as if an after thought. In the middle of the wall, a single-paned window offered the only alternate exit. A rickety wooden chair placed under it for a step if need be, provided the bare minimum of a fire code. A yellow chintz curtain framed the opening.

"Ohhh" was all she could get out before being misunderstood.

"Told you, not fancy," their host said again, "but clean. And the wood box is full."

"Oh, Ms. Ingram . . . Alice, it's perfect." Then another discovery brought a squeal of delight. "Look, Ben! A feather bed!"

An iron bed frame with peeling brass-colored paint dominated the center of the opposite wall. Resting on it was the telling mound of a feather bed carefully covered with a patchwork quilt and overstuffed pillows. Unable to contain herself, Amber plopped onto the bed, and it seemed she would disappear as the feather-stuffed mattress billowed up around her.

"You'll have to pardon her, ma'am. She's a bit daft." Ben smiled at Alice, who was smiling now too. "Now, where did you say that chowder place was?"

"It's just down the road a ways, Mr. uh . . . ."

"Riley. Ben Riley, but please call me Ben."

"Riley?" A confused expression came over her face, and just as quickly vanished. "Yes, okay Ben, then. It's about a mile or two down the road toward the water. Just this side of the fishing village near the bluffs."

"Taggie, you like it too, don't you?" Amber was saying, as Tag, deciding it was time to exit her pocket, began exploring the hills and valleys of the huge bed. "And Ben, look at this. Did you hook this rug, Ms. Ingram?" She knelt and fondly caressed the rag rug that lay on the scarred wooden floor next to the bed. "My grandmother used to hook rugs like this. In her day, she used to say, nothing was to be wasted and rags made sturdy rugs."

Alice was obviously touched by Amber's enthusiasm with her simple dwelling. "Yes I did, dear. Hooked that myself out at the bluff house. And I'd be pleased if you'd just call me Alice."

"Of course." Amber smiled, still inspecting the rug. "Just hard to break old childhood manners."

"Abby, could you please quell your excitement long enough for us to go find this food?" Ben broke in. "I need my strength if I'm going to have to stoke a fire all night long." Turning to Alice, he tipped his walking hat graciously. "Care to join us, Miss Alice?"

"Oh, no." She almost blushed. "But thank you. You two go eat now before total darkness falls. While you're gone, I'll make sure the water gets hot and freshen the sheets with

277

some outside air. Besides, the old dog in there will get a bit worried if I disappear without the truck firing up."

"Can we at least bring you back something, Alice?" Amber asked. "And I'd like to pay you for the room now, before we leave, if you'll tell me what we owe."

"Oh, I suppose twenty dollars would be fair. That'll cover the costs of the wood chopping boy and the water heating with a bit of profit to boot."

"That's more than fair, Alice. I'll get my purse out of the car." She stood. "Come on, Tag. Let's go."

"Abby? Please."

"I'm coming, I'm coming. Sheesh! Does he look starving to you, Alice?" She patted Ben's midsection and rolled her eyes and the two women grinned.

Alice walked back to the car with them and after placing Tag in the console, Amber dug thirty dollars out of her purse and handed it to her. "We'll be back in an hour or so. Does that give you enough time?" she asked. "And I'll bring you some chowder. You can always have it tomorrow."

"Abby, will you please!" Ben sat behind the wheel, tapping it impatiently.

"I'm coming, Ben. Damn, I'm coming!" She gave her new friend a wink over the black convertible top as she slid into the car.

Alice stood by her front door waving as they pulled out onto the highway. As they gained speed, Amber turned to look back.

"Hon?" She covered Ben's hand on the gear shift with her own.

What now? If you've forgotten something, forget it. I'm not going back until I've had food."

"No, I haven't forgotten anything, nothing at all. Actually, I'm remembering something. I'm remembering how it felt when I first saw you. A connection, like I'd known you for a long time but hadn't. It's strange. I feel that way now, that same kind of connection to Alice and that place. As if we were kind of led here."

It was Ben's turn to roll his eyes. "Some grits and fish will cure that, you'll see."

Yeah, she thought. We'll see.

"It's a beautiful fire, hon." She was stretched out on a small lumpy sofa which sat just far enough back from the pot-bellied stove to serve as a room divider from the feather bed. Ben was carefully placing the split wood inside so as not to cause sparks to fly out the small opening. She envisioned smoke curling out of the little metal chimney on the roof as she watched the warm fire light reach into the corners of the room. Postcard perfect, she thought.

"Oh, yeah," he reminisced, "tended many a stove fire in my day. When I was a kid my grandparents had a wood stove in the old home place and I used to vie with my brother for the job of chief fire starter. I've always loved making a fire. I suppose it's an innate thing in humans, going back eons." He reflected for a moment. "He's dead now, my brother."

She saw the brief flash of sadness in his eyes at the mention of his brother.

Satisfied that the flames were just right to catch all the logs, he joined her on the sofa and they fell quiet for a time, recollecting, and absorbing the character of their surroundings. Tag lay curled in a ball between them.

"I like it here, hon. I hope you don't mind, but I've already asked and paid for another night. When I took Alice the chowder. Figured we could spend tomorrow just exploring and it might help her out a bit, too."

"It's okay with me, and that's why we're here, babe. To check out the area, I guess."

"You guess?" she laughed. "You wanted to come to Maine. We're in Maine. Unless you've extended our destination to Nackiwac, New Brunswick, I see no need to keep moving." She gave a slight nudge to his ribcage with her elbow.

"Humph. You mean you don't want to continue on to the great white north and tame a Polar Bear or two? Team up a dogsled of wolves and run them to the strains of ZZ Top?" His face showed mock surprise as he nudged her back.

She snuggled into him. "No. I like it right here. There's something about this place, the fishing town, the bluffs. And Alice. I told you, I feel something has drawn us to that woman; a reason we stopped at these old cabins."

"Yeah? Well, while you figure all that out, I'm going to test that old shower stall and then that bed full of feathers. I don't know about you, but I'm beat."

He rose, stoked the fire, then ruffling her hair, he picked up one of the towels Alice had folded neatly on the dresser. Again, she noticed his avoidance of the esoteric discussion. It sort of puzzled her in a way as she recalled things he'd said in his letters. She looked down at the gull flying through the shadows across her chest and smiled.

Hours later, Ben snoring softly at her side, she lay watching the dance of the embers left by the burned logs in the stove. She felt a coolness on her face as the cabin began to fill with the chill of the night.

"It's going to be cold in here in the morning, Tag. I better get up and throw a couple more logs in that stove," she whispered.

Pushing herself up and out of the feathery nest was no easy task, and she stifled a giggle at the attempt. Once up, she kneeled and placed two more pieces of wood on the coals. They hissed, as the cold wood met with the heat inside the stove. The flames caught and she marveled at Tag's eyes watching her, the reflection lighting them up orange, as if flames themselves. She stared into them, and then at Ben stirring now in her movement.

I don't know what led us here, but tomorrow we'll visit the sea and the wind will speak to me. Lead the way around the next bend in the road.

A noise outside drew her attention. She listened for a moment, and then looked out the small window. Alice was taking a few pieces of wood from the shed to her house. Poor thing, she thought. To be all alone out there in the cold.

She grabbed her clothes, quickly pulled her sweater over her head and hobbled to the door while stepping into her jeans. Just as quickly, she was making her way across the frosty yard. Barefoot.

"Alice," she half-whispered, but the older woman didn't seem to hear. "Alice," she called again. Alice turned just as she caught up with her.

"What are you doing up, dear? And you'll have pneumonia dressed like that," she cautioned.

"Here, let me help you." She took the wood from Alice's thin arms.

"Ah, don't bother yourself now, I been doing it a long time. But since your up, how'd you like some strong New England coffee to ward off the chills?"

"Oh, thank you, Alice, but I ought to get back. You're right; it is cold out here." She suddenly realized she'd run out without shoes, a Florida habit she'd have to break.

The old woman smiled. "You'll get used to it. Come in and sit a spell." She moved toward her door, not looking back to see if Amber was behind her.

Inside, the house was much like the cabins. Rustic, charming in its way. It was slightly larger than the others, with a small kitchenette and a closed door indicating another small room beyond that. The walls held knick-knacks and what-nots and several old photos of a handsome young man in uniform.

"Sit here," Alice said, offering her a rocker by the wood stove. "It'll just take a minute to get us some coffee." She went into the little kitchen and started filling a speckled-blue pot with water.

"Thank you, Alice. Your home is charming." She sat in the cushioned rocker, cuddling her cold feet under her, watching Alice. She smiled at the tinware coffee pot she'd seen in so many farm kitchens, and then continued looking around. It was the house of a recluse, all right, of one who'd lived alone for a long time. It was cluttered but tidy, and she liked it. She began to relax, almost feeling at home yet strange, like a deja vu. What stories these walls could tell if they could only talk, she imagined.

Alice was holding out a mug of coffee to her, breaking into her musings. She took it gratefully, her cold bare feet now causing her entire body to shiver. She sipped at it and almost choked.

Alice smiled at her again. "Been awhile since you had some real coffee, that so?" She was dragging a straight-back chair up to the other side of the wooden end table by the rocker.

"Yes. Yes it has, I usually drink instant now. Boy, this packs a wallop. Thank you." She smiled back at her.

"Got some med'cine in it, is why. Wards off those shivers you got."

She could smell the *med'cine* and guessed it to be about eighty proof. "So," she began, but Alice cut her off as if reading her thoughts.

"Yes, sure was. Born and reared in these parts. Been in this house awhile, don't remember how long. My dad left this place when he died. Before that I lived on the bluffs many a year." She cupped her mug in her hands to warm them. "Me and the dog there."

Amber turned. She'd forgotten all about the dog, and now saw it lying against the door to what must be Alice's bedroom. It looked like a bloodhound, and as old as its owner. It was sound asleep, oblivious to their company.

"Mind if I ask you something, Alice?"

"Best to say what's on your mind, I suppose."

She fidgeted in her chair, her skin flushed. She wasn't sure if it was the fire, the *med'cine,* or the way Alice's eyes seemed so piercing, almost as if they could read her mind. She seemed slightly senile, yet sharper than most, a knowingness about her.

"Why are you here? I mean, alone and all. Did your husband die?"

"No, dear, I never had a husband. I mean I did, but not really. Jeff went off.

Goosebumps rose on her neck at the name. "W-who?"

"Jeff. That was . . . is his name, my fella. Jeff Riley. He went off to that war and got himself lost, and I been waiting for him to come back ever since."

Jeff Riley? So that's why Ben's name caused hesitation when he'd introduced himself, she thought. "You mean World War Two?" she asked, sensing that Alice was at least eighty.

"That's the one." Alice sipped at her coffee.

"Oh. I'm so sorry. You've stayed alone ever since?"

"It's all right, dear. Some things just take longer than others is all. And sometimes things come in a different way than we expect, I guess. But you already know about that, don't you? Maybe I'm just learning it, looking at you and all." Alice smiled, then turned serious. "But why not say what you want to say instead? Something is bothering you?"

"Yes, you're right. What I meant was I have this strange feeling that you were supposed to be here, is what I mean, if you know what I mean." She stammered, not knowing how to say what was on her mind. "That I . . . Ben and I were led to find you and we couldn't have if you weren't here. Does that make sense?"

"Lots of things make sense, lots don't. Depends on the person, I'd say, wouldn't you? Take your fella there, Ben, is it? He's a tough one, on the surface anyway. He's been through a lot, so have you, just not the same as you is what. So he sees what he wants to see, and you see what you need to see, hoping he'll come around. He does the same."

She was on the edge of her seat now, staring back into Alice's eyes. *How could this woman know these things about her and Ben?* "What do you mean, Alice?"

"I'd say you already know what I mean." She got up and poured herself more coffee but made no move to fill Amber's cup.

"Yes." She looked down at the cup in her hand. "Yes, I know about that, and a lost love."

"And now maybe you've come to find that love again, hey? Some think things are measured in time or place. But they aren't, not really. They're measured in love, so it don't

283

matter about time or place. Why, it don't matter what heart it's found in neither, that's what I'm learning. Same love, different place, different time is all."

Amber looked up. "Are you saying a certain love is all that matters? Not who, but just that we love? That love like that has no starting and ending, but just is? Maybe it can go where it wants, be in anyone it wants, or be anything it wants even from other places? And once we've had it in us, we'll know it when see it again? It never dies, can't die? Something like that?"

Alice nodded. "Yeah, something like that."

Her voice faded off as if she was thinking about what Amber had just asked and understanding something at long last herself. Then, as if by impulse, she turned in her chair.

"I want to give you something." She reached behind Amber to a small cabinet and withdrew a piece of yellowed paper, paper that looked as if it had been a wrapper at one time. She held it up to the light to make sure it was still legible. Satisfied, she handed it over.

"What is it?" Amber asked.

"You'll see. In time you'll understand. So will your fella."

"Alice, I need to ask you one more thing. How do you know these things?"

But Alice didn't answer. "Now if you don't mind," she said rising from her chair, "I think I'll go onto bed. I've been up an awfully long spell and it's time I rested now that you're finally here."

"Finally? I don't . . . ."

"You'll see, I told you. Trust me, you'll see," Alice said. "Now, I must say goodnight." She showed Amber to the door, gave her a strong hug, and then closed it behind her.

Half-stumbling across the yard, back to their cabin, she was certain now that they'd been led to this place and Alice. Led by what or who she didn't know, anymore than she'd ever known, but she knew.

And Ben? She had felt the same about him, their meeting, and the subsequent events of their life together so far. Was it all just a series of random events? Coincidental? She didn't believe in coincidence. Even Ben, unknown to him, had played his part in this latest connection by suggesting they go to Maine.

Back inside the cabin, kneeling by the open door of the stove, she carefully unfolded the paper that Alice had given her, obviously a treasure from long ago. In the dim light of the fire she began to read the masculine scrawl, an almost familiar scrawl, and suddenly her lungs ached in the attempt to breathe.

My dearest A. Here are the directions to a little house by your precious sea. I bought it as a surprise, but I've been called away before I could show you. Go there and know love until I return.

It was signed, Jeff.

THERE! THAT MUST BE IT

The morning billowed in a mushroom cloud over them. The road, wet with dew, sauntered through the hardwoods bordering the shore. Ben was driving cautiously on the damp asphalt and softly humming a tune.

She held the yellowed message from Jeff carefully folded in her hand. She hadn't mentioned the note's contents, waiting for the right time. To him it was just another day of leisurely exploring. Tag, perched on Bear's shoulder stretching to see out the rear window, was wide eyed with feline curiosity. Trying to hide her impatience, she kept reminding herself it was their day, too.

They'd eaten breakfast in a little diner in the fishing town and Ben had fallen in love with the picturesque look of the place. Rows of fishing boats bobbed at docks in the harbor, which was really a bay gouged into the rocks of the coastline.

A number of small variety shops, a three-story red brick hotel, a maritime museum, two cafes, and a barber shop made up the main street. It was squared around the town hall on a mound of land in the center. Yellow Marigolds, now frost-burned rust, bordered the gravel walkways surrounding the statue of a seaman in front of the building. A lone seagull, fittingly perched on the statue's shoulder, caused her to cup one hand around her own pendant while pointing to the bird with the other.

"Ben, look!" she announced excitedly, "there's a Jonathan Seagull to greet us."

"Yes, Abby." He smiled at her as one would a child, "It's a seagull. I'll bet you sent him a telepathic notice of our arrival, too, didn't you?"

"As a matter of fact, I did," she retorted, playing his sarcasm game. "Why, hello there, bird friend," she called as they passed. "As you can see, we made it just fine." She giggled somewhat insolently at Ben. "And there's the turn for the cliff road just ahead, hon. Turn right."

The highway was rising now, and twisting to flow with the land's edge. The relentless pounding surf chiseled indiscriminately into the rock coastline determined to claim for its own whatever would give way. The road tunneled through the rock at one point near the top, and the walls hugging both shoulders for near a mile were like a corridor, an entry shaft, she thought. They cleared the burrow through the rock, and stretched before them now lay the open expanse of the Atlantic. Wild sky and rolling grass knolls framed the water. Angry water.

The splendor before them enveloped her. The smell, the sound, the raw power of the sea. The distant surface was a slate gray blending into blue and green pipelines that rolled in to crash against the cliffs, sending giant plumes of spray high into the air. Her pulse quickened and even Ben's eyes widened at the sight.

"Damn! Would you look at that!" was all she could say.

"Yeah, damn is right," he murmured. "Kind of grabs you in the gut, doesn't it?"

"Oh, yes," she whispered back.

As the road wound through the knolls, she saw it then, nestled in a nook of land below them and just above the cliffs. It was a rather small structure but appeared defiant, as if challenging the sea and its storms. The clapboards of the exterior were blackened by salt spray and bent by the tests of gales, but it stood strong and proud in a foreign world. A few hearty shrubs at the corners hinted at loving hands digging in an unyielding soil long ago. A soil deposited, over time, by erosion and the droppings of the multitudes of sea birds hovering over its niche in the rocks.

She leaned forward to better see. The house made a statement to her. A testimonial of one determined to commune with something larger than itself. Suddenly she knew why they'd come to Maine.

"There! That must be it." She was on the edge of the seat now.

"Must be what?" he asked at her abrupt excitement.

"The bluff house, hon. Alice's bluff house."

A pullover off the roadside offered a stop. It was guarded by a weathered split-rail fence warning of the drop-off a few feet farther. He slowed and pulled off the road. The car had barely stopped before Amber was swinging her legs out the open door.

A rocky path led down to the house and warded off any but the adventurous soul, but she didn't seem to notice. The wind swirled her long hair and billowed her jacket out behind her. She hugged it back to her body, holding the pocket and Tag close to her as she began the trek to the old swing she'd already noticed on the porch.

He stood on the gravel beside the car, holding his hat, useless in the wind, watching her go. Shaking his head, he stepped carefully onto the first stone step of the path and began to follow her down.

She was already on the swing by the time he reached bottom and joined her. Her face was serene as she moved to and fro. It seemed she belonged here; why, he didn't know. He looked at the house, the rocky cliff, the wind-swept ocean before them.

"So, this is it? This is what you've been so antsy about all morning?"

She opened her eyes and smiled, and patted the seat beside her. "Can't you just feel it?"

"Feel what? All I feel is the damp from the ocean," he said as he reluctantly joined her.

"The energy, Ben. Can't you just feel it all around?"

He started to answer but thought better of it. She seemed taken with the place, why ruin it. He had in mind maybe a small farm in a clearing, but it didn't really matter. That they were together was the main thing.

"I think we'd be eating a lot of fish if we stayed here. Although, I am an expert fisherman, you know," he joked, referring to the bent pole and pin from a previous stop.

"Just think. From here we can watch the ocean anytime we want. We can explore the coast, the lighthouses, the forests," she said.

"The cold, the pneumonia, the broken bones from falls on slippery rocks," he added.

"Oh, pish posh. You're the one who wanted to come to Maine, remember?"

"Uh, yeah. Maine does have farms, too, you know? But since we're here, want to look around some, go inside? Alice gave you a key, right?"

"Yes. Guess she knew we'd want to go inside," she said and rose and headed for the door.

"Hope it works. The lock looks pretty rusty to me?

She shrugged and inserted the key. "It'll work," she said over her shoulder, then pushed the door all the way open and stepped inside.

It was deserted, yet welcoming at once, small but efficiently laid out. There was one large room that served as a kitchen, eating and living area, but it was sectioned off with various sized room dividers made of knotted pine shelves. Like oversized shadow boxes, they held a few mementos and old books covered in dust.

"Been awhile since anyone stayed here," he said, drawing a face in the grit collected on a drop leaf mahogany table just inside the door.

"Yeah, probably years," she agreed, moving left toward the kitchen area. "Look, hon. The window over the sink looks right out to the ocean. And look here, there's a small refrigerator right under the counter. Reminds me of the built-in dishwasher at home. Oh and . . . ."

She was back in the "Oh, Ben look" mode as when digging around in country shops, talking more to herself than him. He grinned at the wind-tousled hair hanging down her back as she turned to look in what appeared to be a small pantry, and decided to look around on his own.

He moved opposite into the small sitting area. Now he could see the low fireplace that had been obscured by the makeshift shelves. It was framed in rocks, probably taken from the cliffs outside. A circular hearth of honed slate seemed to form a smile on the opening that still held an iron log basket. Above it, a milled log served as a mantle.

Two high-backed winged chairs, dingy now, sat at either side, their arms draped in yellowed doilies of crocheted lace. He crossed the room and inspected one of the chairs. Satisfied it was much sturdier than it looked, he sat down to study the room.

"Hey, Abby. Come see the fireplace," he called, but his only response was the sound of opening and closing cupboard doors. "Damn woman will be in that kitchen all day," he muttered to Tag who leaped into his lap. "That's okay, Taggie boy. You and me, we'll just sit here and have a look around."

The walls were covered in a barn wood paneling that mocked the clapboard exterior. A large fish net, painstakingly nailed into a geometric design, covered most of the side wall. A rusty anchor formed its center point and his interest was captured. He loved maritime relics and thought of his own brass running light packed away in a box somewhere in a west coast storage facility.

The old shrimp boat is sinking in a storm. A young Ben is getting the people off and onto his patrol boat. The captain, his wife, their dog, and a deckhand with a peg leg. As he desperately yanks the last one to safety, the shrimp boat sinks, leaving just its red running light aglow beneath the turbulent water.

"Tag! Ben! Oh, there you are." She sighed, relief flooding over her. She ran to where the two of them had dozed off in the chair, scooped the kitten up and covered his face in kisses.

"What on earth are you going on about?" he asked, startled. "Jesus!"

"You scared me to death! I thought you'd gotten out and fallen off a damn cliff!"

"Who? Me?"

"No. Tag, silly."

"Aaah. That figures," he joked. "But now that you've finally decided to join us, would you look at this great fireplace? I wonder if it's intact and safe to burn a fire. Looks kind of dilapidated in here."

"Does not. It's a wonderful place, and in surprisingly good repair."

"Says who? How would you know, anyway?"

"It just needs a good cleaning that's all, and the electricity turned on."

"Electricity? Babe, this is an old house. I doubt that—"

"Does, too, I saw the pole up on the road. Alice probably turned the power off because of the storms out here. And there's plenty of outlets, I looked. See, she lived here once and must have updated it for him over the years for when he returned."

"What? When who returned? Now what are you talking about?"

"Tell you later. And, I checked the little pump house while you were dozing and the pump looks fairly new."

"Dozing? Me?"

"Sound asleep is more like it. That's when I thought Tag had gotten out, because I looked in all the cupboards thinking I had shut him in, and he was with me in the bedroom, and then I—"

He burst out laughing.

Amber blushed. "I'm sorry. I guess I got carried away, didn't I?" She smiled back at him. "But really, what do you

291

think? Do you like it? It's already got quite a bit of furniture and we can get what we need."

"Abby, aren't you getting a little ahead of yourself here? How do you know Alice wants to rent this place out? And, you haven't even looked at anything else to compare it to."

"I don't need to look at anything else as long as you like it, and Alice will be expecting us to stay."

"How do you know that? Plus, it's desolate out here. Bleak, even. Not exactly what I was thinking when I mentioned Maine to you."

"You liked the town and it's not far. You like the sea and it's just outside the door. There's a housing development just a bit farther on. Alice said. And yes, look at that wonderful fireplace. Great for a chief fire starter like you." She smiled down at him. "Please, let's just see what Alice has to say. If you don't like it after a month or so we can leave. But, you will. I know you will. I think we were led here, Ben."

"Not that again. How come you keep saying that? We could have been led to any number of places this past three weeks or so. Why here?"

"Because this is Maine. And, because of this." She put Tag back in his lap and dug into her pocket. She took the paper and handed it to him. "Read what it says."

He squinted in the dim light inside the house and began to read . . . *My Dearest A. Here are directions to a little house by your precious sea. I bought it as a surprise, but I've been called away before I could show you. Go there and know love until I return. Jeff.*

"What's this?"

"It's a letter to Alice from her fella, as she called him, before he went off to World War Two and never returned."

He handed it back to her. "So? What's that got to do with us and where we live?"

"Don't you see, hon? This house has been standing empty all these years, waiting for us to live in it. That's why Alice came into our lives. That's why you decided on Maine in the first place."

"Oh, for crying out loud. I picked Maine on a whim. Alice's house just happened to be on the road we were on. You're getting as batty as she is."

She carefully folded the paper as if it was some precious treasure. "No. We were meant to come here; why, I don't know, but we were. I felt it when I saw the house from up on the road. I felt the connection to Alice. And look at the name of her lost love. Isn't it too coincidental that his name was Jeff, same as mine? And, his last name was Riley, same as yours! Alice told me. I tell you, this is where we belong."

He threw his hat on the floor, exasperated. "This is nuts, Abby. Pure nuts! If you want us to live here, fine, but don't go getting us involved in some odd couple from long ago. Some wacky story from some wacky old lady!"

She swallowed her own irritation at his reaction. "Why must you be so negative? How do you explain—?"

He cut her off. "I Don't! I gave up trying to explain. I live life as it comes and goes. I don't attach to shadows on walls or fairies in woods, for Chrissakes!"

She turned, looked out at the sea, then back at him imploringly. "It's like everything else so far, Ben. How we met, rainbows, you getting better after being so sick, the fox, the bear, even this pendant you gave me." She pulled the seagull on its chain from inside her sweater. "You read Richard, so I know you believe in these things."

"I read Bach because he spins a good yarn, and because I'm interested in the esoteric parts. But that doesn't mean I treat his work or anyone else's as gospel. They're just possibilities spun from someone's imagination, that's all, not reality. Same for this Alice shit. She's not some ghostbuster, some other world connection; she's just a lonely old woman with a head full of memories and what could have beens." *And, if you only knew that I'm not all better, he thought.*

"And it means nothing to you that her name and my name both begin with an 'A', or that it was signed by someone named Jeff Riley? Or that she just happened to have a house for rent, and we just happen to need one? Next to the sea! In Maine!" Her voice was rising now.

"ARGGHHH! You're driving me crazy, you know that? Now, I've heard enough about this. If you want to dwell on this, this crap, fine, but I'm not going to. If you want the goddamn house, then let's go rent the thing and be done with it. Okay?"

Amber shrugged, gathered Tag into her arms and walked toward the door without a word. She started to climb the path to the car.

"Lunatic," he mumbled, catching up with her.

"Hardhead," she whispered under her breath.

They left the house as they had found it, standing empty. He drove carefully on the way back, while she wanted to fly. Neither spoke, but it wasn't something between them now, as their other arguments had been. It was, she felt, a connectivity arriving, the pieces falling into place, like a patchwork quilt, perhaps. She wasn't concerned about it whatsoever, for happy times were ahead. She was certain.

THE PATCHWORK QUILT

"Here, over here," she directed as they labored to maneuver the large armoire into the bedroom. She'd found it at an antique shop in town and just had to have it. It reminded her of the old free-standing closet her grandmother had when she was little.

"Easy for you to say," he puffed. "Thing weighs more than you do."

"Does not, and besides, it'll go with the other furniture. There, stop where you are. That'll be perfect."

He eased the big piece against the wall, stood back and wiped his brow. "If I may ask, just why in the hell did we have to have this?"

"Hmmm? Because, silly, haven't you noticed this house has no closets? Just where do you think you'll hang your clothes?"

"I plan on going naked the entire winter."

She burst out laughing, and then he did, at the thought. "Damn," she said, "I can just see it now."

"Humph. Damn woman doesn't know a sexpot when she sees one." He pretended disdain.

"Oh yes, I do." She laughed and hugged him close.

The note from Alice hadn't been mentioned again. He'd driven her back to Alice's place, but sat in the car while she went inside. Whatever she wanted to do now, even moving into the little house, was fine with him. Time was too precious to argue. She'd come from Alice's beaming, fairly jumped into the car, and he'd seen Alice watching them leave from her doorway in his rearview mirror. She's a strange one, he'd thought, but said nothing.

They'd spent the next couple days cleaning, getting the power turned on, and a telephone hooked up. The house needed linens, towels, utensils, but they already had most of that, having brought it along. Amber hung her few knick-knacks on the walls, placed them here and there, adjusted this and that, and they'd gone into town for the rest.

He'd paid to have the store deliver the armoire and a new mattress for the old brass bed frame, which they did. By nightfall of the third day following the discovery of the house, everything was in place and he was exhausted, but not her. She was as excited as a woman with her first home.

"Don't you just love it?" She beamed while looking around. "Oh, Ben, we're going to be happy here. I can feel it."

"Right, sure we are," he grumbled, without knowing why. Maybe to keep in character. For the time being anyway.

His remark caught her off guard and she slowly turned, her face serious. "What do you mean by that? This is our home now. What you wanted, a place only ours."

"Oh, nothing. Just teasing you. It's a fine house, babe. Drafty, old, probably loaded with bugs and the roof probably leaks, but if you like it, I like it." He didn't want to get her going on the *I can feel it* remark again. He crossed the room and put his arms around her. "What's for supper? Johnny Bull Pudding? Squaw bread? Moose?"

She relaxed and leaned into him. "You already know, since you bought them. Hot dogs. Hot dogs and tea. Tomorrow we can go into town and stock up; I just didn't think about it today."

"Yeah, and we'd better get used to stocking up for long winter nights, weeks, months." He grinned. "Lay in the coal oil, wood, water maybe. Bear grease, hog jowls, pig's feet and such. You know, get into the swing of things."

"Oh, quit. You sound like we're living a hundred years ago. But you're right about the winter. We will need to stock some things when the time comes." She looked up at him. "Tell me you're happy here, Ben."

He kissed her forehead. "I'm happy here. How's that?"

"Good," she said, untangling herself from his arms and walking into the kitchen. "After supper can we sit on the porch and watch the evening and smell the ocean?"

"Sounds exciting all right," he teased.

"It will be, you'll see. The seabirds come in at dusk to nest, flocks and flocks of them."

"What?" he said as he moved toward the kitchenette. "How do you know that?"

She paused, thinking it over. "I don't know. I guess because that's what birds do at night. Why would it be any different here?"

"Yeah, suppose it wouldn't," he agreed. "Tag'll love it."

They sat at their table eating hot dogs, pork and beans, and drinking tea, him gulping his down, her taking small bites and sips. At dusk they sat on the swing, and just as she'd predicted, the birds came in one flock at a time and settled below and above them in the cliffs and rocky outcrops.

Strange looking birds, he thought, nothing like he'd ever seen before but in pictures. Was that a flock of Loons? Amber had put Tag on his leash, and the kitten didn't know which way to go first.

When the moon rose it was but a sliver of ivory, just enough to paint reflections on the sea before them. Enough to see that the ocean was now just a series of swells, and not whitecaps except for the breaking of the surf on shore.

"What did I tell you? Even the ocean is glad to see us. See how calm it is out there?"

He nodded. It was a captivating sight.

"I'm going to make us a patchwork quilt for winter, so we can snuggle under it when we're out here."

"Yep. We'll sit out here in our Long Johns and boots and shiver our asses off together," he quipped. "You must be mad, woman, if you think a patchwork quilt can withstand a Maine winter, even on a porch. Hell, we'll be sitting here with a portable heater under us and only our eyes showing through headscarves, earflap hats, and our teeth chattering."

She mock punched him in the arm. "Hush, silly." But by now he was laughing, and she began giggling with him.

"Hiya, get your morning paper. Two skeletons were found this spring," he said between laughs. "Both had their mouths open and were holding what appeared to be tea cups. It seems both people froze to death while having a conversation. No one knows what they were discussing, but it's rumored they were talking about heading south for the winter."

"God, you're funny," she said, wiping away a tear. "I can just see it. You want coffee now?" she asked, trying to stop giggling.

He nodded, still laughing, as she disappeared into the house. The pain hit him then—hard, and he nearly doubled over.

"Christ!" he yelled out involuntarily.

"What?" she called from the kitchen.

"Nothing." He managed to sit back down on the swing, his groin feeling as if it was on fire. It scared him. Grin and bear it. Don't let her see.

"Here it is," Amber said cheerily as she returned with their coffee. "With vanilla, no less."

He was trying to straighten himself upright. He took his cup from her but looked the other way, so she wouldn't see his strained face. She'd taken him from the hospital, saved his life even, but although he went along with her esoteric ways for the most part, he didn't really believe. Life was mortal and things like foxes and rainbows were of the imagination, not reality. He knew it was only a matter of

298

time, but it would be their time and he wouldn't spoil it for her.

Unknown to her, he'd gotten a powerful pain-killer while in Los Angeles. He'd only had to use it a few times since, and it was often behind the occasional urgency for food, but now he needed it desperately. Yet, how could he get to it without her seeing? He kept the bottle of pills rolled up in a sock, and the sock at the bottom of his bag.

He stayed turned away from her and stared out to sea while he sipped his coffee, wincing as little as possible, fighting back the pain. It would pass, he knew, but it meant the tumor was growing and would eventually take him, as it did many men. Where would they be when it happened? What would they be doing? If there was only some way to stretch out the years, give her a full life again, before.

"A dollar-twenty-six-fifty for your thoughts," she interrupted.

"Huh?"

"Ben, what's the matter? A minute ago you were near rolling around laughing and now you're sullen. What's wrong?"

"Nothing's wrong. I'm just tired all of a sudden. Overdid it today, I guess, with all that heavy lifting."

She sipped her coffee and watched him, sensing otherwise. She didn't know what, but something was definitely bothering him.

"Is it the house that's worrying you?"

"No. I told you, nothing's wrong."

"Are you having a change of heart about running off to the ends of the earth with a lunatic?" She tried to recapture the previous levity.

"I need to go to bed, that's all."

There was a sudden flash out over the ocean, followed by a rumble of thunder. It looked like a front was moving their way from what he could see in the pale moonlight. He was grateful for the diversion of her questions as Amber turned attention to the flash as well.

She loved storms, loved the change they brought with them, the intensity. She felt him get up but said nothing. Whatever was bothering him would pass, and maybe he was right; it had been a long day. She shouldn't be pressing him. He moved by her without a word and went inside. She heard the rattle of his cup as he sat it on the table even as the wind suddenly blew in from seaward, followed by rain and then more thunder, sending Tag leaping into her lap.

He half-limped into the bedroom and dug around in his suitcase until he found what he needed. He quickly popped a pill in his mouth and swallowed it without water, afraid she might see if he went to the kitchen for a glass. Just as quickly, he hid the pills again.

Outside, she watched the rain sweep across the ocean like a broom, its wind moving it one way then the other. Ben appeared on the porch and handed her the yellow wind-breaker.

"If you're going to sit out here, might want to keep dry."

She looked up at him and smiled. "Thanks, hon," she said, taking the jacket and draping it over her shoulders. "I thought you were going to bed?"

"I am. Just coming to say goodnight."

"I'll be in shortly. I just like watching the rain. It reminds me of us." She looked around, but he was gone.

A DAY TO GRASP FOREVER

He woke early as usual, but this morning was different. Amber was not in her place beside him and Tag was not pouncing on the movement of his feet beneath the covers. The room felt strange.

Gratefully, he noticed the pain was entirely gone. Maybe today will be a day for simply the living of it, he thought, a day to enjoy the dance with this woman who at once drove him nuts and made him happy. A day to pretend they really did have forever in their grasp.

Grabbing his robe from the foot of the bed, he made his way to the kitchen. The smell of bacon and coffee wafted in as soon as he opened the door, and he smiled at the thought of her already up and bustling about. She was so like a kid when excited about something, and it didn't take much to excite her. He envied that quality in her.

He poured himself coffee. "Wish I had a paper," he said to no one. He looked through into the living room. "Abby?" he called, but the only answer was a pounding coming from outside. "Tag?"

He moved toward the door to look out and saw her then. Or half of her. She had pulled a barstool chair out on the porch and his eyes met her waist as he looked out the door.

301

"Good God, woman, what are you doing out there, trying to break your neck?" he asked, sticking his head out the door.

"About time you got up, sleepyhead." She ignored his question. "I'm almost finished. Wait'll you see." There was a sudden sound of hammering that hurt his ears.

"Ow! See what? You lying flat on your back when that stool gives way?"

Amber didn't hear him as she pounded again, and he couldn't get out the door without knocking her over for sure.

"Okay, it's up now. Come look." She climbed down and pulled the stool clear of the door. "Are you coming? Ben?"

"I'm coming, I'm coming! Calm down." But he grinned as he said it, seeing the huge smile of satisfaction on her face as she backed away to view whatever it was she'd risked her neck to hang. He stepped out onto the porch.

"Oh Ben, look," she swooned. "I just knew I was supposed to get this. I was drawn to it the minute I saw it."

He crossed the porch to where she was standing and looking up, he saw the whittled owl she'd nailed on a small piece of driftwood and now had mounted over the door.

"See, hon? And, I bet the lady at that shop is just as tickled with my lamp. This is gonna be our little birdhouse. How fitting; I've moved from a treehouse to a birdhouse." She laughed at the thought.

"Uh-huh," he mumbled, as he sipped from his coffee.

"I've got to go into town and get a wood sign made real soon. Maybe today, even. You know, one of those they burn in the letters. It's going to say *Ben and Abby's Nest*."

Before he could comment one way or another, she threw her arms around him and planted kisses all over his face, spilling his coffee down the front of his robe and her yellow jacket.

An hour later they were on their way to town, Amber driving, her Metal keeping beat, and he looking at the scenery. On one of the curves, the car skidded.

"Whoa!" He sat straight up, reacting.

302

She laughed, seeing his face. "Oh, quit worrying, will you? Nothing's going to ruin this day, not even my driving." She went into the next curve the same way.

"JESUS CHRIST!" Ben shouted.

She slammed on the brakes and skidded to within feet of where the moose stood in the road, staring at them. It was huge. Its antlers were huge. It didn't seem happy at the car's intrusion. She turned the key and the engine, and the music, went silent.

"See, goddamnit? If you'd hit that thing, it would have been all over for us."

"It's not just a thing, Ben. It's a magnificent male moose." The near miss had startled her. "And, you're right, because it would've been over for him too. I've got to remember the wildlife up here when driving. Damn, would you look at the rack of antlers on him!" She stared, mouth open, in awe.

"For Christ's sake, Abby." He started to protest again.

"Shhh, don't scare him," she said. "He'll move, now that he's seen us. Don't worry."

"Oh, I'm not worried! I'm fucking delirious with happiness, aren't you?" he added sarcastically, but in a whisper.

The moose stood its ground, apparently not intending to move. A small cloud of vapor from its nostrils hinted at his agitation.

"Now what, Jane?" Ben said, frustrated. "It looks like that thing's not going anywhere and this is the only road to town. Are we going to have a standoff? Is it high noon yet? Christ! Blow the damn horn."

"No. If I do that it'll scare him. Do you want him charging?"

He guessed the thing in excess of a thousand pounds and five feet at its shoulder. Having it charge them was definitely not a good idea. Damn cloth convertible top was going to be the death of them yet. "It's not mating season, is it? Maybe it thinks the car's name is Sheila."

"Shhh."

The moose threw its head back and emitted a high-pitched squeal, something that sounded to him like a cross between a trumpet and a chain-saw. "Uh-oh."

"He's just telling us who's in charge. Once he sees we aren't a threat, he'll move on. Don't worry," she said.

Before he could reply, the moose turned around and lumbered off the road into the woods. Ben noticed that he didn't even bother to look back, as if totally unafraid of them, totally unconcerned, once he'd established his superiority.

"Good," he said quietly. "Now, how about slowing down on the next curve, in case it has kinfolk I'm not anxious to meet."

"Wasn't he simply grand?" she said, ignoring him.

"Hard to tell when looking at antlers that big. Did you notice one was cracked, a tip torn off, something? Probably from a fight over who would stand in the road to scare the shit out of lunatics in silver cars. He must have won."

She began driving slowly away. "No, all I saw was how splendid he was. So stately, like a king. By the way, why do you always see the threat, never the beauty? I've noticed that about you."

He shifted in his seat. "I see beauty when it isn't a threat. Told you that before. When you look at an alligator, do you see the teeth or the tail first? I see the teeth."

"Hmmm, I guess I'd have to say I just see an alligator. Not a threat, not anything. I see it as a work of art, a part of Nature just like us."

He chuckled. "And if that gator was chasing you, would it still be a work of art? You'd see the teeth then, alright, and you could either stand there until it devoured you, or get the hell out of its way. Problem is the gator wouldn't see you as a work of art; it would see you as lunch."

"Yes, I suppose that's true." She glanced at him, then back to the road. "But it wouldn't be chasing me. It would be chasing you. It would know you were afraid, and because you were, it could sense that you were vulnerable. Animals smell fear. They see it in posture, movement. If you aren't afraid of them, if you intend no harm, as long as you aren't

304

part of their food supply, they won't hurt you. And, I've told you *that* before."

"Hogwash. Is that why bathers on beaches get attacked by sharks? Why snakes strike? Listen, there was a young adventurer who went to film the grizzlies in Alaska every year, all alone. He moved among them, knew their habits, was unobtrusive. For the most part they tolerated him.

"Your point?"

"Then one night for no apparent reason, one came and ate him. Now why, when they sensed he wasn't afraid, when they saw he meant no harm, when he wasn't part of their food chain, did that happen, hmmm?"

She thought about it. "I don't know. But there must have been a reason not apparent."

"Sure there was. It's what I said before. Humans and animals aren't on the same wavelength. It might have killed him simply because he didn't belong in the bears' domain. Same for shark attacks, snakes, anything. Ever think about that?"

She was quiet for a minute. "But why aren't we all on the same wavelength? That's what I'm saying. If we were, those things wouldn't happen. They don't when we are."

"Oh? Don't we do the same thing? When something threatening enters our domain, don't we instantly kill it?" Before she could answer, he went on. "Maybe it had a toothache, a thorn in its paw, hadn't been laid in awhile, or maybe was just crazy."

The little town came into view and she began slowing. "You've made my point again. We do the same things. The same things we berate an animal for, we do ourselves. But we do it on a much larger scale. Animals can get sick, too, you know. Act out of character. And I suppose there are instances when putting one down would be kind, as well as necessary. Yet, where an animal will confront or size up only the danger standing in its face, we have a tendency to condemn entire species. One bear or wolf attacks, so that must mean all bears and wolves are bad and serve no value or purpose. Better off rid of them. And, to that I say hogwash!"

"Ahhh, nuts." He said no more, but his face said that he was, once again, considering her remarks.

"You ready to go shopping?" She spotted a parking place near the docks and was pulling in.

They spent the rest of the morning in the small specialty shops lining the harbor, and stocking up in the town's one grocery chain store. Amber found a small shop where a placard in the window announced *Specialty Signs.* She'd gotten lost in the stories the retired logger told of the local woods, as he skillfully burned her requested letters into a polished pine plaque.

Ben, meanwhile, wandered across the street to a maritime antique store he'd spotted while looking out the window in the sign shop. Next to flying, his other love was anything nautical. Amber joined him, her new sign under her arm, as he was bargaining for a hand-carved figurine that looked like it had once adorned the bow of some sailing ship from the last century.

"What's that monstrosity?" she asked.

"Monstrosity?" He winked at the store's proprietor, a short man in his eighties if he was a day. "Hell, woman, this thing once guided sailors across entire oceans. This Lady of the Sea led men into ferocious sea battles with sword and musket." He struck a fencing pose and a menacing gaze.

She burst out laughing. "Pirates, huh?"

The proprietor coughed. "Actually, that came off a mercantile that went down off the rocks in the Thirties. Use to run bolts of cloth up and down the coast."

Ben stared. "You people just have no imagination, no imagination at all."

"Hundred and fifty," the man said.

"What? Not for some old mercantile. Maybe if off a pirate's ship, but not for a mercantile." he thrust his hands in his pockets with an air of defiance.

The haggling began, and Amber spotting a table of lanterns from the days before electricity, was already moving

306

across the store leaving the men to their business. "Oh, look at that antique oil lantern," she said, her voice trailing off.

"A hundred and no more," Ben said.

"One twenty-five and I'm taking a beating at that price. May not last through the winter."

"One fifteen and we'll be on canned goods for a month at that."

"On second thought," the proprietor added, "seems to me I do recollect now that she came off a rum runner that was sunk by the Coast Guard during Prohibition."

"That's better," he said, withdrawing his wallet.

Half an hour later, the sign, the three-foot Lady, and the lantern were packed in the trunk and they were pulling into the strip center at the edge of town. Ben had spotted a TV and satellite service store next to the grocery and insisted on going in.

They'd finally finished all their shopping and were starting home when Amber saw a banner hanging over the street she hadn't noticed before. It announced the town's Columbus Day Festival to be held over the weekend.

"Ben, look. Can we come? You'd enjoy that and it'll give us a chance to take part in the town's activities." She was excited again.

"I don't see why not, and they'll probably have lots of chowder booths and other food, too." He winked at her knowing she liked to tease him about his fixation with food.

"Good, I'll take that as a yes," she said, turning to smile at him.

They drove the next few miles in silence enjoying the ride along the bluffs. As they neared their pullover, she reached over and patted his knee.

"The man at the shop said the satellite guy would be here this afternoon so you should have TV this evening. Then, maybe you'll feel at home," she said.

"Hell, by the time I get done lugging all this stuff you bought down the side of a cliff, I'll be too tired to watch TV," he countered.

"Bitch, bitch, bitch," she teased. "You're the one who bought at least half the grocery store. If left to me, some coffee and fruit would've done nicely, maybe a little cheese and crackers. And cat food and bacon for Tag. I hope you plan on cooking all that because I have no intention of developing an obsession for Emeril." She grinned at him as she pulled the car close to the split rail.

"Who?"

"Never mind. We'll have to hurry unloading to be done by nightfall." She chuckled as she pulled the trunk release.

Ben lifted the trunk lid and started grabbing bags. She reached around him and took a large basket with a handle she'd bought because she was sure it would *come in handy for something.* Filling the basket with smaller bags, she grabbed her new sign and headed down the path.

"Hey! Is that all you're taking?" he yelled at her back.

She nodded in response, laughing.

She managed to turn the doorknob, then pushed her way in. "Tag? Ohhh, Taggie. We're back," she called. "Where are you hiding?" She set the basket on the table and immediately decided it would be a wonderful bed for the kitten. "Come, Tag. We bought you something." Tag appeared in the doorway leading to the bedroom, stretching and yawning in response to the news.

"There you are." She scooped him and kissed his nose. "Here I was worrying about leaving you alone for the first time and look at you. Just sleeping away and not scared at all. Guess *you* feel at home here anyway."

Ben came through the door laden with sacks and packages. He dropped the load on the table and collapsed onto the chair. "That's it; the rest is yours. Only been two days and already there's enough shit here to start a thrift shop."

"Fine. You can start putting the groceries away while I go get the rest. I'll take my coffee black, thank you." She kissed the top of his head and was out the door before he could argue.

"Heh," he answered. "Look what I brought you, Tag." He pulled a small packet from his pocket, tore the cellophane open and held up a ball of purple feathers tied with a bell and attached to a pliable stick. "You like this?" he asked, shaking the toy.

The kitten leaped on his new-found prey and Ben laughed aloud at the ensuing antics. "Aw damn, you're something else. I see that's gonna keep you busy awhile. I guess I better boil some coffee water and see if the shopping queen needs more help." Tag agreed by knocking his toy to the floor and leaping on it, batting it back and forth in a frenzy, as if his survival depended on it.

Ben roared. "Ahhh, life is good and then you nap, right Tag?"

Traipsing back up the path to help Amber bring the remaining bags to the house, he half smiled. "It's starting to feel like home here after all," he whispered to the wind and the waves splashing below. "And, the day has been pain free. Could Abby be right?" Did he dare to hope?

He made supper while Amber again mounted her bar stool chair and nailed the new sign over the whittled owl and positioned the Lady in the fish net. They'd eaten, cleaned up, made a fire, and now he was flipping channels on his TV, while she snuggled next to him watching the flame in her red lantern.

The room fell silent as he announced nothing was on worth watching and turned the TV off. They watched the lantern's red glow together. The bottle candle, a taper of green melting its color down the sides, glimmered at them from the mantle.

"It's been a wonderful day, Ben. Thank you for bringing us to Maine."

He squeezed her hand and continued staring into the light. Yeah, he thought, a day to grasp forever.

FESTIVALS, SQUALLS, AND POTTED MUMS

Amber opened her eyes to sunrays sparkling through the just-washed window at the foot of their bed. She stretched what felt like a mile and rolled to her side causing Tag to fall off her chest. He'd taken to sleeping there with his cold nose nuzzled in her neck, and his basket bed now held his toys.

"Shhh, don't wake Ben," she whispered in the kitten's ear.

Ben was breathing the slow, even breaths of sleep at her side. She smiled at his serene face. She worried over his all too frequent nightmares, but he resisted her questions. Rising quietly, she made her way to the kitchen and coffee, Tag at her heels.

The kitchen window promised a spectacular day as she filled the kettle for more coffee and rinsed Tag's bowl. Perfect for a festival, she thought, as she dialed the handset on the portable phone. The beautiful day made her think of her sons.

She was bending over, taking something from the oven when he walked up behind her and encircled his arms around her tiny waist. The long auburn hair lay unbraided down her back and she had tied it back with a pale yellow bow. He buried his face in it and breathed in the smell of her.

"Sure been doing a lot of talking out here," he whispered into her ear.

She had jumped at the contact. "Damn! Don't sneak up behind me like that," she blurted. "Scared me to death!"

"Sheesh. You edgy or what?"

"Guess I lived alone too long is all. Sorry, I didn't mean to snap."

"That's okay, Abby." He felt kind of sorry for her. For all her energy, she was fragile. "I heard you talking out here and thought Alice had called to see how you'd settled in."

"No, I planned to go see her tomorrow. I called the boys to give them the new phone number and tell them about the house. Maybe you could call your son, too?"

"Yeah, maybe," he said. "All okay with yours?"

"Yes, they're fine with it since meeting you and learning you're not Jack the Ripper." She smiled and kissed his cheek. "Now, eat your breakfast because it's festival day and maybe I can find some potted Mums. We need some flowers around here."

"Sure, and I'll do some chowder tasting while you dig among plants. Looks like it is going be a great day," he said, bending to look out the window.

The streets were crowded with people and vendors, and she was surprised at the turn-out. "People must come from miles around," she said, linking her arm through his as they walked into the throng.

"Plenty to look at and eat," he agreed. "Quite a doing for such a small town."

They spent an hour or so looking in the booths and watching the people. Amber found yellow Mums, a huge pumpkin, and tied bundles of Indian corn. When she wasn't watching, Ben bought an old hand-held fog horn with a future joke in mind. They walked back to the car, put things in the trunk, and decided to look for a place to sit and have coffee, Ben grumbling about the lack of a Starbuck's.

"Hey, hon, look over there." She pointed to a sign with an arrow toward the docks offering sightseeing boat rides. "Can we go? Oh, please," she begged, pulling him in the direction of the sign.

"Abby, we can't do everything in one day."

"Why not? It's still early enough. We can at least go find out where it's going and how long."

"I'm sure there's a long wait to even get on," he argued.

"So? Can't we just find out?"

"Damn stubborn-ass woman. Never satisfied. Think life has to be lived in one day."

"You never know when it does, hon. Come on." She went on ahead of him.

"Shit," he mumbled as he quickened his step. But her last remark had struck a nerve.

As the boat pulled away from the dock, Amber noticed Ben sitting quietly, not taking in the view. She'd insisted they go out on the converted excursion boat, hoping to get a glimpse of their bluff house. He'd been reluctant, even agitated, but eventually had given in. They'd boarded the boat, a large commercial-type built for fishing, just as it was leaving.

"Isn't it nice, hon?" she asked.

"What, the boat? It's okay."

"No," she said sliding in beside him on the bench, "the ocean. Look around. Doesn't it just invigorate you no end?"

"I suppose."

"You suppose? What kind of answer is that? You're not enthused at all; I thought you loved the ocean."

"I do."

"Well, then, what? You sure don't act like it. Here I thought you'd be pleased to be on it again." The loud clangs of a buoy made her turn and look.

"That's the channel buoy," he said. "It marks the harbor entrance. It means we're now officially at sea."

"How do you know that?"

"Because all harbors have them in one form or another." The boat began to rise and fall with the swells.

"Oh," she answered, interested. "Good, maybe the captain will swing down the coast now so we can see our little house." She gave him a peck on the cheek. "I'm going up to the front where I can see. Are you just going to sit there?"

He nodded.

"Okay for you, then," she said and hurried away toward the bow.

He looked first out to sea, then at the clouds, his face frowning. He got up and made his way to the wheelhouse up a flight of stairs, ladders as they're called in maritime jargon, and looked in at the captain. He turned and looked down at the bow, saw Amber practically hanging off it, and cringed. He hollered at her to no avail, turned back and knocked at the wheelhouse door.

Inside, the captain, a thin and salty looking man in his forties or fifties, motioned him to enter.

"Help you?" the captain said.

"Oh, not really. It's been awhile since I was in a wheelhouse, and thought maybe you wouldn't mind if I just took a look."

"Nope. Don't mind."

"Thank you," he said, scanning the interior. There was the brass binnacle housing the compass in front of the spoked wheel, the throttles and prop controls, a horn rope, radio and radar, a fish finder. Regular stuff. "What's the water out here?"

"Deep, bit of a chop. Current's pretty strong," the captain answered, concentrating on the waves and not his questions.

"I see." Ben grunted, looking up at the sky. "I'm not from around here, but seems those clouds look to be storm clouds."

"Yeah," the captain answered. "Get them all the time."

"Is it a squall?"

He glanced at Ben, then back. "Maybe. I'm kind of busy, if you don't mind."

"Sure, not trying to interfere. As said, just haven't been in one of these in awhile. Thanks for allowing me." He excused himself and hurried to find Amber.

She was leaning over the bow as he came up behind her.

"What are you doing?"

"Ben, look! Dolphins! Dolphins right under the bow, keeping up with the boat. Damn! I didn't think about dolphins up here in the cold water. Whales maybe."

He eased her back, smiling. "Sure. Dolphins like to play around boats. I've heard they scratch their backs on the keel, but doubt it. Probably they like surfing the wave the bow provides. I'd bet if you went aft, I mean back to the stern, you'd see them in the boat's wake as well."

"Really?" I've only seen them in the passes and the Intracoastal. Sometimes close to shore."

"Let's go look." Before she could answer he gently pulled her away, and toward the rear.

"What's the rush?" she protested. "We've got all afternoon."

"Rush? No rush, babe. Just thought you'd like to see." They hit a large swell and both had to grab the handrail to keep their balance. The boat turned at the same time, and the rocky coastline came into view. He guessed them out maybe a mile.

"Look over there." He pointed. "See it?"

"Oh, yes. Isn't it beautiful? I mean, look how rugged it is, like the beginning of the world." The boat went into a trough and then back up. "Wow," she said. "Damn!"

"Just the swells, babe, that's all. But make sure you hold onto something from now on, so you don't fall down or worse, get thrown off."

The boat rolled again, and Amber was delighted. "Oh, yeah," she said as they continued along the passageway. "Isn't it great?" Spray hit her in the face and she laughed while Ben held onto her and guided her toward the stern, which was under a sun canopy made from canvass.

"It might be raining in awhile," he said as they came into the covered area. "We probably ought to stay under this thing to keep dry."

"Rain? Pish posh. Not on a perfect day like this."

The boat took another large roll and Ben's face said he was worried. But Amber in her excitement broke free from him and ran to the stern, eager to see if anything was in the boat's wake, as he'd said.

Goddamnit, he thought. She's bound and determined to fall off this fucking thing. Shit. Shit! He hurried back and came up beside her.

"Hi, seagulls," Amber yelled. "Looking for something to eat, are you?" A flock of seagulls was following the boat and occasionally diving into its wake. "I don't see any dolphins."

"Maybe they're aren't any there; it's getting rough."

The boat took a long roll in a trough, throwing them into each other. "How long is this ride, anyway?" he asked. "Did you ask when you got the tickets?"

"Huh? No, I don't know. Didn't think to ask because I didn't think it mattered," she answered. "Probably an hour or so. The sign said coast tour, so . . . ."

The boat dove through a wave and showered them with sea water.

"Shit."

"It's just ocean. You can shower when we get back. Pretend it's the Gulf and you have a flower garden shirt on." She winked at him.

But he wasn't thinking of taking a shower or flower garden shirts. He was thinking, wondering, actually, if this captain knew what he was doing, running them along in troughs with a storm moving in. Hell, he's a native, he thought. What am I worried about? He probably knows these waters like the back of his hand. Yet he didn't like the way the water was getting rougher and suggested that maybe they ought to take a seat beneath the canopy. He was afraid a sudden pitch would throw her overboard, and he didn't relish the idea of diving into rough sea. Or any sea, for that matter.

He began to sweat and looked around for the life jacket station.

"Abby, do you know how to swim?" he asked, pulling her to a chair.

"What? Why ask that? Of course I know how to swim. Er, sort of." She laughed. "I can belly float and swim on my back. Told you that before. But, quit worrying, will you? Nothing's going to happen out here except that we're going to have a good time and see our house."

"Yeah." He looked around until he saw it. "I'll be right back. Stay here, will you? Watch the waves or something." With that he was moving toward the container marked Life Preservers. He grabbed two and made his way back cautiously, as the boat now was heaving on the swells and the sky was beginning to darken.

"Here," he said to her, putting his on. "Just in case."

"In case of what? I don't want that thing on. It'll take all the fun out of it. I don't see anyone else running for one"

"Put it on!" he almost shouted, trying to contain himself. "This isn't a fucking lake, it's the goddamn ocean!"

"See if I ever invite you for another boat ride, damned grump." She reluctantly struggled into the orange life jacket with him helping, miffed, as the boat took more water over the side, spraying them, even under the canopy.

"It's getting rough, so it's for your own good." Before she could answer, the wind came up, lightning cracked, and it began to rain.

"We're gonna get soaked out here, even under cover with this much wind. Come on, we're going inside?"

"Why? I love storms. They make you feel so alive."

"Right, but we'd be better off inside," he said watching the swells now rising almost to the boat's gunwales. "We're in for a pretty good one, it feels like." He was trying to hide his growing panic as another wave came crashing over the rail and spray was whipping around them. "Hell, Abby, everyone else is inside but us. We must look like dumb tourists. Come on, let's go."

"Oh, all right. Geeze. Seems they would've canceled the ride if there was a dangerous storm coming?"

He noticed fog beginning to creep in and obstructing their view of the coast. "We're gonna have to turn back anyway. Look there."

She turned to look, but the boat took a long dive under another wave as she did and almost threw her to the deck.

"Whoa! That was a big one," she said, suddenly startled.

"Told you! We're going inside right now," he yelled, beginning to sweat profusely. He grabbed her with one hand and held onto the bench seat with the other. "Don't stand up. Stay crouched and pull yourself along the seats. Stay away from the railing."

They moved carefully toward the cabin door, maybe fifteen feet away. The boat was rocking now, no longer riding the swells but diving into them, and wave after wave hit them as they made their way slowly forward. Amber no longer protesting.

When they'd almost made it to the door, Ben looked out at the water and froze. A huge comber was bearing down on them and would broadside the boat if the captain didn't turn into or away from it in time. Suddenly he was in another time, another place. . . .

He's in his twenties. He and two other crew members stare through their boat's windshield at an enormous wave approaching them in a storm. "Jesus!"

Amber suddenly realized they were in danger after all and cried out. "BEN?" It brought him back.

"HOLD ON," he yelled as he covered her with his body. "GRAB HOLD OF SOMETHING! ANYTHING!"

She grabbed onto one of the air vent pipes sticking up beneath the gunwale as the boat shuddered, turning into the oncoming wave. It began to rise as it started up the wave, like going up in an elevator or a roller coaster, and they were nearly lying on the deck from its angle.

"Damn!" Amber swore, really concerned now.

317

The boat seemed to point vertically momentarily, and it was all he could do to hang onto her and the pipe with his free hand. She tucked herself into a fetal position, now clutching the pipe with both hands, and he wrapped around her like a spoon. The boat suddenly topped the wave and plummeted down the other side, throwing them forward.

"Goddamnit! Hang on, and let's try to get into the cabin on three when it levels out again." He looked out at the sea as the boat rode up one swell and down another, each, it seemed to him, bigger than the last. "One . . . two . . . NOW!" he yelled, and they both half-stumbled, half-groped their way to the cabin door. He jerked it open and almost shoved her inside, slamming it shut behind them just as another wave crashed into it.

The other passengers were clearly worried and all had their life vests on, each hanging onto something as well.

"Ben?" Amber said quietly, her face now showing strain.

"What?"

"This thing can't turn over, can it?"

The boat with Ben and the other two young sailors on it is lifted by the wave and catapulted backwards, throwing them into the sea. Ben surfaces, gasping for breath and looking wildly around. "Maddox! Jones!" A wave carries him away from their upside down patrol boat, its twin propellers still turning.

"No," he lied. "But just make sure you keep hanging onto something so you don't get bounced into the bulkhead. We've run into a squall, that's all. It'll pass."

He knew better. This was no squall; this was a gale and how long it would last was anyone's guess. He also knew the captain would probably try to ride it out, rather than make a run for port, and while the safer move in the long run, he could only hope the boat could take the sea's pounding.

"You're not worried, are you?" he forced a smile. "I thought you liked storms."

"Oh, I do, I do," she said. "But the idea of drowning isn't appealing to me." Her face said she was worried now.

"Ah, you're not gonna drown, babe. I won't let you. Besides, you're too damned ornery to drown," he teased, trying to ease her fears. Across the cabin a woman began a low moan, clearly frightened.

He heard the engines increase, and knew the captain was trying to make headway into the storm, that it was probably pushing them back toward the shore. And the rocks. Shit.

"Back in a bit. You stay right here," he told Amber as he turned for the cabin door.

"No, wait," she began, but he was out the door and clutching his way to the wheelhouse ladder before she could say any more.

This time he didn't knock but forced the door open against the wind and slammed it behind him. "What we got, Captain?" he asked as the boat dove through another wave. "I can help."

"Southeaster," the man said grimly, struggling with the wheel. "Caught me off guard, like they often do." He glanced quickly at Ben. "Can you read a radar scope? I'd make a run for the harbor if I could see it."

Ben looked out through the windows. Fog was thickening. Shit. "Yes sir, I can. I can also steer, if you'd rather look yourself."

"Good," the Captain said, motioning for him to take the wheel. "Deckhand's out drunk, lazy bastard, else I'd have me some help. Keep her heading into them waves while I take a peek."

Ben nodded and took the wheel while the captain went to the radar scope and looked at its glowing screen. "There it is, up about a half-mile," he said, taking the wheel from Ben. "Let me know when we're dead opposite."

Before he could reply the Captain turned the sixty-foot trawler with the skill of a professional. The boat yawed at first, then swung around in the trough and was angled out before the next comber lifted them into the air again.

"Hell of a ride, ain't it?" The Captain laughed, but it was an uneasy laugh.

Ben got on the scope and studied the coastline as the boat maneuvered its way through the storm. The Captain was making a tack, running into the storm, then away from it, as a sailboat would do in a headwind. Ben knew he was trying to avoid being rolled over by the monstrous waves while still making headway. At the right moment, the boat would turn and run for the harbor with the waves behind them. With this kind of boat and waves this big, he also knew that if they misjudged, they'd hit the rocks instead.

"How we doing?" the Captain asked as he spun the wheel one way, then the other and alternated the throttles.

"Just fine. Another quarter mile, I'd say."

"Okay. Let me know when you see the cut and I'll crank her over."

"You got it," Ben said, wondering and worried about what Amber was doing below.

Amber sat holding the woman in her arms as the woman sobbed hysterically. "I knew we shouldn't have come out on this . . . this death ship!" the woman bawled.

"Shhh, shhh," Amber said quietly. "We'll be fine, dear, nothing to worry about. Why, I've been through lots of storms like these, and I'm still here. See?" She smiled at the woman.

The woman looked up at her. "You have?"

"Sure. Lots of them," she said, but she was trembling as she said it.

"Now!" Ben yelled to the Captain.

"Hope you're right, bub," the Captain said as he spun the wheel and added power.

Ben felt the stern lift high as a comber passed beneath them, then settle down into the following trough. Me too, he thought.

"Here," the Captain said.

Ben took the wheel as the captain quickly looked into the scope. "Come right a bit. Hold her there. Now left."

Ben cranked the wheel over hard.

"Stop!"

Ben's hands were shaking remembering the last time he'd been in a gale, but he held the wheel tightly and felt the waves pass beneath them, lifting them and throwing them forward as if a cork on the water.

"Here we go," the Captain said as he quickly grabbed the wheel. "Get out there and watch for the buoy. Or the rocks, whichever." He pointed to the door.

He stepped out on the small bridge that surrounded the wheelhouse and stared into the fog. Nothing. Shit. He heard the engines slowing as the captain idled down. He's going to let the waves carry us in if he can, he thought, until the last moment. Then he'll gun it and run for the harbor. If he's wrong, by being at idle, he'll be ready to throw the engines into reverse, not that it would help much in a storm this size, but he felt better at the Captain's technique.

He squinted into the fog. His heart suddenly leaped into his throat as the black, steel and extremely large sea buoy suddenly appeared directly in front of them.

"LOOK OUT!" he yelled, pointing.

The boat instantly swung to the right, barely missing the tall contraption, close enough to where someone on deck, had they been stupid enough, could have stepped onto it.

The Captain throttled up again, about half-power, Ben guessed, and within a minute or so, the entry rocks guarding the channel appeared through the fog. He pointed again and looked back at the Captain. The man nodded and winked, as if it had been a game for him. Game, he thought? I ought to wring his fucking neck for taking us out in bad weather like this. But he realized that this probably wasn't bad weather to an older seaman like the Captain, a man probably used to storms, a man who might have seen hundreds.

He thought as well that maybe the wink had been one of relief, and let his anger subside then, thinking instead of Amber. He hurried back to the cabin.

They passed the entry jetty light as he opened the cabin door and knew they'd entered the harbor. He had no idea what Amber had been doing, and only hoped she was all right, and not been knocked unconscious or something.

"Where've you been?" she said as he shut the door behind him.

He turned to see her standing at a grill by an open window inside the cabin. She was making hot dogs. A woman stood beside her, putting mustard on buns with trembling hands, her face streaked with dried tears. Amber was humming as if at a picnic. The other passengers were behind them, waiting their turns.

It was all he could do to not laugh out loud at the scene. Leave it to her, he thought. Making hot dogs when they'd nearly all drowned.

"Want one?" She winked, as if not concerned in the least, but she was shaking as she said it.

As they stumbled away from the docks, soaking wet, reeling in the storm as it swirled the festival litter around them, both noticed they still had their lifejackets on. They looked at each other and laughed. When they got to their car, he held her close and kissed her.

"What was that for?" she asked over the rain and wind.

"Nothing," he said. "Just glad you're still with me, I guess."

"Want to go out again tomorrow?" She grinned up at him.

"Lunatic!" he bellowed, pretending puffery as she snuggled into him. "That's what you are, a goddamn lunatic."

"Yeah," she smiled. "Ain't I?"

CORN SHUCK RUGS AND AUTUMN THINGS

Amber was sprawled in the middle of the porch surrounded by a mound of corn stalks, her fingers deftly weaving shucks into a growing circle in her lap. The pile crackled beside her as Tag emerged in hot pursuit of the braided husk trailing from her hands.

"How am I ever going to finish our doormat if you keep breaking my strands?" she scolded him. "I made you a ball to play with so I could finish this before Ben gets home from the drug store." Tag showed no concern for her predicament as he landed square in the middle of the round mat draped across her knees.

"Oh, okay. I guess I'll have to put this up for later and go check on the soup." She kissed the top of the kitten's head and pushed the stalks aside, carefully laying the half-finished mat under them.

"I think I see Ben coming now," she said, once on her feet. "Look, Tag." The silver car caught a sunbeam as Ben pulled off the road. "There's your buddy." His topaz eyes followed her finger up the hill.

The kitten scampered up the path toward the car just as Ben was closing the door. She stood laughing at the sight of him, more like a dog running to greet his master. "That

323

animal never ceases to amaze me," she said out loud. Shaking her head, she moved through the door to check on supper.

The big toothy grin of the jack-o-lantern flickered on the counter, its innards now boiling on the stove. The triangle eyes winked at Ben as he came through the door, Tag leaping at the package he carried loosely in his hand.

"See you've been carving on the pumpkin," he said as he tousled her hair.

"Yes, and wait'll you taste the soup." She stood on her tip toes and kissed the top of his forehead. "Did you get what you needed?"

"What? Oh . . . yes. Yes, I did." The bottle of pills suddenly felt like a watermelon in his pocket. "I've been out of paper tablets," he said, tossing the bag holding two yellow writing pads on the table. He picked it back up then. "Guess I'll go put these in my bag instead of cluttering up the supper table."

"Okay, and wash up while you're in there; it's almost ready. You promised we could take a walk on the shore after we eat so I fixed it early."

"So I did," he answered as he closed the door leading to the bedroom and bath.

The wind off the water wrapped them in a chill as they strolled just above the rolling surf.

"What are you thinking?" she asked him, seeing him in some kind of deep thought.

"Me?"

"Yes, you. Who would I be talking to, some seagull?"

He laughed. "It wouldn't surprise me. Nothing surprises me about you anymore."

She pushed him in the arm.

"Are you about ready to head back, Abby? A cup of hot chocolate and the swing is looking pretty good to me now. I'm cold." He gave an exaggerated shiver and hugged his jacket close.

"Sure, hon. It is a bit nippy this afternoon, isn't it?" she agreed. "And, I have pumpkin pie to go with the hot chocolate, too." She took his hand as they turned and retraced their own footprints in the sand.

Their house came into view above them and they wound through the rocks to the path that led steeply up the side of the cliff.

When they reached the top, Ben headed toward the porch and the swing. "Pumpkin pie, did you say?" he asked, visibly out of breath. He settled into the swing while she went inside. "If you need any help, give a holler. I won't come, but it'll make you feel good." He chuckled at his own jesting.

He heard her muttering some kind of retort from inside and smiled. Within a minute she re-appeared, pie, plates, and forks in hand. "Now you can go bring out the hot chocolate," she said, setting the plates between them on the swing.

"Me? Oh all right," he feigned annoyance while getting out of the swing and heading inside. "I have to do every-thing!"

She grinned and took a bite of her pie

A Harvest Moon as golden as new cheddar rose over them as they sat snuggled together sipping their chocolate, enjoying the night and being together.

"Know what I was thinking?" he finally said. "I was thinking about the time I drew out the entire universe with a piece of chalk on a sidewalk. I was probably eight or so. Used a shadow off a fire plug and started making little white dots for stars. Of course, I didn't have the slightest idea if I was right; I just drew what I'd seen in the night sky, you know? But I didn't care. It was my universe and that's all that counted. You ever do something like that?"

"No, I was interested in the faces in clouds. I'd lie for hours sometimes figuring them out."

"Yeah."

"What do you want for Christmas?" he asked.

"Christmas? It hadn't crossed my mind. Why do you ask that?"

He shrugged. "Just curious."

"Ben, look," she said, pointing to the sky. A shooting star arced above, clearly observable in the dark of night.

"Wish I may . . . wish I might," he began.

"Have this wish I wish tonight," she finished.

Ben went inside and returned with coffee for them both.

"What would you wish for if wishes came true?" he asked taking a sip.

"But they do, hon. Haven't you ever had wishes come true?"

"Yes and no. Not regularly though, and often not in the form I wished them. But what would you wish for? A million bucks?"

"No," she said, lowering her eyes.

"What, then?"

She took his hand, still looking at the sky. "I'd wish . . . she began, hesitating. "I'd wish we'd met sooner. I was alone two years. Or, I'd wish . . . ."

He guessed where she was going with the thought. She'd wish her husband hadn't died as he had, leaving her alone at all. He squeezed her hand in silent understanding.

A slight smile came at his perception; a hint of moisture welled in the corner of her eyes.

"I guess not all wishes come true. At least, all the time," he said. "Me, I'd kind of like another swipe at old life, too. Undo what I've done, re-do what I should have. I think when we want something badly enough it turns up. I can't really say, but I've had things come into my life that I wanted, and some, not. I've looked into it some, but never found any answers."

"Maybe there aren't any absolute answers," she agreed.

"If there are, they haven't shown themselves to me with any clarity. I've tried religion, the occult, positive thinking. I've actually watched things appear out of nowhere when I was desperate, but on the flip side, couldn't make things happen no matter what. How do you explain that?"

She thought it over. "I can't. Like you, I've seen the same. I've never figured it out either. But I know *something* exists."

"Guardian angels?" he asked.

"Could be. I don't rule it out."

"Luck?"

She shook her head. "I don't think there's such a thing as luck. Chance might be a better word. I've had my share of bad and good, and sometimes the end result was the opposite of what I'd expected. So really not bad or good at all. More a situation and how I chose to deal with it."

"Yeah. I know what you're saying. Not sure I agree, though."

He draped his arm around her shoulder and pulled her closer. "Must be some reason then why the assholes seem to get away with everything and the good suffer," he continued.

"Oh, I don't think they get away with it; just appears that way. You know I'm a proponent of what goes around comes around. I think eventually you get back what you throw out. I can always remember my mom telling me "if you dance, you must pay the fiddler." Yet, life would be pretty dull without some music, wouldn't it, hon? I like that quote they use with sports . . . 'It isn't about if you win or loose, but how you play the game'."

"Aaah, my eternal optimist," he kidded.

Another shooting star passed over. "Maybe," she went on, "desire and imagination is from both the past and future. Maybe we've lived before, and before you protest, what I mean is maybe it's a dimensional thing. Maybe imagination is really just memory. You know, like Richard likes to contemplate."

"That everything is and always has been alive, that nothing ever dies, all that?" he asked.

She nodded. "That it's all about parallel universes, and that we just jump from one to another, life to life."

"Then how do you explain the varying amounts of people on earth at a given time? Seems like it would remain constant," he added, taking a sip of his coffee.

Amber laughed. "If there are many dimensions, the flow between them doesn't have to be a constant. Nor are we limited to just people. Energy can take any form it chooses. I choose to come back as the wind next time, or maybe a rainbow." She turned to look at him.

"Might explain ghosts," he went on, not commenting on her last, "if there's some kind of portal, some kind of door from one life to another."

"I don't believe in ghosts as such, not the haunting kind. But I think spirit energy can be anything it wants, you know that." She smiled at him. "And doesn't it seem strange to you that with all there is to learn, we'd only live one life?"

He put his cup down and his other arm around her. "You chilly?"

She shook her head. "Not really."

He sat back and pushed the swing with his feet. "All religions in one form or another speak of it," he continued. "All the ancients, and now, in a way, the physicists. But I kind of think it might fall more in the nothing can be destroyed idea about energy. Then again, I'm neither religious nor a physicist. But I am ancient," he smiled down at her.

"Are not. Just cantankerous." She kissed his cheek.

"That, too." He smiled. "And these bones are telling me I need my . . . what do women call it? Beauty rest, and in my case, lots of it."

"Does that mean you're going off to bed and leave me out here with an unanswerable question? Huh? Are you, huh? Damned old coot."

"And you're a damn stubborn female who talks to animals, birds, and the wind."

"What's wrong with talking to the wind?" she kidded him.

"Oh, absolutely nothing. I often talk to shadows, myself. They're quite interesting, you know."

"Stop it. You're making fun of me again."

"Yeah," he said, brushing her lips with his own. "Now I'm off to bed. Try not to stay up all night if you can."

328

"Okay, hon. I probably won't be far behind. Night," she said as he went inside.

She turned again to the sky, her thoughts lingering on their conversation. "Twinkle, twinkle, little star," she sang softly, and one of them seemed to do just that. She smiled. "There you are. I wondered where you'd been all this time," she whispered into the night.

Inside, Ben replaced the cap on the pill bottle, crawled between the covers and pulled them up to his chin. He peered around the room and whispered to the shadows. "Wish I may, wish I might, live this love another night. Aaah, Abby, how I wish I had your faith. How do I tell you of the peril growing within me?"

'TIS A WONDROUS THING

Amber sat with her coffee scribbling Ben a note. Time had slipped away of late, lost any significance, but it was Saturday if her calculations were correct, and the local farmers would have their booths set up around the town square. She needed more Indian corn to complete her Halloween decorations, and the late October morning was beckoning her to get started early.

She propped the message next to his oatmeal bowl, carried her mug to the sink, then quietly peeked in the bedroom. Ben, Tag beside him, was still curled beneath the covers as the first light filtered through the window and hovered over the bed. Perfect, she thought, listening to the even breathing of his sleep. He'd been fidgety during the night again and had gotten up once to take an aspirin or something.

Grabbing her yellow jacket from the coat stand, her purse and keys from the table, she slipped noiselessly out the door. The cool morning air was invigorating and she breathed deeply, filling her lungs with its energy as she fairly skipped up the path to the car.

Now moving north on the highway toward town, she relaxed and scanned the landscape around her. The tufts of iridescent yellow and scarlet hardwoods appeared as giant balloons tied to the forest floor among the spiral evergreens. The pine tops pierced the crystal blue sky before it fell into the ocean somewhere off to the right side horizon. The leaves, already past their color peak, were starting to fall. They carpeted the ground like a rug, protecting the plant roots from heavy snows that were sure to come.

She shivered at the prospect and wondered how she'd acclimate to a harsh winter after so many years in the tropics. Even the few spent at the farm in the southern Appalachians were mild. The Mainers would scoff at what the South called winter. Smiling at the thought, on impulse she pulled into one of the small coves sculpted in the rocks and lowered the top of the convertible. A flock of sea birds bustling around the ledges stopped their squawking and stared at her, unsure but not alarmed.

"Hello there, bird friends," she called out to them. "'Tis a wondrous thing to have such a beautiful day for riding the wind with only the open sky overhead, don't you think? What? A bit chilly, you say?" she asked as they resumed their calling. "Aaah, yes, but it gets the blood pumping; makes you know you're alive." The birds seemed to nod their agreement and went on about their squabbling or whatever it was they were doing.

Pushing an *Aerosmith* CD into the player, she waved to the birds and pulled back onto the highway. As the wind struck her face, she suddenly realized that she'd been craving this time alone with her car and her music. She suspected that Ben, too, was eager for some solitude with his yellow pads and his thoughts.

They'd been together almost incessantly since leaving the Florida treehouse, and she'd noticed his being preoccupied on more than one occasion lately. Writers, she knew, were solitary beasts at heart and she didn't want to ever intrude on his private space. Given that, perhaps he'd write her a ghost story to read by the fire on Hallows Eve. That thought, too, brought a smile. For one so damn pragmatic,

Ben sure had an affinity for ghosts and spooky things, almost trepidation.

As she accelerated and the car responded, she suppressed the urge to give it its rein, her mind envisioning a powerful stallion galloping through a canyon after breaking loose from a pen. Ben always scolded her penchant for driving too fast. He'd been even more skittish about it since the day they'd encountered the moose, although that experience had made her more cautious, too, if only for the sake of the animals. But she was past that point in the road now and had clear vision of the town lying below the bluffs. She threw her caution to the wind, and her spirit soared in tune to the music and the tires squealing on the asphalt as she raced to the bottom.

She pulled into a parking space not far from the temporary farmer's market set up around the square. A couple walking by watched her with surprised expressions as they glanced at her license plates.

"Tourist," the woman stated, somewhat distastefully, to her partner.

"Bit nuts, I'd say," the man replied, but grinned as he said it.

"Good morning, folks. Isn't it simply an incredible day?" she called. Noticing them staring at her, she remembered to lower the volume on the player.

The woman barely nodded and the man, looking briefly around, said, "Why yes, I suppose it is." He smiled over his shoulder as the woman pulled him on their way.

Unable to resist the vixen in her, she winked at him and yelled, "Enjoy yourselves, folks."

Laughing to herself, she pressed the button that would raise the top. "Friendly old crone, wasn't she? I'll never understand why most people take affront at anyone daring to step outside the lines of convention," she said out loud, then reprimanded herself. "Gads, they *will* think I'm a loon if I talk to myself." Still smiling, she gathered her purse, locked the car, and headed toward the bustle around the stands in search of Indian corn.

A few booths later she was laden with sacks of yellow squash, bright colored corn, and ornamental pumpkins. She bought apples, sticks, and the makings of caramel coating to dip them in. She chatted amicably with the various vendors and learned of a haunted house being set up by the local Chamber of Commerce. Maybe Ben would like that, she thought. She was thoroughly excited at the crackle of cold in the air, and the festive rattling of paper ma'che witches and goblins hung from the booths to mark the upcoming holiday.

She decided to take some fruit and fall vegetables to Alice, and bought extra apples for pies and cobblers. Alice could definitely use some calories to go with her *medicine* coffee, she thought with a grin, and maybe a pie would pack an extra pound or two on her delicate frame for winter. And why not a pumpkin for carving too? She'd help her do it if need be, then share her recipe for pumpkin soup.

"Amber? Amber!"

She was caught off-guard at hearing her name in the crowd of strangers and turned to see a small woman with white hair flying in the breezes waving at her from across the street.

"Alice! Hello," she called and started to cross over to where Alice stood smiling at her. "I was just thinking of bringing you some treats and here you are."

She was genuinely glad to see her friend and trotted the rest of the distance between them. She wrapped her arms, bags and all, around Alice and the weight of it all took the balance from under their feet causing them both to stumble.

"Ooops, I'm sorry, Alice. I'm so happy to see you I almost wiped you out with a cob of corn and a soon-to-be-jack-o-lantern." Both women laughed and moved to a nearby bench where Amber could drop her load of packages. "It's so funny, I was just thinking of coming by your house and here you are! Talk about a coincidence!"

"I thought you didn't believe in those things, dear." Alice winked, her eyes sparkling in the bright autumn sun.

"I don't." Amber laughed. "Would you like to get some hot cider? I saw a booth selling it fresh-made."

"I should get on home. Don't like to leave the old dog alone too long, and I got what I came to town for. But, if you planned on coming by, why not follow me if you're done your shopping?" Alice looked questioningly at the pile of bags on the bench next to them.

"Yes, yes I will. I have some things for you here." She looked at the small bag Alice was carrying. "I hope you didn't buy apples because I just bought enough for the whole town. Where are you parked?"

"Oh, just around the corner, not far at all." Alice stood and patted Amber's cheek. "You know the way. I'll just go on ahead and see you at the cabins. That okay?"

"Okay. I'll be close behind you." She started reloading her arms with the sacks and watched Alice head for the corner. "Nope. I don't believe in coincidences at all," she whispered to her retreating friend's back.

She pulled into the graveled parking area in front of the rental cabins a short time later and unloaded what she'd gotten for Alice. Smells of strong brewed coffee greeted her before she could even knock. She was glancing fondly over her shoulder at the cabin she and Ben had stayed in their first few days there when Alice opened the door.

"Get yourself in here before those bags break your bones, my dear." Alice stood aside so Amber could pass by, motioning her arm in a welcoming gesture. "What a treat to have some company on such a lovely afternoon. I'm so glad I ran into you, Amber."

"Me, too." She smiled as she put her treats on the counter, then plopped in the chair she'd sat in on the night of their arrival. "I've meant to get over here sooner, but I confess, I got so involved with settling in the house. Thank you so much, Alice. I'm so happy there. Just wait until you see how we've fixed it up, and Ben has been such a dear to help."

She tucked her feet under her and looked around the cabin. The dog, after sniffing in her direction, returned to his rug by the bedroom door. Satisfied, she guessed, that he'd found her familiar enough, and Alice in no danger.

"How is Ben taking to the place? I mean, does he seem really content?" Alice asked. "I fear he wasn't as enthusiastic as you at the idea of moving in there at first. You warm enough by the way? I could stir up the fire if you get a chill."

"I'm fine, hon. Why don't you sit with me for a minute and then I'll help you carve the pumpkin. And go easy on the *medicine* in my coffee. I have to drive home this time." She winked, leaned forward, and patted the chair Alice would pull up next to her.

"Okay, think I will. Been on the old legs all morning. And, Ben?" Alice renewed her question as she handed Amber a mug, then sat.

"Oh, he's a bit cantankerous now and then, but I think he's happy too."

"You think? You're not sure?"

She couldn't quite read Alice's face. Was it disappointment causing the slight narrowing of her eyes?

"Alice, Ben isn't one you can be sure of. He holds back a part of himself, even from me. Especially from me. I just enjoy each day we have, trust he'll see one day. But I fret a little when he isn't looking, I'm afraid. Something still eats at him from deep down. He doesn't share our feelings of connections. Thinks I'm a bit of a nut. I don't know what it is he's hesitant about, or trying to forget, or trying not to. But, it's something, and I don't know if he's running from me or to me at times. I wonder if he knows."

She got up. She didn't really want to talk about Ben, and Alice seemed to be pondering her answer, and forming her next question. "You sit." She patted Alice's shoulder. "I'll get you more coffee. And where do you keep your carving knives? That pumpkin's got a big smile hiding in that orange skin of his and I love smiling jack-o-lanterns." She bent over and kissed the old woman's forehead on her way to the kitchen.

Ben was sitting at the table, his hair disheveled, still in his robe, typing away on the laptop computer as fast as he could type . . . .

The monster came out of the woods, its great horn glistening, surrounded by a swirling mist of gossamer clouds. Leto tried to draw his sword and couldn't, the pain from his wound overwhelming him. He cried out in fear and anger, falling to his knees in the sandy loam, cursing. It wasn't going to take him as it had the others, he swore to himself.

The beast came forward, nostrils flaring and shooting red flames as it breathed, its heavy, cloven hoofs causing deep impressions in the earth. It was as horrible looking as Leto had been told and he tried to shrink away but couldn't. It stopped and looked down at its small adversary, then threw its head back and howled. The scream sent shivers through Leto's body as he fumbled unsuccessfully for the amulet beneath his shaggy coat.

If a sword can't stop it, maybe this can. Leto's hand wrapped around the golden object on its chain around his neck, desperately trying to free it from the confines of his clothing as the swirling mist enveloped him . . . .

Ben pushed himself away from the table. "Hmmm," he said, rising and going into the small kitchen for more coffee. He waited as the water boiled, seemingly perplexed and scratching at his beard, thinking.

"Too pedantic," he said. "Too weak. Something." He poured the boiling water into his cup and returned to the table, looking at what had been written on the screen. He continued typing . . . .

The beast stood looking at him, undecided as to how it would take him, Leto thought. Would it be a single thrust from its great cornu? Would the creature play with him first, making the kill even more agonizing?

Leto, still on his knees, suddenly withdrew the amulet from his coat and held it up for the beast to see. "Go, damn you, go!" He felt the amulet coming to life, its sonic hum penetrating the mist and parting it in a circle around him. The beast shrank back, first one step, then two, as Leto struggled to keep the charm held high. "Go! You have no power over me this day! Go!"

It grudgingly turned and Leto could see its massive backside and tail as it left, taking the mist with it and leaving him alone in the clearing again. Leto couldn't keep his arm up any longer and collapsed into the earth, sweating profusely . . . .

"Ah, shit," Ben swore as he leaned back in his chair. "What a goofy story. Leto, Smeto, Great Beasts and pumpernickel, bah, humbug. No one's going to believe that. It's too set, it's too corny."

He stood. "I need some fresh air, that's what I need," he said, moving toward the bedroom. Alone in the kitchen, Tagalong jumped onto the table and looked down at the machine lying before him. He stuck out a paw and played with the keys.

The sleek nose of the *Spyder* hugged the road, as if breathing in the scent of home, with her sudden urge to return to Ben's side. She'd enjoyed her day at the market, her visit with her friend, although some of the unasked questions in Alice's eyes had disquieted her. Should she press more to open pages in a book he seemed intent on keeping unread? Did Alice sense more, know more, than she was letting on? Was it merely Ben's contentment level that concerned her?

"Pish," she chided herself. "Quit looking for ghosts just because you've been carving pumpkins!"

He was cautiously moving down the rocky path toward the ocean below. "It's harder going down than coming up," he said. "Or I'm getting old." The sea before him was a royal blue and he marveled at how it changed colors so often, from wild and frothy gray to aqua-green to blue. Once on the beach he walked along, watching the sand. He was looking for hermit crabs to dart in and out of their burrowed confines as he approached.

"Hiya! Come on out, Mr. Crab. I know you're there." He reached down to inspect a small hole in the sand. "Arrhggg," he groaned as he doubled up in pain, nearly falling onto the protruding rocks before catching himself on the way down. Looking around, he saw no one on the beach but him. He looked back to the path that led to their house and began to half-limp toward it, sweat beading on his forehead. The climb back up the path was tortuous, but he eventually made it and staggered inside.

Amber drummed the steering wheel with her fingers and increased her speed. The need for space, and giving Ben his, was gone. Now she wanted only to be where he was. She turned on the winding coast road, forcing herself to slow down. The gull on its chain felt cold against her flesh as the wind off the water blew in the car. She pushed the button that would raise the window and swallowed hard, hoping to dislodge the lump forming in her throat. Something, she didn't know what, but something, was wrong.

The pills were shaken from his hidden bottle and gulped, then re-hidden. He collapsed onto the bed until the pain subsided, his eyes staring blankly at the ceiling. "This isn't going to work. It just isn't."

In the distance he heard the familiar bass thump, then silence, then a car door close. Resilience washed over him, replacing the fear. The pain had once again passed and Abby was home. "It has to work. For her, for us. It has to, dammit."

He rolled over and pushed himself up and went into the bathroom, splashed some water on his face and was entering the kitchen just as she stumbled through the door backwards.

"Ben? I'm home. Ben . . . Tag?" she called, thrashing with the bundle of cornstalks resisting the door.

"Jesus! What are you yelling for? And why are you trying to carry the entire farmer's market in one trip?" he said as he moved to help. It was all he could do to sound stern as he stifled a laugh at the sight of her.

Amber whirled around, almost hitting him in the face with the dried corn. "Ben, you're here," she said, dropping her burdens in a pile at their feet. She captured his face between her hands, stood on her tiptoes, and kissed him long and hard.

"Hey, what's the matter with you?" he said, putting his hands up in mock defense. "Where did you think I'd be? Settle down, will you?" Then he hugged her tight against him and wondered if the trembling he felt was hers or his own.

Stepping back, satisfied that he was okay, she recovered. "Nothing's wrong, for Pete's sake. I just wondered why you didn't charge up the hill and help me with all this stuff. I've got supper to fix and decorations to finish and pumpkins to carve and . . . Tag! No! Don't wreck the corn." She reached down and scooped up the awakened kitten now intent on attacking the strange intruder.

"Why is it bedlam seems to follow you like a shadow?" Ben chortled. "I guess I'll just have to take matters into my own hands here." He bent to gather the bags off the floor, relieved that he felt no pain.

"Good. Just what I need, a man that takes control." She laughed, hugging Tag to her. "What say we have an omelet for supper since *you* are the champion egg cooker around here? I bought yard hen eggs at the market if they aren't all broken by now."

"Omelet it is. By candlelight even. How's that? Now get all that crap out of my way. Damn lunatic." God, he was glad she was home.

"And I see you've been working," she said, noticing the laptop and yellow pads spread on the table. "Can I see?"

"Absolutely not! You'll jinx my masterpiece." Forgetting he'd left the computer on, he rushed to block her view. "Now away with you," he ordered as he saved and closed his word processor, grinning at seeing the long row of garbled letters at the end of his manuscript. Even the cat's a wannabe writer, he laughed to himself as he closed the lid.

"Fire or swing?" He spoke softly in her ear as he encircled her shoulders from behind.

She was hanging the dishtowel as he approached her. Twisting to face him, she laid her head on his chest. "Fire. It's chilly, don't you think?"

"I thought so, too, and just got it going. Come on."

He guided her toward a billowy comforter spread before the hearth without releasing her from his arms. A pile of pillows were thrown in a heap to form a back rest and they positioned themselves in front of the warmth.

"And what did I do to deserve this display of romantic behavior, may I ask?" She hid her face in the soft place between his neck and shoulder, her lips against his skin.

"I haven't figured that out since you spend most of your time driving me nuts." He smiled at the top of her head. "Actually, I wanted to talk to you about something but I've suddenly forgotten what it was." He thought he noticed a catch in her breath, but ignored it.

"What's wrong, Ben?" She pulled back and their eyes locked in that uncanny way they'd done so many times.

The firelight danced in her eyes and glinted off the auburn highlights of her hair. His heart caught in an overwhelming rush of emotion. Feelings that he'd kept buried far too long, for reasons even he misunderstood, rushed tumultuously to the surface. No, he thought. They would have this moment, this hour . . . this night. He'd allow nothing to tarnish it.

"Nothing is wrong, Abby. Except that maybe I've never really told you how much I love you." He brushed her hair back off her face and kissed her gently on the forehead.

"Oh, Ben. You don't have to say anything."

"Hush now. I know I don't have to say. Not having to is why I must. And, you must promise me you won't ever forget it." He tried to pull her close but she resisted.

340

It wasn't like him to be so serious and he was scaring her. She forced eye contact again. "Must? Promise I won't forget? Of course I won't forget. What aren't you telling me?"

"I haven't told you how you've given meaning to my life when I'd lost any. How you've filled a cold, dark place with warm sunshine and gentle mornings. Barren nights with presence and serenity."

"Oh, Ben. I—"

"No. Don't say anything. For once, just listen."

"Okay." She relaxed and cuddled into him, watching the firelight create dancing shadows around the room.

"When I'm restless and waken," he went on, "old hauntings are forgotten when I feel you next to me. Smell the scent of your hair; listen as your breathing mingles with my own. That's what I'm not telling you, and I fear I've taken you for granted."

He reached into his pocket and brought out a polished oyster shell, shaded in coral, and hinged in gold with a small gold clasp holding it closed. "Abby, I can only hope to give you back a small portion of what you've given me. I hope this helps adorn your life as you've adorned mine."

She leaned forward and took the shell from him. "How beautiful. Look at it sparkle in the light." She held it out in her palm, so the shadows could play on its surface.

"Go ahead. Open it." He watched her, his eyes moist with the emotion he'd so long suppressed.

She gently released the clasp. Inside, on a bed of velvet, laid a solitary cultured pearl. She gasped at its exquisite, yet simple, beauty.

"It's a gift from the sea you so love, Abby. And I'm honored to be the one to give it to you."

She caressed the pearl with a quivering finger as her tears fell on the soft velvet lining of the shell. "Oh, thank you, Ben. I love you, you know that don't you?"

"Yes, I know." He couldn't say anymore.

She carefully closed the shell, held it close, and then stretched over him to place it on the end table by his chair.

He pulled her down and held her next to him. Overcome, she strained to fill every inch of her length with the touch of him. Suddenly they were grasping, then clinging, to one another almost frantically.

Time hung suspended and the room went away. Any barriers left standing, any fears still buried, and all the secret longings kept hidden, slowly dissolved into nothingness. The two of them drifted slowly through a vacuum into a new space, a new realm, where nothing else existed, had ever existed before them.

She felt the heat of him then, entering her own. Two distant lifetimes, two separate beings, at last, truly merged their spirit. A new and single entity was born in the succumbing, and it languished, reveled in its birth. Slowly, its aura rose out and away from them and lingered among the fire shadows.

She woke what must have been hours later. The room was dark but for the red coals smoldering on the fireplace floor. It looked almost unfamiliar to her. She felt Ben beside her, now sleeping peacefully, and then she remembered. She snuggled closer, listening to the surf break against the rocks, and watching a new dawn come through the window.

CARAMEL APPLES ON STICKS AND
SLOW DANCING

"No, Abby, I don't want to go to some fool haunted house like a goddamn teenager. Look at this place. It looks like the goddamn decoration aisle at Wal-Mart!"

He threw his hat on the table and waved his arm around the kitchen, accidentally slapping the witch with blinking red eyes hanging from the light fixture. It cackled at him haughtily in response to the movement.

"Okay. Okay, dammit, we don't have to go," she snapped back, "not that it might do you good to get out and act like a teenager, you damned old grump ass."

Amber was standing before an array of apples, inserting sticks and dipping them into a bubbling pot of caramel. "It was only an idea for something to do. Just forget it. Go plop your ass in your chair and watch your stupid tube. Expand your knowledge base so it will match your soon to be expanding waistline if you don't start getting some exercise!" She tossed the pointed sticks on the counter, some rolling off onto the floor causing Tag to pounce.

"And it would be an even better idea if you'd grow the hell up. We aren't fucking kids anymore. Jesus!" he spat back. And what're you making so many apples for? I hate apples."

"You hate everything that is good for you. So what the hell else is new? But I happen to like them, and here's a news flash for you, Mr. Riley. Life isn't just all about you."

"Fuck you, Amber." He stomped to the bedroom and slammed the door.

"Oh, it's *Amber* now, is it?" she grumbled to herself. Her anger rose to intense. "Yes," she yelled through the closed door, "why don't you fuck me, Ben? Afraid you might get a little exercise?" An answering thud from the door, as something was thrown from the other side, took the fight out of her.

She sat at the table, again setting the cackling witch off. "Damn!" she snarled. She'd gotten it for Tag mostly, but now she reached up, yanked the witch down and threw it in the direction of the trash can. Leaning back, she wiped at the tears of frustration welling in her eyes. Suddenly, the witch *was* silly. Everything was silly, and for all her efforts at gaiety, Ben's mood wasn't improving. Tag jumped onto her lap, nuzzled and purred into her ear as if to reassure her that all would be okay. It was weird how the animal could sense when something was amiss.

"Oh, Taggie boy, what is wrong with Ben?" she implored, hugging him close. "Something is bothering him, and he won't say. He keeps telling me everything is fine, and it isn't. He's as restless and irritable as when I first met him. Tag purred his answer but she didn't understand him anymore than she understood Ben.

He dampened a wash cloth and wiped the cold sweat from his brow. As fast as he'd blown off, he was sorry. He considered taking a pill but the pain was gone; only the dread of when it would hit again wore on his nerves. Instead, he walked to the window and looked out over the ocean wondering how he'd make it up to her this time.

Abby devoted herself to loving him and making them a home, a home like he'd never had in his entire life. The last

344

thing he ever wanted to do, he was doing. His own fear of losing what they had was the driving wedge causing it to happen. "I'm going to have to talk to her," he told himself.

He turned to sit in the chair. Take a few minutes to calm down and then go hold her close and tell her the damn truth, he thought. At least then she'll know, and we can cherish what time we have left rather than this bickering.

He rested his chin in his hands and fought his own tears. "I've tried to believe she could heal me just with her will, her mindful will, and her damn spirit foxes, and her damn rainbows. Goddamnit, it isn't working for me," he whispered to Bear. "The pain is more frequent now and I never know when it might hit. That's why I can't go with her to some damn fool haunted house!"

The big animal, perched on the antique window seat Abby had recently found at an auction, stared blankly back at him, offering no saving solutions. He couldn't help but smile as his mind wandered back to the first time he'd met him, sprawled in a cream-colored rocker and looking out over the wooden deck at the rear of a tree house. It seemed like eons ago, yet just last week. The tears came now, and he didn't bother to fight them.

The apples were lined in neat rows on a baking tin cooling. The witch no longer hung over the table and no candle burned in the jack-o-lantern. And why did he miss it? He stood at the sink still wondering on how to approach her. How to approach the entire mess, really.

He found her on the swing, Tag curled in the crook of her crossed knee. "I've decided to forgive you," he said, sitting beside her and draping one arm across her shoulders. At the sound of his voice, Tag crawled onto his more ample lap.

"I figured you might, long about suppertime." She didn't have to look at him to know he was smiling.

"Yeah, I see you're prepared to start force feeding me apples. And, after I changed shirts to take you out for fish, too."

"Good. You can have apples for breakfast instead." She looked at him then. "You don't have to take me out, you know."

"I know. I'd like to, though. I was kind of rough on you earlier. Not that you didn't have it coming, of course." He ruffled her hair as he said it.

She laughed in spite of herself. With Ben, humor was the sincerest form of apology, or flattery for that matter. Still, she felt uneasy. It was also one of his ways of avoiding an issue.

"I'm going in to change sweaters before you change your mind." She stood and walked inside, but not before bending to kiss his forehead.

"Christ," he muttered when the door shut. "Why does she make this so goddamn difficult?" And now he felt fine, which made it more so. "Aaah shit, Tag, let's go in. It'll wait one more day."

They'd eaten chowder and codfish by the wharfs, kept their bantering playful. She declined stopping at the haunted house after all, saying she was happy at just the touring of the town streets and seeing the festivities. Ben was at his charismatic best, and she was ready to go home.

"Abby, do you ever wonder what you'd be doing now if you hadn't wandered into a book store on a certain Saturday morning?" They were driving home slowly, with Ben behind the wheel.

"Oh I don't know. Never really think about it. Probably would still be doing what I was doing before." She was gazing ahead watching for the reflection of tell-tale eyes that would warn of a deer or moose crossing the road. "What would you be doing if you hadn't done the same?"

He didn't answer. "Funny, how a chance encounter can change everything, huh?" He glanced at her out of the corner of his eye.

"Chance? What is chance? Absolute or oblique. You know I don't think anything happens by chance. Oh, ninety percent of the time we don't pay attention to circumstances

346

around us, so what might have been doesn't always materialize. But the stage is set more often than we know, I'd say." She looked at him. "Why do you ask anyway?"

"Just wondering what you'd be doing with your life if I weren't in it. I worry sometimes that my pragmatism strikes you as hard. You think I see only in black and white with no possibility of gray, no room for mystery."

"I think you worry yourself with it more than me, hon," she said, smiling at him.

"What's that supposed to mean? There's just no understanding a woman." He chuckled and took her hand.

"It only means I think you know there's beauty and awe behind the intellect of the system, a magic, if you will. But, if something hasn't been scientifically proven, if you fail to see exactly how and why it works, you feel you must discount it. Like chance, connections, and meant to be's."

"Not really. I just try to show that no matter the awe about something, there's physicality behind it." He cleared his throat. "We are limited to the laws of a physical world."

"Ben, there's no research, no science, no proof that can answer all questions. Answers only lead to more questions, for Pete's sake. What is proven at all, ever? Only what was and maybe what is. What about beyond, and what will still be? And, even *was* and *is* are open to debate and perception."

"There you go talking in riddles again."

"Not riddles at all. You talk of gravity, that gravity always pulls down. Well, if you're the sun and I'm the earth, then gravity pulls up." She paused. "All depends on point of reference, wouldn't you say?"

Suddenly it wasn't funny. "Okay, go on, I'm listening."

"Well, it's got to do with limitations. If you limit the possibilities of an esoterical force, a transcendence between dimensions, life to only physical, you're doing the same thing as a fundamentalist who limits God to a doctrine. You're limiting science to what has already been proven. For me, some of the answers lie in the magic that is yet unknown. And the connection, the *why* we both wandered into

347

a bookstore on a Saturday morning, lies in that magic. Best I can do, darlin'." She squeezed his hand and turned the volume on the music, signaling an end to the discussion. She wanted him to think about what she'd said.

She is unique, the damn lunatic, he thought. Her ease and clarity of thinking often amazes me. I wish I had her simple trust in the higher things. I wish I could be well for her, grow much older with her. How I wish she could be right.

"Want coffee or hot chocolate?" Amber called from the kitchen.

"Hot chocolate." He was starting a fire in the fire place and lighting the oil lamps with long matchsticks.

"What? No comforter and pillows on the floor tonight?" she teased, coming into the room and setting the mugs on the coffee table.

"I was thinking of listening to some soft music for a change." He smiled at her. "Perhaps I could entice you into a dance. We haven't danced since the waterfall, and I admit you did show some promise," he teased. What would you like to hear?" He was thumbing through the few CDs that weren't in the car.

"You choose, you lead, and I'll follow," she said, sipping on her cocoa and smiling at him. "I'm not taking any chances at blowing this rare display of your more lustful side."

"Damn nut." He feigned annoyance. "What do you mean, rare? How's this?" He stood and held out his hand to her as the familiar voice of Elton John drifted from the speakers of the small player they'd gotten at the TV shop.

"That's perfect," she answered, walking up to him, hand extended.

He held her hesitantly at first, and then moved her slowly in the standard steps . . . forward, right, back, left. Again. He gently pulled her closer, and she leaned into him. Back, left, forward, right. Again.

His breath was caressing her ear, and she leaned her head and swayed into its warmth while his hand trailed down her back and the music entered her veins. She closed her eyes and followed a neon highway of sound in her mind, the flow of them moving effortlessly. Around, back, around again, each turn connecting more, the flesh of them. From somewhere she heard the words of the music.

> *"I saw you dancing out the ocean,*
> *running fast along the sand*
> *A spirit born of earth and water,*
> *fire flying from your hand.*
> *In the instant that you love someone,*
> *in the second that the hammer hits*
> *Reality runs up your spine,*
> *and the pieces finally fit . . ."*

He abandoned himself to the movement, to the touch and the scent of her. The heat embraced him. Was it from her, from within, the fire? It didn't matter, nothing mattered, but this life he was holding in his arms.

> *"And all I ever needed was the one,*
> *like freedom feels where wild horses run*
> *Where stars collide like you and I,*
> *no shadows block the sun*
> *You're all I ever needed,*
> *Babe, you're the one. . .*

Her fingers wandered up the back of him and guided his face to hers. She opened her eyes, leaned back and searched into his, seeing the very Soul of him for a brief moment.

He pulled back then and buried his face in her hair, tears mingling in the waves of it. If only this night, this warmth, this woman, could have always been, could last for all eternity. The words were singing his life, and his delicate future was swaying before and under him.

"There are caravans we follow,
drunken nights in dark hotels
When chances breathe between the silence,
where sex and love no longer gels
For each man in his time is Cain,
until he walks along the beach
And sees his future in the water,
a long lost heart within his reach.
Oh you're all I ever needed,
ooh Babe, you're the one.

He kissed her then, deeply, not missing a bend in the movement, not loosing a word of the song, a note of the music, as it came to its end. They stood then, their feet no longer moving, their bodies still swaying with the flames of the fire and the shadows. His hands unwound the braid in her hair letting it fall over her shoulders. Words were redundant then, their hearts did the speaking for them, but he spoke them anyway. Words he'd said rarely in his lifetime, words he feared he wouldn't have time to say enough in what was left of it.

"I love you, Abby."

She wanted to answer, but knew he needed her not to. Instead she moved into him again, and returned his kiss. Just as deeply.

SO MANY SECRETS

It was November and shorter days brought colder weather, though still unseasonably mild for Maine. Mornings, Ben and Amber still bundled up and shared their coffee and philosophies on the swing under the promised patchwork quilt. She'd grown accustomed to his moodiness both in conversation and behavior, light and humorous one moment, reflective and distant the next. Romantic and passionate after that.

Worried about his restlessness at first, afraid that he was unhappy, she'd questioned him, and inevitably he'd lost his temper, followed by an apology. A ritual in itself, it was demeaning to both of them. Now she left it alone, trusting he'd talk to her when he felt ready. Jeff had always talked to her about anything, but she'd chided herself that Ben wasn't Jeff.

Instead of nagging, she busied herself with caring for him, their new home, and watching closely when he'd have restless nights. Visions of the bout in the Texas hospital were still all too clear, and it had been but a few months since he'd been so ill. Determined to love and feed him back to health, she'd spotted an old apple press at a flea market and decided that homemade cider would entice him to eat an apple a day.

"What's that contraption?" he asked, as she lugged it through the door. "Won't be long before I'll have to move to the porch for all the paraphernalia you keep dragging in here."

"It's an apple press," she announced proudly at his question, ignoring the quip following. "I'm going to make hot apple cider all winter instead of that damned iced tea you want with dinner."

"I hate apples, you know that."

"You do not. You hate the skin on them is all, and you're going to love cider because I said so," she teased, throwing a bag of cinnamon sticks on the table where he sat with his laptop.

Afternoons, she and Tag poured over bulb and seed catalogs planning a spring garden, or created decorations and crafts with stuff, as Ben called it, discovered during their explorations. They visited nearby towns, markets, or took long strolls in the woods that bordered the other side of the highway. She thought of trying to get a job in the village but decided to wait until after Christmas, and also when she was more sure of Ben's health and moods.

He spent a good deal of time working on his laptop, and his imaginative writings fascinated her. Often she spotted her own truths lingering between the lines of his fiction, and was convinced that her healing philosophy was beginning to take root. She hoped that he was writing another wonderful story like he'd shared with her on Halloween Eve. Although a myth, when Leto overcame the beast with the amulet, she'd thrown the yellow pad into the air, and her arms around Ben's neck.

"Oh, Ben, see? Leto did believe in the power of his amulet. It was a symbol of his Spirit."

"Hogwash," he'd chortled back. "Leto was a superstitious old fool and he overcame the beast because it was a story. Make believe. You can do anything in make believe, Abby. The story was corny and written for fun."

But she would have none of it and at her urging he'd sent it off to his agent. They were thrilled when it had sold almost instantly, she, of course, saying it was meant to be. And she was convinced that the encounter with the bear and the moose had been his inspiration.

Evenings, Ben would watch the news on TV while she cleaned supper dishes and tidied the kitchen. Always a fire crackled in the fireplace, always oil lamps and candles burned, and he would tease that she was a sorceress in disguise. Occasionally, they'd read to each other from the latest book she simply "had to have," or he'd read poems and short stories he'd written for her on an impulse. She was certain he'd been seriously overlooked for a Pulitzer, and when she expressed so to him, he'd guffawed at the thought.

"Writing has made me a decent living since I quit flying planes, but the world of the written word and publishing, my dear Abby, is fraught with talent. Sadly, it's not always what you pen, but who you know, what circle you travel in, that determines the kind of success that wins Pulitzers." He smiled at her almost wistfully.

"Doesn't seem fair to me," she countered. "Sounds more like politics."

He grinned at her innocence. "It is politics, Abby, at that level. You may sell some, get published some, achieve merit awards even, but for every *New York Times* bestseller there are tens of thousands of books in print, and twice that many submissions just for the printing."

"Tens of thousands?" Her eyes widened. "In that case, that you've sold any, made a decent living as you say, speaks volumes of your talent." She smiled at him with admiration.

He feigned humility. "Oh, how blind art the eyes of a woman in love," he teased and hugged her to him.

Nights they lay close, sharing their dreams and their gratitude for the finding of the other until sleep would come. She always silently implored the Powers That Be that Ben would rest peacefully. And he would for a while, but rare was the night that he wasn't up pacing in the other room before dawn. Yet it didn't seem to be nightmares waking him like before. It was more like something lying heavy on his mind. *So many secrets he keeps, she thought.*

He stood over the sink fighting nausea. He guessed it was caused as much by wrangled nerves and the stress of trying to keep up a front for Abby as anything growing inside of him. In actuality, he'd only had one bad attack that day, and the pills were still able to abate the pain. But he knew the time would come when they wouldn't. Then what would he do to keep up the charade?

Tag, attacking the dangling tie of his robe, brought him back to the present. "Okay, ruffian, we better go back to bed before we have Abby out here asking her infernal questions." He bent and scooped up the cat, noticing how he'd filled out, seemingly overnight. "Growing into a fine feline, you are," he whispered. "Guess I can depend on you to keep her good company if something happens."

"You okay, hon?" she asked as he slid back into bed.

"Fine. Just needed a drink of water is all. Go back to sleep."

"Alright. Wake me if you need something. Promise?"

"I promise," he answered, knowing he couldn't ask her for what he needed.

She heard him in the bathroom as she was propping a note by his oatmeal bowl. She was dressed and ready to pick up Alice to take her to the doctor, but stopped to pour his coffee.

"Morning, babe," he kind of grumbled from behind as she placed the pot back on the warmer.

"Hey, you," she replied, turning to smile at him. "I was just leaving. You have the morning to yourself."

"Leaving? Where you off to so damned early?"

"Oh, Ben, don't you remember anything? I told you Alice has a terrible cold and I insisted she go get some real medicine. She's too frail to let a bad cold get a hold of her, and she won't go unless I lead her by the hand."

"Yeah, I do recall you saying she sounded like a frog croaking when you called. When will you be back? I have to go to town for a few supplies myself later," he answered noncommittally.

"I can pick up anything you need if you like."

"No, you can't, and no I wouldn't like, Abby. There are a few things I'd still like to do for myself. Jesus!" he snapped.

"Okay. I'll be back shortly after lunch," she answered, stung by his snarl. "I guess you can get your own breakfast, too." Without another word, she grabbed her jacket off the coat stand and went out the door.

"Abby . . . ." He started to call after her and then stopped. "What's the use? Shit," he muttered. He was doing her more harm with his short fuse than if he just sat her down and told her he was dying. Why was it so damn hard?

He poured his coffee and put the oatmeal bowl and juice glass back in the cupboard. None of it was doing any good anyway. Her and her damn healthy food wasn't doing one goddamn bit of good. Grabbing his own jacket, he carried his coffee and cigarettes out to the swing. Looking out over the endless water, oblivious to the chill in the air, his mind raced for a solution. He didn't know if he was more afraid of dying or of loosing Amber. Why now, he lamented, when he'd finally found the contentment he searched years for? So much in his life yet to do? So much in his life started and left undone? So much fucked up.

He considered praying and decided against it. Who would listen? He leaned forward, elbows on knees, and buried his face in his hands fighting tears, fighting rage, despair. He looked up then, out over the water and toward the sky. A massive bank of gray clouds nestled on the water at the horizon, its top thinly lined in brilliant silver as the sun lingered slightly below and behind. Every cloud has a silver lining, he thought. Suddenly, he remembered her rainbows and he willed one to appear and bring a miracle into his life as it had hers. It didn't.

The town appeared ahead and below her as she rounded the last curve on the bluff highway, as they'd taken to calling it. She'd fought her anger on the ride in, but her resilience was weakening. Ben's continual snarling, often at the most innocent of provocation, was wearing. Her own volatile nature was ebbing much too close to the surface.

Something was wrong. It was affecting their relationship and needed to be addressed. She made up her mind to discuss it with him that evening and then concentrated on cheering up for Alice. Turning at the intersection in the Town Square, she noticed some workers stringing lights for Christmas decorations and thought of her sons. Perhaps they would come for Christmas. She could invite Ben's son too.

He came back into the house, refilled his coffee, and sat down at his laptop again. He attempted to work but his muse wouldn't come, couldn't penetrate the dilemma that was consuming him. Finally, he closed his word processor and connected on line. *Cancer Treatment*, he typed into the search engine, and began to scroll. And scroll. His eyes rested on one in particular, and he grabbed a pen and paper and wrote down a number. His hand was shaking violently as he pushed the buttons on his cell phone. It had to be done.

"McBride Research Center," the voice answered. "How may I direct your call?"

Minutes later, he heard a car door up on the road and guessed it was Abby returning. He hid the paper in a pocket and cleared the screen. He'd found out what he needed to know.

"Car's back if you need it," Amber said, as she hung her jacket back on its hook.

"How's Alice? Did she get her antibiotics?" he asked, trying to break the frost of her mood.

"She'll be okay. We got her medicine, some fruit and orange juice, and I stopped at the café and got her enough chowder to have a couple hot meals. What time will you be back for supper?"

"About an hour or so, I suppose. Just have to pick up a few mailing supplies." He'd called ahead for his pain prescription and it would be ready when he got there. "Sorry I snapped at you this morning, Abby. I just need to get out and about now and then, too," he offered.

"Of course, you do. Let's just forget it, okay?" she answered. Not this time, Ben, she thought. Sorry doesn't get it anymore. We'll talk after supper.

He watched her move around the kitchen. He'd built a fire and was sitting on the small sofa instead of his usual chair. He patted the space beside him as she carried mugs of coffee into the sitting room.

"Sit by me here, Abby. I have something to talk to you about."

A pit formed in her stomach at the seriousness on his face, but she smiled and sat, resting her head against him. She, too, had decided to get what was bothering him out in the open, but she wasn't prepared for what came next.

"Abby, I've told you before that there were things unfinished in my life. I've tried to put them aside, behind me, and concentrate only on us and the future, but it isn't working. I'm going to have to go away. Back to the west coast. I don't know beyond that." There, he'd said it. Not the entire truth, but he'd gotten it out that he must leave. And without scaring her as to his dying. He thought he felt her body start to tremble and braced himself for her response.

She was staggered, bewildered. Her voice locked in her throat. Had she heard him right?

"Abby?" He turned to look at her. "It isn't you, Abby. No one has ever come close to fulfilling in me what you have. Please don't think it has anything to do with you. It's beyond my control."

She still said nothing. It was as if the blood had drained from her body and she couldn't concentrate. The room took on the feel of a dream, illusory. She stared, first at the fire, then him, trying to understand, trying to focus, as the room began to spin.

"Abby, dammit, say something. Don't stare at me like that." He was startled now, she seemed about to faint. He shook her. "Amber!"

She'd heard him wrong. That was it. "What did you say, Ben?" she asked, her voice calm. "I don't think I heard you right."

He was intense now. He wasn't prepared for her reaction, more for anger, more demanding an explanation. "I said I have to leave, go away, for awhile anyway. Something's come up but it has nothing to do with you."

"Nothing to do with me?" she mumbled. "How could that be so? How could anything in our lives now not have to do with the other? I don't understand."

Shit, he thought, how do I answer her without telling her everything? "Abby, there are things I have to do. Since we began this venture, you've known it was on a trial basis."

She moved to the edge of the sofa, almost slinging his arm away. "Venture? Trial basis? What am I? Was I? A fucking experiment?" An agony was rising within her.

"No, goddammit. You aren't, weren't, a fucking experiment. Not you! But this life, this move was. And, I can't go on with it until, unless, other things are settled. It isn't even fair to you to try."

"And walking away is fair? No explanation, no reason, just that you have things to *do*? That's fair? Don't do me any favors, Ben. Don't lie. There's more to this than you're telling me, or else it *is* me. Simply, that you don't want to stay with me. That you aren't happy. I don't know if I can believe that, so what aren't you telling me? Why the nightmares, the pacing the floor at all hours? Are you sick again? In trouble? Tell me! For Christ's sake, tell, or at least face, the truth for once in your miserable life." Out of nowhere, a suppressed rage broke through and she jumped up, her coffee mug falling to the floor.

"You have no idea what you are saying. No idea of what I have to do, or why." His eyes flashed his own anger as he spoke.

"Perhaps you're right, damn you." She paced back and forth in front of him. "I have no idea what you have to do because you've never told me of your secret life. Maybe it's yourself that you are running from, not what you think, and

358

justify, that you're gonna fix and make right. Is that it? Are you just afraid you won't be able to control the outcome of everything you do, everything that happens to you, how you live and when you die, every relationship you surrender to?"

"You really are nuts, you know that?" he yelled back. "You accuse me of wanting to control? All the while, you run around like a goddamn fairy, a mystical nymph, force-feeding your fairy dust down my throat. Have you ever faced anything realistically in your own fucked up life?"

He was furious now. A fury built out of his own frustration at the truth of her words and his guilt for not being able to do as she said. Tell, or face the truth once in his whole miserable life.

"Okay, Ben, do what you must. I can't see anything to be gained by beating each other up. Best we just don't talk anymore."

She bent over and picked up her mug and went to the kitchen to get a towel to wipe up the spilled coffee. Ben, his anger again dissolving as fast as it had risen, sat and stared at her unable to absorb the scene that had just taken place between them. All he was trying to do was save her more heartbreak. He couldn't comprehend that what he was doing was giving her more than the truth would have.

Amber robotically finished cleaning the spill, scooped Tag out of his basket, and walked toward the bedroom. He watched the fire ebb, and then followed her.

*****

He forced himself back to the present. He didn't want to think of the first time he'd left her on a rainy night. He didn't want to remember how he'd struggled with the decision to come back to the little burg in Florida and ask Abby to live with him. It was all different now. The last thing he ever wanted to do was leave her.

Abby had left him sitting alone. He heard her talking to Tag in the kitchen and wondered now back over the day. The morning argument on the swing, her running off to town or where ever she went in that infernal car, quiet for a time, then the arguments again. And now she'd told him she may stay here a month, may stay until after Christmas when pressed about her plans.

Maybe he shouldn't wait until the end of the month to leave. If he left right away, maybe he could be back by Christmas. If he was going to come back at all, prolonging it until the end of the month wasn't going to help. He envisioned every day being just like this day had been.

There would be endless debates over his reasons for going. They'd be clinging to each other one minute and fighting the next. Eventually, he'd break and tell her about the cancer eating at him when she asked over and over again if he was sick or in trouble. Could she even deal with him dying too? Wouldn't it be better to let her think he'd just left?

If the treatment worked, he could come back sooner, or at least let her know before she had time to leave the bluff and go back to the treehouse permanently. If it didn't, she wouldn't want to stay here without him anyway.

MILES TO GO BEFORE I SLEEP

His reservations were made. Abby was waiting to take him to the airport. I must go now before I change my mind, he thought. But, one thing remained undone. He had to explain to her the only way he knew how. Then she would understand, would know it wasn't because of her that he was leaving. He wiped the sweat from his brow brought on by another wave of agony, picked up his yellow pad and began to write.

My Dearest Abby,
I'm writing this to try and explain what I haven't been able to say in conversation. About my leaving, I mean. You think it has to do with fixing my past. It doesn't. It has to do with fixing our present, and our future. Had I explained, you'd panic thinking of Texas. You'd give me that 'you won't die one day sooner than you're supposed to' line that you did back in your treehouse. Well, babe, maybe this is my time because for all you've said and done, for all I've tried to believe, it hasn't worked.
If I'm dying, and there are reasons to believe I am, then best you not have to go through it again. Even these words will hurt, this I know, but I can't just leave you hanging with no

answer as to why I'm leaving. I'm going to another doctor, this time near Los Angeles, and yes, one I found on the Internet. He has a new procedure and, anyway, my love, it's now or never. He will cure me or I will die there, it's that simple. He is, in effect, my last chance. So rather than go into details, I'll come back to you and we can live out our natural lives together or you will continue on without me. You will get a phone call in a few days either from me or him.

Please, please, please don't let this weigh you down as I know it must, as it would me if the situation was reversed. Instead, think of that poem I wrote you called The Bow. Or as you often say, "whatever's meant to be will be."

He wrote another line, then scratched through it. It said *Until.* Instead, he signed it *Your Ben, Forever.*

He tore the page from the pad, put the pad into his suitcase with the rest of his belongings for the trip, closed it, and carried it into the other room where she was sitting, her back to him. He slipped the page under the vase on the table.

"Ready?" he asked.

She nodded, got up stiffly, and walked out the door. He looked at Tag asleep on his pillow, then around the room.

"I'll be back, little guy" he whispered. "Someway. Somehow. I'll be back."

He quietly closed the door to their house, their home, and climbed the path. She'd already started the car and he saw her face was expressionless. He gathered his resolve not to break and got in beside her.

"Okay," he said to her, but she just looked straight ahead and slowly accelerated.

Not a word was uttered on the way to the airport. He stared out the side while she stared ahead. The moon overhead seemed to wink at him as it darted in and out of the fast-moving clouds coming in off the water, and he wondered if it would be snowing by the time she returned. He started to mention it but checked himself and remained quiet. Why talk about life at a time like this? His mind

362

wandered back to when they'd met, to the hospital, and what she must be thinking. When she reads the note she'll understand, he reassured himself.

Amber pulled into the airport and parked. She was going to let him go in by himself, but something inside wouldn't let her. This may be the last time she saw him. Ever. With what little strength she had remaining, she got out and accompanied him, just wanting to be near him. He seemed to understand. When they reached the entry doors he turned and kissed her, but it wasn't his regular kiss. It was lighter, yet deeper all in one. The kiss seemed to be saying something to her, but what?

Without a word, she turned and began walking, yet again, away from him. Forcing her pace to quicken, she refused to turn and look back, wondering if he was doing the same. The hum of the jet engines, with their almost undetectable high-whining whistle, droned through the air, taunting her, as the plane he would board sat on the tarmac just beyond the small terminal building.

She forced her eyes toward the silver car glistening under the yellow parking lot lights. She laughed sardonically at the *Short Term Parking* sign. The lot was farther from the terminal than the long term lot. Airports. Did they purposely confuse so you wouldn't think about who was leaving and who was left?

Moments later the hum of the convertible's engine rescued her from the drone of the jets. She angled to the exit and the drive back to the little house they'd shared. For what? Three weeks? Three months? Or what was to be their lifetime? It didn't matter now. She tried to concentrate on the predawn blackness in front of her, interrupted only by the beam of the head lights. The wind off the water was challenging the little car. Maybe she wouldn't have to wait long to see a 'Nor'easter' after all. And still be home by Christmas.

She parked the car, hugged the yellow windbreaker around her, and started down the path to the house. The dim light inside silhouetted the now-empty swing. It was swaying gently by itself as if a ghost of Ben's essence pushed it with an invisible foot. She concentrated on the door and thought of other dawns.

Inside, the smell of him lingered along with the cigarette smoke. His half-empty coffee cup sat cold on the counter. A hard boiled egg he'd boiled for her lay untouched on the drain board as if to remind her to eat something. Tag lay curled on Ben's couch pillow, breathing him in.

"Damn you, Ben! Damn you!" she suddenly burst out. The contents of her purse clattered to the floor as she threw it across the room, her frustration turning to a rage. Startled, Tag stared at her wide-eyed, and beyond her, at no one. Seeing his little face, she dissolved into tears, picked him up, and hugged him to her.

"I'm so sorry, Tag," she whimpered. So sorry for everything. But don't you worry. Everything is going to be fine. It is, I promise."

She sat on the sofa and laid her head back. Staring at the ceiling, she continued her croon to the cat. "How would you like to live in a treehouse by a warmer sea? You can make friends with all the critters, and maybe even old Fred will show himself once he gets used to you poking around."

Tag looked at her and, sensing she was upset, buried his face in her neck.

"Is that a yes, fella?" Tears were streaming down her face now, anger gone. "Okay. We'll start packing this afternoon, but you go back to sleep now. I have to go ride awhile, sort out my plans. It's cold in here, empty but for you. Yes, cold. Maybe emptiness is cold."

She put him back down on the pillow and petted him back to sleep. Outside, the first snowflake melted on the warm hood of the car.

Astonishing, she thought, looking around, how a small house could so quickly be filled with the memories of a lifetime, their lifetime together anyway. Her eyes went to the Lady of the Sea still in the fishnet as he'd left her. Her painted eyes stared back, void of emotion.

She's mocking me, sneering almost, at my being so gullible, so easily deceived by life's currents that I blindly positioned myself to be thrown upon the rocks yet again. This lady who guided men through entire oceans would hold no pity for one so naive. Looking away, she tried to swallow the fear beginning to build in the pit of her stomach.

"Has everything been a lie? All my hopes, my dreams?" she cried out, looking back into those mocking eyes. "Has the very soul of me been nothing but a big joke? How could I have been so wrong, so misled?" The figurine didn't answer.

The wind, now rattling the windows, taunted, too. It blew through the worn siding like one of Ben's story ghosts. Like claws, the cold dug into her and wrapped around her heart. She turned toward the fireplace, grabbed an iron poker from the stand and stirred the coals. A few sparks swirled and then died.

"Everything dies. I've been such a fool," she whispered to the smiling hearth and started to back away. Then she thought of Tag; he would need the warmth.

She piled a few small pieces of wood, teepee style, in the dying embers, and looked around for something to ignite it. A page torn off a yellow writing tablet lay on the nearby table. Not realizing, she balled up his last words to her, unread, and dropped it in. A corner of the thin paper caught, and his fine-point scrawl curled and dissolved into the renewed coals.

The kindling teepee surrendered to the flames, their heat already warming her face. Once certain that it would burn, she stood and walked to the fishnet wall. She removed the Lady of the Sea from the netting and carried her to the fire.

Numb now, robot-like, she filled Tag's food bowl and freshened his water. A thought of calling Alice fleeted through her mind, and left as quickly. She decided to wait until after a ride cleared her head.

"I'm not anxious to tell her I'm leaving," she said to the empty room. "I dread telling her that all her waiting for a love to return was a waste of her life. Inner voices saying nothing, only fostering silly delusions. Or maybe they are the delusions."

She spoke in whispers through clenched teeth as she bent to collect the scattered contents of her purse. "All the damn connections are merely random chance after all; fucking ships passing in the night, fucking coincidence! Why, you'll break Alice's heart . . . Aaa-bby."

The last came out in an exaggerated rasp. "Abby? Shit! Easier to say than Abigale, is all. To think I've been dumb enough to think his calling me that had significance. Damn.

She was beginning to fill with a chill as biting as the ghost seeping through the house cracks. The initial rage, then despair, was turning to bitterness now. Still, a remnant of compassion held as she thought of Alice. I can't destroy her dreams. She's alone, nowhere to go, just her and the old dog and she's been so kind to me. Let her have her stupid dreams for what little time is left. I'll just say something unexpected came up and I have to return to Florida, that I'll write to her. Now, I have to concentrate on getting Tag to the treehouse. I've got . . . what's the old poem . . . *miles to go before I sleep.*

She looked at Tag asleep again on the pillow, his fur a deep russet in the hue cast by the fire. He looked forlorn and she went to the bedroom to retrieve Bear. She noticed that Ben had forgotten his robe at the foot of their bed.

"Oh, well, you won't need it in sunny LA, or wherever the hell you're going." Her voice again echoed desolation, defeat. She lifted Bear from the window seat and gathered the robe, draping it around his body. Maybe the scent of Ben would console Tag while she was gone.

The setting before her now, Tag wound in a circle, Bear perched protectively beside him wrapped in the robe, the soft firelight in a room that held the now shattered heart of her, was more than she could endure. She had to escape, to ride fast where she could be free of it. She'd go see Alice rather than call her, get gas for the car, and leave early as soon as she'd packed what few things there were to take back. She wanted nothing that would remind her of this voyage through a dream that ended in his walking away yet again.

A loud crash on the porch startled her. Because hope springs eternal, she rushed to the door and pushed it open against the wind gusts, now determined to lock her in.

"Ben? Ben, is that you?" she yelled above the roar. Only the empty swing, blowing into the wall of the house with a thump, answered her.

She stepped farther onto the porch to see up on the road, stumbled and looked down. The muted light of daybreak, struggling to penetrate the black clouds, fell on the whittled owl. Still grasping the log, it had fallen and landed face down. The wood-burned sign announcing *Ben and Abby's Nest* had split and lay in two pieces on the porch boards alongside. The sight of it was like a knife stabbing the depths of her as she bent to pick it up.

She turned back inside to get her purse and check the fire that would keep Tag warm. Not to raise sparks, she gently placed the bird and the broken pieces of her life on the charred remains of the Sea Lady. Her eyes were no longer mocking her.

Bits of snow pelted her face like needles in the howling wind. The path up to the car was getting slippery and each step was precarious. Her hair flew wildly, the long strands lashing her cheeks and stinging her eyes. She turned her head away from the direct force of it and barely could see the water, a hard, steel gray, pummeling the rocks below. The heavy sweater under her windbreaker failed to warm the seagull still riding on her chest. Its cold metal flesh scorched her own as she bowed into the gale force and inched toward the car, no longer a glistening silver, but dull, gray like the water.

The elements she'd held so dear now battered her like they pounded the boulders at the cliff bottom. The scream of wind and ocean now seemed a din of malevolent laughter. No longer did she love the storm. A cluster of pebbles gave way and she stumbled to her knees, feeling the warm ooze of blood before it, too, burned her with its cold.

A voice deep inside asked of the wisdom in venturing out onto the highway in such weather, but she ignored it. She'd never listen to inner voices again; that much she finally learned. A fleeting vision of Tag alone in the house passed through her mind's eye, and she pushed it away. Into some closet where hung sense and reason. "It's just for a little while; I won't be gone long," she moaned into the deep recesses of thoughts that might cause her to hesitate.

Her feet slipped again just at the top of the embankment and only the fence guarding the drop-off kept her from sprawling on the rocks, sliding back down. One final thrust and her arms clutched the split rail. She regained her balance and held tight with one hand, digging for her keys with the other.

The yellow running light flashed with the press of the remote on the key ring, signaling the door had unlocked. She lunged for the car, yanked the door open, and literally fell inside, letting the comfort, always there like a suit of armor, embrace her.

The snow flakes were growing larger, softer, in the tunnel of light from the headlamps. The engine, not idle long since returning from the airport, spewed heat onto her stinging knees. She began to relax, feel out the surface beneath her tires, and increased her speed slightly. Her mind began touring the corridors of memory trying to discover what signs she'd missed that would have aroused her from her fantasies. She found none.

A CHILL AS DEEP AS DEATH

Inside the airport terminal, Ben sat waiting for his plane to begin loading. It was already an hour behind schedule due to an approaching storm, he'd been told. As he waited, he couldn't keep his mind off Abby.

Godamnit, I'm doing this for her, he thought. For us. He'd tried to force himself to think of the treatment that lay ahead of him instead, but it wasn't working. He read in one of Bach's books, he walked around, bought a cup of coffee.

"Passengers for Flight 337," he heard the voice come over the loudspeaker, "can now board." He grabbed up his bag, slung it over his shoulder, got his ticket out, and headed for the loading gate.

He could see through the windows that it was now snowing hard. Icing conditions, no doubt, had kept the ground crew busy clearing the runway and delaying his flight. Or was it something else?

He was near the back of the line now waiting to board, the passengers ahead of him going through the boarding process. His mind raced. Shut up! He told his runaway thoughts.

She drove in silence, content to listen to the wind. She thought of the two times past when Ben had seemingly run from the feelings and the commitment those feelings might entail. But it was different then, or so she'd thought. After their brief time together in the beginning, even she didn't understand the emotions their strange meeting had evoked in her, so had accepted the confusion that prompted his first departure into a rainy night.

But then there were the letters and his reaching out to her; the subsequent trip to Texas and the hospital, his returning to her home. Then a signal she'd missed hit her as the car fishtailed slightly on the next curve. *He'd come under protest and only because he was too weak to return to his life on the west coast. He'd left again as soon as he was strong enough.* Why hadn't she seen it then? Why didn't she see it when he was gone so long without any word at all? Was it because she hadn't wanted to see it? To have done so would have meant her esoteric beliefs were questionable and those beliefs had come to be her survival without Jeff. Just like Alice had survived an adult lifetime on a dream.

"No," she cried out. "I did listen to the inner voices and they lied. Or was it me who lied? To myself?" Tears blinded her vision again, but her mind wouldn't stop. Love does die and you can't bring it back. Maybe it was Alice who knew that all along and accepted what I couldn't. And she knew I couldn't, so she encouraged me with Ben, even to renting us the bluff house so dear to her.

He burst through the airport doors and looked wildly around for a cab. None. The wind was up, blowing snow at a forty-five degree angle. This was no ordinary snowstorm, his mind said. He'd never been through a blizzard before, but guessed this must be one, or one forming. He ran back inside the terminal.

The wind was picking up and the snow falling harder. The daylight wasn't coming, or was that what was making the snow field in front of her all the more blinding and hard to see through? She pushed the button for the fog lights and the road surface stared back her, easier to see now. She'd get gas and head back to the bluff, pack for the trip while the snowstorm passed, call Alice after all, and she and Tag and Bear would leave. Leave this cold, empty place and go home where her life could be warm again. Still, the thought of leaving gnawed at her heart.

He came quickly through the airport doors again, bag over his shoulder, car key in hand. Against the protestations of the rental employee, and a slipped hundred dollar bill into the employee's hand, he'd managed to rent a car. To hell with the operation, he thought. If I'm going to die, I'll do it with her. How stupid of me not to share this with her. How wrong I've been not to let her be a part of this as well, if that is what's meant to be.

What am I saying? I'm beginning to sound like her. Fuck it, he thought, as he slipped and slid his way toward the rental in the lot, now covering with snow. Death is part of life. He brushed the snow from the car's windshield, got in, started it, and began driving, and sliding, toward the airport exit. He turned on the car radio and frantically dialed around, listening for local news and weather.

"I don't want to think anymore," she sighed out loud. "It's over, it's done." She reached automatically into the console and dug out a CD, any CD, to sooth her shattered nerves. To drown out her mindless questioning with the beat of the beloved classic Metal. She pulled one from its case and shoved it into the player. The car swerved with the distraction and she noticed the fog lights now revealed a snow-encrusted road just beyond the nose of the car. She switched to high beams but that only magnified the wall of white in front of her.

"Damn, why isn't it getting daylight?" she mumbled just as the first strains of music from the speakers sent a chill down her spine. "Oh no, not that. Not now," she cried softly.

Bocelli, the magical voice Ben so loved, would speak for him . . . *Time To Say Goodbye*.

She started to eject it, then stopped. Fitting, that of all the CDs, I'd blindly grab this one. Maybe I need to listen, was her thought. She gave in to it, melded into the seat, tears forming, anger leaving. Unconsciously pressing the accelerator, she momentarily forgot the weather and did what was second nature to her. Became one with the music and the car.

The car's aerodynamics, the wide tires, the power in the heart of it, carved through the wind as if a blade. The tires gripped the snow-covered road, now illuminated in fog-light yellow, with a seeming vengeance. She penetrated the storm and became lost in it. Bocelli, like the wind outside, carried her aloft, into the sky above it all.

He managed to find his way to the coast road, the wipers beating furiously but not all that successfully. He'd seen few cars, but for a sheriff's car that had passed him in the opposite direction, its headlights almost blinding him just after he made the turn south. He fumbled in his bag, looking for the pills, as a wave of pain swept over and through him making him nauseous.

"Fuck it! Just fuck it!" He found the bottle, popped the top and threw two inside his mouth, the rest scattered endlessly onto the seat and floor. He was nearing the curvy part of the road and he slowed, shifting into a lower gear to let the car's weight help with the needed traction. God, what a time to learn how to drive in snow, he thought.

As he cautiously entered the first sharp curve, two pinpoints of light haloed in a topaz yellow coming toward him suddenly loomed large, too large. The damn thing was coming straight at him.

"Shit!" By instinct he cranked the wheel over hard, but the car slid forward instead. "SHIT!"

He quickly reversed the wheel but continued sliding forward, and the approaching car was nearly on him, its headlights now like yellow spotlights in his eyes. He threw one hand up to shield his eyes from the glare, or to protect himself from the crash, he didn't know which. At the last second the oncoming car missed him, but its draft from the excess speed, and the slippery surface, spun him around, out of control, toward the guard rail and the raging ocean below.

"SHITTT!"

The drift saved him. The car came to an abrupt halt as it plowed into the snowdrift covering the rail, throwing him sideways against his seatbelt. He recovered and tried to move the car, but it was hopelessly stuck. "Damn! Damn! Damn!" he yelled in frustration, slapping the steering wheel.

Headlights coming at her around the curve careened her back to Earth. Pulling the wheel right just in time to avoid the collision, her momentum carried her past the oncoming car before she swerved. She flattened both feet on the floor and steered into the skid. Keeping her foot off the brake, she rode into the slide to regain her control. She veered to the drift on the left, opposite the cliff's edge, just enough for the snow to reduce her speed but not pull the car off the road into the ditch, and prayed another car wouldn't come from the opposite direction.

The window went down quickly and he looked out, then around. The drifts were piling up in the swirling wind, but he thought he recognized the area, thought he wasn't all that far from their bluff house.

"I'll make it," he said to himself. "I have to."

He pulled a cap from his bag, the one he'd always worn, the one he'd been wearing when they met, and snuggled it onto his head. Climbing from the car, he began to walk, bending into the wind. The cold of it hit him all at once and he shivered almost violently.

He began to run on the road as best he could but kept falling down. He looked to the woods, then to the road ahead, and headed into the woods thinking it would help shield him from the wind and snow that now ripped at him.

She forgot her own miseries as the car slowed. She was sure she'd run the other car off the road. Damn! I've got to go back, she thought. Someone may be hurt. Her mind raced wildly. I've got to turn around without getting stuck myself. She couldn't see well enough to determine how close she was to the cliff wall but knew it was there, somewhere. She cursed herself for not always leaving the CB radio in the car, for shunning cell phones.

"I've got to chance it," she said out loud. "No, wait! The bird cove! It's just ahead, I think. I can turn there."

She pulled away from the drift that slowed her, checked her traction, and regained speed. Her eyes strained to see the turn-off to the right. The cove itself, she reasoned, may have protected the road there, held down the drifts. She hit the high beams again, but it didn't help. She turned the headlights off altogether and tried running with just the fog lights. A dull hint of the struggling dawn seemed to help a bit.

The turn-off should be coming up now, she thought. I need to go just a little faster in case I have to pass through a drift. "Oh, I'm coming, I'm coming back. Please be all right," she cried out to whoever may be waiting for her, hurt or trapped. "Damn! *Where* is that turn?" Her eyes burned, blurred.

"There! There it is." She could barely make out the cliff side marking the wall of the cove and the turn. She pulled the wheel to the right, fed the accelerator and the brake at once, to force a half donut turn. She heard, no felt, a thump. Resistance. She'd hit something . . . good.

She plowed through the drift and yanked the wheel left. "Turn! Dammit, TURN!" she yelled as the car suddenly lunged forward and seemed to be gliding on the snow, powerless to turn. Then it broke free, as if flying. Suddenly there was an explosion of light in her head. She heard her own voice in the distance. "Damn, its cold . . . Bennn . . . ."

He was hopelessly lost and he knew it. He was exhausted, his breath coming in gasps. His face and hands were covered with snow and even the coat flap partially covering his face didn't seem to help. I'm going to die right out here, his numbed brain said. He was knee-deep in snow, yet kept on, moving in a zigzag, unable to see. "Abbby . . . ."

The whine of the engine propelled the sleek machine forward into the wind. Severed by the intrusion, the gale force of it slid over and under the metal nose in a conflict of uplift and downdraft. The silver fuselage shimmered in the sun with the vibration of its thrust. She laid her head back and dissolved into the seat, letting the Spirit of the machine have its head. To take her wherever it wanted to go. Then it was free, the wheels releasing their grip on the surface.

The pain took him then as before, doubling him over, and he went head-first into the snow, unable to even yell.

"No, dammit. Not like this." The snow quickly tried to bury him in it. He was panting, his face and hands white, his head down. The chill was shaking him brutally, like a doll, the pain like liquid fire within him. "Abbby . . . ."

It soared upward, a streak of silver becoming one with the sky, causing hawks to swerve and billowy clouds to open channels into their inner sanctums. She languished there as in a vacuum, cataleptic, not there, but nowhere else. A time to say goodbye . . . .

The convertible sailed through the guardrail as if a gate had opened, and headed for the ocean two hundred feet below. As if in slow motion, its nose going over and trunk coming up from behind.

He imagined hearing a soft "thud" nearby. He shook his head. What would make that sound, out here, now? He heard it again, a definite "thud" like something pawing the snow. He struggled to look up, to see in the blizzard whiteout, and saw a dark shape before him not ten yards away. He squinted as it began to take form. "It must be death come for me. God, it's big."

The car hit the water almost inverted, the music still playing through the storm's howl . . . *Time to Say Goodbye.*

As his vision cleared, the moose they'd encountered on the road appeared before him, its broken antler dripping icicles, its nostrils flaring, its breath coming out in puffs. It suddenly turned and began to walk away though the deep snow.

"Wait," he called, trying to get to his feet. "WAIT!" But the large animal continued on, slowly disappearing into the whiteout. By the time he was halfway standing again, the animal had been swallowed by the storm.

"COME BACK!" he yelled as best he could, but his only answer was the wind and blinding snow. He nearly collapsed again, sick with agony and despair. "Abbby . . . ." He fell to his knees.

The car began to sink, the ocean turning to a yellow foam from its lamps, its wheels still rotating, struggling for life . . . *Time to Say Goodbye.*

After a moment, he looked up into the storm, then down again, and saw the hoof prints of the moose deeply embedded in the snow. *Her face came to him then, perfectly clear in his mind. She was smiling at him.* He looked at the tracks again, his face showing recollection of their many arguments. "Oh my God! She was right. Oh Jesus, she was right after all. The fox, the rainbow, the bear, now the moose. But, you must believe the magic! You just have to believe!"

He struggled to half-stand, then began clumsily trying to follow the animal's tracks, which seemed too distinct in so much snow. Much too distinct. The pain left him then as suddenly as it had come, but this time he sensed it had left for good. He stopped, felt his body, his face brightening. "Good God! Abby, it's gone. GONE, DO YOU HEAR?" he yelled, nearly laughing. With a new-found energy he began to half-run. "I'm coming, Abby. I'm coming home."

There emitted a soft sigh from the car's escaping steam as a wave rolled over it, and the silvery shimmer was gone. Swallowed by the waves, lost forever in the ocean's depths.

Frost came from his mouth, his lungs burned from the raw air as he continued on, the animal's tracks becoming fainter and fainter. He tried to run even harder; his cap came off for his effort, exposing his head to the storm. He stopped briefly to wipe the snow from his face, and when he looked out again, the tracks were gone.

"NO, DAMMIT! NOOO!"

Now beside himself with frustration and worry, unable to go on, out of strength, out of breath, again out of hope, the resignation hit him that he wasn't going to make it after all.

"Oh, why in hell did I ever leave her?" He looked skyward. "DAMN YOU!"

He was ready to collapse, ready to give up, when he heard her voice in his mind . . . "Ben, his last words to me were 'never give up.' Never, never give up, Ben."

He looked up again. The storm was beginning to lessen, and through the trees he could see an open space ahead, illumined by a now timid dawn. He rubbed his eyes. It was near the pullover by the path to their house, he was certain. He trudged on and soon broke out onto the road.

"Yesss," he managed to say as he saw smoke coming from a chimney not far away. The storm was passing over him and continuing on. Daylight was beginning to rise full. "Abby, I'm home," he called, again trying to run toward the house.

He burst into the living room. "ABBY? ABBY, IT'S ME! I'M BACK! I DIDN'T LEAVE, ABBY, I DIDN'T LEAVE AND I'M NOT GOING TO! NOT EVER!"

"Meowww."

He turned and stared at Tag looking back at him, the kitten's eyes questioning. "Where's your momma, little guy?" But Tag stared past him, as if seeing something he couldn't.

He surveyed the room and noticed the Lady of the Sea in the fireplace, nearly destroyed by the now dying flames. A partially-burned owl and her beloved sign propped next to it.

"Abby . . . ?"

He ran into their bedroom, then back out, frantic. Then he remembered . . . he hadn't noticed her car up on the roadside pullover. Outside the window, the sun was trying to shine, but he suddenly felt a chill as deep as death come over him. He crumpled into the chair and rested his face in his hands. It came up from the depths of his soul then, a great wellspring and he couldn't stop it. Some great agony was about to . . . had to be released. His body heaved with sobbing. He cried out, a guttural sound, desolate in its nature and desperate in its plea.

"NOOO, it can't be. NOOO! GOD . . . it just can't be.

Alone but for the orange kitten sitting at his feet, he stood at the cliff's edge overlooking the sea. The wind was freezing his face into a set, but unfelt, harshness. The eyes that rivaled the blue of the sky were soft now, and a lone tear trailed downward only to be quickly dried by the force of air striking his cheek.

Below him, the surf swirled and battered the rocks, and he watched the water dismiss the obstacles that stood in its path. Much like life itself, he thought. A rock, no matter how firmly planted, could not impede the forces intended to move it. When weary of trying, it will release its hold and go where the water carries it.

He clutched the small bundle in his arms, not yet ready to part with it. But part, he must. With all that was left in him, he flung the carefully wrapped contents out to the wind, as if an offering, holding tight to the pale yellow windbreaker that held them. A sprinkling of dust glistened, caught by a sunray peeking over the clouds on the far horizon. A small bird of brass and gold, free of its chain, wings outstretched, flew out over the ocean. His heart smiled faintly as the little bird she'd worn around her neck so long took flight, soaring higher than ever before, and then was lost to his sight.

He gripped the chain in his pocket and searched far into the distance, hoping for one last glimpse of the gull, and then he saw it. His breath caught in his throat. There, just over the cloudy horizon, it was forming before his eyes. A bow. A radiant double rainbow was extending its arcs outward from a point of sunlight, beginning to encircle the panorama in front of him. It seemed to be reaching for him in an embrace. He rubbed his eyes. A rainbow in winter? In Maine? How could it be?

And then he understood . . . finally understood the magic. The tears came unabashed now. He lingered there, he didn't know how long, until the bow slowly grew faint and finally disappeared.

Turning around, his eyes looked down and south. The small and weathered cottage on the next bluff seemed lonely in its emptiness. The house that had given them, such as it was, their time, seemed to call out to him. "Come on, Taggie boy. Let's go home."

SPRING FLOWERS

Ben jabbed the small spade into the rocky soil around the base of the flowers in the garden Alice had begun so long ago. The one Abby had tended since, which he was tending now. The spring flowers had sprung up without a care following, but for the blizzard, a mild winter. For Maine anyway. Bright flowers, beautiful and large, crocuses, and ones he'd never even seen before. He paused to wipe his forehead with one of her bandanas, smiling down at the plants that seemed to thank him for loosening the soil around their roots.

The little bluff house had a new coat of paint, white with green trim and green shutters, and the path up to the road was now steps of red brick. The old chimney was as it had been since being built, but there was a new roof and a new porch railing as well. And a new sign above the door.

He heard the brief honk of the mail truck signaling he had mail, so he took off his work gloves, laid them beside his digging trowel, and climbed the steps to the mailbox. He took out the single envelope and looked at the address, then shut the door to the box and patted it before descending the twenty-two steps to the house below, opening the envelope as he went. The envelope's return address was the name of a clinic, a clinic in Bangor he'd been to not long after the storm.

Dear Mr. Riley, it began. *We are happy to inform you that all of your recent follow up tests came out negative. There appears to be no trace of any pathogen or carcinoma anywhere in your body. Please see the lab results enclosed, and if you have any questions, feel free to contact us.*

The letter was signed by some Chief of Staff at the hospital, but he didn't really notice who. He stopped before the door, noticing the sign had tilted again, and moved to straighten it. "There," he said, still missing the whittled owl that had burned in the fire.

He folded the letter and put it back into the envelope and stuck it in his pocket. He sat in the same swing and looked out over the sea. What a difference time had made, he thought. Time, the healer of all wounds, the lineal stretch that guided everyone's life, more or less. His thoughts drifted back to that night and the next day when it had all happened.

He was being pulled out of an obscure place by a knock on the door, a loud, insistent knock. He must have drifted off to a troubled sleep from pure exhaustion and despair. His head lay on the arm of the chair where he'd twisted and curled, almost to a fetal position. A position of defeat. He stirred at the sound and raised his head, unsure of where he was, his face drawn and streaked. The knocking continued.

"Abby?" He sprang from his chair and bolted for the door. "ABBY?"

He jerked on the door, relief nearly consuming him. "Abby, you had me scared to death," he said as the door literally flew open. But it wasn't Amber on the porch doing the knocking. It was the local sheriff, a short man with a protruding stomach and large moustache.

"Excuse me," the sheriff said, "but are you Mr. Riley?"

He froze at the sight of the sheriff, his mouth unable to speak, his body stiff, like a corpse. Then he felt himself slipping away, sinking toward the floor, his legs refusing to hold him. His mind refusing to hear what words would come next.

He rose and walked to the end of the porch. He peeked around to see if the boys had returned with the car. The corners of his mouth arched into a slight grin as he caught himself still thinking of the sons as boys. If good things come from all our tragedies, he thought, surely the bond he'd rebuilt with his own son, and the friendship he'd formed with Abby's, had become such a prize.

The aroma of her pumpkin soup recipe wafted from the kitchen, and he was so pleased she'd thought to freeze the meat from the Halloween jack-o-lanterns. His heart softened at the thought of her as he stepped over the corn shuck mat, back in its place in front of the door. He sat again on the swing as his thoughts returned to that fateful morning.

"Mr. Riley, are you alright?" the sheriff bolstered him with a strong arm. "There's been an accident. I think you need to come with me. "You are Ben Riley?"

He stared at him, saying nothing.

"I found your identification in the rental car where you went off the road. This is the address on the papers. Mr. Riley?" The sheriff shook him gently, but roughly at once. He could only nod in agreement.

"Please come with me, sir. We're needed at the hospital. There's been an accident."

Still in his jacket, he turned and pulled the door closed. The last sound he heard was Tag meowing softly by a now cold fire. "I'll be back for you, little guy. I'll be back," was all he could say.

"Okay, let's get going, Mr. Riley, but maybe you'd better get your hat."

He nodded, dazed, and turned, then turned back again. "I-I don't have one."

The sheriff looked at him strangely. "Let's go then. My car is warm enough, I suppose."

382

He numbly followed the sheriff up the path to the patrol car. As they rounded the curve on the road near Amber's bird cove, he saw the hole in the drift and the guard rail.

"Is that . . . ?"

The man nodded. "Car went through it in the storm."

He leaned back in the seat, silent tears coming down his cheeks. "Did anyone . . . ?"

"Won't be long now, Mr. Riley. A few more miles."

A meow brought him back to the present, and he chuckled to see Tag stumbling over his garden boots to rub against his leg. Tail straight up and back arched, the now grown kitten registered his annoyance at being ignored. With the boys gone to town and the activities inside the house temporarily quiet, Tag seized the opportunity for his full attention.

"Look at you with dirt on your face," he crooned, mocking Amber. "What would your momma say if she knew you were rooting in the gardens like a pup? And, what did you do? Run those boys off? They should be back here by now." He ruffled the orange fur as Tag curled on his lap for a nap. His attachment to the kitten, too, took him back.

The cruiser turned into the hospital lot and the sheriff came to a stop at the Emergency Room doors. He started to get out, hesitated, and then turned around.

"I've got something you might want to have before we go inside. Found it up on the rocks by the accident scene." He dug in his jacket pocket, then extended his closed fist. "I'll go in ahead and let them know we're here. Come to the Nurse's station; I'll meet you there in five minutes."

A blast of arctic wind struck his face when the sheriff opened the car door. It was all that kept him from crying out his agony as he felt the cold metal chain make contact with the flesh of his palm. The slam of the car door closing was as a gunshot to his heart as he looked down at the seagull he'd given her in a letter a lifetime ago. It lay lifeless now in his hand, gleaming faintly in the florescent lights over the entrance doors.

He pulled the chain down over his head, gently placing the seagull against his own chest, forced himself out of the car and made his way to the entrance. Hope does spring eternal in the soul of a human and once inside he began looking around for Abby, but she wasn't there. Just people getting bandaged and put into casts, victims of icy roads and sidewalks.

The sheriff stood waiting for him at the desk as promised, and they continued on down a long hallway until arriving at door number 122. He pushed the door open and motioned for Ben to enter.

He wants me to identify her body, he thought. He stopped. "I can't do this."

"Mr. Riley," the sheriff said, and then took his arm. "It's going to be okay."

He nodded and walked slowly in.

"Ben?"

"Ben?" the younger man said again.

"Hmmm? Oh, sorry. I was daydreaming," he said, turning as the younger of Amber's sons joined him on the swing. "Did you get it?"

The young man nodded. "Yep, Bro's up there adding the finishing touches."

"Good. Guess I'd better go inside and check on the progress of dinner." He rose and moved toward the door, then turned back. "You sure all is according to plan?"

"Yep, again. Will you quit worrying? How long before we should leave to pick up your son at the airport?"

He looked at his watch. "The flight is due in about forty-five minutes; guess you two could leave any time now," he said as he walked to the end of the porch to wave at the boy's brother.

"Okay, we're off and we're starved. Make sure dinner's on when we get back," the young man teased as he moved to join his brother up on the pullover.

"Will you quit worrying?" he teased back. "And don't forget to pick up Alice," he called as he entered the house beneath the small sign that hung over the doorway. *Ben and Abby's Nest*, it said, burned across the wings of a seagull in flight.

She was bending over, sticking something in the oven when he walked up behind her and encircled his arms around her tiny waist. The long auburn hair trailed down her back and she had tied it back with a pale yellow bow. He buried his face in it and breathed in the smell of her.

"And just what kind of mischief are you three planning out there?" Amber inquired with a laugh. "And shouldn't you be leaving for the airport?" She turned in to him and rested her cheek on his chest.

"What? And leave you here to slave over a hot stove all alone? Perish the thought!" He twirled her around the kitchen in a waltz. I assigned that duty to your young'uns."

"I'm so happy, Ben. It's going to be wonderful having all the boys together. You know something? I think I love you. Have I told you that before?"

"Not nearly enough, Abby. Not nearly enough." He held her close and didn't even try to stop the tears that fell on the yellow ribbon beneath his chin. One more time, he allowed his mind to wander back . . . .

Abby was lying in bed, her head bandaged, her eyes closed. A few strands of auburn hair had managed to escape the gauze strips and lay curled on her thin shoulders now flecked with burns from an exploding air bag.

"I found her in a snow bank on a rock ledge just below where that car went through," the sheriff said. "She was unconscious, still is, so I brought her here. It's a miracle I even noticed it in that storm. Strange, too, that I decided to make one more patrol of the coast road. She would've frozen to death by morning."

He nearly collapsed with relief. "Abby! Oh my God!"

He rushed to her side and clutched her free hand between both of his own. The other was in a cast that reached just beyond her wrist.

"Guess she got thrown out of the car when it went through the guardrail. Probably wasn't wearing her seat belt," the sheriff continued.

He burst out laughing. "That would be a good guess, sir, a really good guess," he said, lifting her hand in his. "For once, her damnable stubbornness has saved her life."

She's alive, was all he could think as he stared down at her. "Thank you, sheriff," he said. "You'll never know how much."

Amber's eye lids flickered as Ben spoke. They opened slowly and stared up at him.

"Ben? You're here?" she whispered faintly.

"Lunatic," he softly murmured, bringing her hand to his cheek. "I couldn't leave you. I just couldn't."

"Ben? Oh Ben, is it really you? I just had the most wonderful dream. I flew higher than ever before."

"Yes, you did, my darlin' Abby. A most wonderful dream at that." He bent over and gently brushed her lips with his own. "And the best part is, the dream's only just begun. We are going to fly higher still." He smiled before kissing her again, their tears mingling on her cheeks.

EPILOGUE

Night had fallen. Inside the bluff house, Ben, Amber, their sons, and Alice could be seen sitting at the table, laughing as they ate supper. The pleasant smell of pumpkin in the air drifted across the road and into the edge of the forest where a pair of yellow-green eyes glowed in the light of the rising moon. They watched the festivities below with curiosity and seeming satisfaction, yet a bit of sadness, too.

The fox turned then and retreated silently into the woods from which it had come. It stopped and looked back briefly, then began to trot into the forest until it had disappeared. Even as a shooting star shot through the Heavens high overhead. Even as the ocean below calmly lapped at the shore beneath the house. Even as a new silver convertible wrapped with a huge red bow sat in the little pullover by the split rail fence above the bluff house.

Waiting . . . .